THE RANGE DETECTIVES
HANG THEM SLOWLY

THE RANGE DETECTIVES
HANG THEM SLOWLY

WILLIAM W. JOHNSTONE
with J. A. Johnstone

PINNACLE BOOKS
Kensington Publishing Corp.
www.kensingtonbooks.com

PINNACLE BOOKS are published by

Kensington Publishing Corp.
119 West 40th Street
New York, NY 10018

PUBLISHER'S NOTE
Following the death of William W. Johnstone, the Johnstone family is working with a carefully selected writer to organize and complete Mr. Johnstone's outlines and many unfinished manuscripts to create additional novels in all of his series like The Last Gunfighter, Mountain Man, and Eagles, among others. This novel was inspired by Mr. Johnstone's superb storytelling.

All Kensington titles, imprints, and distributed lines are available at special quantity discounts for bulk purchases for sales promotions, premiums, fund-raising, educational, or institutional use. Special book excerpts or customized printings can also be created to fit specific needs. For details, write or phone the office of the Kensington sales manager: Kensington Publishing Corp., 119 West 40th Street, New York, NY 10018, attn: Sales Department; phone 1-800-221-2647.

PINNACLE BOOKS, the Pinnacle logo, and the WWJ steer head logo are Reg. U.S. Pat. & TM Off.

ISBN-13: 978-0-7860-4489-4
ISBN-10: 0-7860-4489-6

First printing: November 2016

10 9 8 7 6 5 4 3

Printed in the United States of America

Electronic edition:

ISBN-13: 978-0-7860-3816-9 (e-book)
ISBN-10: 0-7860-3816-0 (e-book)

CHAPTER ONE

Trouble hung in the air like smoke drifting in from a distant fire. At least, it seemed that way to the young man dressed in well-worn range clothes who rode slowly along the main street of Wagontongue, Montana.

It was a busy day in the settlement. A number of wagons were parked on the street, especially around the two mercantile stores. Many of the hitch racks were almost full, too. The young man reined in, swung down from the saddle, and looped his horse's reins around the last available spot at the rail in front of the Silver Star Saloon.

Strains of music from what sounded like a player piano drifted past the batwings into the warm afternoon air of the street. The tune was a sprightly, enticing one, but the newcomer didn't need much encouragement to step into the saloon. He'd had a long ride, and his throat was dry from thirst.

The tension he had sensed as he rode into town was even thicker inside the Silver Star. He felt it as soon as he pushed through the batwings. The music continued—it did indeed come from a player piano tucked into a corner—but the low buzz of conversation in the room tailed off and then stopped as the customers turned to look at him.

He saw right away that three distinct groups occupied the saloon. Ten men sat around a large, round table in the back, covered with baize for poker playing although a game wasn't going on at the moment. They were drinking instead. A couple partially full bottles of whiskey sat on the table, along with an empty one.

A like number of men stood together at the bar, shot glasses and mugs of beer on the hardwood in front of them. They seemed more interested in using the long mirror on the wall behind the bar to keep an eye on the men at the table than they did in drinking.

The feelings of hostility between those two bunches were so thick they were almost visible in the smoke-hazed air.

The other group in the saloon consisted of the bartender, a couple young women in short spangled dresses who worked there, and several men who sat at some of the tables scattered to the newcomer's left. They looked like townsmen, except for a lean, saturnine man in a frock coat who sat alone, lazily dealing a hand of solitaire on the table in front of him. The newcomer figured he was a tinhorn gambler, but the atmosphere in the saloon was too tense for anybody else to be interested in a card game.

The townies—too stubborn to be run out . . . yet— looked nervous but unwilling to finish their drinks and leave. If a ruckus erupted, more than likely they would dart through those batwings almost quicker than the eye could follow.

All that information flashed through the young man's brain in a heartbeat. He'd barely paused as the batwings swung closed behind him, then strode to the bar and stopped at the closest end, several feet away from the group of men who stood there.

The people in the saloon started talking again, figuring him for a nobody. Just a drifter. Another saddle tramp.

That was what he looked like in his run-down boots, faded denim trousers, patched shirt, and sweat-stained hat. He wore a gun, but it was an old Colt single-action in a plain holster, worn high enough to make it obvious that he wasn't any kind of fast draw. The brown stubble on his jaw and the layer of trail dust on his face and clothes made it obvious he had been traveling for quite a while.

The bartender, a gray haired man with creases and gullies in his face that looked like a river had carved them out, came over to the newcomer and asked, "Somethin' for you, mister?"

"Beer," the young man said. "How much?"

"Two bits."

The young man reached into a pocket, brought out a coin, looked at it, and heaved a wistful sigh like he was saying good-bye to an old friend. He slid it across the hardwood. The bartender filled a mug and set it in front of the newcomer while his other hand deftly scooped up the coin.

The young man took a sip of the beer to cut the trail dust in his throat. Then, since the bartender was still standing across from him, he leaned forward, lowered his voice, and asked, "Is it just me, or is everybody in here wound up a mite tight?"

The bartender turned so his back was partially

toward the rest of the saloon, leaned an elbow on the hardwood, and said in a confidential tone, "It's sort of like waitin' for a thunderstorm to burst on a hot, still day, ain't it?"

"I'd say so."

The bartender leaned his head toward the big table in the back.

"That's the Rafter M crew yonder. Some of 'em, anyway. The ones most on the prod. The ones here at the bar are the Three Rivers bunch." The bartender shook his head. "Ain't no love lost between 'em, I can tell you that for a fact."

"Is there going to be a fight?"

"I hope not. Mort Cabot, the fella who owns the Rafter M, and Keenan Malone, the boss of the Three Rivers, are good about payin' for damages, but I'd just as soon not have to go through all the bother of cleanin' up. Name's Cy Hartung, by the way. This is my place."

"Vance Brewster. I'm glad to meet you, Mr. Hartung."

"Grub line rider?"

"Yep. Anybody around here hiring?"

"I'm not sure about that," Hartung said. "I think the Three Rivers just hired a couple new hands, but they may be full up now."

"You said the boss is named Malone? Is he here?"

Hartung shook his head. "Naw. He ain't much of a drinker. These fellas are just some of the punchers who work for him."

"Pretty good spread that Malone has?"

"One of the biggest and best in these parts. He don't own it, though, just runs it. Somebody back east actually owns it. Don't know if it's one man or one of those . . . what do you call 'em? Syndicates. Some ranches here in Montana are even owned by *Englishmen.*"

Both men shook their heads as if to ask what the world was coming to.

"I reckon the Rafter M must be pretty big, too," Vance said. "It's natural that big spreads would have a rivalry. I've seen it plenty of times before. Last place I rode for, down in Colorado, the fellas couldn't stand the men who worked for the next ranch over, and the feeling was vice versa."

"It ain't just a rivalry." Hartung lowered his voice. "There's been trouble—stolen cattle trouble—with both sides blamin' the other."

Vance took another sip of his beer and frowned.

"You make it sound like the best thing a fella could do is to mount up and ride outta this part of the country. If all hell's gonna break loose, it can do it without me." He sighed. "Problem is, I'm near flat busted. I got to have some work and earn some wages."

"Might be you could get something clerkin' at one of the stores."

The look Vance gave the bartender made it clear he would never stoop that low. Any job that couldn't be done from horseback just wasn't worth doing, in the opinion of most cowboys.

Vance had a feeling somebody was watching him. He glanced along the bar and saw that one of the Three Rivers punchers was slouched forward over the hardwood, idly toying with his beer mug while he looked toward Vance. The man was tall and lanky, with a hawk-like face and a thick black mustache that drooped over his wide mouth. He wore a collarless shirt and a black leather vest, and a battered black hat was thumbed back on a rumpled thatch of dark hair. He gave Vance a friendly nod and a half-smile, then turned his head to say something to the stocky, red-headed man who stood on the other side of him.

Vance forgot about those two a moment later when one of the Rafter M men stood up from the table and sauntered toward the entrance.

The man moved like a big cat and had the same air of menace about him, an attitude that said he could strike swiftly and dangerously at any second, with no warning. His lean, handsome face had a slightly lantern-jawed cast to it. His black hat was cocked at a jaunty angle on his sandy hair.

"Who's that?" Vance asked Cy Hartung.

"Dax Coolidge." A frown of disapproval creased the saloon man's already wrinkled face. "He's a gunman."

"I thought you said those fellas all rode for the Rafter M."

"That's where Coolidge draws his wages, all right, but Mort Cabot didn't hire him for his ropin' skills, if you know what I mean. With trouble brewin' between Cabot's spread and the Three Rivers, I reckon it makes sense he'd want some gun-handy fellas workin' for him."

"So he brought in Coolidge?"

Hartung scratched his jaw. "Well, come to think of it, Coolidge had been in these parts for a while when he signed on with the Rafter M. Had sort of a shady reputation, too, but I reckon that didn't matter to Cabot. You could even say that helped make up Cabot's mind."

"The more I hear, the better that clerking job is

starting to sound." Vance took another drink, licked his lips, and added, "I don't want any part of a range war."

"I don't blame you there." Hartung glanced toward the door, then caught his breath. His hands, which were lying flat on the bar, pressed down harder in reaction to what he saw.

Vance couldn't help but turn his head to look. Dax Coolidge had stopped short a couple steps from the entrance when the batwings swung inward to admit someone else.

A young woman stepped inside. Hair the color of a sunset brushed her shoulders and hung partway down her back. She wore a man's shirt with the sleeves rolled up a couple turns, a brown vest, and a brown skirt split for riding astride. Her hat dangled behind her head from the chin strap around her throat.

Vance figured he knew a ranch girl when he saw one, and a pretty one, at that, even with the scowl displayed on her face as she looked at the man who blocked her path.

"I'll thank you to get out of my way, Mr. Coolidge," she said.

He gave her a mocking grin in return. "Here I thought *you* were the one in *my* way, Rose."

She blew out an exasperated breath and started to step to the side.

Coolidge moved to block her again.

"Blast it," Cy Hartung muttered. "I was startin' to hope there wouldn't be any trouble."

"Who's that?" Vance asked again.

"The girl? Miss Rosaleen Malone. Her pa is old Keenan Malone, the boss of the Three Rivers I was tellin' you about."

"Coolidge acts like he knows her."

"Shoot, everybody in these parts knows Rosaleen. She was born and raised here. Malone had her on a horse before she could walk. She was born sort of late in life to Malone and his wife, and she's the only youngster they ever had. Folks figure Malone wanted a son, so he tried to make Rosaleen as much like one as he could."

Vance shook his head and said in an admiring tone, "Nobody's ever going to mistake her for a boy."

"No, not likely."

While Vance was talking to the bartender, Rosaleen Malone had tried to move the other way and go around Coolidge, but once again he had placed himself in her path.

She was starting to look more than frustrated. She was getting mad. "You need to get out of my way."

"I could do that," Coolidge said. "But you're gonna have to do something for me first."

"I don't think so."

"It's nothing bad. Just have a dance with me, Rose." Coolidge nodded toward the player piano, which was still cranking out a merry tune.

"No," she said flatly.

From the table where the rest of the Rafter M men were sitting, one of them called, "Leave the gal alone, Dax."

Without looking around, Coolidge said, "You stay out of it, Harry. This is none of your business." His voice held a distinct tone of menace, even though it was directed at a fellow member of the Rafter M crew.

Clearly, Dax Coolidge was a man who didn't like to be crossed—by anybody.

The men at the table looked uneasy, and Vance

knew why. On the frontier, a decent woman was treated with the utmost respect, even by the most hardened range riders. Too few of them were around to do otherwise.

Evidently Coolidge didn't believe that code of conduct applied to him. With the Three Rivers men standing along the bar watching, he reached out and closed his left hand around Rosaleen's right arm.

"Oh, no," Cy Hartung said. "He's laid hands on her."

"Dance with me, Rose," Coolidge said as he pulled her closer to him.

Since he had hold of her right arm, her left hand flashed up and cracked across his face. His head jerked to the side, he uttered a curse, and reached for her with his other hand.

What he intended to do next, nobody ever knew. The men from the Three Rivers exploded away from the bar, furious shouts erupting from their throats.

CHAPTER TWO

As the Three Rivers punchers swarmed toward Coolidge, one man bounded ahead of his companions, grabbed Coolidge's shoulder, hauled him around, and yelled, "Get your hands off her, you no-good son of a—"

Coolidge's fist crashed into his face and knocked him back into the arms of his friends.

At the same moment, the Rafter M crew leaped to their feet and waded in, tackling and slugging.

Vance had seen the disapproval on their faces as Coolidge accosted Rosaleen Malone, but regardless of that, men such as these rode for the brand, and when one of their own was under attack, they sprung to his aid.

As Vance expected, every customer in the place who didn't belong to one of the two ranch crews scurried to get out of the saloon. A bottleneck backup formed at the entrance as shoulders wedged together, but then the two men who were stuck popped through and the rest stampeded after them, including the frock-coated gambler.

Squealing, the two saloon girls darted behind the bar and ducked down in case any chairs started flying, which was always possible in a brawl. Cy Hartung ran back and forth, shouting futilely at the battlers to take it outside.

Vance looked for Rosaleen Malone but didn't see her. He supposed she had ducked out, too, while Coolidge was distracted and she had the chance.

He was the only neutral party on his side of the bar. He gave some thought to slipping out, too, but he wanted to finish his beer first.

He had just picked up the mug when one of the Rafter M crew, reeling from a punch, crashed into him. Vance caught him, but the beer that was still in the mug flew into the man's face. Sputtering, he pushed loose from Vance's arms and yelled, "Try to drown me, will you, you Three Rivers skunk!"

His fist came up and smacked into Vance's jaw, knocking the young man's head back.

Vance reacted instinctively. With the empty mug still in his hand, he lifted it and brought it down on the man's head. The mug shattered, and the cowboy dropped like a stone.

Another Rafter M man saw that and howled, "That fella just killed Pete!"

Vance looked at the mug's handle, which was all he still had in his hand, and then tossed it aside to meet the attack of the three men who charged at him.

He knew he couldn't hope to defeat all three of them, but he planned to give a good account of himself.

Before the Rafter M men could reach him, two figures appeared, one on each side of him.

The man to his right said, "We'll back your play, son."

It was the tall, lanky, mustachioed cowboy Vance had noticed looking at him earlier. The other unexpected ally was the short redhead. Their arrival made the odds even.

Fists lashed out. Flesh and bone thudded together. Men grunted with effort as the combatants stood toe-to-toe, slugging it out. It wasn't the first fight Vance had ever been in, and he did a good job of blocking his opponent's blows and delivering punches of his own.

His two newfound friends were veritable devils when it came to fisticuffs. The tall cowboy looked too scrawny to pack much heft into his punches, but they landed with devastating power. A right and a left drove into the belly of a Rafter M rider and doubled him over, putting him in perfect position for a sizzling uppercut that lifted him off his feet and deposited him on his back in a limp sprawl.

The man fighting with the redhead had an advantage in reach, but the redhead just lowered his head, hunched his shoulders, and absorbed the punishment the other man dished out as he bored in, arms working like pistons and fists pounding into the man's midsection.

That left Vance to handle the man in the middle. Leaning his head to the side so a blow grazed off the side of his skull, he landed a quick left-right combination to sternum and jaw. Another combination consisting of a left hook to the stomach and a second hard right to the jaw made the Rafter M man's knees fold up. He tried to tackle Vance around the thighs as he collapsed, but Vance shoved him away.

Putting his back against the bar, Vance looked at the tall cowboy and the redhead and grinned. "Pretty good fight while it lasted."

"It ain't over!" the tall cowboy said. "Duck!"

Vance ducked as part of a broken chair sailed over his head and crashed into the back bar, breaking several bottles. Cy Hartung wailed in dismay.

"At least there hasn't been any gunplay," the red-head said.

"Yet," his friend said.

Dax Coolidge had a reputation as a gunman, Vance recalled. He looked around and spotted Coolidge sitting on the floor, his back propped against an overturned table. He was shaking his head groggily.

Rosaleen Malone stood nearby, holding an empty whiskey bottle by the neck.

She hadn't fled when the fight started after all. Vance couldn't help but wonder if she had walloped Coolidge over the head with it. He figured that could be why the gunman looked stunned.

Cowboys were still pounding away at each other as they stomped around in a litter of broken chairs and tables. Hartung would be collecting damages from Mort Cabot and Keenan Malone, that was for sure.

"By God, that's enough!" a man roared from the entrance. When that didn't do any good, he raised the shotgun in his hands and emptied one of its twin barrels into the ceiling.

Cy Hartung whimpered a little in the echoing silence that followed the blast.

The man lowered the Greener and strode into the saloon, followed by two men who were armed the same way. The battle was forgotten as cowboys from both spreads eyed the newcomers warily. The menacing presence of those double-barreled scatterguns was enough to make anybody nervous.

The shot had had been fired by a man with a badge

pinned to the shirt stretched over his barrel chest. He had a rugged, rough-hewn face with a bristled slab of a jaw. "Sorry about putting buckshot holes in your ceiling, Cy," the lawman said. "Seemed like the quickest way to get these loco mavericks to settle down."

"It's all right, Sheriff," Hartung said. "You've got to keep the peace."

The lawman chuckled. "That's what they pay me to do, all right. What started this ruckus?" Before Hartung could answer, the sheriff went on. "It doesn't really matter, I guess. I see Rafter M and Three Rivers are both here, so that's really all it takes, isn't it? Didn't I tell you boys to drink in different saloons from now on?"

Still holding the empty bottle, Rosaleen stepped forward and set it on a table that was still upright. "I'll tell you what started it, Sheriff, or rather *who*. It was Dax Coolidge."

One of the Three Rivers punchers said, "That's right, Sheriff. He was molestin' Miss Malone, and when we stepped in to put a stop to it, the rest of those Rafter M polecats jumped us."

"That's a lie," Coolidge said as he pushed through the crowd. He had gotten his wits back about him. "All I did was ask Miss Malone to dance with me, and she slapped me. Even after that, I didn't do anything until the whole bunch from the Three Rivers attacked me."

"Now you're lying." The words came out of Vance's mouth before he could stop them. "You had your hands on Miss Malone. The only reason she struck you was to protect herself."

Everyone in the room looked at him in surprise.

Coolidge's lips curled in a sneer. "What business is it of yours? You're a stranger here."

"I may be a stranger," Vance said, "but that doesn't mean I'll put up with a woman being manhandled. Where I come from, we just don't allow things like that."

"And where's that?"

Vance shrugged. "Last place was Colorado. Before that, all over, I reckon you'd say."

With the heavily armed deputies flanking him, the sheriff broke open his shotgun, took out the shell he'd fired, and replaced it with a fresh one. As he snapped the weapon closed, he said, "You've been warned about causing trouble, Coolidge. You're going down to the jail to cool your heels overnight."

Coolidge stiffened. "Blast it, Jerrico—"

"I didn't ask for an argument. Hand over your gun."

For a second, Vance thought Coolidge was going to draw and start shooting rather than surrender the weapon. But then his shoulders rose and fell in a little shrug, and he took the gun carefully out of its holster, reversing it and handing it to one of the deputies.

"Things are liable to be different one of these days, Sheriff. You might not always have the odds on your side."

"I've always got the odds on my side against the likes of you." Sheriff Jerrico jerked his head toward the batwinged entrance and told his deputies, "Get him out of here and lock him up."

When the deputies were gone with their prisoner, Jerrico looked at the bartender. "You want me to have these fellas empty their pockets, Cy, or would you rather send bills to Cabot and Malone?"

"I'll just take it up with the cowboys, Sheriff," Hartung said. "It's not the first time this has happened."

"Yeah, but it better be the last," Jerrico said with a warning glare directed at both ranch crews. "If there's a next time, I might just lock up all of you for a month!" He stepped aside and nodded toward the entrance. "All of you get out of here and go back to your spreads. Rafter M first. I don't want the fight spreading into the street. You boys get out of town and then Three Rivers can go."

"That ain't fair," a Rafter M man said. "What's to stop them from gettin' an extra drink before they go?"

"I am," Hartung declared. "Bar's closed for now."

Jerrico nodded. "That's what I was just about to say. Get moving."

With sullen expressions on their bruised and somewhat bloody faces, the Rafter M riders filed out of the Silver Star.

The sheriff followed, pausing in the entrance to tell the Three Rivers bunch, "I want you men out of here in ten minutes. I'll be keeping an eye out to make sure you leave." The batwings flapped closed behind him as he went out.

The tall, mustachioed cowboy grinned at Vance. "Looks like you're the only one who don't have to hightail it, since you don't belong to either bunch."

"I was wondering if maybe I could change that," Vance said.

"Lookin' for work, are you?"

"I could use a riding job. My pockets are so empty they're starting to echo. You reckon the Three Rivers could use another good hand?"

"I don't rightly know. Wilbur and me just signed

on not long ago our own selves. You'd have to talk to Mr. Malone about that, I reckon. But it can't hurt anything that you jumped in to give us a hand against those Rafter M varmints. My name's Stewart, by the way. They call me Stovepipe."

"On account of he's so tall and skinny," the redhead said.

Stovepipe chuckled and pointed a thumb at his friend. "That short-growed runt is one Wilbur Coleman. We been ridin' together for a spell."

"Yeah, ever since we were trying to duck posses at the same time," Wilbur said. "But I don't reckon we need to talk about that, do we?"

"I disremember what you're talkin' about," Stovepipe said with a smile on his deeply tanned face. "I've always rode the straight and narrow trail."

"Yeah, that's what we'll call it."

Vance said, "Since you fellas are already riding for the Three Rivers, maybe you could put in a good word for me with the boss."

"Sure, I reckon we could do that," Stovepipe said. "Can't guarantee it'll do any good, though."

"Neither can I," a voice behind Vance said, "but it might help if I spoke to the boss, too."

He turned to find Rosaleen Malone smiling at him.

CHAPTER THREE

Vance snatched his hat off his head. "Uh, Miss Malone . . . It's an honor—"

"Don't go falling all over yourself, son," she told him. "I grew up around cowboys, so I know you're all rough as a cob even though you try to pretend to be polite around us female types. But there's no need in my case."

"It's a hard habit to break," Vance said. "And it truly is an honor and a pleasure to meet you. I've heard a lot about you."

She frowned slightly. "Didn't you just ride into town today? I don't recall seeing you around before."

"Less than an hour ago, in fact."

"And you've been gossiping about me already."

Quickly, Vance said, "Well, I wouldn't exactly call it gossiping—"

She stopped him with a grin. "Don't worry. I'm just joshing you, son."

Vance wasn't sure how he felt about being called *son* by a woman who was probably a year or two younger than him, and a mighty pretty one, to boot.

Stovepipe stepped into the conversation by saying, "Miss Malone, this here is Vance Brewster. He took our side in the fight. Coldcocked Pete Decker with an empty beer mug."

Rosaleen's green eyes widened. "Did that kill him?"

"No, I saw him get up and walk off under his own power," Stovepipe said. "Reckon he's got a skull as thick as the door of a bank vault."

"And Stovepipe would know about bank vaults and how hard it is to get into 'em," Wilbur said.

"You hush," Stovepipe said with a quick glare at his friend. "You'll have these folks thinkin' I used to be some sorta owlhoot, when I've always been the most law-abidin', peaceable hombre you'd ever hope to find."

"Uh-huh," Wilbur said.

"Anyway," Vance went on, "I *am* looking for a riding job, Miss Malone, so anything you say to your father that might help would sure be appreciated."

Rosaleen nodded. "I'll see what I can do, but like I told you, no promises."

Cy Hartung rested his hands on the bar and said from the other side of it, "Uh, I hate to bother you, Miss Malone . . ."

She turned toward him. "That's all right, Mr. Hartung. Don't worry. The Three Rivers will pay its share of the damages. Would you like me to tell my father how much?"

"I haven't figured it up yet. Would it be all right if I just sent word to him tomorrow?"

"That's fine. I'll tell him he can expect to be hearing from you."

"I'm much obliged to you, miss."

Rosaleen shook her head. "The fight was sort of my fault. I'm the one who came in here looking for the boys so I could tell them we were ready to head back to the ranch."

Vance spoke up right away. "It's not your fault at all. Coolidge was to blame. He's the one who acted like a complete boor."

"He's that, sure enough. But I saw the Rafter M brands on some of the horses tied up outside. I should have known things would be pretty tense in here."

Stovepipe said, "I reckon if you comin' in hadn't popped the cork on that fracas, something else would've. Those fellas from the Rafter M were spoilin' for a fight."

"Of course, all the Three Rivers crew wanted was a peaceful drink," Rosaleen said with a smile.

"That's right. Just a little tonsil lubrication 'fore we all headed over to the weekly meetin' of the Ladies Quiltin' Society."

Rosaleen laughed at Stovepipe's words, then grew more serious. "It's been ten minutes since Cabot's bunch left. Three Rivers, let's go."

"Me, too?" Vance asked.

"Of course," Rosaleen answered without hesitation. "You fought on our side. Even if my father decides not to hire you, you're getting a good supper and a bunk for the night in return for your trouble."

"It was no trouble at all, Miss Malone."

"It made you some enemies . . . including Dax Coolidge."

Vance offered, "I've heard it said a man can be judged by his enemies."

"In that case," Stovepipe said, "you rate pretty high, amigo, 'cause Coolidge is a bad man to have against you."

The Three Rivers crew emerged from the Silver Star and saw no sign of any Rafter M riders, but Sheriff Jerrico stood across the street in front of a hardware store, leaning on one of the posts that held up the awning over the boardwalk. The lawman still had that Greener tucked under his arm. He gave the group a curt nod.

The men went to the hitch rack to untie their horses. Rosaleen angled across the street toward a wagon parked in front of Hampton's General Mercantile. A middle-aged woman as round as a ball, wearing a dress and a sunbonnet, was perched on the wagon seat.

As Vance loosened his reins from the rail, he heard the older woman say, "I take it there was trouble in the saloon, dear?"

"A little, Aunt Sinead. Nothing I shouldn't have expected, though, when I saw Cabot's men were in there."

"I saw Charlie Jerrico's deputies hauling that terrible Dax Coolidge out of there and knew something must have happened. Thank goodness you're all right, girl. Keenan would never forgive me if anything ever happened to you."

Rosaleen jerked the reins of a good-looking sorrel loose from the rail in front of the mercantile and replied with a note of annoyance in her voice, "I can take care of myself just fine. It's not your responsibility."

"I doubt if your father would see it that way."

Vance watched and listened to that exchange as he swung up into the saddle and settled into the leather

Stovepipe eased a rangy paint up next to Vance's horse and said quietly, "The lady on the wagon is Rosaleen's Aunt Sinead O'Hara. Older sister of Malone's late missus. Aunt Sinead handles the cookin' and the housekeepin' and is the general factotum around the place. You don't want *her* for an enemy, neither."

"I don't go around *looking* for enemies, you know."

"Most folks don't. They make 'em anyway, sorta in the natural course o' things."

"And Stovepipe would know," Wilbur added as he brought a sturdy roan up on Vance's other side. "He's made a heap."

"There you go again, makin' me sound like a wild desperado."

"Just making sure Vance understands how trouble seems to gravitate to you, Stovepipe."

"So I can keep my distance?" Vance chuckled. "I think I'll take my chances. You two seem like good fellas to have for friends."

"Don't say nobody warned you," Wilbur said.

When Rosaleen was mounted on the sorrel, Aunt Sinead slapped the reins against the backs of the team hitched to the wagon and got them moving. The two women led the way out of the settlement, heading northwest toward a range of low hills.

As they rode with the other cowboys, Stovepipe nodded toward the distant hills and told Vance, "Three Rivers lies amongst those. Spread got its name from the three streams that meander through the hills. They ain't hardly big enough to be called rivers, but they do a good job of waterin' the range land. Plenty of grass in the valleys all year 'round, and there's good graze in the higher pastures durin' the summer, too."

"You seem to know a lot about the place for somebody who just signed on not long ago," Vance said.

Wilbur said, "Those jug handles on the sides of his head have a purpose. Stovepipe's a good listener. Picks up on all sorts of things an hombre without such big ears might not."

"I've never thought my ears were that much bigger than most fellas'. I just know how to use 'em, and my eyes, too. It's called payin' attention. Some folks seem to forget how to do that."

"Who needs to with you around?" Wilbur asked with a shrug.

"What about the Ralter M." Vance asked. "Where in it located?"

Stovepipe pointed to the northeast, where the terrain was flatter. "It's even bigger than the Three Rivers, but Malone and Cabot run about the same size herd because the range ain't as good over yonder and it takes more of it to support each cow. I ain't sayin' it's *bad* range, mind you. It just ain't as good as the Three Rivers, which is might' near heaven on earth for raisin' cattle."

Vance nodded. "I'm glad to hear it. It sounds like I'm headed for a good place . . . *if* I get a job there."

"Worry about that when the time comes. Like Miss Rosaleen said, you get a good meal and a bunk for the night no matter what else happens. Grub line riders like us got to take life one day at a time. That's all it gives us, anyway, no matter who we are."

The ride to the Three Rivers ranch took the rest of the afternoon. Stovepipe spun yarns most of the way, with the occasional interjection of dry wit from Wilbur. Vance enjoyed listening to them. From the sound of the stories, the two drifters had been almost everywhere on the frontier.

"From the Rio Grande to the Milk River, and from the Mississipp' to the blue waters of the Pacific," as Stovepipe put it.

The sun had almost touched the hills by the time the wagon and the riders headed up a long valley toward the ranch headquarters. The main house was a sturdy two-story frame structure with whitewashed walls. Several cottonwoods grew around it for shade during the summer. In addition were a long, low bunkhouse, a couple barns with attached corrals, a square, stone building that appeared to be a black-smith shop, some storage sheds, and a smokehouse.

Pretty impressive, Vance thought. As they came closer, he could tell everything was well-maintained. It was obvious Keenan Malone ran an efficient opera-tion around here.

Stovepipe pointed toward one of the barns. "That's where the horses go. Head in that direction. Malone's got a good remuda built up. Of course, you've got your own mount, like me and Wilbur, but if you sign on, you'll be able to rest him some."

"Sounds good," Vance said, nodding. "Is that a garden I see over there on the other side of the main house?"

"Yep. And there's a little chicken house back there,

too, so we've always got fresh eggs and plenty o' vegetables in season. I ain't much on rabbit food, but some taters and carrots and onions always liven up a pot of stew. Ain't nobody cooks up a stew like the Irish."

"I'm starting to think I'm going to like it here," Vance said with a grin.

A brawny, broad-shouldered man walked out of the other barn and strode toward Rosaleen and Aunt Sinead as they veered toward the main house. He had a thick white mustache, bushy brows of the same shade, and walked with the rolling gait of someone born to the saddle.

"Keenan Malone," Stovepipe told Vance. "Fine man, from what I've seen of him."

Rosaleen reined in the sorrel while Aunt Sinead drove the wagon around the house, probably so the supplies she had picked up in Wagontongue could be unloaded into the kitchen. After a moment, Rosaleen turned in her saddle and beckoned to Vance.

"Looks like she put in that good word for you," Stovepipe said. "Good luck, son. Hope you get that job."

"Thanks." Vance turned his horse and heeled it toward the Malones.

Rosaleen had dismounted by the time he got there, so he swung down from the saddle, too.

She said, "Dad, this is Vance Brewster."

"Good to meet you, Vance," Malone said as he stuck out a big hand.

Vance clasped it and returned the rancher's firm grip. "It's my pleasure, sir. This is a really fine-looking spread."

"I've been takin' care of it for many years, just like

I've been lookin' after Rosaleen here." Only the faintest hint of an Irish lilt could be heard in Malone's voice.

"Like I told Aunt Sinead, I'm getting a little too old to need looking after, Dad," Rosaleen said.

Malone just shook his head. "A child never gets old enough for a parent to feel that way. You'll understand that yourself, one of these days."

Since the sun was low enough in the sky to give everything a bit of a rosy hue to start with, it was hard to tell if Rosaleen blushed at her father's comment, but Vance thought she did.

"My daughter tells me you pitched in on our side during that scrape with Cabot's men in town," Malone went on.

"Yes, sir."

"Might not have been the wisest thing to do, you bein' a newcomer to these parts."

Vance shook his head. "My only regret is that I didn't get to wallop that skunk Dax Coolidge like Miss Rosaleen did."

Malone's eyebrows rose as he looked at his daughter. "You did that?"

She grinned. "With an empty whiskey bottle. He had it coming."

"I don't doubt it for a second. Bust his head open?"

"No . . . unfortunately. I knocked him silly for a while, though."

"Good girl." Malone turned back to Vance. "Rosaleen tells me you're lookin' for a job."

"That's right."

"Top hand, are you?"

Vance said, "I won't lie to you, sir. I'm not a top hand, but I've always been willing to work hard, and I pick up on things pretty quickly, if I do say so myself. I'd rather be honest, though, if you're thinking about hiring me."

"I'm thinkin' about it. I figure this spread can always use a young fella who's willin' to work hard." Malone extended his hand again. "Welcome to the Three Rivers, Vance. You've got a job . . . for now. We'll see how it goes."

CHAPTER FOUR

Over the next few days, Vance earned his keep on the ranch. Like the rest of the crew, he was up before the sun every day and spent long hours in the saddle, riding the range to check on the stock, roping calves who had gotten stuck in the mud along the rivers and pulling them free, pushing cows from this pasture to that one and generally doing whatever Keenan Malone ordered him to.

Malone served as his own foreman, although he had a *segundo*. Andy Callahan rode herd on the crew when Malone wasn't around. Malone worked with the cowboys every day, since he wasn't the sort of boss who would ask his men to do anything he wasn't willing to do himself.

The third day after Vance signed on, Wilbur watched with narrowed eyes as the young cowboy walked from the barn toward the bunkhouse. "The youngster looks to be a mite stiff and sore," Wilbur said to Stovepipe as the two of them ambled along a short distance behind Vance.

"Yeah, I noticed the same thing," Stovepipe said. "You can tell he's rode and roped before, but I got a feelin' he ain't spent quite so many hours in a saddle as he's doin' these days."

"What do you reckon that means? That he didn't ride for all those other spreads like he claimed?"

Stovepipe's bony shoulders rose and fell. "I reckon it'd be goin' too far to say the boy's a liar."

"I didn't say he was a liar. I just wondered if he'd stretched the truth a mite. *You've* been known to do that, and I wouldn't call you a liar."

"Let's just figure he'll bear keepin' an eye on," Stovepipe said. "Can't deny he's a hard worker, just like he said he was. He throws himself full blast right into whatever he's supposed to do and does the best he can."

"Yeah. You can't help but like him. He sorta reminds me of a big ol' friendly puppy."

Stovepipe grinned. "Even a puppy's got teeth and knows how to use 'em if he has to. Be interestin' to see what kind of bite Vance has got."

"You mean if there's more trouble?"

"I reckon it's more a matter of *when* than *if*," Stovepipe said.

The hands took their meals in the big dining room in the main house with Malone and his daughter and sister-in-law. That evening at supper, Malone stood up and said, "Tomorrow we'll be starting a gather of all the stock in the northern section, boys."

"Are we puttin' together a trail herd, Mr. Malone?" Andy Callahan asked.

"That's right. All of you know, except the three new men, that there was a mighty nice calf crop this spring. We're gonna need to sell off some older stock so there'll be plenty of grass for those hungry little critters. Plus, I'll be writin' my midyear report for the owners pretty soon, and they like to see a little cash flow."

"They oughta come out here and see it for themselves," one of the men said.

"I reckon those men have better things to do than tramp around a ranch," Malone said. "Anyway, they've got jobs of their own that have to be taken care of.

In a half-whisper, Vance said to Stovepipe, "I'm not sure I'd call sitting behind a desk in an office a real job."

From the head of the table, Malone asked, "You got something to share with us, Brewster?"

Vance looked abashed and shook his head. "Uh, no, sir. Sorry."

"Well, then, as I was sayin' . . . we'll put together a herd of about five hundred head and drive it over to the railhead at Miles City. Ought to get a decent price for it and make everybody happy. So I hope you fellas are ready to work. We won't be loafin' around like usual for a while."

Vance sighed at Malone's description of what they had been doing. *Loafing* didn't seem quite right to him.

Later, he and Stovepipe and Wilbur stood by one of the corrals and leaned on the rail fence as they enjoyed the evening air. Since the three of them had been on the ranch the shortest amount of time, they had gravitated together naturally and become friends.

"Ever been on a trail drive before, Vance?" Stovepipe asked as he looked up at the stars twinkling in the deep black sky overhead. Montana Territory was called big sky country, and the heavens loomed just as large at night as they did during the day.

"Sure I have," Vance said. "I helped push several herds up the Chisholm Trail from Texas to Kansas. I drove cattle to market in Colorado, too."

"Why, this won't seem like much of a chore to you at all, then. It ain't near as far to Miles City as it is to the railheads in them other places."

Wilbur said, "Yeah, a few days of being in the saddle fourteen or sixteen hours a day ought to get us there."

Vance winced slightly at that comment, but neither Stovepipe nor Wilbur seemed to take any note of the reaction.

A soft step behind them made them turn. Enough light came from the moon and stars for Vance to recognize Rosaleen. She was wearing a dress rather than her riding getup.

He had thought she looked lovely at supper, and reached for his hat, yanking it off without even thinking about what he was doing. "Miss Rosaleen," he greeted her. "Good evening."

"Vance," she said. "Mr. Stewart. Mr. Coleman."

"Miss," Stovepipe said. "It's a beautiful evenin', made more so by your presence."

"You're a flatterer, Mr. Stewart," she said with a smile.

"No, miss, just a truthful man."

"What brings you out here?" Vance asked, then added quickly, "Not that I'm complaining."

"I wanted to check on my horse and make sure he's in good shape for tomorrow."

"Tomorrow? Were you planning on going somewhere?"

"I'm coming along on the roundup, of course."

Stovepipe, Wilbur, and Vance exchanged glances in the moonlight. It was obvious all three men wanted to say something, but they were reluctant to do so.

Stovepipe finally took the plunge. "Miss Rosaleen, I ain't sure it's a good idea for you to get mixed up in a deal like that. It's liable to be a lot of hot, dusty, dangerous work."

"I know what a roundup is like, Mr. Stewart. I've been around them before." She squared her shoulders. "It's just that I intend to take part in this one, instead of being merely an observer."

"Does your pa know that?" Wilbur asked.

"He'll find out soon enough."

"When he does," Stovepipe said, "he might just lay down the law and tell you, you ain't goin'."

Rosaleen's chin came up defiantly. "He'll have a fight on his hands if he does. He's the one who made sure I know how to rope and ride and treated me like a boy, much to my mother's dismay. If he doesn't like the way I act now, he's got no one to blame but himself."

"Can you shoot?" Vance asked.

"I always have a saddle carbine with me, and I'm a good shot with it, if I do say so myself. I shot the head off a rattlesnake once at fifty feet."

"That's good shootin', all right," Stovepipe said. "You've got me might' near convinced, Miss Rosaleen."

"And if I do get into any trouble," she said, "I'll have a bunch of cowboys around to help me, won't I?"

"I reckon they'll be linin' up to give you a hand," Stovepipe said.

Vance Brewster would probably be the first one in that line, he thought.

Aunt Sinead prepared an especially big breakfast the next morning, since the men would be in their saddles just about all day and would have to make do with what they could carry for a midday meal. When they had stoked themselves with coffee, flapjacks, eggs, and thick steaks, they went out to the barn to get their horses ready.

Keenan Malone's only concession to the fact he was the boss was letting the ranch's horse wrangler, a stove-up old hand named Asa, saddle his mount for him. When Malone came out of the house and strode toward the barn, Asa had a big, sturdy dun ready for him.

"Thanks, Asa," Malone said as he took the reins. He checked the cinches although he knew there was no real need to do so. The wrangler was absolutely trustworthy, but it was a habit of decades' standing, and Malone wasn't about to quit.

Asa had gone back into the barn, but he came out again before Malone could mount up. The old wrangler was leading a saddled sorrel.

"Wait a minute," Malone said with a frown. "That looks like—"

The sound of the house's front door closing interrupted him. He looked over his shoulder and saw Rosaleen walking quickly toward him. Her riding outfit was the same as any of the other hands'—a man's shirt, thick denim trousers, and high-topped boots. Her hair was tucked up in the high-crowned hat she wore with its strap taut under her chin.

"Aw, no," Malone said as he began shaking his head. "Not hardly!" He raised his right arm and pointed toward the door. "You might as well turn around and march on back into the house, missy!"

Rosaleen's chin jutted toward him. "Or what? You'll turn me over your knee and spank me like I was a little girl?"

"You ain't too big for me to do that if I have to, that's for dang sure!"

"Yes, I am, and you know it. Just like you know there's no good reason why I can't help you with the roundup. I ride as well as most of the men do, and I'm a better hand with a rope than some of them."

The members of the crew, all mounted, drifted over from the barn in time to witness most of this confrontation. A hint of a knowing smile tugged at the corners of Stovepipe's mouth under the drooping mustache. Things were working out pretty much the way he had expected. Keenan Malone was being stubborn . . . and Rosaleen was being stubborner.

Andy Callahan nudged his horse forward. "It's true, boss. I've seen Miss Rosaleen handle a lariat, and she's better than, say, Brewster here."

"Hey," Vance said. "I've done all right so far."

Malone narrowed his eyes at Callahan. "Andy, you won't be offended if I tell you this ain't none of your business, will you?"

"Nope. You're the boss. You can say whatever you want. I'm just sayin' Miss Rosaleen would give us an extra hand, that's all."

"We got plenty of men to handle a roundup."

Callahan shrugged. "That's true, too. Why don't the rest of us head on up to the north range and leave you two to work it out however you want?"

Malone agreed. "That's what I was just about to say."

Callahan lifted his reins, turned his horse, and motioned with his head. "Come on, boys." He rode north away from the ranch with the rest of the crew in a loose bunch behind him.

"I sort of wanted to stay and see how the argument came out," Wilbur said as he rode alongside Stovepipe and Vance.

"I'll bet you when Mr. Malone catches up, Rosaleen is with him," Vance said.

"No bet," Stovepipe said. "Man'd be a fool to buck the odds on a sure thing."

CHAPTER FIVE

The northern section of the Three Rivers ranch was mostly hilly terrain, but a broad, level pasture lay in the center of those hills. It was there Andy Callahan led the cowboys.

"We'll hold the gather here," he told them. "It shouldn't take more than a couple days to round up five hundred head like the boss wants. Leave the calves and their mamas where you find them. We just want steers."

He split up the crew into two groups, one bunch to work the hills to the east, the other to head west. Before they could set out, two riders appeared to the south, riding in their direction.

Callahan tried not to smile as he said, "Looks like here comes the rest of the outfit."

From a distance the newcomers appeared to be two more punchers, but Stovepipe recognized the dun and the sorrel they were riding.

So did Vance. "Looks like Miss Rosaleen won the argument."

"I don't reckon anybody here expected any different," Stovepipe said.

The newcomers rode up and Malone said, "The boys got their jobs laid out, Andy?"

"Yep. Half goin' east, half goin' west."

Rosaleen said without hesitation, "I'll go west."

Stovepipe wondered if her decision was because he, Wilbur, and Vance were with that group.

"One man will have to switch," Malone said. "You and I are stayin' together."

"You think I want my father watching over my shoulder all day?" Rosaleen asked with a toss of her head. "I don't see any reason why we can't split up, Dad. You trust all the men who ride for you, don't you?"

"Of course I do!"

"Then I ought to be just as safe with them as I am with you. You go east and I'll go west."

Malone looked like he wanted to argue, but he had already come out on the short end of the stick in one such discussion this morning, so he gave in. "All right. Just be careful."

"You don't have a thing to worry about."

He let out a dubious snort and turned his horse to join the cowboys who would be combing the hills to the east of the pasture.

Rosaleen nudged her horse in the other direction. "This is going to be fun," she said as she fell in alongside Vance, Stovepipe, and Wilbur.

"I've been on many a roundup," Stovepipe said. "I ain't sure I'd describe any of 'em as fun."

"This isn't a real roundup. If it was, we'd have a chuck wagon out here and we'd make camp and sleep under the stars. We'll all be back in our own beds tonight, except for the men who have to ride nighthawk." Rosaleen shook her head. "This is just a little chore. I'm not sure why Dad is determined to make such a big deal out of it."

Stovepipe said, "Well, he worries about his little girl. Reckon that's natural enough."

"He needs to learn I'm not a little girl anymore." She patted the smooth wooden stock of the carbine that rode in a sheath under the saddle fender. "And anybody who makes that mistake is liable to regret it."

The hills were rugged and thickly wooded, and the valleys and draws between them were often choked with brush. Before the morning was half over, Stovepipe and Wilbur had pulled thick leather chaps from their saddlebags and strapped them on, and so had Rosaleen. Vance didn't have any of the protective garments, so he spent most of his time yelping as the brush clawed and scratched at his legs.

"How come you don't have any chaps?" Wilbur asked him. "I never knew a Texas boy who didn't carry a pair with him. A fella can't go into that *brasada* down there without 'em."

"I'm not *from* Texas," Vance said. "I just worked there. Anyway, I, uh"—he lowered his voice and looked at Rosaleen, far enough away to be out of earshot if he didn't talk very loud—"I had to sell mine. I've been right on the edge of being broke for a good while now."

"Well, I guess it could've been worse. You could've sold your saddle." Wilbur's contemptuous tone made it clear what he thought of any cowboy who would resort to that desperate measure.

The work was as hot, dusty, and dirty as they had all known it would be. The cattle had a habit of hiding in

the brush and were stubborn when the cowboys tried
to chouse them out of it. They had to ride into the
undergrowth after the beasts and often had to take
their coiled ropes and wallop the cows with them to
get them to move. Sometimes they had to dab a loop
around a steer's neck and drag it into the open, where
some of the other hands would then haze it toward
the gather.

Rosaleen didn't shirk or complain. By the time the
sun was almost directly overhead, her shirt was soaked
with sweat and the upper half of her face was covered
with a layer of dust. Like the others, she had tied her
bandanna around the lower part of her face to keep
some of the dust out of her nose and mouth.

Working a canyon with Vance, Stovepipe, and
Wilbur, she was approaching a dense tangle of brush
when an old bull suddenly broke out of the thicket
with a crackle of branches. The proddy old bull knew
something was going on and didn't like it, whatever
it was.

Stovepipe recognized the type. "Best be careful,
Miss Ros—"

An angry bellow from the bull interrupted him.

"I can handle him," Rosaleen said as she kept her
horse moving forward.

The bull launched into a charge toward her, head
lowered as he continued bawling in fury.

With not much distance between her and the bull,
Rosaleen yanked the sorrel aside. The horse was
nimble enough to get out of the way, but it was a close
thing.

Too close for comfort, in fact. The bull veered to
the side and crashed his shoulder into Rosaleen's

mount. The sorrel squealed in fright and pain and went down.

With the skill of an experienced rider, Rosaleen kicked her feet out of the stirrups and threw herself out of the saddle as the sorrel fell. That kept the horse from landing on her, but she slammed down hard on the rocky ground. A good fifty yards away, Stovepipe could tell she was stunned. Wilbur was even farther away.

Closer, Vance jammed his heels into his horse's flanks and sent the mount plunging toward Rosaleen. He shouted at the bull as he rode hard, leaning forward in the saddle, but the massive animal ignored him.

Having overrun the spot where Rosaleen and her horse had fallen, the bull slowed and turned back toward the young woman. His brain might be small, but he knew he was mad and that anger was directed at Rosaleen. He charged again.

Vance flashed in front of the bull and leaped from the saddle while his horse was still moving. He jerked his hat off and waved it in wild, sweeping motions. Drawn by the movement, the bull turned toward him. Pounding hooves seemed to shake the ground as the bull continued the attack.

Vance held the hat away from his body and kept waving it around. The bull lowered his head and aimed for the hat. Vance was able to pivot smoothly out of the way as the brute thundered past.

"Get Miss Rosaleen!" he shouted to Stovepipe.

Already on his way to do exactly that, the cowpoke closed in on Rosaleen, who climbed shakily to her feet. Stovepipe thought she still looked like she wasn't quite sure what was going on. He thrust his arm down. "Miss Rosaleen! Grab hold!"

The fog seemed to clear from her brain. She realized what Stovepipe was telling her and raised her hands to grasp his arm as he rode up to her. A quick heave lifted her onto the back of the horse behind the saddle. Stovepipe turned the mount toward Vance and the bull.

Rosaleen gasped. "What in the world is he doing?"

"Looks to me like he's bullfightin', like them Spaniards do, only with a hat instead of a cape. I never knew that would work."

"You've got to help him! He's going to be killed!"

"No, miss. He'll be all right. Wilbur's there to lend a hand."

The redheaded cowboy was shaking out a loop in his rope as he galloped toward the bull. When he had it ready, he hauled back on the reins to bring his horse to a skidding stop, whipped the lariat around over his head a couple times, and let it fly. The loop sailed out to settle over the bull's horns as it turned toward Vance again after another narrow miss.

The bull was too big and heavy to take down, but as Wilbur's well-trained horse dug its hooves in, the rope went taut and pulled the bull's head around sharply. The huge creature came to a stop and stood there, nostrils flaring in anger.

"Get back on your horse, Vance," Wilbur told the young man. "You can dab a loop on this proddy old varmint, too, and we'll take him down to the gather."

Vance was breathing heavily from his exertions. He swung up into the saddle, took his rope loose, and lassoed the bull.

Stovepipe rode up beside him with Rosaleen still behind the saddle. "That was some mighty fancy footwork you was doin' out there. Where'd you learn to bullfight?"

"I didn't. I'd just seen it done down in Mexico, only with a cape, not a hat." Vance shrugged. "I didn't know if that would work, but it seemed like it was worth a try."

"You saved my life, Vance," Rosaleen said. "You and Mr. Stewart."

"No need to give me any credit," Stovepipe said. "That ol' bull would've stomped you 'fore I could ever get there if it hadn't been for this young fella."

"I thought about trying to pick you up like Stovepipe did," Vance said, "but it didn't seem like enough time for that. The quickest way was to distract the bull."

"And maybe get trampled yourself in the process," she said.

"I was willing to run that risk."

"Thank you. I don't know what else to say."

Vance grinned. "That's plenty."

Rosaleen looked around and asked, "What about my horse?"

"He's back on his feet," Stovepipe told her. "We'll go take a look at him while Vance and Wilbur get this bull down to the gather. I don't know if your pa will want to sell him or not, but we can get him out of the way while we're workin' up here so he won't cause no more trouble."

They rode over to Rosaleen's sorrel.

Stovepipe dismounted, then reached up to help her slide down from the horse's back. He turned to the sorrel and examined the animal closely, sliding his hands up and down the horse's legs and prodding its side where the bull had rammed it.

"Don't seem to be any broken bones," he said after a few minutes. "He'll have a nice sore bruise on his side, but I reckon he'll get over that. You were both lucky."

Rosaleen rubbed her horse gently. "I know. Maybe I shouldn't have insisted on coming along after all."

"Well, it's hard to say. Trouble can crop up wherever you are and whatever you're doin'. There was nothin' foolish about you wantin' to help us. Cowboyin' can be dangerous work, and that's all there is to it."

"Well, I enjoyed the morning, even as hot and sweaty and dusty as it was, right up until that bull came after me," Rosaleen said with a wan smile. "I suspect this incident will be the end of the roundup for me."

"Because of your pa?"

"When Dad finds out what happened, they'll probably hear the explosion all the way down in Wagontongue."

Keenan Malone bore a distinct resemblance to the bull that had tried to trample his daughter. He was practically breathing fire and his angry bellows sounded very familiar to Stovepipe, Wilbur, and Vance as they stood at a distance and watched the confrontation between father and daughter.

Stovepipe could tell the young woman was trying to defend herself, but there wasn't a lot she could say. It was an incontrovertible fact that if the men hadn't intervened, she probably would have died up in the hills.

Finally, she turned, stalked over to her horse, mounted up, and prodded the sorrel into a trot back toward the ranch headquarters. For a long moment, Malone watched her riding away.

Then he turned and walked over to the three cowboys. "I reckon I owe you fellas more than I can ever repay. Anything you want, just tell me, and if it's in my power I'll see that you get it."

"Shoot, Mr. Malone, we already got ever'thing we want," Stovepipe said. "We got good ridin' jobs, and for a cowboy nothin' else much matters."

Wilbur nodded, and Vance said, "I'm just glad we were there."

"You and me both, son," Malone said. "There'll be a little extra time off for you three, once we get this little trail drive done."

"Does that mean my job's permanent now?" Vance asked.

"For as long as you want it to be, Vance. You've got a home on the Three Rivers." Malone clapped a hand on Vance's shoulder, squeezed hard for a second in gratitude, then nodded curtly, turned, and walked away to get back to work.

"Don't get too much of a swelled head," Stovepipe told the young man. "We've still got a heap of cows to rassle with, and they don't know a thing in the world about Mr. Malone feelin' obliged to you."

"He doesn't have to feel that way," Vance said. "I didn't do it for him. I don't think I could stand it if anything were to happen to Miss Rosaleen."

As they walked back toward their horses to resume

the roundup, Stovepipe and Wilbur exchanged a glance behind Vance's back. It was pretty obvious that Vance had fallen in love with Rosaleen, but the course of young love seldom ran smooth, Stovepipe thought.

Especially in country that was still primed for a range war.

CHAPTER SIX

By late that afternoon, they had a little more than three hundred head gathered in the pasture. Malone looked them over, nodded in satisfaction, and told Andy Callahan, "We ought to be able to finish tomorrow without any trouble."

"We'll need to leave some fellas out here to ride nighthawk," Callahan said. "Ain't likely these cows would stray too far, but I'd just as soon not have to gather any of 'em up again tomorrow."

Stovepipe, Wilbur, and Vance were sitting on their horses not too far behind the ranch manager and the segundo. Stovepipe nudged his horse forward and said, "I reckon we could do it."

"Blast it, Stovepipe," Wilbur said. "Didn't your ma ever teach you anything about volunteering?"

"I recollect she thought it was a good idea. She was a fine one for helpin' others, my ma was."

Malone turned his horse and said, "I appreciate the offer, Stewart, but I wanted you men to have some time off in return for what you did for Rosaleen. I don't want to saddle you with an extra chore."

"You wouldn't be doin' any such thing. Fact of the matter is, I like ridin' nighthawk. It's plumb peaceful bein' out under the stars and singin' a song to them cows."

"Peaceful for you, maybe," Wilbur said. "You don't have to listen to yourself sing."

Malone looked over at Vance. "What do you think, Brewster?"

Vance shrugged. "Stovepipe and Wilbur have sort of taken me under their wings. I'm happy to go along with whatever they think is a good idea."

"It's settled, then," Stovepipe said. "We'll handle this chore."

"All right," Malone said. "You'll need some grub. I'll have somebody ride out here from the ranch with it."

"Maybe you could tell Aunt Sinead to put in a dozen of those biscuits of hers," Wilbur said. "They're some of the best I've ever had."

"I reckon I can do that."

Malone and Callahan trotted off, leaving Stovepipe, Wilbur, and Vance to look out over the herd, which at the moment was grazing peacefully.

"What worm of an idea do you have crawling around in that brain of yours, Stovepipe?" Wilbur asked. "Despite what you said earlier, I never knew you to volunteer for anything unless you had a good reason for it."

"Watchin' over them cows ain't a good enough reason?"

"No, it's not. If I had to guess, I'd say you've got one of those hunches of yours." Wilbur turned to Vance. "Stovepipe gets hunches. Sometimes it seems like they come on him out of nowhere, but nine times out of ten they're right, so I've learned to put some stock in them."

Vance said, "When I first rode into Wagontongue, the bartender at the Silver Star said something about rustling being a problem around here."

"That's right. Wilbur and me ain't been around these parts for all that long our own selves, but we've heard the same thing, ain't we?"

"The Three Rivers blames the Rafter M, the Rafter M blames the Three Rivers," Wilbur said.

"I wouldn't have any trouble believing Dax Coolidge is a rustler," Vance said, "but there's nothing like that going on over here."

"Try tellin' that to Cabot and his boys. Chances are, they ain't gonna be in the mood to listen."

"Is that what your hunch is about, Stovepipe?" Vance asked. "You think rustlers are going to hit this herd?"

Stovepipe crossed his hands on his saddle horn and leaned forward to ease muscles grown weary from the long day. "Herd this size is a temptin' target. It's big enough to be worth stealin' but small enough that half a dozen men could handle it."

"But how would Cabot's men even know we've been rounding up some of the Three Rivers stock?"

"Didn't say it was the Rafter M bunch we've got to worry about. It's still too soon to make up my mind about that. But whether it is or it ain't, whoever's wide-loopin' beef around here could have somebody posted up in the hills with a pair o' field glasses, keepin' an eye on what's goin' on." Stovepipe's bony shoulders rose and fell. "O' course, this is all just speculation.

Chances are, nothin'll happen tonight 'cept we'll lose some sleep. And that'll be just fine with me."

The sun had set just a few minutes earlier, leaving a rosy golden arch over the hills to the west, when Rosaleen drove up to the meadow in one of the ranch wagons. She was wearing a dress again instead of the range clothes she'd had on earlier, and her fiery hair was brushed out so that it hung free.

"Well, this is a plumb pleasant surprise, miss," Stovepipe told her. "Have you come to bring us our supper?"

"That's right." Rosaleen stepped down from the wagon and lifted the basket that had been riding on the seat beside her. "Fried chicken, biscuits and honey, and peach pie."

Stovepipe grinned "You're fixin' to leave me lickin' my chops, miss."

Vance stepped up and took the basket from her. He carried it to the back of the wagon and set it in the open bed. The four of them gathered around it as he asked, "You're going to join us, aren't you, Miss Rosaleen?"

"I thought I would. I told Aunt Sinead to pack plenty. You ought to even have some left over for breakfast in the morning." She lifted the cloth that covered the basket and added, "I've got a jug of lemonade in here, too."

"Better an' better," Stovepipe said.

Rosaleen moved to sit in the wagon bed next to the basket.

Vance didn't hesitate. He took hold of her under

the arms and lifted her, setting her gently on the boards. Then he took a quick step back, removed his hat, and said, "Sorry if I overstepped my bounds there, Miss Rosaleen. I reckon you just, uh, bring out the chivalry in me."

Stovepipe heard the mischief lurking in her tone as she said, "That's all right, Vance. And I think you could probably just call me Rosaleen and forget about the *miss* part. You *did* save my life earlier today, you know."

"I wouldn't want to do anything improper."

"You should've figured out by now we don't stand on a lot of ceremony around here. The Three Rivers is sort of like a family."

Vance grinned. "I like the sound of that."

As they ate, Stovepipe asked, "Has your pa gotten over that close call you had with that ol' bull?"

"I don't think he'll actually get over it for a while, but he's sort of run out of steam, I guess you'd say. He's stopped huffing and blowing about it." She sounded crestfallen as she added, "But now I may never get to help with the ranch work again. To tell you the truth, I've thought about how I might be the one running this place someday."

"You really think so?" Vance asked.

"What, you don't think I could do it? You don't think a woman could run a ranch just as well as a man?"

"I didn't say that, but it'd be pretty unusual, wouldn't it? I don't know how a salty bunch of cowboys would take orders from a woman."

"They'd take those orders and like them, if I was

the one giving them. I can be pretty salty, too, you know."

Stovepipe said, "I ain't doubtin' it. 'Course, in the case of the Three Rivers, it ain't really up to anybody out here. The spread's owned by some hombres back east, ain't it?"

"That's true. But when the time comes for my father to step down, I plan to make my case to the owners." Rosaleen shook her head. "That's a long time in the future, though. Dad's never going to retire until his health forces him to, and he's still in his prime."

"Well, if that's what you want, all I can say is good luck to you," Vance told her. "Maybe I'll still be around here when that day comes." He grinned a little sheepishly. "Although I've never really stayed in one place for too long at a time."

Night had fallen by the time they finished the meal. Rosaleen wrapped up the food that was left and stuck it in one of Stovepipe's saddlebags.

Vance was frowning as he said, "You're going to have to drive that wagon back to headquarters in the dark by yourself."

"Yes, and I've lived on this ranch my whole life and know every foot of it as well as I know the inside of our house. Besides, my carbine's up on the seat, too, if I run into any trouble."

"I don't know, Rosaleen—"

"I told you, you didn't have to call me *miss*. I didn't say you could start fussing over me. I get more than enough of that from Dad, thank you very much."

"Speakin' of your pa," Stovepipe said. "After what

happened today I'm a mite surprised he agreed to let you come out here."

"You're assuming I told him. All I said was that I'd talk to Aunt Sinead and see to it you fellows got some supper. He was in his office, hunched over some paperwork, when I left."

"Then there's liable to be some fussin' when you get back."

"Yeah," Wilbur said. "It's a sure bet the boss has realized by now what you did."

"I'm not worried. In case Keenan Malone hasn't figured it out by now, he's not going to run every little bit of my life!"

A few minutes later, Rosaleen climbed to the seat, turned the wagon around, and got the team moving. She lifted a hand to wave good-bye in the light of a rising moon.

As the three cowboys stood and watched her go, Vance said, "Maybe I'm worrying too much, but I still don't like the idea of her driving around by herself at night like this."

"Neither do I," Stovepipe said. "That's why I'm gonna go after her."

"She's liable to pitch a fit if she knows you're following her."

"She won't know unless Stovepipe wants her to," Wilbur said. "He's sneaky that way."

Rosaleen was quickly out of sight, although the faint sound of the team's hoofbeats could still be heard.

Stovepipe drifted toward his paint. "You boys go ahead and start ridin' around that herd. I'll be back in a while and spell one of you. I probably won't follow Miss Rosaleen all the way to headquarters."

"What about that hunch of yours that there might be trouble tonight?" Wilbur asked.

"I ain't forgot. I ain't fond of splittin' our forces this way, but we'll just have to do the best we can. You fellas keep a sharp eye out while you're ridin'." Stovepipe rubbed his chin. "Never know what you might run into."

CHAPTER SEVEN

Stovepipe had been right about riding nighthawk being a peaceful job . . . at least most of the time. Vance was enjoying it. The air had a pleasant hint of coolness about it after the heat of the day. A few night birds sang in the trees up on the hillsides.

Vance and Wilbur sang, too, low-voiced ballads as they circled the herd, one always opposite the other. Those were the only sounds other than the faint thudding of hoofbeats and an occasional bawl from one of the cows.

So far Vance's stay on the Three Rivers had gone about like he'd expected it to . . . with the exception of Rosaleen Malone. He hadn't expected her at all, and his reaction to her was even more surprising. He sure hadn't come looking for romance, but when he first laid eyes on her, it felt like somebody had just slugged him hard in the gut. His heart had started pounding, and he couldn't quite seem to get his breath.

Vance wasn't a total innocent. He had been involved with women before, but none had been anything like

Rosaleen. When he'd seen that bull bearing down on her, intent on trampling the life out of her, the fear he felt froze the blood in his veins. All he'd been able to think about was saving her, no matter what the risk might have been to his own life.

He jogged along slowly, thinking he would have liked to follow her back to the Three Rivers head-quarters and make sure she got there safely, but he knew Stovepipe was more suited to the job. Vance would have bumbled along and somehow tipped off his presence to her, he was sure of that. Knowing she was proud, he also knew she would be offended they didn't think she could get back by herself.

The thoughts running through his mind didn't keep him from continuing to sing. He preferred a more sprightly tune, but the purpose was to keep the cattle calm, not to entertain him. He finished one melancholy ballad and launched into another one. Most of the songs were about cowboys' lost loves—probably a good reason for that. It wasn't exactly a life favorable to romance and settling down.

Stovepipe tracked as much by instinct as by his senses. He could hear the team's hoofbeats and the faint rattle of Rosaleen's wagon wheels, and occasionally he caught a glimpse of the vehicle in the moonlight. But as much as anything else, he just *knew* he was on the right trail. Everything worked together. It was a skill he had developed over a lot of years.

Being alert didn't stop his mind from drifting to Vance Brewster. Stovepipe felt a natural liking for the young cowboy, but at the same time something was off about him. The boy was asking for trouble, too, by allowing himself to fall for Rosaleen Malone the way he so obviously had. Stovepipe was pretty sure her pa had somebody better in mind for his daughter than some forty-a-month-and-found cowpuncher. Maybe not anybody in particular at this point, but somebody better than that, anyway.

Stovepipe turned his thoughts in a different direction, pondering the trouble that had descended on those parts in the past months. He and Wilbur had heard about the missing cattle, the potshots taken at cowboys out riding the range, the escalating animosity between the Three Rivers and Mort Cabot's Rafter M.

Since they had drifted in and signed on with the Three Rivers, Stovepipe hadn't yet laid eyes on Cabot, but he wondered if he might recognize the man from somewhere else, maybe even someone he'd known by another name. If that proved to be the case, it could provide some answers to the questions gnawing at him.

As Vance rounded the herd, he was pointed back in the direction Stovepipe had gone and spotted a rider coming toward him. It didn't seem like enough time had passed for Rosaleen to have made it all the way back to headquarters, but Stovepipe had said he might not follow her the entire distance. Vance wanted to find out, so he broke away from the herd momentarily and rode toward the man on horseback.

The moonlight was deceptive, especially since a few clouds drifted through the sky and created shifting shadows. Vance was fairly close to the newcomer before he realized the horse wasn't Stovepipe's paint.

He hauled back on the reins, cried out, "Hey!" and reached for the gun on his hip. "Who are—"

Colt flame bloomed in the darkness as the man opened fire.

Stovepipe hadn't seen Cabot, but he had gotten a couple good looks at Dax Coolidge and was convinced of one thing.

The man was a killer.

Whether or not the rest of the Rafter M hands were as bad, Coolidge was a gun-wolf, plain and simple, and sooner or later, Stovepipe would have to deal with him.

That grim thought was percolating in his head when instinct and senses worked hand in hand once more to make him haul back on the paint's reins. He had heard something out of place. As he turned his head to look back in the direction of the pasture where the gather was being held, he heard it again.

A gunshot, followed swiftly by several more.

Vance was no fast gun, but he was young and his re-actions were good. As the stranger charged him, he ducked. Bullets whined over his head and past his ears. He yanked his well-worn old revolver from its holster, lifted the gun, and started thumbing off shots with it.

The big revolver boomed like thunder. As the peal-ing reports rolled across the pasture, the gathered stock began to shift, lurching a little one way and then the other. More of the cattle started to bawl nervously.

Muzzle flashes dotted the night as more attackers

swooped in from the shadows. Across the outside of his upper left arm, Vance felt an impact and slashing pain that twisted him halfway around in the saddle. He knew he'd just been shot but didn't think the wound was serious.

It certainly wasn't going to keep him from putting up a fight.

Stovepipe's gaze darted toward the wagon carrying Rosaleen Malone. He felt himself being tugged both ways. He wanted to make sure the girl was safe, but sporadic shots continued to drift through the night, telling him that hell was breaking loose behind him. His friends were in danger.

Biting back a curse, he wheeled the paint around and sent it plunging through the night in a hard run.

Although it was difficult, Vance forced his left arm to work, hauling on the reins and pulling his horse in a tight turn as he continued firing with his right hand. He could see three or four men on horseback. They spread out as they rode toward him, and he knew they intended to surround him.

Over the gun-thunder and pounding hoofbeats, Vance heard Wilbur's ringing shout. "Hang on, Vance!"

The little redheaded cowboy galloped around the herd and flashed into view a moment later, riding like a demon as he controlled his mount with his knees. His hands were busy with the Winchester that spouted flame and lead as fast as he could work its lever and pull the trigger.

As he joined forces with Vance, the raiders jerked

their horses back toward the trees. It seemed like they were meeting more resistance than they'd expected.

Vance's revolver was empty. He took advantage of the momentary lull to dump the empty brass and thumb fresh rounds into the weapon. "Looks like they didn't expect us to put up this much of a fight!" Excitement made his heart pound and sent his blood coursing along his veins. He was afraid—only a fool could hear that many bullets whining around him and not feel at least a twinge of fear—but he was exhilarated, too.

Wilbur twisted around in his saddle as shouts and gunfire broke out on the far side of the herd. "It was a trick!" he cried. "They wanted to get us both on one side so they could stampede those cows at us!"

The dark mass of the herd shifted suddenly. Any excitement Vance felt quickly vanished, replaced completely by fear. Three hundred cattle didn't amount to a huge herd, but if they stampeded and swept over him and Wilbur, the two cowboys would wind up looking like something that wasn't even human, their bodies chopped, flattened, and ground into the dirt.

"Head for the trees!" Wilbur dug his heels into the roan's flanks and sent the horse leaping forward as the cattle surged toward them.

He picked up speed, Vance right behind him as they fled in the same direction the raiders had gone a couple minutes earlier. Trying to stay out in front of the stampede, Vance and Wilbur made almost perfect targets as they raced toward the gunmen hidden in the trees.

Orange flame gouted from the shadows. Wilbur angled his horse from side to side to make it more difficult for the hidden gunmen to hit him, and Vance followed suit. That maneuver slowed them down and allowed the stampeding cattle to rumble closer.

Vance had heard people talk about being caught between a rock and a hard place. It was one of those situations if ever there was one!

Suddenly, like an unexpected bolt of lightning from a clear blue sky, Stovepipe flashed in from the side and shouted, "This way, boys! We got to turn 'em, not run from 'em! I'll cover you!"

It was one of the most magnificent sights Vance had ever seen. Stovepipe and the paint seemed linked together as if man and horse could read each other's thoughts. The paint ran full-out and never missed a step as Stovepipe twisted in the saddle, thrust his Winchester at the trees, and unleashed a long, rolling wave of flame and lead.

Wilbur and Vance turned their mounts to ride to the inside of Stovepipe's gallant race. All three headed across the face of the stampede.

Wilbur called, "Get the leaders!"

They aimed for the spooked steers in front of the others. Wilbur and Vance angled in, turned their horses back into the flow of the stampede, and matched the frantic pace. A misstep would be fatal for both horse and rider.

Wilbur yelled, snatched his hat off his head, and leaned over to swat one of the racing steers with it. The animal pulled away from him, but Wilbur crowded in, forcing the steer to turn more and more.

Turning a stampede back on itself was the only reliable way to stop a dangerous panic. Vance followed the same tactics, and in moments, the cattle were curving back and moving away from the trees at the edge of the pasture. It was only a matter of time until the breaking point was reached and the stampede would collapse into a milling mess.

But . . . the stampede hadn't started by itself. Men on horseback had started it. They came out of the trees and galloped along the edges of the turning herd, opening fire on Stovepipe, Wilbur, and Vance.

The three cowboys were still caught between forces that wanted them dead.

CHAPTER EIGHT

"Keep 'em bunched," Stovepipe shouted to Wilbur and Vance. "I'll hold off those other fellas!" He jammed his empty Winchester into the saddle boot, whirled the paint, and surprised the pursuers by charging straight at them. His Colt leaped into his hand and geysered flame.

Three attackers came up on horseback. Stovepipe didn't know how many were still hidden in the trees or whether more riders were on the other side of the herd, but it was clear that he and his companions were heavily outnumbered.

That didn't matter. Stovepipe intended to keep fighting. He knew the rustlers wouldn't want to leave any witnesses behind, so surrendering wouldn't do any good.

Besides, the idea of backing down always stuck in his craw. If his number was up, he intended to go out fighting.

He came upon the three pursuers quickly, In order to avoid a collision, they had to split up and let him gallop between them. Shots slammed in his direction as he spurted through the opening. He felt one of the slugs sizzle through the air beside his ear, but none tagged him.

He reached back a little with his gun, fired, and hammered a bullet into a man's shoulder. The would-be killer reeled in the saddle and had to grab the horn with his free hand to keep from falling off.

A bullet plucked at the side of Stovepipe's shirt as he jerked around in the saddle and triggered again. One of the riders hunched over, obviously wounded in the midsection. Like the first man, he almost fell from his horse. He wound up clutching the animal's mane to stay mounted.

That left just one man to face Stovepipe. Having seen the tall, lanky cowboy's deadly accuracy with a six-gun, he decided he didn't like the odds. He whirled his horse and lit a shuck.

The other two men, already wounded—one of them perhaps seriously—didn't want any part of it any longer. They swayed in their saddles but managed to turn the horses and gallop after their companion.

Stovepipe let them go. He could have thrown a few shots at them to hurry them on their way, but he was more concerned about how Wilbur and Vance were doing with the stampede. He headed toward the herd.

The spooked cattle had slowed as they continued turning. The stampede was almost under control. Stovepipe rode after his two friends, noting that the gunfire from the trees seemed to have stopped as well. Either the rustlers had decided it wasn't worth the blood they were spending to steal those cattle . . .

Or they had already gotten what they came for.

The herd began to mill instead of run as the stampede collapsed on itself.

Stovepipe rode up to the obviously weary Wilbur and Vance. "Mighty good job, fellas. Vance, it takes a good hand to help stop a stampede without gettin' hisself trampled."

"Thanks, Stovepipe, but you're the one who came up with the idea."

"What happened to those rustlers?" Wilbur asked. "Why'd they stop shooting at us?"

"Reckon they must've lit a shuck. We'd best take a look at this herd and see how many head are left."

"Wait a minute. You mean—?"

"I mean when those varmints lit out, they may not have left by themselves."

"Blast it!" Wilbur said. "We don't have to count. In all the commotion, they took off with some of the stock, didn't they? I can feel it in my bones, Stove-pipe!"

"I'm gettin' the same feelin', but we'll take a look to be sure."

Wilbur pointed toward Vance. "Better check the young fella's arm first. I think he was hit."

"It's nothing," Vance said. "Just a scratch—"

"Yeah, I see the blood on your sleeve now," Stove-pipe said. "Looks to me like it might be more than a scratch. Get down off that horse, son, and let's have a look."

"I'll scout around while you're doing that," Wilbur said as his companions dismounted.

"You can take your shirt off, or I can cut the sleeve off," Stovepipe said.

"Let me take it off. I don't have that many spare shirts. Might be able to wash the blood out and mend the place where the bullet tore it." Vance winced in pain several times during the process, but he managed to get the shirt off.

Stovepipe snapped a lucifer to life and used the match's flame to study the wound. It was a shallow furrow in the flesh, just deep enough to draw blood.

"Looks like it's already stopped oozin' crimson. That's good. It'll probably be stiff and sore for a few days, but it oughta heal up just fine, so you'd never know it happened except for the scar. That is, if you don't get blood poisonin' from it. We can take steps to keep that from happenin'." Stovepipe went to his horse and reached into one of the saddlebags, bringing out a silver flask.

"Hold that arm straight out from your shoulder so I can pour some o' this whiskey in the ditch that bullet left behind," he told Vance. "It'll sting a mite. Well, actually, it'll burn like blazes, but I reckon you knew that."

"Just do what you need to do." Vance lifted his arm and positioned it the way Stovepipe told him.

Leaning closer, Stovepipe carefully poured a small amount of whiskey into the wound.

Vance groaned. Through clenched teeth, he said, "You weren't kidding about it burning like blazes."

Stovepipe put the flask in the young cowboy's other hand and said, "Here. This Who-hit-John is good medicine from the inside, too, as long as you don't take too much of it."

Vance downed a slug of the fiery liquor, then shuddered, He drew in a deep breath as he lowered his wounded arm. "You know, I don't think it hurts quite as much now."

"Good for what ails you," Stovepipe said as he took

the flask, replaced the cap, and stowed it away in his pocket. "Now we need to tie a bandage around there just in case it starts bleedin' again."

By the time he had done that, Wilbur returned from his check on the herd. The redhead was muttering curses under his breath.

"The dirty sons made off with some o' the stock, didn't they?" Stovepipe asked.

"Hard to say for sure in the dark, but my guess is they got about a hundred head. Probably cut them out while the others were busy with Vance and me, then headed those cows off in one direction while they stampeded the rest at the two of us. Maybe that was their plan all along. I think they attacked Vance to draw me around to this side of the herd so they could catch both of us in the stampede."

Stovepipe shook his head. "Nope. The graze on Vance's arm proves they were really tryin' to kill him. No man alive is a good enough shot to simply graze a man on purpose in the dark. They'd have killed both of you right from the get-go if they could have, and been pleased with their own selves for doin' so. Then they could've driven off the whole three hundred head. But since it didn't work out that way and you fellas put up a strong fight, they just adapted and done the best they could."

"Which was making off with a hundred head," Vance said. "We have to go after them."

"Must've been close to a dozen of the fellas. We'd be outnumbered."

"That doesn't matter. We can't let them get away with Three Rivers stock."

Stovepipe nodded slowly "All right. Here's what

we'll do. Vance, you figure you can ride with that wounded arm?"

"Of course. Like I told you, it doesn't hurt as bad as it did."

"Then you and I will go after that bunch. Wilbur, you ride back to headquarters and let Mr. Malone know what happened. I reckon him and most of the boys will be strappin' on six-shooters and throwin' saddles on their horses mighty quick-like after you do."

"Wait a minute," Wilbur said. "Why do I have to go for help? Vance is the one who's hurt. Send him instead."

"Well, that was my first thought, but then I realized you'd be more likely to be able to pick up our trail in the dark and lead the boys to wherever those rustlers went. I'll leave some sign to make it easier for you." Stovepipe paused. "No offense, Vance, but I don't know how good you are at trackin'. Wilbur's plumb fine."

"No offense taken," Vance said. "Your reasoning makes sense."

Wilbur said, "It always does . . . blast it. All right, Stovepipe, I'll do like you say. It'll mean leaving these cattle here without anybody to keep an eye on them, but I reckon going after those rustlers is more important. You think they'll push that beef all night?"

"Wouldn't be surprised. They'll want to put as much distance as they can between us and them."

"Yeah, well, if they do stop and hole up somewhere—"

"Vance and I will be around to spot the hideout."

"I was gonna say the two of you don't need to jump them until I get back with the crew from the Three

Rivers," Wilbur said. "Wouldn't be fair for you to hog all the fun for yourselves."

Stovepipe and Vance swung up in their saddles as Wilbur headed back in the direction of headquarters.

Stovepipe took the flask from his pocket. "You need another dose of this medicine before I put it away?"

"I'm tempted, but I'd better not. It's possible there might be more gunplay before the night's over, and I should have a clear head for that."

"Seems like you handled yourself pretty well," Stovepipe said as they nudged their mounts into motion. "Ever been in a fight like that before on the other spreads where you've worked?"

"No, not really. Not against rustlers. A brawl now and then with some other crew, like the one in Wagontongue the day I rode in, but other than that . . ." Vance's shoulders rose and fell.

He rode along quietly for a moment, then added, "It's scary, being shot at like that."

"Durn right it is. I've heard fellas claim they got used to hearin' bullets zing past their heads, but I ain't sure I believe it. That's happened to me quite a few times, and I sure ain't got used to it."

"You make it sound like trouble follows you around."

"Or I follow it." Stovepipe shrugged. "Either way, we wind up in each other's company a whole heap."

They circled the herd to the other side of the pasture. Stovepipe pointed to a stretch of ground where the grass was beaten down enough that it was visible even in the moonlight. "Looks like that's the way the rustlers headed. One thing about stealin' cattle . . . it's hard to move 'em very much without leavin' some sort of trail."

They followed the route of the stolen stock. The

trail led north toward a high ridge that marked the boundary of the Three Rivers ranch in that direction.

Stovepipe pointed out the ridge. From where they were, it was just a thick, dark line on the horizon.

"What's on the other side of it?" Vance asked.

"Don't rightly know. Haven't ever been up there, that I recall."

Vance laughed. "I thought you and Wilbur had been everywhere, judging from the stories you tell."

"Well . . . I reckon you could say we've been in the *vicinity* of everywhere, but there are particular spots here and there where we ain't ever set foot. Now, I got a question for you."

"Sure. Anything I can answer, I will."

"I know it ain't likely, but did you happen to get a good look at any of those rustlers while you was swappin' bullets with 'em? Sometimes you might catch a glimpse of a face in a muzzle flash."

Vance shook his head. "No, I'm afraid not. Everything happened so fast. I wouldn't be able to recognize any of them if I saw them again."

"I was thinkin' more along the lines of maybe you'd seen some of 'em before."

"You mean at the Silver Star in Wagontongue, the day of that fight with the Rafter M bunch? I wish I could say I recognized Dax Coolidge, so the sheriff could arrest him for rustling and attempted murder, but I didn't see him or any of the other Rafter M hands from that day." Vance paused. "Of course, Coolidge is the only one who made a real impression. If some of the others were with the rustlers tonight, I might not have recognized them even if I saw them."

"Fair enough, I reckon. We'll know 'em when the time comes, if it ever does."

"What time is that?" Vance asked.

"The time when we've caught up to 'em and taught 'em a little lesson about how it ain't smart to steal from the Three Rivers." Stovepipe rested a hand on the butt of his Colt.

CHAPTER NINE

Wilbur rode hard up to the main house at the Three Rivers headquarters. The roan's hoofbeats drummed steadily on the ground as horse and rider approached.

It was late enough that everybody had turned in. The main house and the bunkhouse were dark. The dogs, a pair of rangy black-and-tan mutts that were part hound, heard Wilbur galloping in and set up a loud, baying commotion. As he reined to a halt in front of the house, a light appeared in one of the windows.

Before Wilbur could even dismount, the front door swung open and Keenan Malone stepped out onto the porch, lantern in one hand and double-barreled shotgun in the other. "Who's there?" the cattleman demanded. He raised the lantern in his left hand so the circle of yellow light washed over the yard in front of the house.

"It's me, Mr. Malone. Wilbur Coleman."

"Coleman! You're supposed to be out there keepin' an eye on that herd with Stewart and Brewster." Malone stomped down the steps to the ground. "Blast it! Somethin's happened, hasn't it?"

"Yeah—"

"Is Vance all right?" Rosaleen asked before he could explain. She stood on the porch, holding a dressing gown closed around her.

"Yes, ma'am, mostly."

"Mostly! What does that mean?"

"He got grazed a little by a rustler's bullet, but Stovepipe tended to him and he'll be fine."

"Rustlers," Malone said, followed by a curse. He swallowed the rest of the furious response that obviously wanted to come boiling out of him. "So they hit the herd, did they?"

"Yeah. Ambushed me and Vance a while after you left. Then stampeded the herd right at us. When the dust cleared, we'd winged a couple of them and drove them off, but they took about a hundred head with them."

Malone set the lantern on the top step so he could hold the shotgun with both hands. "Rafter M's gone too far this time!" he said as he brandished the weapon. "We'll saddle up and ride over there and read from the book to Cabot and his bunch of no-account thieves!"

"No offense, Mr. Malone, but we don't *know* it was the Rafter M behind the raid. We never got a good look at any of the varmints."

"Well, who else could it be? We ain't had any trouble except with Cabot's bunch!"

Malone always blamed Cabot for everything bad that happened, whatever it was, Wilbur thought. Cabot was the same way when it came to Malone. That deep-seated hostility didn't really prove a thing on either side, though.

Malone wasn't likely to see the logic in that, however, especially when he had a burr under his saddle. To make him see reason would require another approach.

"Stovepipe and Vance went after those rustlers," Wilbur said. "Stovepipe was sort of counting on me taking some help back with me."

"You said Vance was wounded," Rosaleen said. "He shouldn't have gone chasing off after rustlers in the dark!"

Wilbur shrugged. "Well, miss, like I told you, he wasn't hurt bad. And Stovepipe figured I could pick up the trail better than Vance could." He looked at Malone. "All due respect, boss, but it seems like going after the fellas who actually stole the stock would be better than heading for the Rafter M to raise a ruckus."

Malone chewed his white mustache furiously for a second before he said, "You're right, blast it."

The men in the bunkhouse had realized that something was going on. Several of them approached, led by Andy Callahan, who called, "Is there some sort of trouble, boss?"

"The worst sort. Rustlin'! Tell the boys to pull their boots on and grab their guns. We're ridin'!"

Aunt Sinead had come out to see what the commotion was about, too. From the porch just behind Rosaleen, she said, "I'll get some coffee ready. You'll need it before you ride out."

"Just don't take too long about it," Malone said. "Every minute we waste, those varmints are gettin' farther away."

"Yeah, but Stovepipe's on their trail," Wilbur said.

He'll leave some sign for us to follow. Wherever those cow thieves go, we'll be able to follow 'em."

"And I'm bettin' it's right back around to the Rafter M!" Malone said.

By the time they had been on the trail of the rustlers for a few hours, Vance was even more impressed by Stovepipe than he already had been. The lanky cowboy's tracking abilities seemed to verge on the supernatural. Most of the time Vance couldn't see any indication at all of where they should be going, but Stovepipe led them forward confidently.

When the moon finally set, however, Stovepipe reined in and said, "Reckon we'd best wait for daylight in a couple hours. I hate to let those varmints lengthen their lead on us, but we risk losin' 'em entirely if we try to track 'em in the pitch dark."

"I think it's amazing you've been able to bring us this far," Vance said. "They'll have to let the cattle rest at some point. We'll have a chance then to catch up, or at least shorten their lead again."

"Yeah. We'll let our own mounts rest." Stovepipe swung down from the saddle and arched his back to ease his muscles. "It'd be mighty nice to build a fire and boil a pot o' coffee, but I'd just as soon not risk it. Got some jerky in my saddlebags, if you'd like to gnaw on a piece. Or maybe you'd rather just get a little shuteye."

"That doesn't sound bad. We can take turns sleeping."

Stovepipe waved a hand. "Don't worry about that.

Fella gets to be my age, he don't sleep as much as he used to."

"You're not that old."

"It ain't the years so much as it is the miles, I reckon," Stovepipe said with a chuckle. "And I've covered a heap of 'em."

They loosened the cinches on their saddles and let the horses graze. Vance sat down with his back against a tree trunk, pulled his hat brim down over his eyes, and soon began to snore softly. Stovepipe hunkered on his heels and thought for a spell.

Wilbur figured Rosaleen would want to accompany her father and the rest of the Three Rivers crew when they went after the rustlers, but to his surprise she didn't even ask. He supposed she knew she would be wasting her time arguing with Keenan Malone, especially after the close call she'd had with the bull.

Malone designated three of the older hands to remain at the ranch headquarters and keep an eye on the place. It was unlikely the raid on the herd had been designed to pull the crew away from headquarters and leave it open to an attack, but anything was possible. He was just trying to make sure no trickery was involved.

Wilbur thought that was a good idea and would have suggested it himself if Malone hadn't come up with it.

Before they rode out, Wilbur switched his saddle to another horse. He had ridden the roan hard on the way back, and the animal deserved some rest. Besides, there was no way of knowing how long the chase they were embarking on might last, so it was best to start out with a fresh mount.

The sky gradually turned gray in the east. While the dim light strengthened, Stovepipe picked up several small rocks and arranged them on the ground in the shape of an arrow. He knew Wilbur would notice the sign instantly, as soon as he saw it.

So did Vance, once he woke up after Stovepipe nudged his boot with a toe. He nodded toward the rocks. "You left that for Wilbur, right?"

"Yeah. I've been breakin' branches as we went along, too. He won't have no trouble followin' those signs, but I figured since I had the time I might as well leave him somethin' even better."

"I wonder how long it'll take him and the others from the Three Rivers to catch up to us."

"I imagine they'll come along as fast as they can. Keenan Malone's gonna be mighty hot under the collar when he hears about what happened. Only thing that old fella's more devoted to than the ranch is his daughter."

"I can understand that. About Rosaleen, I mean."

"Yeah, I knew what you meant." Stovepipe glanced at the sky. "It's light enough we can pick up the trail again. We'd best get started. Want a piece of that jerky and a biscuit now?"

"Still no coffee?"

"We'd be burnin' daylight."

"I'll take the jerky, then," Vance said as he reached for the strip of dried beef Stovepipe held out to him.

* * *

It wasn't long until dawn when they reached the pasture. Wilbur was relieved to see that most, if not all, of the cattle were still there, just as he and Stovepipe and Vance had left them after stopping the stampede.

"Show me what happened," Malone ordered in a curt voice. "Just don't take too long about it."

With a few waves of his hand, Wilbur sketched in the events of the night before. He concluded by pointing to the stretch of ground where the grass was beaten down. "We ought to be able to pick up the trail over there somewhere."

"Andy, check it out," Malone said. "The rest of you fellas, get down off those horses and let 'em blow for a minute."

Callahan said, "Come on, Wilbur. You and Stovepipe are pards. You'll know what to look for."

The two of them rode around the herd and across the pasture. It didn't take long at all for Wilbur to spot the trail, even in the gray predawn light. They hurried back to where Malone was waiting.

"The trail's there, boss," Callahan said. "We can get started whenever you want."

"Let the horses rest a couple more minutes. Once we start, I don't aim to stop until we've got them cows back. Pick out a couple of the boys to stay here and keep an eye on this bunch until we get back."

The two men Callahan selected for that task grumbled about being left behind and missing all the action, but they didn't disobey. They sat there disconsolately in their saddles as the rest of the bunch rode off a short time later.

* * *

As the sun rose, Stovepipe spotted the dust haze hanging in the air north and pointed it out to the young cowboy. "They're on the move . . . and not more than a few miles ahead of us. They must've got to feelin' confident last night and decided they could afford to rest for a longer spell than I expected."

"They probably figured we'd go back to the ranch headquarters for help, so it would be a while before we were able to get on their trail." Vance grinned. "They probably didn't count on you being able to track them in the dark, either."

Stovepipe reined in and pulled his field glasses out of his saddlebags. He lifted the lenses to his eyes and studied the ridge that marked the ranch's northern boundary. "There's a gap in the ridge that looks big enough to drive cattle through," he said after a moment. "It likely leads up to what I'm bettin' is a stretch of tableland beyond the ridge."

"Where's the Rafter M from here?"

Stovepipe lowered the glasses and hipped around in the saddle to point to their right. "Yonder a ways."

"How far does that ridge run?"

"Not far enough to border Cabot's range. It peters out somewhere before it gets there, and so does the higher ground."

"So if the rustlers are from the Rafter M, they could drive the cattle up into that high country and then swing east until they were able to drop down onto Cabot's range."

"They could," Stovepipe said. "Ain't nothin' in that direction to stop 'em, as far as I know."

Vance frowned in thought as he rubbed his chin. "Seems like an awfully long way around, unless they're just trying to throw us off their scent. And if they are, it's not working very well, is it? Rafter M is still the first bunch we suspect."

"Keenan Malone will be even more convinced Cabot's bunch is behind it. I figure when Wilbur got there, the boss's first impulse was to ride on Rafter M with all guns blazin'."

"Without any proof?"

"Out here folks mostly act on what they believe is true accordin' to their hearts and their guts. They don't worry overmuch about proof that would stand up in a court of law. That's changin', slow but sure, but it ain't completely there yet.

"I wouldn't worry, though. Wilbur will have convinced him it's better to come after those stolen cows than it would be to raid Cabot's place."

"You seem pretty sure of that."

"Wilbur's a mighty persuasive little cuss when he wants to be. Besides, he's sneaky. He can generally talk a fella around to doin' whatever he wants, and he'll make the gent believe it was all his own idea to start with."

"I'll bet he can't do that with you."

"Well . . . not too often." Stovepipe chuckled. "Or maybe he's just so good at it I don't know when he's doin' it." He stored the field glasses back in his saddlebag and they continued riding on the trail of the stolen herd as they talked.

After a few minutes, Stovepipe said, "You know, I got an idea percolatin' in my brain."

"If Wilbur was here, he'd probably say that was something to worry about."

"He might, at that. But I'm thinkin' we can move faster, just the two of us on horseback, than a hundred head of cattle can."

"I should hope so, but why does that matter? If you're thinking we ought to go ahead and catch up to them, the odds would be really heavy against us, wouldn't they?" Vance needed some clarification.

"Sure, if we came up on 'em from behind and they knew we were comin'. But if we took 'em by surprise and held the high ground, too . . ."

Vance's face lit up with understanding. "You think we can beat them to that gap in the ridge!"

"I think there's a good enough chance we ought to give it a try. If we can hold 'em at the gap, that'll give Wilbur, Malone, and the rest of the boys time to catch up. Once we do that, we've got those rustlers smack-dab where we want 'em, right in the jaws of a bear trap."

"I'm all for it," Vance said with an emphatic nod. "They're liable to give us quite a fight, though."

"And we'll hand it right back to 'em," Stovepipe said. "Come on!"

CHAPTER TEN

Wilbur, Malone, and Callahan were in the lead. The tracks left by the stolen cattle were easy to see, especially once the sun came up and light flooded over the landscape. Here and there the trail led into a rockier patch where it was more difficult to follow, but on each of those occasions Wilbur spotted a broken branch on a bush and knew Stovepipe was sending them in the right direction.

Stovepipe and Vance swung to the west, deeper into the hills that eventually turned into a range of small mountains. The rugged terrain gave them plenty of cover as long as they were careful not to let themselves be skylighted on higher ground. Stovepipe's uncanny instincts seemed able to tell them exactly where they needed to go in order to cover the ground quickly and yet remain out of sight of the rustlers.

They pushed their mounts as hard as they dared,

and gradually came abreast of the dust cloud marking the location of the stolen herd.

Stovepipe pointed it out. "We're fixin' to be ahead of them."

"And not any too soon," Vance said. "Seems like the ridge is getting closer a lot faster than it was before."

"Distances are deceptive out here. But unless somethin' happens to slow us down, we ought to make it to the pass a good quarter of an hour before they do."

Once they were well past the herd, they were able to turn back to the east, toward the gap in the ridge. Stovepipe kept his eyes open. It was possible the rustlers had sent scouts out ahead, and he didn't want to run into them without any warning.

It was late in the morning when they reached the ridge without seeing anyone. The rocky bluff was taller and more rugged than it had appeared from a distance. Its steep surface was riven with cracks that would make it impossible for a horse or cow to climb it.

The only way up was through the gap, a sloping passage twenty yards wide and about seventy yards from bottom to top. The walls were irregular, and slabs of rock lay here and there along the base where they had landed when they'd sheared off sometime in the distant past.

"Wonder what sort of geological event carved this out," Vance said as he gazed up the slanting trail.

"Not much tellin', 'cept that it was a long time ago." Stovepipe nudged the paint into motion and rode slowly through the gap with Vance following him.

When they reached the top and turned around, they could see a long way out onto the flats in front of the ridge. From that perspective, the hills were to the right. To the left were the plains that stretched out seemingly to infinity. The stolen herd was visible as a dark blotch moving slowly toward them.

"Looks like they're headed toward Massey Plateau," Callahan said after a while.

"What's that?" Wilbur asked.

"That's right. You haven't been around here long enough to know all the landmarks yet." Callahan pointed to a dark line on the horizon. "That's Buzzard Ridge."

"Mighty appealing name for a place," Wilbur muttered.

"People started calling it that because buzzards would sit on the edge of it and watch for something dying out here where we are."

"Oh. Well, that's nice."

Callahan grinned. "The name stuck. The ridge is the northern boundary of Three Rivers range."

"Yeah, I seem to remember Stovepipe saying something about that. He's a wonder for learning all he can about whatever place he happens to be. I've seen him sit and study maps for hours. Just for the sheer fun of it, he says!"

"The Massey Plateau is the tableland on the other side of the ridge," Callahan went on. "Named after an old fur trapper who decided to get out of that business and start raising cows instead. One of the first cattlemen in this whole part of the country."

"How did he do at it?"

"Oh, not good." Callahan grinned. "The Blackfeet killed and scalped him less than a year later."

Wilbur shuddered. "I'm glad those days are over and done with. Stovepipe and I have had a few run-ins with hostile Indians over the years, but most of 'em are peaceable now."

Malone grunted. "Less than ten years since Little Bighorn."

"Well . . . that can be a lifetime out here," Wilbur said.

Stovepipe and Vance dismounted. Following Stovepipe's order, Vance led both horses away from the upper end of the gap and picketed them where they could graze but still be out of the line of fire from any bullets that came flying up the trail.

Stovepipe took his field glasses from the saddlebags and found himself a patch of deep shade where there was no chance of sunlight glinting off the lenses to warn the rustlers someone was up there. He studied their quarry as the men drove the stolen stock closer.

"Looks like ten men pushin' 'em along," Stovepipe said when Vance rejoined him, carrying both rifles.

"I think there were at least a couple more of them when they hit the herd."

"Could be the others are back there somewhere in shallow graves . . . or no graves at all. If they didn't make it, their pards could've just let them lay where they fell."

"That would be a terrible thing to do."

"These ain't exactly choirboys we're talkin' about. They're more interested in gettin' those cows wherever they're goin' than in anything else."

"But we're not going to let them do that, are we?"

Stovepipe grinned and reached for his rifle. "Nope, we sure ain't."

Riding between Malone and Wilbur, Callahan had heard enough storytelling and changed the subject. "Do you think they're takin' those cows up on the plateau, boss?"

"Yes, and then they'll drive east and drop back down onto Cabot's range. Mark my words, boys, that's where they're headed!"

"We'll get behind these boulders," Stovepipe said, pointing out two of the huge rock slabs to Vance, "and stay outta sight until they've got those cows inside the gap. Once they do, we'll throw down on 'em and call on 'em to surrender. If they don't . . ." His shoulders rose and fell in an eloquent shrug.

"With a pair of rifles, we ought to be able to close up this gap pretty effectively," Vance said. "They won't have much room to maneuver or retreat, caught between stone walls like that. It's like a military tactic."

"Know somethin' about military tactics, do you?"

"I've studied them some . . . when it was too long between paydays and I didn't have any money for whiskey or dance hall gals or bucking the tiger. Got to pass the time somehow, you know."

"Sure," Stovepipe said. "I've poked into plenty of odd things myself. Now, better fill your pockets with cartridges and find a comfortable spot to wait behind that rock. If you listen close, you can hear horns clackin' together out there. They'll be here soon."

Each man made sure he had plenty of ammunition for his Winchester, then they retreated behind the stone slabs, making sure they could see each other from where they waited. Stovepipe nodded to Vance to let the young man know he was in good position.

Stovepipe could see through the gap all the way down to the bottom of the trail. He waited patiently as the sun neared its zenith and the heat grew. A vagrant breeze swirled past him, and on it he could smell the leading edge of the dust kicked up by the plodding hooves.

The rustlers riding point came into view, followed a few yards behind by the same old bull that had tried to trample Rosaleen Malone. Stovepipe wasn't surprised to see that the grizzled critter had taken the first position. The bull was plenty ornery enough for that.

Surrounding the herd were the two rustlers at point, three pairs of flankers, and two riding drag.

Stovepipe waited. As soon as the two dust-eaters had entered the passage, he stepped out into the open next to the boulder, leveled his rifle, and shouted in a clear powerful voice that carried over the rumble of hooves, "Elevate, you dirty sons! You've wide-looped your last cow! Throw down your guns and hoist your hands, or—"

He didn't really expect the rustlers to surrender, but giving them a chance to was the decent thing to do. That didn't mean he was foolhardy about it. The Winchester already had a round in the chamber, and Stovepipe had lined the sights on the chest of one of the rustlers as soon as he called out.

When the man howled a curse and clawed at the

gun on his hip, clearly not intending to throw it down and give up, all Stovepipe had to do was squeeze the trigger and blow the varmint right out of the saddle . . . which was exactly what he did.

The next instant, a wave of gun-thunder and its resounding echoes filled the gap.

CHAPTER ELEVEN

Wilbur came up in his stirrups. "Stovepipe and Vance may not have a chance to get to that plateau you were just talking about."

"What do you mean?" Callahan asked.

"Listen!"

They all heard it then—the faint popping of distant gunshots drifting through the midday air.

"What in blazes!" Malone said.

"My guess is that Stovepipe arranged a little reception for 'em!" Wilbur said. "Let's go!"

He spurred his horse forward and the others followed.

Stovepipe and Vance hadn't discussed which of the rustlers each of them was going to target, but it played out just as efficiently as if they had. As Stovepipe had blasted one point man off his horse, Vance fired at the other and drilled him through the right arm. From the way the man screamed and the arm flopped around, Vance's bullet had shattered the elbow.

Vance grimaced. He'd been shooting to kill, not wound. But with such a serious injury, the rustler was out of the fight anyway, so he supposed that was all that mattered.

The cows had spread out nearly from one side of the gap to the other, which made it difficult for the flankers to get past and rush forward to help their friends. The rustlers fired their revolvers over the heads of the stock, throwing a lot of lead at Stovepipe and Vance, but the bullets all splattered harmlessly against the boulders as the two cowboys had ducked behind the massive rocks.

The gunfire had an unintended effect. With each shot that slammed out and rebounded from the gap's walls, adding to the thunderous racket, the cattle became more panic-stricken. They lunged back and forth, running into each other, and pressed steadily forward. The rustler Vance had wounded looked back over his shoulder and let out a frightened shout as he realized the herd was moving faster . . . and heading toward him.

The man tried to wheel his horse around and gallop out of the way, but the injured arm made his movements slow and awkward. The old bull crashed into the horse, making it leap wildly in fear. Unable to hold on, the rustler screamed as he flew out of the saddle.

The horse bounded clear and ran for the top of the trail, outdistancing the steers. Its rider wasn't so lucky. He disappeared under the mass of horns and hooves and tails.

Vance shuddered at the man's fate.

Meanwhile, the other rustlers were still shooting at the men behind the boulders. Stovepipe edged his rifle barrel around the rock and squeezed off a shot that broke a man's shoulder.

Vance fired as well, and although he didn't hit flesh and bone, his bullet came close enough to send a startled rustler's hat flying off his head.

That was enough to break their nerve. As the cattle stampeded through the gap, the men who had stolen them the night before turned and fled. The flankers pressed their mounts close to the walls to avoid being trampled as they worked their way back along the fringes of the herd.

Stovepipe and Vance sent a few more shots in their direction, but they couldn't tell if the bullets found their targets. The gap was filled with too much chaos.

The spooked herd rumbled between the boulders where Stovepipe and Vance had taken cover, safe from the stampede.

The panicky charge didn't last long. It began to dissipate as soon as the cattle reached the top of the trail and started to spread out on the bench beyond. The brutes forgot they were scared and went right back to grazing.

Stovepipe and Vance kept an eye on the gap, which was empty except for the grisly remains of the two men who had died.

"Where did the others go?" Vance asked.

"Took off for the tall and uncut, would be my guess," Stovepipe said. "They figured out we had 'em penned up in here and decided a hundred head of stock just wasn't worth it."

"I thought we could keep them bottled up and wait for Wilbur and the others so we could catch them."

"That was my plan, all right . . . but where cows are concerned, it don't take much to ruin a fella's plans.

They ain't always predictable critters." Stovepipe came out from behind the boulder with the rifle held at a slant across his chest. "I'm gonna walk down there and have a look around."

"The rest of those rustlers could still be lurking around."

"They could be, but it ain't likely. They had no way of knowin' how many men we had up here." Stovepipe grinned. "If they'd knowed there was just two of us, they might've been more stubborn about not lightin' a shuck."

Telling Vance to cover him, Stovepipe walked down the slanting trail with his Winchester ready for instant use. Even before he reached the bottom, he spotted riders coming fast from the direction of the ranch headquarters, but they were still about half a mile away.

That gave Stovepipe a chance to take a good look around before Wilbur and the others got there. He was especially interested in a cluster of hoofprints he found not far from the bottom of the trail. It looked like the rustlers had paused there for a moment, probably to discuss what they were going to do next.

They had done what outlaws nearly always did when facing capture—they scattered and took off in several different directions at once. Stovepipe knew they would be difficult if not impossible to track down, but that didn't stop him from hunkering on his heels to study the hoofprints.

He had just straightened from that task when the bunch from the Three Rivers galloped up, led by Wilbur, Keenan Malone, and Andy Callahan.

"Stewart!" Malone boomed. "What the hell happened here?"

"Are you all right, Stovepipe?" Wilbur asked.

"Fine as frog hair," Stovepipe answered with a grin. "Mr. Malone, all those stolen cows are up at the top of this trail, scattered around and grazin' now."

"Where are the no-good sons who took 'em?"

"Well, two of the hombres are layin' up yonder on the trail, or what's left of 'em, anyway. Anybody whose stomach is on the sensitive side probably hadn't ought to look at 'em. They ain't a pretty sight."

Malone grunted and said, "I'm not gonna waste any sympathy on a couple of blasted rustlers. As far as I'm concerned, they got what they had comin' to 'em. Although I wouldn't have minded if they'd lived to hang nice and slow, kickin' out their lives at the end of a rope. That's a fittin' end for rustlers. What about the others?"

Stovepipe shook his head. "Gone. Vance and me figured it was more important to recover that missin' stock. Anyway, we took the shots we could at 'em. Couldn't do much more than that."

"No, I don't reckon. What about Brewster? Coleman said he was winged earlier."

"He's up at the top of the trail, coverin' me. He'll be all right. Just got a scratch on his arm."

Callahan said, "Miss Rosaleen will be mighty glad to hear that."

Malone scowled at his segundo for a second, then said, "Maybe we can trail the rest of that sorry bunch of cow thieves."

"Not likely," Stovepipe said. "They scattered hell-west and crosswise."

"Don't reckon it really matters. We know where they came from . . . the Rafter M."

"You sure about that, boss?"

"Who else could be responsible for this except that blasted Mort Cabot?"

Stovepipe didn't answer that, but a frown creased his forehead.

Andy Callahan held out a hand to him. "Swing up here behind me, Stewart. I'll give you a ride to the top of the trail."

Stovepipe accepted the invitation. The whole group rode through the gap and found Vance waiting for them at the top. Stovepipe slid down from Callahan's horse to reclaim his paint.

"Good work, Brewster," Malone told the young cowboy. "How's the wing?"

Vance moved the wounded arm and nodded. "A little sore, but it works all right."

"You can take it easy for a day or two when we get back to the ranch. Let it rest and heal. You got ventilated defendin' Three Rivers stock, so you deserve a break."

"That's not necessary, boss. It'll be fine—"

"You can argue with me all you want, boy, but you'll have to argue with my daughter and sister-in-law, too, and that's a mighty formidable chore."

Stovepipe smiled and told Vance, "Might as well admit defeat, son. The ladies will have their way. Right now, though, maybe you'll give me a hand with a little errand."

"Sure. What is it, Stovepipe?"

"Let's see if we can find the horses those two rustlers were ridin'. They ran on up here after those fellas met their unfortunate ends, and it ain't likely they wandered too far."

"Good idea, Stewart. If those nags have Rafter M brands on 'em, that ought to be enough to get Charlie

Jerrico after Cabot and his sorry bunch." Malone turned in the saddle and waved an arm. "The rest of you boys start gatherin' these cattle so we can drive 'em back to where they belong."

Stovepipe and Vance mounted up and went in search of the rustlers' horses. As Stovepipe had predicted, the animals hadn't gone far. They had found each other and were less than a mile away, grazing in peace and contentment, unaware that their previous owners were both dead.

Stovepipe caught the reins of one horse while Vance took charge of the other. From the saddle, Stovepipe studied them and located unfamiliar brands. Neither horse wore Rafter M iron. He pointed that out to Vance.

"That doesn't really prove anything, does it? Isn't it possible that when Cabot's men set out to steal Three Rivers stock, they would use horses with brands that don't come from around here? That way, no trail would lead straight back to them . . . in a case like this?"

"That makes sense, all right. A remuda strictly for rustlin' purposes. That wouldn't be cheap, but a big enough operation could justify it."

Stovepipe tugged at his right earlobe for a moment, then rasped his thumbnail along his dark-stubbled jawline. Those little habits were indications he was deep in thought. After a few seconds, he smiled and shook his head. "Oh, well, we wouldn't want all the answers to just fall right into our laps, would we? If a fella got what he wanted without havin' to fight for it, he'd likely feel it wasn't worth very much."

"So you're saying it's the journey that's worthwhile, not the destination."

"Reckon a fella could put it like that, if he was of a philosophical bent. Which I ain't. Come on. Let's take these cayuses and get back to the others."

Malone met them with avid interest on his rugged face. "Tell me those are Rafter M horses."

"Can't do that, boss. The brands they're wearin' ain't quite as bad as Mexican skillet-of-snakes marks, but they ain't any I've ever seen before, either."

Malone and Callahan checked out the brands with similar lack of recognition.

Malone didn't bother trying to hide the disappointment he felt. "So we can't just charge over to the Rafter M and settle things with that sorry bunch."

"Ride in there with guns blazin', and Cabot would have an excuse to call the law down on your head," Stovepipe said.

Malone smacked his knobby-knuckled right fist into his left palm with a resounding pop. "Blast his eyes, that's probably just what the sorry son is hopin' we'll do! Well, he ain't gonna get his wish . . . this time." He looked around at the other men. "But I'm tellin' you this, boys . . . I've had enough. The next time Rafter M makes a move against us, it's war! And if it comes to that, I plan on wipin' the whole blasted lot of 'em right off the face of the earth!"

CHAPTER TWELVE

It was late in the afternoon before the men made it back to the Three Rivers headquarters. They had driven the recovered stock to the pasture where the rest of the herd was being held. Keenan Malone left half a dozen men there to watch over the cattle, including Andy Callahan. They would be on high alert, and if the rustlers tried to strike again, they would find themselves facing a hot lead welcome.

Stovepipe, Wilbur, and Vance were with the bunch that returned to headquarters. The dogs pitched their usual barking fit as the riders approached, so Rosaleen and Aunt Sinead were on the porch waiting with anxious expressions on their faces as the men reined to a halt.

"Dad, are you all right?" Rosaleen asked as she went down the steps and then put a hand on the shoulder of her father's horse.

"I'm fine," Malone said. "Didn't hardly come close enough to trouble to even hear the shootin'." He nodded toward Stovepipe and Vance. "These two had already done for a couple of the cow thieves and routed the rest of 'em by the time we got there."

Rosaleen turned to Vance. "I know you're hurt."

He lifted the arm with a bloodstained rag tied around it as a bandage. "It's not enough to worry about." He grimaced a little as he moved the arm, though.

"I'll be the judge of that," Aunt Sinead said in a tone that made it clear there would be no argument. "Get down off that horse and come in the house, young man. I'm sure Mr. Stewart did the best he could, but that injury needs to be cleaned and bandaged properly."

"Yes, ma'am, it sure does," Stovepipe said. "My skills as a sawbones are kinda limited."

"Don't worry about your horse," Wilbur told Vance. "We'll take care of it."

With the two women fussing over him, Vance was ushered into the house.

Malone turned to Stovepipe and Wilbur. "I meant what I told you earlier. You boys can take it easy for a day or two."

"That sorta goes against the grain for us," Stovepipe said. "We're used to workin' for a livin'."

"We can probably force ourselves to ease up a mite, though," Wilbur said. "If we really try."

Malone said, "I'll count on you, then, Coleman, to pound some sense into your scrawny partner's head. I'll see you at supper. If Sinead don't already have somethin' special planned, I'll see to it that she does."

While they were unsaddling their horses, Wilbur said quietly to Stovepipe, "I saw you taking a good long look at something on the ground when we rode up. Hoofprints?"

"Yeah. Appeared those rustlers stopped for a minute to palaver 'fore they went hellin' off hither and yon."

"Did you recognize any of the prints?"

Stovepipe shook his head and said, "Nope. Most of 'em had nothin' to set 'em apart from a thousand other hoofprints. But a few were distinctive enough I reckon I'd know again, happen I was to lay eyes on 'em."

"Did you see anything to indicate the Rafter M *wasn't* behind the raid?"

"Nary a thing. But there's no proof Cabot was to blame for it, either."

Vance came up behind them and asked, "What are you fellas talking about?"

"Oh, nothin' important," Stovepipe said. "Got that arm tended to?"

Vance held up his left arm, which sported a clean, fresh bandage around the upper part where the bullet had grazed him. "Yeah. Aunt Sinead said you did a really good job patching it up. She seemed a little reluctant to admit that, but credit where credit is due, she said."

"Stovepipe's tended to plenty of bullet wounds in his time," Wilbur said. "More than his fair share."

"That's because we keep wanderin' into trouble," Stovepipe said. "You wouldn't think that would happen to a couple peace-lovin' hombres like me and Wilbur."

Wilbur snorted at that idea. Vance just grinned. He would have had to be pretty dumb not to have figured out already that peace and quiet seldom lasted long around his newfound friends.

As it turned out, Aunt Sinead had spent the afternoon baking pies, in the hope they would have something to celebrate when the men returned to ranch headquarters, so supper was indeed special.

Wilbur was groaning from feeling a mite overstuffed as they headed back to the bunkhouse. "I reckon both your legs must be hollow," he said to Stovepipe. "I never saw a man who could eat as much as you do and stay so skinny. How many slices of pie did you have, anyway?"

"I disremember," Stovepipe said with a grin. "All I recollect is that they were good. Anyway, I burn up what I eat by thinkin' so hard."

"What are you thinking about these days?"

Stovepipe pursed his lips but didn't answer.

"I get it," Wilbur went on. "You don't have everything figured out to your satisfaction, so you're going to clam up and keep it all to yourself like you usually do."

"It ain't that I'm clammin' up. I just don't know anything for sure yet. I got a few ideas, mind you, but until I can prove 'em, it might be better to play my cards close to my vest."

"And if somebody blows a hole in that vest and you wind up buzzard bait, nobody will ever know what you were thinking, will they?"

"We'll just be careful and not let that happen," Stovepipe said.

"Because we have such a long tradition of being

careful." Wilbur sighed. "I'm wasting my breath. You've got a certain way you do things, and nobody's going to budge you from it."

"It's worked out pretty well so far."

"I'll give you that."

Since the Three Rivers had plenty of hands to finish the roundup without them, Stovepipe, Wilbur, and Vance agreed to stay close to headquarters the next day and take it easy, the way Keenan Malone wanted them to.

Vance's wounded arm was stiff and he was glad he didn't have to go out and help with the gather. In a few days, the Three Rivers crew would be driving the herd into Wagontongue to ship the cattle to market. He hoped that with some rest, his arm would be healed enough for him to take part in the drive. Actually, he didn't mind the time off.

Malone had less luck getting his daughter to do what he said. After the dangerous incidents during the past thirty-six hours, he didn't want Rosaleen anywhere near the gather. She knew that.

At the same time, she wanted to see what was going on.

Vance could tell Stovepipe and Wilbur were restless. They were the sort of men who felt like they ought to be accomplishing something all the time, especially when they weren't hurt.

Vance watched them walk to the barn then followed them inside. They were saddling their horses.

"Where are you two going?"

"Just thought we'd scout around a mite," Stovepipe said. "With all the activity goin' on up on the north part of the ranch, troublemakers might figure it was a good time to get up to mischief somewheres else."

That was actually a good idea, Vance thought. He started toward the stall where his horse was kept. "I'll come with you."

"I reckon not," Stovepipe told him. "Hours in the saddle ain't gonna do that arm of yours any good, and if that wound busted open and started bleedin' again, Aunt Sinead would be liable to skin me alive. No, you just stay here and take it easy."

"You didn't like it when Mr. Malone told you to do that."

"No, but we ain't been shot, neither. He feels grateful to us, but that maybe ain't the best way to express his gratitude."

Stovepipe and Wilbur swung up into their saddles, waved in farewell, and rode out from headquarters. Vance watched them go, shaking his head.

It looked like he was stuck at ranch headquarters, whether he liked it or not.

Facing a long, boring day, he went back to the bunkhouse, found a pad of paper and a pencil, and figured he would write some letters. The first one was to his father, telling the old man all about what he'd been doing, trying not to embellish the tale too much.

The thought that someday she might be running the ranch still nagged at Rosaleen's brain. It wasn't likely the owners back east would ever entrust the Three Rivers to a woman . . . unless she could demonstrate beyond a shadow of a doubt that she was the best person for the job.

With those thoughts going through her mind, she slipped out to the barn around the middle of the morning, dressed in range clothes again.

From the corner of his eye, Vance spotted movement through the window facing the barn. The glass was pretty smudged and grimy, but he was able to make out the shape of a slender cowboy walking toward the barn.

Something about the figure's movements struck him as surreptitious, so he set the letter aside, stood up, and moved closer to the window. The cowboy disappeared into the shadows inside the barn.

Making a close study of the fella from behind convinced Vance of one thing. That was no fella. The curve of the hips in those denim trousers was distinctly feminine. Since there were only two women on the ranch and the one he'd just seen definitely wasn't Aunt Sinead, that left only one answer.

Rosaleen was skulking around the barn . . . and she was dressed for riding.

She was going to disobey her father and ride out to the roundup again. Vance was sure of it.

Malone had ordered her to stay close to home, but Rosaleen didn't like being told what to do. Vance hadn't known her for long, but he had already figured out that much about her.

* * *

Rosaleen saddled one of the ponies she usually rode and led it well away from headquarters before mounting up and heading for the hills where the rest of the gather was taking place.

When she didn't emerge from the barn for several minutes, Vance left the bunkhouse and walked over there. He found the door in the back of the barn open, and through it he spotted a person on horseback moving away in the distance to the north. He didn't need Stovepipe's field glasses to know who the rider was.

Some of the older hands who worked at headquarters most of the time were around, but Vance didn't even consider telling them what he'd seen. He just went to his horse's stall to saddle the animal.

The sore arm made the task more difficult, but he managed without damaging the wound . . . he hoped. Once he was mounted, he left through the back door, too, and followed the rider he could barely see ahead of him.

It was a glorious day with a vault of blue sky arching overhead, dotted here and there with fluffy white clouds. The air had just enough of a bite to keep the sun from being too warm. Rosaleen felt a sense of prideful possession as she rode over the rolling landscape. She knew the spread wasn't hers—she was well aware it belonged to those nameless, faceless tycoons back east—but in all the ways that mattered, this was her home. It was where she had grown up and where she planned to spend the rest of her days.

Her father had wanted a son and had raised her accordingly, but she bore no grudges against him for that. She'd always been glad she could ride and shoot and dab a loop on a steer if she needed to. Those were useful skills for anyone to have on the frontier, male or female.

She hadn't ignored the more feminine aspects of life. She barely remembered her mother, but Aunt Sinead had always been there to make sure she learned what she needed to know. The way Rosaleen saw it, she had the best of both worlds . . . as long as nobody tried to pen her up in either of them.

In a way, Vance hoped he was mistaken and that Rosaleen was still back at the ranch, safe and sound. Deep down, though, he knew his hunch was right.

He became more convinced when he saw she was headed for the area where the roundup was taking place. Even after everything that had happened, she didn't like to be shut out of the ranch's activities. Whatever was going on, she wanted to be right in the middle of it.

That put a grin on his face. He could understand the feeling. He was much the same way, most of the time.

He thought about urging his horse to a faster pace and catching up with her, but he stayed back. Honestly, even though he was used to riding, bouncing around in the saddle made his wounded arm ache and twinge. He didn't want to hurt it worse by galloping unless there was a good reason.

Really, he had followed her only to make sure she was all right, Vance thought. He could trail her, keep an eye on her, and accomplish that goal. It might also be a good idea not to let her know he had appointed himself her guardian. Likely, her proud nature wouldn't like that.

They rode for several miles, with Vance getting a little closer but not much. He still had Rosaleen in sight all the time. Had she looked back, she might have seen him, but she didn't seem to be paying much attention to her back trail.

Vance frowned. She ought to be more cautious, he thought, especially with tensions running so high between the Three Rivers and the neighboring Rafter M. Cabot's men would know they weren't welcome on Three Rivers range . . . but that wouldn't stop them from riding there anyway.

Rosaleen was lost in her thoughts, musing on having the best of both worlds—that of a woman and that of a cowboy—when she realized someone was riding along parallel with her. He was on top of a small, pine-dotted ridge about fifty yards away.

Without thinking, she slowed abruptly, giving away that she had spotted him. He reined his mount down the slope and angled to intercept her.

Part of Rosaleen wanted to wheel her horse around and run, but her pride wouldn't let her. She was on Three Rivers range, after all. Her home. She had no reason to be afraid or to flee. She brought her horse to a stop and waited to see what the rider was going to do.

He headed straight for her.

CHAPTER THIRTEEN

Vance suddenly straightened and rode taller in the saddle as he spotted a man on horseback atop a ridge, ahead of him and to the left. The rider seemed to be keeping pace with Rosaleen, but then as she abruptly slowed her mount, the man turned his horse and headed down off the ridge. When he reached level ground, he angled so his trail would cross Rosaleen's.

Vance didn't like the looks of that. The stranger seemed bent on accosting Rosaleen. Of course, he might be one of the Three Rivers crew, and she wouldn't be in danger from any of them. The whole bunch of cowhands seemed to think of her as a niece or a little sister.

Vance urged his horse into a fast lope. He wanted to be sure what was going on.

As the rider came closer, Rosaleen saw that he wore a blue shirt and a black hat and vest. The hat with a tightly rolled brim was cocked at an angle on his head, giving him an arrogant look. She told herself she was leaping to conclusions, but she really didn't think that was the case.

After a moment, she was able to see his face. Dax Coolidge. He was a handsome man, in a rough-hewn way, but his deep-set eyes and the way his mouth twisted in a smirk worked against that.

He wasn't one of her father's men . . . and that meant he had no business riding around Three Rivers range.

The man reined to a halt about fifteen feet from her. He reached up and pinched the brim of his hat as he said, "Miss Malone." The gesture had no real respect in it. Rather, his whole attitude seemed mocking.

"Mr. Coolidge," she said. "What are you doing here?"

"I could ask you the same thing."

"No, not really. My father is the manager of this ranch. I have every right to be here. You work for Mort Cabot, and you're a long way from the Rafter M,"

"Not that awful far, as the crow flies. Anyway, can't a fella pay a friendly visit to the neighbors every now and then?"

"Cabot and his men aren't welcome on Three Rivers range," Rosaleen said. "I know that's not very hospitable . . . but most folks don't invite snakes into their front parlor."

Coolidge's pale blue eyes narrowed. Rosaleen felt a shiver of fear go through her, although she tried not to show it.

"Ma'am, that's downright unfriendly, especially when I haven't done a thing except greet you politely. You didn't even answer my question about what you're doing all the way out here alone."

"I'm not alone," she answered instantly. "There are half a dozen of my father's cowboys nearby."

Coolidge crossed his hands on his saddle horn, leaned forward, and looked around. An arrogant grin creased his tanned features. "Whereabouts? I don't see anybody except you." He nudged his horse closer. "Fact is, the way you came back so quick with that answer tells me you really *are* by yourself."

"You had better leave me alone and get out of here." Rosaleen hated herself for sounding nervous, but she couldn't help it. "If you ride out now, I won't tell my father or anyone else about you being here where you don't belong—"

Again he moved his mount closer to hers as he said sharply, "That's where you're wrong, Miss Malone. I *belong* wherever I damned well happen to be. Dax Coolidge rides where he wants to, and nobody tells me different."

Anger flared up inside Rosaleen. *She* would be damned if she let anybody crowd her, even a notorious gunman like Coolidge. She jerked her horse back and reached for her carbine at the same time. Once she was looking at him over the barrel of the repeater, he would sing a different tune.

But he didn't just sit there and let her pull the carbine from its sheath. In almost one motion, he jabbed his heels into his horse's flanks, the animal leaped toward Rosaleen's horse, and Coolidge yanked it into a tight turn alongside her. He reached over, looped his left arm around her waist, and jerked her out of the saddle even as an involuntary scream ripped from her throat.

Vance heard that frightened cry, and combined with the sight of Rosaleen struggling in the man's grip, it made anger explode inside him. He forgot all about his injured arm as he leaned forward and sent his mount racing toward them.

Hearing the swiftly drumming hoofbeats as Vance galloped toward them, the man jerked his horse around to face the newcomer.

Close enough to see the man's face, Vance realized it was familiar somehow, but he wasn't sure where he'd seen the hombre before. None of that mattered anyway. No matter who he was, Vance wasn't going to let him get away with manhandling Rosaleen!

The man reached for his gun, making Vance realize what a disadvantage he had. Even with a Colt on his hip, he was no gunman. He'd been able to blaze away at the rustlers with a rifle, but a showdown with six-shooters was much different.

Besides, the man had hold of Rosaleen. Vance couldn't start throwing lead. He'd be just as likely to hit her, and he couldn't risk that.

The stranger, on the other hand, didn't have to worry about being careful. Flame spurted from the muzzle of his gun as he triggered a pair of shots at Vance.

Neither bullet found its target. The man's horse was moving around skittishly from carrying double and Rosaleen was still struggling to get loose from the man's grip.

As he tried to bring the horse under control, she finally twisted enough to bring an elbow up sharply under his chin. The impact of the blow jerked his head back and loosened his arm around her waist. She planted both hands against his chest, shoved hard, and toppled to the ground as she broke free.

Vance's heart leaped as he saw her fall. She was in

danger of the horse stepping on her, especially if the hard landing stunned her.

But as soon as Rosaleen hit the ground, she was moving. She rolled away from the horse, putting several yards between her and the steel-shod hooves.

Vance was closing in, dividing the stranger's attention between him and Rosaleen. That gave Vance the chance to close the gap between them. The man jerked back toward him at the last moment, and Vance got a good look at him—Dax Coolidge, the gunman who worked for the Rafter M.

Coolidge's gun came around toward him.

Moving too fast to stop, Vance kicked his feet free of the stirrups and dived at Coolidge. The man's revolver blasted at the same instant, so close that Vance felt the heat of the shot lash against his face.

A fraction of a second later, Vance crashed into Coolidge and drove him from the saddle. Vance rammed Coolidge into the ground as they landed and Coolidge's gun flew out of his hand.

Vance's injured arm throbbed, but in his fury over Coolidge's treatment of Rosaleen, he barely noticed it. He lunged for Coolidge's throat with his other hand. The landing had knocked the breath out of the gunman's lungs, and Vance intended to keep him helpless and gasping for air.

Vance assumed none of the bullets had hit him. He didn't feel any new injuries as he closed his right hand around Coolidge's throat. Coolidge's eyes widened as Vance began to choke him.

With a lot of experience at brawling, Coolidge brought his right leg up, wedged it across Vance's chest, and broke free with a convulsive movement of his entire body. Vance sprawled on his back.

Coolidge rolled onto hands and knees and paused for a couple seconds to drag in several deep breaths. At the same time, Vance tried to push himself up and without thinking put his left hand on the ground to take some of his weight. Pain shot through that arm, and the muscles refused to work. He fell back awkwardly.

Coolidge's questing gaze found the gun he had dropped, and he lunged for it. Vance knew that if Coolidge got his hands on the weapon, he was as good as dead. He scrambled up and dived onto Coolidge's back.

That stopped Coolidge from getting hold of the gun, but he writhed like a snake, rolling over and throwing Vance off again. Vance landed within kicking distance and slammed the heel of his right boot into Coolidge's left shoulder. The gunman yelled in pain.

Bigger and heavier than Coolidge, Vance threw himself at the gunman again and sledged a punch into his jaw. If he'd had the full use of both arms, he could have hammered Coolidge into senselessness.

Coolidge wasn't just as lithe and wiry as a snake, he was as treacherous as one, too. His knee came up and sank into Vance's groin. Blinding pain exploded through Vance. He curled up around that agony, knowing that he had to shake it off but unable for the moment to do so.

Coolidge hit him on the chin with a right and sank his left into Vance's belly. Vance summoned all the strength he could muster and surged up onto his knees. A one-armed tackle brought Coolidge down again and Vance butted him in the face.

That stunned Coolidge. Still hurting something fierce, Vance forced his mind and muscles to work and lifted himself to look around for Coolidge's gun.

Spotting it on the ground, he went after it. His hand closed around it and he reeled to his feet. As he turned toward Coolidge, he saw the gunfighter had managed to stand up, too.

Coolidge had another pistol in his hand. His thumb was on the hammer and his finger was wrapped around the trigger.

All Vance could think was it must have been hidden in Coolidge's boot or in a holster at the small of his back. The weapon was a smaller caliber, but it was no less deadly . . . and the revolver in his own hand was pointing at the ground. He had no chance . . .

"You're holding a gun," Coolidge said as an ugly grin stretched across his face. "That makes it self-defense, kid."

His finger tightened on the trigger.

CHAPTER FOURTEEN

The roar of a shot filled the air, but it didn't come from Coolidge's gun. Coolidge's arm jerked and he cried out in pain. The pistol flew through the air and landed several yards away, its cylinder smashed by the bullet that had struck it.

Vance looked around in confusion and saw a rider galloping toward them. Farther back, another man sat on horseback, holding a rifle. That man nudged his horse into motion and rode forward at a more deliberate pace. Vance recognized him right away as Stovepipe Stewart.

Not surprisingly, the first man was Wilbur Coleman. He brought his roan to a sliding halt and was out of the saddle before the horse came to a complete stop. He covered Coolidge with a Colt. "You all right, Vance?"

"Yeah, I . . . I reckon." Vance looked down at his arm, saw crimson seeping through onto his shirt sleeve. "Aunt Sinead's not gonna be happy when she sees I've busted open this wound, though. But I had a good reason—" He stopped short and looked around for Rosaleen. She stood nearby, leaning on the pony she had ridden and holding on to the saddle. Her face was pale.

Vance hurried to her side, "Rosaleen, you're hurt—"

"No," she told him with a shake of her head. "That fall just . . . knocked the wind out of me. I'll be fine. But your arm is bleeding."

"It's nothing to worry about. I'll just have to be patched up again." He grinned. "Seems like I'm making a habit out of it."

"Don't joke about it. Coolidge could have killed you."

They turned to look at the gunman, who stood there scowling at Wilbur. The gun in Wilbur's hand was rock-steady as he kept it pointed at Coolidge. Coolidge shook his right hand a little, like he was trying to get feeling back into it. It stung from having the pistol shot out of his grasp.

That was some incredible marksmanship, Vance thought. Since it was Stovepipe who had made the shot, somehow he wasn't surprised.

Stovepipe rode up in a deliberate manner and reined in his paint. "Everybody all right here?"

"Vance is bleeding again," Rosaleen said.

"Well, I ain't surprised, since him and Coolidge was engagin' in such strenuous fisticuffs. Don't appear he's on the verge of bleedin' to death, though."

Vance looked down at his arm again and shook his head. "I'll be all right. It does kind of hurt like blazes, though."

"What happened here?"

Rosaleen said, "Coolidge attacked me. There's no telling what he might have done if Vance hadn't come along when he did."

Coolidge's lips twisted in a snarl. "That's a damned

lie. I was just talking to the girl when she started to haul out her rifle and shoot me. All I was doing was trying to stop her, and then this loco cowboy came along and tackled me."

"You're the one who's lying," Vance said. "I saw you drag Miss Malone out of her saddle. On top of that, you're trespassing. Rafter M riders aren't welcome on Three Rivers range."

Coolidge sneered at him. "Talking mighty big, aren't you, boy? You're just a grub line rider. You don't give orders around here."

"Vance is right," Rosaleen said. "You're trespassing, and if my father was here, he'd back that up."

"Sounds like plenty of reason to get the law involved," Stovepipe said. "Climb up on that nag o' yours, Coolidge. We're takin' a little ride to Wagontongue."

Coolidge cursed at him and ranted. "You're not going to turn me over to the law!"

Still holding the rifle, Stovepipe turned it slightly so the barrel was pointed straight at Coolidge. "Be even less trouble to haul you in slung over your saddle, instead of ridin' it." The icy tone of his voice left no doubt he meant the threat.

Still muttering curses, Coolidge turned to his horse and mounted. Wilbur holstered his gun, then picked up the pistol Stovepipe had shot out of Coolidge's hand and took the gunman's other revolver from Vance. "Reckon we'll turn these over to the sheriff."

"Miss Rosaleen, can you see to it that Vance gets back to headquarters and has that wounded arm tended to?" Stovepipe asked.

"Of course," she said. "I'm feeling better now. I'm not as shaken up anymore."

"Much obliged to you, then. Wilbur and me will take Coolidge to see Sheriff Jerrico. This varmint belongs behind bars."

"No jail's gonna keep me in," Coolidge said.

"We'll see about that."

"Stovepipe," Vance said, "the last time I saw you and Wilbur, you were riding south. What are you doing up here on this part of the ranch?"

"Just call it a hunch," Stovepipe said. "I got to feelin' there might be some trouble up here, so Wilbur and me decided to come check it out."

"You mean *you* decided," Wilbur said from the back of his roan. "You were the one with the hunch."

"And it's a good thing you did," Vance said. "If you hadn't come along when you did, I'd probably be dead now."

"And there's no telling what Coolidge would have done to me," Rosaleen added.

"Glad to be of service," Stovepipe said as he ticked a finger against the brim of his hat. "Now come on, Coolidge. You got a date with the law."

Coolidge didn't do much on the ride into town except snarl curses now and then. Stovepipe and Wilbur rode behind the gunman and ignored him, other than keeping an eye on him to make sure he didn't try to escape.

"What do you reckon Miss Rosaleen was doing up there on that part of the range in the first place?" Wilbur asked.

"Goin' to poke her pretty little nose into the roundup,

of course," Stovepipe said. "She's got that—what do you call it?—feminine curiosity, in spades."

Wilbur snorted. "I never saw anybody more curious than you, Stovepipe, and you're not the least bit feminine."

"I'll take that as a compliment. And I admit, I sorta like to stick my nose into things, too, whether it's wanted or not."

"Somebody's liable to try to cut it off one of these days."

"They'll have a fight on their hands if they do."

The two cowboys rode along in silence for a few minutes, then Stovepipe went on. "Ain't no doubt about it now. Vance is plumb smitten with Miss Rosaleen. Don't reckon anybody could blame him, either. Why, if I was twenty years younger—"

"Thirty's more like it."

"Well . . . give or take. Anyway, he's stuck on her, and I reckon the feelin's startin' to get sorta mutual. Be interestin' to see what happens when her daddy figures out the same thing. He won't be too happy about some grub line rider courtin' his little gal. Of course, Malone don't know the full story yet."

"And you do."

"I'm gettin' there," Stovepipe said. "Slowly but surely, I'm gettin' there."

It was the middle of the afternoon by the time they reached Wagontongue.

Coolidge had started to complain about being hungry. "I never got any lunch, you know. I was too busy being attacked for no good reason."

"Yeah, you go on spinnin' that yarn," Stovepipe told him. "We'll just see how many folks believe it."

"You'll get supper tonight, Coolidge," Wilbur said. "In jail."

Despite being the county seat, Wagontongue didn't have a courthouse. The most substantial building in town was the redbrick train station on the southern edge of town with corrals and loading pens on the other side of the tracks. County business was done out of a frame office building on Main Street, and next door was a sturdy stone building that housed the sheriff's office and jail.

Riding with their Winchesters across the saddles in front of them, Stovepipe and Wilbur drew a lot of attention as they rode along the street with their prisoner. Everyone in Wagontongue knew who Dax Coolidge was, and most of them were afraid of him. Even, when it was obvious that he was disarmed, they stared nervously at him, as if they were worried he might explode into violence at any moment.

Coolidge cooperated, though, other than looking back over his shoulder every now and then to curse or smirk at Stovepipe and Wilbur. "You won't keep me in jail."

"Not our job to keep you there," Stovepipe said. "That'll be up to the sheriff."

Coolidge just let out a contemptuous laugh at that.

Stovepipe noticed several men hurrying ahead of them toward the sheriff's office, so he wasn't surprised to see slab-jawed Charlie Jerrico standing on the boardwalk in front of the office, waiting for them. Gossip had moved faster than the riders.

Jerrico hooked his thumbs in the gunbelt slanting

across his hips and scowled at the three riders. "What the hell is this all about?"

Stovepipe, Wilbur, and Coolidge reined in.

"Got a prisoner for you, Sheriff," Stovepipe said.

Even as he was speaking, Coolidge bulled in verbally. "I want to file a complaint, Jerrico. These two saddle tramps kidnapped me!"

"Kidnapping's a pretty serious charge." Jerrico looked at Stovepipe. "You're one of those Three Rivers men, aren't you?"

"That's right. Name of Stewart. This here's my pard Wilbur Coleman. I reckon you could say we made a citizen's arrest on Coolidge. He was about to murder Vance Brewster, another hombre who rides for the Three Rivers."

"That's a lie," Coolidge said in a scathing tone. "Brewster had a gun in his hand. If I'd killed him, it would have been self-defense."

"Not hardly," Stovepipe said. "A gun-wolf like you against a kid like that? That's murder, any way you look at it."

Coolidge sneered. "Not according to the law."

"And we ain't even mentioned nothin' yet about how you tried to molest Miss Rosaleen Malone."

That drew surprised, scandalized murmurs from the crowd that had gathered in the street in front of the sheriff's office.

Jerrico frowned and jerked his head toward the door. "Inside now, all three of you. We're not gonna conduct law business on the street."

Wilbur dismounted first, then kept his rifle pointed in Coolidge's general direction as the gunman climbed down from the saddle. Stovepipe swung down last.

"Leave those rifles out here," Jerrico told them.

"I don't rightly trust Coolidge," Stovepipe said.

"I don't care. Nobody walks into my office waving guns around. You can consider Coolidge to be in my custody. I'll be responsible for him."

"You're arresting me?" Coolidge demanded.

"I'm holding you until I find out what happened. Get inside, now."

Stovepipe and Wilbur returned their rifles to the saddle boots, then all four men trooped into the office.

Jerrico pointed to Stovepipe. "All right, Stewart, I'll listen to your version first."

Coolidge said, "That's not fair!"

"Shut up, or you can tell your side of it from inside a cell."

Stovepipe explained about riding up on the brutal battle between Coolidge and Vance Brewster. He concluded by saying, "Vance went to pick up the gun Coolidge had dropped, and Coolidge grabbed a hideout gun he had in his boot. He was about to shoot the boy, like I said before, when I shot the gun outta his hand."

"You shot the gun out of a man's hand?" Jerrico asked in evident disbelief. "How far away were you?"

Stovepipe shrugged. "Fifty yards or so, I reckon." He shook his head. "Didn't say I did it a-purpose, mind you. I could've been aimin' for his head and missed. But either way, it worked out all right."

Jerrico looked at Coolidge. "So you claim that's a lie?"

"What Stewart told you was true enough, I suppose," Coolidge said with obvious reluctance, "but he and Coleman came up at the tail end of the trouble. They didn't see the Malone girl try to grab her carbine and shoot me, just because I was on Three Rivers range. She was loco, Sheriff, pure loco."

"I've never known Miss Malone to act like that," Jerrico said.

"Well, she did today. And then Brewster came along and jumped me. All I was doing the whole time out there was trying to defend myself."

Wilbur let out a disgusted snort, making it plain what he thought of Coolidge's claim.

Jerrico glared at him for a second, then asked, "Where are Miss Malone and Brewster now?"

"She took Vance back to the ranch headquarters so he could get his wounded arm patched up again," Stovepipe said. "He got hurt a few nights ago fightin' rustlers."

"How come I haven't heard about that?"

Stovepipe shrugged. "I reckon Mr. Malone ain't got around to reportin' it yet."

"Let him know he'd better ride in and tell me about it."

"I can do that," Stovepipe said. "What about Coolidge?"

The gunman pointed at Stovepipe and Wilbur. "I want to file charges against these two, and against Brewster and the Malone girl, too."

"Nobody's filing any charges until I've talked to everybody involved, and that includes Brewster and Miss Malone. They need to come in and give me a statement, too."

Stovepipe was anxious to get the gunman behind bars. "What about Coolidge in the meantime? You gonna let him run around loose and cause more trouble?"

"No, I'm going to hold him, for now."

Coolidge exploded. "What! You can't do that. Damn you, Jerrico—"

The sheriff thrust his face up next to Coolidge's and said through clenched teeth, "You'd better just shut up right now, mister, unless you want to land in even more trouble. If Miss Malone hadn't been involved, things might have been different, but you can't go around manhandling women, no matter what reason you think you have. You can cool your heels in one of my cells until I get to the bottom of this."

Coolidge looked like he wanted to argue, but he didn't say anything else. He went along without putting up a fight as Jerrico gripped his arm and led him into the cell block behind the office. A moment later an iron-barred door clanged shut behind him.

"What were you doing on the Three Rivers, anyway?" Jerrico asked through the bars.

"That's my business," Coolidge said sullenly as he sat down on the bunk in the cell. "It's still a free country, isn't it?"

"Yeah, but maybe not for you. Not for a while, anyway."

Stovepipe and Wilbur were standing in the open cell block door watching the exchange. Jerrico came back into the office and closed that door, too.

"In a couple days, the Three Rivers is gonna be bringin' in a herd to be shipped out," Stovepipe said. "Will that be soon enough for Malone and Brewster and Miss Malone to talk to you?"

"Fine with me," Jerrico said with a shrug. "Coolidge

may complain about having to stay locked up that long, but I don't particularly care. I'm tired of him strutting around here like he owns the whole territory."

"Thanks for takin' our word over his about what happened."

"I'm not taking anybody's word. I gave some serious thought to locking you up, too, Stewart. You're the only one who actually fired a shot in the whole melee, right?"

Stovepipe smiled. "Come to think of it, I reckon I am. It was in a good cause, though."

"We'll see." Jerrico nodded toward the office door. "Get out of here, and don't cause any trouble while you're in town."

Stovepipe and Wilbur went outside. Stovepipe frowned at Coolidge's horse and stuck his head back into the office.

"Sheriff, you got a little corral out back where you and the deputies keep your horses, ain't that right?"

"Yeah," Jerrico said from behind the scarred old desk where he had sat down. "So what?"

"Want me to put Coolidge's horse back there for you?"

"Well, that would be helpful, I suppose. Thanks, Stewart."

"Glad to do it, Sheriff."

Stovepipe went to the hitch rack, untied the reins of Coolidge's mount, and started toward the corner of the building.

"Now what are we doing?" Wilbur asked.

"Just helpin' the sheriff for a minute." Stovepipe led the horse to the corral, opened the gate, and shooed it inside. He closed the gate and leaned on it for a moment, head down and frowning.

"If you stand there brooding for much longer, it's going to be dark before we get back to the Three Rivers," Wilbur said.

"Yeah, you're right." Stovepipe turned away from the corral and took the reins to his paint from Wilbur. They mounted up and rode away from Wagontongue, heading north toward the Three Rivers spread.

"You made a bad enemy today, Stovepipe," Wilbur said when the settlement was behind them. "So did Vance."

"You mean Coolidge?"

"Yeah. Varmints like that always hold grudges."

Stovepipe shrugged. "Ain't the first time some bad man's had a hankerin' to ventilate me. Probably won't be the last."

"The way you go around hunting trouble . . . I reckon you can count on that."

CHAPTER FIFTEEN

Shadows were settling down over the range by the time Stovepipe and Wilbur got back to the Three Rivers. The yellow light from the windows looked warm and welcoming in the gathering darkness.

The dogs announced their arrival. Several men came out of the bunkhouse carrying rifles, among them Andy Callahan.

The segundo raised a hand in greeting when he recognized who the newcomers were. "Figured you boys would be coming back in this evening. You didn't miss supper by much. I'm sure Aunt Sinead has been keepin' some food warm for you."

"Sounds good," Stovepipe said as he swung down from the saddle. "Where's Vance?"

"Inside talking to the boss and Miss Rosaleen." Callahan chuckled. "When the boss found out what had happened, we had our hands full keepin' him from charging over to the Rafter M to have a show-down. He's been proddy lately anyway, what with all the trouble, and this was almost the last straw. Vance pointed out that Cabot may not have sent Dax Coolidge over here. Ever since he's been in these parts, Coolidge has done pretty much whatever he wanted."

Stovepipe agreed. "Pretty smart thing for Vance to say. The boy's got a good head on his shoulders. Goin' to war against the Rafter M oughta be a last resort."

"Yeah, but if it comes to that . . . all of us intend to win," Callahan said with a grim note in his usually affable voice.

Stovepipe couldn't argue with that sentiment. A couple men offered to take care of their horses, so he and Wilbur turned the mounts over and went into the house.

Aunt Sinead greeted them by saying, "When I heard the dogs carrying on, I figured it meant you boys were back. There are plates of food on the table for you, still nice and hot, and plenty of coffee left in the pot, too."

"Ma'am, you're a godsend," Wilbur told her.

"After you eat, Keenan wants to see you in his office. Rosaleen and young Mr. Brewster are in there with him now."

Stovepipe and Wilbur went into the dining room and tackled the food, which was delicious as always, washing it down with sips of hot, black coffee. The meal helped restore vitality that had been sapped by all the riding they had done.

Finished, they went to Malone's office at the side of the house. A pair of windows looked out at the bunkhouse and barn across the ranch yard. The door was open a few inches, but Stovepipe knocked on it anyway and Malone told them to come in.

A rolltop desk sat against one wall, with a table in the middle of the room. Vance and Rosaleen sat on one side of the table while Malone stood near the windows with his hands clasped together behind his back. He nodded to Stovepipe and Wilbur as they came into the room. "I understand I owe you fellas another debt of thanks for steppin' in and helpin' my girl."

"That was mostly Vance's doin'," Stovepipe said. "He'd already lit into Coolidge before Wilbur and me ever got there."

"Yeah, and Coolidge was about to kill me, too," Vance said. "Don't be modest, Stovepipe. You saved our lives, more than likely."

"Stovepipe's just naturally humble," Wilbur said.

"And a trick shooter, to boot," Malone said. "I heard about that, too."

"Luck," Stovepipe said.

Malone's skeptical grunt made it clear he didn't consider the shot to be luck at all, but he let it go and directed his questions to Stovepipe. "What happened when you took Coolidge to town?"

"The sheriff locked him up."

"I'm surprised. Charlie Jerrico's been bendin' over backwards to stay neutral in the trouble between the Rafter M and the Three Rivers."

"Well, bein' impartial's usually a good thing for a lawman."

Malone snorted. "Not when one side is a bunch of thievin' rustlers and backshooters."

"Cabot and his boys probably say the same thing about you and the Three Rivers crew."

"Maybe, but they're just tryin' to fool folks into thinkin' they're honest." Malone shook his head. "It won't work, especially with me."

"The sheriff wants you to come into town and make a report about that rustlin' a few nights ago."

"Why?" Malone asked with a frown. "It's all over with. We got the cows back, and sent some of those thievin' varmints across the divide."

"I guess Jerrico thinks it oughta be down on record. Anyway, he asked us to tell you." Stovepipe looked at Vance and Rosaleen. "He wants to talk to the two of you, as well."

"About the trouble with Coolidge?" Vance asked.

"Yep. Coolidge claims you attacked him, not the other way around, and he was just defendin' himself."

Rosaleen said, "That's a lie."

"Sure it is, but I reckon the sheriff thinks he's got to hear you say that. Until he's questioned both of you, he's gonna keep Coolidge locked up."

Malone said, "Well, there's that to be thankful for, anyway. Once a judge hears what Coolidge did, maybe he'll wind up in prison where he belongs." The cattleman cleared his throat. "How anxious is Jerrico to talk to us?"

"He said it'd be all right if you stopped at his office when you bring the herd in to ship it," Stovepipe said.

"That'll be day after tomorrow, more than likely. Tomorrow we'll get a good tally and make sure all those critters are branded." Malone cast a stern look toward his daughter. "Until then, I want you to stick close to home, Rosaleen. You got to go into Wagontongue with us and talk to the sheriff, but you can stay out of trouble between now and then."

Her chin jutted out in defiance as she said, "I ought to be able to ride anywhere on this range I want to."

"Maybe so, but where there's one snake, there's usually more. I don't want you runnin' into more Rafter M men."

Rosaleen looked like she wanted to argue, but

then she sighed. "All right. I'll stay here while you finish getting everything ready for the drive into the settlement . . . but that doesn't mean I have to like it."

Malone turned to Vance. "With that bum wing, you can skip the drive and ride into town with Rosaleen on the wagon."

"I'll be all right to help, boss—"

"You've done plenty already. Seems like every time my daughter needs a hand, you're right there to make sure she gets it. How's that happen?"

Vance smiled. "Just lucky, I guess."

"Uh-huh. Lucky." Malone didn't look convinced. He was starting to catch on.

Stovepipe saw the mixed emotions he expected on the old cattleman's rugged face. To Malone's way of thinking, no grub line rider was a suitable match for his daughter . . . and yet, Vance had helped save her life more than once. If things continued, he was going to have quite a dilemma to deal with.

But first there was the matter of getting those cattle to Wagontongue and shipping them off to market.

Stovepipe, Wilbur, and the rest of the Three Rivers crew spent the next day preparing for the drive. Unlike the epic cattle drives from Texas to Kansas during the decade following the close of the Civil War, this journey would be much shorter. They would start early in the morning and with luck would have the cattle in Wagontongue late that afternoon, where they would be driven into the holding pens to await the arrival of the railroad cars that would carry them east to the slaughterhouses. The crew would spend the night in town. A few punchers would remain to help with the loading when the cars came in, while the rest would return to the ranch the next day.

Malone had plenty of guards posted on the herd around the clock, but the rustlers didn't make another try. That came as no surprise to Stovepipe. He, Wilbur, and Vance had dealt the gang a pretty severe blow, and the outlaws would probably spend some time licking their wounds before they attempted another raid.

Stovepipe's gut told him the gang hadn't given up and left that part of the country, though. More trouble was coming; it was just a matter of when.

The morning of the drive dawned bright and clear, perfect weather. The crew had breakfast well before the sun was up.

As they were leaving the house after the meal, Malone said, "Stewart, Coleman, hold up a minute."

"Yeah, boss?" Stovepipe said as they turned back.

"I've got plenty of men to chouse those cows where they're goin'. I want the two of you to stick with my daughter and Brewster."

"They're takin' the wagon to town?"

"That's right. Rosaleen can drive. She was able to handle a team by the time she was six years old."

Stovepipe smiled. "I don't doubt it. You figure they're liable to run into trouble on the way to Wagontongue or after they get there?"

"I don't know, and that's why I want the two of you to ride in with them. Coolidge should still be locked up, but Cabot's got other gun-wolves ridin' for him, and I don't trust any of 'em. I trust the Brewster boy—

he's shown that he'll stick up for Rosaleen—but there's somethin' about him . . . Sometimes he seems almost like a greenhorn to me, even though he claims he's been ridin' the chuck line for several years."

"Well, we can keep an eye on 'em if that's what you want."

"Yeah," Wilbur said, "we're not gonna argue about getting out of eating trail dust all day."

"Don't know how those two younguns will be feel about bein' saddled with a couple nursemaids, though," Stovepipe added.

"As long as my daughter's safe, that's all I care about," Malone said.

Stovepipe and Wilbur went out to the bunkhouse and found Vance awkwardly trying to strap on his gunbelt.

"You can leave that hogleg here if you want," Stovepipe said.

Vance shook his head. "After everything that's happened, I'm not going anywhere without being armed."

"Yeah, but Stovepipe and I are gonna be ridin' into town with you and Miss Rosaleen," Wilbur said.

Vance's forehead creased in a frown. "Chaperones, eh? Or bodyguards?"

Stovepipe chuckled. "Maybe a little bit of both. But we're goin' to Wagontongue with the two of you, anyway. Boss's orders."

After a moment, Vance shrugged. "Fine. I can't say as I'll mind the company. I'd be lying if I said I wasn't looking forward to spending the time alone with Rosaleen, but it's a lot more important that she stay safe."

"That's a practical way to look at it."

"Anyway," Vance said with a grin, "I'll still get to sit beside her on the wagon, won't I?"

The rest of the crew, including Malone and Callahan, were gone by the time the wrangler had hitched the team of horses to the wagon. Their mounts saddled and ready to go, Stovepipe and Wilbur were standing beside the wagon with Vance when Rosaleen came out of the house wearing a riding skirt, shirt, vest, and hat. She carried her carbine.

"Dad told me you two were coming with us," she said to Stovepipe and Wilbur. "I appreciate it . . . even though I think Vance and I can take care of ourselves."

"I don't doubt it, miss," Stovepipe said. "Not to be indelicate about it, but Wilbur and me, we ain't complainin' about not havin' to stare at the hind ends of a bunch of cows all day."

"Come on," Rosaleen said as she climbed onto the wagon seat without giving Vance a chance to help her. "We can get to Wagontongue by the middle of the day and take care of our business with the sheriff before Dad and the herd come in later."

The little group set off for town. As Malone had said, Rosaleen handled the reins skillfully and kept the team moving at a good pace. The trail was wide, hard-packed without too many ruts, and easy to follow. The morning was pleasant.

Stovepipe and Wilbur rode on ahead, staying about fifty yards in front of the wagon. Their eyes moved constantly, scanning the range around them for any signs of potential trouble, but the landscape appeared to be peaceful and deserted.

"You're trying to give those two a little privacy, aren't you?" Wilbur asked after a while.

"Well, mostly just scoutin' ahead," Stovepipe said, "but if it gives them a chance to talk amongst themselves, I don't reckon that hurts anything."

"You're just a big ol' rangeland Cupid, aren't you?"

"You don't see me wearin' a diaper and carryin' a bow and arrow, do you?"

Wilbur shuddered. "No, and I'd just as soon not even think about a sight like that. But you can't deny that you're trying to put those two together, and I'm not sure why. It's just asking for trouble, Stovepipe. Malone's never gonna go along with it, and you know that."

"Maybe. We'll see. Anyway, when you're talkin' about a couple young folks like that, if they're bound and determined to get together, there ain't a whole heck of a lot anybody can do to stop it. Put the gal under lock and key, maybe, but usually that just makes her want the fella even more."

"And you're an expert on romance."

Stovepipe laughed. "Not hardly! Some things you can't help but see, though. Vance has got it bad for that gal, and she's startin' to feel the same way about him. Should be interestin', before it's all over."

Wilbur blew out an exasperated breath. "Interesting is one word for it, all right."

Since the wagon was able to travel much faster than the herd, it was only midday when the vehicle and the two riders reached Wagontongue. Rosaleen drove to the livery stable where they would leave the wagon while they were in town. Stovepipe and Wilbur turned their mounts over to the liveryman, as well.

"Do you want to get some lunch first," Vance asked Rosaleen, "or should we go talk to the sheriff?"

"Let's go talk to Sheriff Jerrico. I want to get that over with. I'll feel better knowing that Dax Coolidge is behind bars and is going to stay there for a while."

They walked along the street toward the sheriff's office. Stovepipe noticed some of the townspeople giving them odd looks and wondered what that was about. If it was anything important, they would find out soon enough, he decided.

The door of the sheriff's office opened as they approached. Jerrico stepped out, just settling his hat on his head. He stopped short and scowled as he saw Stovepipe, Wilbur, Vance, and Rosaleen.

"Howdy, Sheriff," Stovepipe said. "Told you we'd bring back Vance and Miss Malone so you can talk to 'em and get the straight story about what happened with Coolidge—"

"It doesn't matter anymore," Jerrico broke in. "Coolidge isn't here. I had to let him go."

CHAPTER SIXTEEN

It was almost impossible to surprise Stovepipe, but even he looked astonished at the unexpected news. After a moment, he said, "What're you talkin' about, Sheriff? You said you'd hold Coolidge until you had a chance to talk to these two young folks about what happened out at the Three Rivers."

"I know what I said," Jerrico replied, clearly impatient and annoyed. "I meant it, too. But then Mort Cabot heard that I had Coolidge in jail and came into town stomping and bellering like an old bull. He had his lawyer with him, and they claimed I had no right to keep Coolidge locked up."

"Of course you did," Vance said. "You can hold someone for questioning for as long as you deem it necessary."

Jerrico's brawny shoulders rose and fell in a shrug. "That's how it seemed to me, too, and I argued up a storm with them. But then Cabot went to see the judge and browbeat him into ruling that I had to either charge Coolidge or let him go. I couldn't charge him just on hearsay evidence—"

"Wilbur and me saw him fixin' to shoot Vance," Stovepipe said. "That ain't hearsay."

"And neither of you denied that Brewster was holding a gun. Any jury would call that self-defense."

Wilbur said, "So you turned him loose."

"I didn't have any choice. For what it's worth, Coolidge had a falling-out with Cabot and drew his time. He said he was leaving these parts."

"He argued with Cabot right after Cabot got him released from jail?" Stovepipe asked.

"That's right."

"What about?"

"Because Cabot told him to go back to the ranch and stay there," Jerrico said. "He warned Coolidge not to disobey his orders and go anywhere near the Three Rivers again."

Vance said, "So Cabot claims he *didn't* send Coolidge over there that day?"

"That's the way it sounded to me," Jerrico said with another shrug. "I didn't ask him any specific questions about it. By that point, it seemed like a waste of time. Now, if there's nothing else, I was on my way to eat lunch . . ."

"I reckon that's all, Sheriff," Stovepipe said, then added, "Just one more thing. All that happened yesterday?"

"Yeah."

"And you ain't seen Coolidge since?"

"Not hide nor hair. Maybe he really did light a shuck."

That was possible, Stovepipe supposed, but he wasn't quite prepared to believe it just yet.

"Now what do we do?" Vance asked as Sheriff Jerrico walked off.

"Not much we *can* do," Stovepipe said. "Coolidge is gone. He's a low-down rat who oughta be locked up, but that ain't gonna happen now."

Rosaleen said, "I don't like the idea of him being loose again. There's no telling what he might do."

"If he tries anything, he'll regret it," Vance said, mustering up a little bravado. In spite of that, however, all of them were worried.

"We might as well get something to eat," Wilbur said, not letting anything interfere too much with his appetite, as usual.

"And then we can go down to the depot and let 'em know the herd'll be here later this afternoon," Stovepipe said. "Did your pa make arrangements for rollin' stock, Miss Rosaleen?"

"No, but I can handle that. I take care of some of his business. He's always made sure I know about everything that goes on concerning the ranch."

Vance said, "It sounds like he's grooming you to take over for him one of these days."

"And what would be wrong with that?"

Vance held up both hands, palms out. "Nothing. I didn't mean to imply there was. A woman running a ranch would be . . . unusual, I suppose, but that doesn't mean there's anything wrong with it."

Rosaleen smiled. "I'm sorry. I didn't mean to respond quite so sharply. I'm just used to people underestimating me."

"Nobody who's been around you much, I reckon," Stovepipe said.

They had a good meal at one of the cafés, then walked to the redbrick depot at the southern edge of town. If Vance and Rosaleen were still upset about Sheriff Jerrico releasing Dax Coolidge, they didn't show it.

The stationmaster was a short, round-faced, cherubic hombre with a fringe of fuzzy white hair around his bald dome. He looked up from his desk with a friendly smile when Rosaleen came into the office, followed by Vance, Stovepipe, and Wilbur.

"Miss Malone, it's always a pleasure to see you. Is your father with you?"

"Not right now, but he's on his way to town with about five hundred head he'd like to ship out, Mr. Helton."

The stationmaster's smile disappeared. "Five hundred head?" he repeated. "Coming in today?"

"That's right. Of course, we understand it may take a day or two to get the cars here to load them up . . ." Rosaleen's voice trailed off as she saw the way Helton was shaking his head.

"Miss Malone, I wish you or your father had let me know about this ahead of time."

"I don't understand. There's never been any problem before."

"The railroad has only so much rolling stock available, you know, and yesterday Mr. Cabot came in and made arrangements to ship some of *his* cattle in the next few days. I'm afraid it'll be a week or more before we can accommodate the Three Rivers."

"Cabot!" Rosaleen said. "That . . . that . . ."

While she was sputtering to find words in her anger, Vance stepped forward. "Let me understand this. Cabot has all the available cattle cars reserved, is that correct?"

"That's right," Helton said.

"But he doesn't have a herd ready to ship now. I saw the loading pens as we came in. They're empty."

"He said it might be a few days—"

"But the Three Rivers herd will be here *today*," Vance said.

"It's not first come, first served," Helton said defensively. "Mr. Cabot put down a deposit. The Three Rivers will just have to wait."

Rosaleen said, "If we have to keep our cattle in the pens for a week or more, that'll cost just about everything the ranch will make selling the herd."

"There's nothing I can do about that," Helton said.

"You can't send a wire and arrange for more cars to be brought in from elsewhere on the line?" Vance asked. "This is a big railroad. Cabot can't have tied up every single cattle car it owns."

"I'd have to bring in cars from another division. I can't do that without orders from the general manager of the entire line."

"Wire him and ask."

Helton sighed. "All right, but he's just going to turn down the request. I know how these things work, young man."

"So do I." Vance turned to Rosaleen. "It's going to be all right. I'll see to it."

She didn't seem to hear his promise. "Dad should have made the arrangements earlier, I guess. It just didn't occur to him that Cabot would try to tie him up like that . . . Wait a minute! I don't believe for a second this is a coincidence. Somehow, Cabot *knew* we were bringing in a herd. He shouldn't have known, but he did."

"Coolidge," Stovepipe said. "I reckon now we know why he was on Three Rivers range that day. He was prowlin' around, seein' if anything was goin' on. He must've spotted the gather before he ran into you, Miss Rosaleen."

"And he told Cabot," she said. "But I thought he quit riding for the Rafter M."

"Maybe he did," Stovepipe said with a shrug. "He could've still passed along what he knew to Cabot before he rode out."

Clearly uncomfortable at hearing all this, since he had to do business with both ranches, the station-master asked, "Is there anything else I can do for you folks?"

"You can't do anything *else*, when you haven't done anything to start with." Rosaleen leaned her head toward the office door. "Come on."

The four of them paused outside the depot.

Rosaleen sighed. "I don't know what we're going to do now. Nothing has worked out. Coolidge is gone instead of being behind bars where he belongs, and that herd is going to be stuck here for a week or more, eating up all the profit."

"You were going to stay at the hotel tonight anyway," Vance said. "Why don't you go ahead and get a room so you can rest for a while before your father gets here with the herd? I'll walk you over there."

She looked at him defiantly. "I thought you were going to somehow make everything all right. Isn't that what you claimed in there?"

Vance looked a little crestfallen. He swallowed and said, "I, uh, I reckon I was a little too full of big talk. I'm just a saddle tramp, after all. There's not really anything—"

"Oh, hell, I know that," she snapped. "I guess you're

right, though. Might as well get a hotel room and wait for Dad to get here."

Vance nodded and walked with her toward the hotel, heading diagonally across the street and leaving Stovepipe and Wilbur behind.

"Poor varmint," Wilbur said. "He looked like a puppy dog somebody kicked. I reckon that's what happens when you go around acting too big for your britches." He squared his shoulders. "What say we go get a drink?"

"Maybe in a little while," Stovepipe said as he scratched his jaw. "Somethin' else I got to do first."

"Blast it. I know that look. What's going on inside that head of yours, Stovepipe?"

"I ain't rightly sure myself, but I reckon it's time we found out a few things." He turned around and headed back into the train station in a loping walk. Wilbur hurried to keep up with him.

Stovepipe went to the window with a Western Union telegraph operator on the other side of it. The lanky cowboy said, "I need to send a wire."

"That's what we're here for." The eyeshade-wearing operator handed Stovepipe a pencil and a telegraph form. "There's nobody waiting, so you can stand right there and write it out if you want."

Stovepipe licked the pencil lead and quickly printed his message in block letters. Wilbur leaned forward and tried to read it, but Stovepipe's shoulder was in the way. When Stovepipe was finished, he slid the yellow flimsy back through the window to the operator. He took it, counted the words, did a quick mental calculation, then quoted the price. Stovepipe laid a coin on the counter.

A moment later, the telegraph key was clattering as the operator sent the message over the wire.

"Blast it. I never could tell what was in a telegram just by listening to the key," Wilbur said. "Are you gonna tell me what this is all about, Stovepipe?"

"Soon," Stovepipe promised.

When the operator was finished, he asked, "Are you going to wait for a reply?"

"Yeah, for a while, anyway."

Stovepipe went over to one of the benches in the waiting room and sat down.

Frowning, Wilbur followed his friend. "One of these days you're gonna act so blamed mysterious you're gonna fool yourself."

"Could be," Stovepipe agreed with a smile. He sat up straighter. "Hand me that newspaper somebody left, would you? And take a section of it for yourself."

"What in blazes—" Wilbur stopped short, picked up the folded newspaper someone had left on the bench, and handed a section to Stovepipe while he opened the other section and pretended to read it as he lifted it in front of his face. Stovepipe did likewise.

Wilbur said, "We're hiding out from somebody, aren't we?"

"Vance just walked into the depot."

"Then what are you worried about, if it's just him?"

"I want to see what he's gonna do. I've got a hunch . . ."

Both cowboys peeked over the top of the newspaper as Vance walked across the lobby to the telegraph window, evidently without spotting them. The young man spoke to the operator, filled out a message blank, and paid for it to be sent. As he turned away,

Stovepipe and Wilbur raised the newspapers again to keep him from noticing them.

"So he sent a wire," Wilbur said when Vance was gone. "What in the Sam Hill is so interesting about that?"

"Who do you reckon a grub line rider would be sendin' a telegram to?"

"Who knows? I'd tell you to go ask that fella, but I doubt if he'd tell you."

Stovepipe shook his head. "No need. I got a pretty good idea."

"Well, are you gonna share it with anybody?"

"Not just yet. Not until I get a reply from the wire I sent. I figure the whole thing will be clear as day then."

"Maybe for you, but it's clouding up for a storm in my brain."

"Don't worry, Wilbur," Stovepipe said. "It'll blow over."

Chapter Seventeen

An hour later, they were still sitting in the depot. They had read the newspaper from front to back for real, not using it as camouflage. The paper, which came from Denver, was three weeks old. That was actually fairly current for a frontier settlement like Wagontongue, where news from the rest of the world sometimes didn't reach for months.

The telegraph operator leaned through his window, caught Stovepipe's eye, and beckoned him over. Wilbur went along, too, of course, as Stovepipe's long legs carried him toward the window.

"Here you go," the operator said as he extended a telegraph flimsy.

Stovepipe took it, scanned the words on it, and nodded slowly.

The operator asked, "That what you were expecting to hear?"

"As a matter of fact, it is," Stovepipe said.

"Dadgum it!" Wilbur said. "Are you gonna tell me what's going on or not?"

Stovepipe held the wire out to him. Wilbur snatched it and read it, then lifted a surprised gaze to his friend. "Really?"

"Yep."

"And you knew this?"

"I had a pretty good idea," Stovepipe said. "Some things that didn't add up before sort of do now."

Wilbur thumbed his hat back and frowned. "Yeah, I guess so. But what are we gonna do about it?"

"Right now . . . nothin'. I reckon we'll play the hand out and see where it leads."

"All right. You haven't ever steered us wrong yet."

"Got to be a first time for everything," Stovepipe said with a chuckle.

"I wouldn't count on that."

Wilbur handed the telegram back to Stovepipe, who folded it and stuck it in his shirt pocket. They left the train station, pausing just outside.

Stovepipe took a turnip watch from his pocket and flipped it open. "It'll be a couple hours at least before Malone and the boys get here with that herd. Plenty of time for us to mosey up to the Silver Star and wet our whistles."

"I just hope there aren't any Rafter M men there," Wilbur said. "I could do without another brawl right now. We can save that for later."

The saloon was mostly empty on the lazy afternoon. Cy Hartung greeted them warily and drew beers for them.

"I see you've got the place fixed up since the last time we were here," Stovepipe commented as he looked around.

"Yeah, all the damage is repaired. You're not figuring on starting another ruckus, are you?"

Wilbur said, "We didn't start that one. Dax Coolidge did."

"And Coolidge has left town, accordin' to Sheriff Jerrico," Stovepipe added.

"I heard that," Hartung said. "I just hope it turns out to be true. Even without Coolidge around, it still feels like a summer day when a thunderstorm's brewing."

"You don't think the Three Rivers and the Rafter M can ever get along?"

"With so many hard feelings between Keenan Malone and Mort Cabot? I don't see how."

Stovepipe took a sip of the beer. "Those spreads have been in these parts for a long time. Have Malone and Cabot always gotten along so poorly?"

"No, not at all. Oh, they weren't friends or anything," Hartung said with a wave of his hand. "They were business rivals, after all. But there was no real trouble between them. I guess the problem just built up slow, without anybody really noticing. A fight here, some missing cows there, little things that got bigger and bigger."

"Rustling's not a little thing," Wilbur said.

"No, but as long as everybody stays just about even, you don't go to war over it. Hell, the Rafter M and the Three Rivers used to pool their stock to drive to Miles City before the railroad got here. I can't imagine them doing that now, can you?"

"Nope," Stovepipe said with absolute sincerity. "I sure can't."

They nursed their beers and continued to chat with the saloonkeeper. Stovepipe was aware of the time passing, so after a while he drained the rest of his beer and said, "We'd best be goin'." He slid a coin across the hardwood. "Enjoyed the talk, Cy."

"Come back any time," Hartung said. "Except when the Rafter M bunch is here. I'd just as soon you not mix it up with them again any time soon."

Stovepipe and Wilbur stood on the boardwalk outside the saloon and looked to the north.

Stovepipe pointed out the dust cloud rising in that direction. "Herd's almost here. They'll circle around town. Let's go down to the depot and wait for 'em."

When they reached the train station, they found that Vance and Rosaleen were already there, waiting impatiently.

"I wondered where the two of you had gotten off to," Rosaleen said.

"We were close by," Stovepipe said. "Any sign of trouble?"

"You mean Dax Coolidge?" Vance asked. "No, he doesn't seem to be around town. I looked, while Rosaleen was resting. Maybe he actually did leave."

"We can hope so." Rosaleen sighed. "I'm not looking forward to telling Dad about what's happened with Cabot and the railroad cars."

"I was hoping the situation would change before the herd got here." Vance sounded disappointed. "I guess it hasn't."

"What was going to change?" Rosaleen said. "You keep talking like there's going to be some sort of miracle, Vance, but where I come from, such things just don't happen. Cabot outwitted us . . . this time. We'll have another chance at him sooner or later, though. Let's go watch."

They walked through the depot lobby and out onto the platform.

The Three Rivers hands brought the cattle around the western edge of town to avoid having to drive them down the main street. The holding pens along the south side of the tracks were open. With a lot of bawling from the steers and yelling by the cowboys and clouds of dust swirling in the air, the animals were pushed into the pens.

Keenan Malone rode up to the end of the platform and dismounted, looping his horse's reins around a hitching post. He came up the steps, a smile on his dusty, rugged face, and asked without any greeting, "Did you talk to the sheriff? Is Coolidge gonna be behind bars where he belongs for a long time?"

"Sheriff Jerrico had to let Coolidge go, Dad."

Malone's smile disappeared, replaced instantly by an angry scowl. "Let him go! What in blazes did he do that for?"

"Cabot and his lawyer raised a fuss. They claimed there was no real evidence against Coolidge, and they got the judge to agree with them."

"Damn it!" Malone smacked fist into palm. "If we'd known they were gonna try a trick like that, you and Vance coulda come into town yesterday instead of waitin' until today."

"It's too late to do anything about it now," Rosaleen said. "Coolidge had an argument with Mr. Cabot and quit the Rafter M. He seems to have left this part of the country."

Malone frowned. "I don't believe it. This is just more of Cabot's underhanded trickery. I wouldn't believe that range hog no farther than I could throw him!"

"That's . . . actually not the worst of it, Dad." Rosaleen had to take a deep breath before she could go on.

"Cabot's got all the railroad's rolling stock tied up for the next week or more. We can't ship the herd."

Malone stared at her in stunned silence while several seconds ticked by. Stovepipe figured the cattleman was building up to some sort of explosion, and he was right.

Malone's face got redder and redder until his white mustache and bushy eyebrows stood out in sharp contrast to his weather-beaten skin, and then a flood of sulfurous profanity erupted from his mouth. The fact that he would curse so colorfully and vehemently in front of his daughter was a good indication of how upset he was.

Finally, when the storm lost a little strength, he gripped the wooden handle of the gun jutting up from the holster on his hip and said, "Cabot! I'm gonna ride out to the Rafter M and shoot him down like the worthless dog he is! He's pulled his last snake-blooded trick!"

"And what good will that do?" Rosaleen argued. "With that crew of killers working for him, you'd never get off the ranch alive, and you know it! They'd cut you down before you got within a hundred yards of Cabot."

"Not if I took every one of the boys with me!" Malone looked at Stovepipe, Wilbur, and Vance. "What do you say, fellas? You ready to go out there with me and clean up that rat's nest?"

Vance said, "With all due respect, Mr. Malone, you'd just wind up getting a lot of good men killed if we did that."

Malone's jaw jutted out as he glared at the younger man. "What you mean is you're yellow! I thought better o' you than that, boy! I thought you had sand,

and maybe even . . ." Too mad to go on, Malone's ranting trailed off in a choked snarl.

Vance's face paled under the lash of Malone's words. Anger flared in the young cowboy's eyes, but he managed to hold it in. "You've got it wrong, Mr. Malone. I just don't want to see anybody get hurt unnecessarily."

"No, *you've* got it wrong," Malone snapped. "There comes a time when a man has to fight back, if he's any sort of man at all!" His lip curled. "Reckon maybe I *was* wrong about that where you're concerned."

Vance's hands clenched into fists. He looked like he was about to take a swing at Malone, and honestly, Stovepipe wouldn't have blamed him all that much if he did. But it wasn't the time—

"Mr. Malone! Mr. Malone!"

They all looked around at the sound of that urgent call and saw Helton, the stationmaster, hurrying across the platform toward them.

He was red-faced, too, and a little breathless as he came to a stop and held up a yellow piece of paper. "I knew your herd had come in, and somebody told me you were out here on the platform. I suppose Miss Malone told you about the problem with the rolling stock—"

"She told me Mort Cabot's a lying, underhanded, no-good sack of—"

"I just got a wire from headquarters," Helton broke in as he waved the telegraph flimsy. "By special order of the general manager, two dozen additional cattle cars have been diverted to Wagontongue. They'll be here tomorrow, and you can ship your herd then!"

Malone and Rosaleen stared at the stationmaster. The news was like a bolt out of the blue.

But Vance didn't look all that surprised by it, Stovepipe thought as he watched the young man from the corner of his eye.

In fact, Vance looked downright pleased . . . as if this unexpected development was just what he'd been waiting for.

CHAPTER EIGHTEEN

Malone and Helton walked off toward the station-master's office to discuss the details of shipping the herd out of Wagontongue, leaving Stovepipe, Wilbur, Vance, and Rosaleen on the platform.

Rosaleen turned a puzzled frown toward Vance. "What did you do?"

"Me? What do you mean, what did I do?"

"You said you'd see to it the problem was taken care of, and now, out of the blue, more cattle cars show up . . . or they will, tomorrow, anyway." Her frown deepened. "What I want to know is how you managed that."

Vance shook his head. "You're giving me too much credit. I'd love to say that I was responsible for what happened, but think about it. You know that's impossible! I'm just a drifting cowhand. Mr. Helton said earlier that he'd wire the general manager and ask for more cars, so I'm sure that's what happened. And for some reason the general manager agreed." Vance shrugged. "That's all I can figure out."

"Well . . . maybe," Rosaleen said, but she didn't sound convinced.

"Honestly, I'd love to do something to impress you, but this . . . I'm just glad it worked out."

"Me, too." Rosaleen cocked her head to the side. "And just why would you be interested in impressing me, Mr. Brewster?"

"Well, I, uh . . . I sort of feel . . ."

Stovepipe felt a mite sorry for the young man. Rosaleen probably knew good and well how Vance felt about her. She would have had to be pretty dense not to have figured it out. Her question was sort of like a cat tormenting a hapless mouse before it moved in for the kill.

Stovepipe inclined his head toward the holding pens and said to Wilbur, "Come on. Let's go see if we can give somebody a hand with those cows."

"That's a good idea," Vance said quickly, seizing the opportunity to escape from Rosaleen's intent gaze. He started toward the end of the platform and added, "Come on, boys. There's work to do."

That was true, Stovepipe thought. And since he had gotten that telegram, he knew his real work was just getting started.

By nightfall, Andy Callahan had picked some of the men to stand guard over the herd in shifts. It was unlikely that anybody would try to cause trouble on the edge of the settlement, but the possibility couldn't be ruled out completely. Better to be vigilant, even if it turned out to be unnecessary.

Stovepipe and Wilbur volunteered for sentry duty since they hadn't done any of the work of pushing the herd down from the ranch. Vance offered as well, but Callahan turned him down.

"You've still got that sore arm," the segundo told him. "Don't worry. By the time we get back to the Three Rivers, you oughta be healed up enough to start riding the range again. There'll be plenty of work to do. There always is around a cattle spread."

"I'm learning that," Vance said with a nod.

Callahan frowned. "What do you mean, you're learning that? You've been riding the grub line for a while, you said."

"Well, sure. I just meant that every ranch is a little different, and I'm learning how things are on the Three Rivers."

Callahan just grunted, shook his head, and moved on, clearly thinking that Vance was an odd one.

Next to one of the holding pens, Stovepipe and Wilbur were standing nearby and overheard the conversation. Stovepipe looked at his stocky friend and smiled. Like Callahan, Wilbur just shook his head.

The crew spent the night at one of the cheaper hotels. Malone had laid down the law—the Silver Star and the other saloons were off-limits until after the cattle were loaded onto the railroad cars and no longer the responsibility of the Three Rivers riders. Once that was the case, a little blowout might be all right before the men headed back to the ranch.

It was after midnight when Stovepipe and Wilbur took their turn on sentry duty. They patrolled one side of the pens while another pair of cowboys was posted on the opposite side.

"Reckon anybody's gonna try anything?" Wilbur

asked quietly as they walked along with Winchesters
tucked under their arms.

"Not likely, but you can't ever tell for sure until it
happens," Stovepipe said.

"If Mort Cabot has heard that his little trick with
the rolling stock didn't work, he's liable to make some
other move."

"He might. He's bound and determined to get the
best of the Three Rivers. Not much doubt about that,
what with Cabot blamin' Malone for all his troubles."

"Yeah, but Malone's not actually behind any of it,"
Wilbur said. "We'd know that by now if he was."

"I reckon we would. Malone's a hot-tempered old
codger, but he ain't what I'd call sneaky or secretive.
Any moves he makes against the Rafter M are gonna
be out in the open."

"So Cabot's just using that as an excuse to cause
problems for the Three Rivers."

"Maybe—" Stovepipe stopped short, then said in
an urgent whisper, "Somebody movin' around over
there . . . by the far corner of the pens."

Only the flicker of a shadow had alerted him, but it
was enough.

Like a phantom himself, Stovepipe glided along
the pens, holding the rifle slanted across his chest.
Wilbur was right behind him, moving equally as silent.

Stovepipe spotted a sudden spurt of orange. Whoever was skulking around the pen had just lit a match.
Stovepipe's heart slugged in his chest as he saw sparks
start to leap.

He slid to a halt and brought the Winchester to his
shoulder. As the sparks drew back, Stovepipe fired.

The rifle cracked sharply, causing the cattle to stir and bawl. Someone cried out in pain.

Stovepipe saw the sparks still flying, but they were down close to the ground. He dashed forward, knowing he might be running straight into hell. Those sparks had come from the fuse attached to a stick of dynamite. Whoever had lit it had been about to throw the cylinder of explosive into the holding pens when Stovepipe shot and either hit him or at least startled him enough to make him drop the dynamite.

The rapid thud of running footsteps told Stovepipe the man hadn't tried to retrieve the dynamite. He was getting out of there as fast as he could.

"Wilbur!" Stovepipe called. "Headin' toward the depot!"

"I've got him, Stovepipe!" Wilbur replied as he veered in pursuit of the fleeing man. He hadn't realized exactly what was going on. If he had, he would have tackled Stovepipe rather than let his old friend try to reach the dynamite before it went off.

Thoughts flashed through Stovepipe's mind as he ran. If the explosive detonated where it was, it would blow down the corral fence, probably kill some of the cattle, and might even damage the railroad tracks. If Stovepipe could reach it before the blast, he could put out the fuse and prevent the destruction.

Problem was, he didn't know how long that fuse was. The dynamite could go off and blow him to kingdom come just as he got there.

He didn't slow down. He could still see the sparks from the fuse popping and flashing. As long as he could see them, he was all right.

When they stopped would be all the warning he had. That would be only a fraction of a second, not long enough to do anything except realize he was about to die.

His long legs carried him quickly over the ground. Close enough, he left his feet in a long dive and stretched out his right hand as far as it would go.

His aim was true as his hand closed around the burning end of the fuse. He felt its coal sear his palm, but there was no explosion. The fuse was out.

Shots roared over by the depot. Wilbur must have caught up to the would-be bomber, Stovepipe thought as he scrambled to his feet. Ignoring the pain in his burned hand, he scooped up the dynamite and stuck it in his pocket. The stuff was too dangerous to leave lying around.

As he loped toward the station, he heard the sharp crack of a rifle, probably Wilbur's, interspersed with the heavier boom of a handgun. Stovepipe rounded the building's rear corner and spotted the orange glare of a muzzle flash. Return fire came from a dark shape crouched behind some crates stacked next to the brick wall.

Stovepipe wheeled around and went the other way. He bounded up onto the platform, pounded across it, and jerked open the door into the station.

The lobby was deserted. Nobody was on duty except the night operator in the telegraph office. He was kneeling behind his window with just his head showing as he peered fearfully over the counter. His eyes widened at the sight of Stovepipe galloping across the dimly lit lobby.

Stovepipe figured the man who had taken cover behind the crates was Wilbur, which meant the hombre firing around the corner of the building was the dynamiter. Stovepipe's plan was to get the dynamiter between himself and Wilbur. If they could capture him and force him to talk, it could go a long way toward clearing up several mysteries.

Stovepipe stepped out the front door of the station and immediately pressed his shoulder against the wall. He could make out the man crouched at the corner and drew a bead on him. "Drop your gun and elevate!" Stovepipe shouted at him.

The man twisted toward him and triggered a shot. The bullet whipped past Stovepipe's ear. That was good shooting, considering the poor light and the fact that the man was hurrying.

Stovepipe didn't want to kill the hombre, but he wasn't going to stand there and let himself be ventilated. He cranked off three swift rounds from the Winchester, aiming low, intending to sweep the gunman's legs out from under him.

The bullets missed and the man turned to run. Stovepipe blew out an exasperated breath as he tracked the figure with his rifle barrel. Shooting at night was tricky to start with, and shooting at a moving target . . . well, he'd have to have a lot of luck on his side, he thought as he pressed the trigger.

Fire ripped the night apart. A thunderous explosion shook the ground and buffeted Stovepipe, forcing him take a step back against the wall behind him. He wasn't a man given to profanity, but he bit back a curse as he realized the man must have had at least one more stick of dynamite with him. Fate had sent Stovepipe's bullet to the blasting cap attached to the end of it and that had set off the explosive.

They wouldn't be questioning the varmint after all, Stovepipe thought as the echoes of the blast rolled away across the plains around Wagontongue.

The undertaker might not even be able to scoop up enough of him to bury.

And he had a stick of that unholy stuff in his own pocket, Stovepipe recalled. A little shudder went through him as he pulled it out and looked at it. He was tempted to dump the dynamite into the rain barrel under the end of the gutter that ran along the station's eaves, but then he recalled getting wet just made the explosive even more unstable. He wasn't sure what the best way was to get rid of it.

"Stovepipe!" Wilbur called. "Stovepipe, are you all right?"

"Yeah," Stovepipe replied. "Just wonderin' what to do with a little chunk o' hell I grabbed on to."

CHAPTER NINETEEN

The shooting would have been enough to wake up most folks in Wagontongue, but the explosion had finished off the job. At least half of the town's citizens flocked to the railroad station, many of the men carrying weapons of some sort.

"What's goin' on?" one bearded old-timer yelled as he brandished a single-shot rifle. "Have the damn Yankees started another war?"

"Damn Yankees, is it?" another elderly man responded. "It was you Johnny Rebs who started the whole thing by firin' on Fort Sumter!"

"We were just defendin' our sovereign territory from bein' invaded by you blue bellies!"

"Shut up!" Sheriff Jerrico roared as he stalked through the crowd. "Everybody pipe down!"

People got out of the way of the angry lawman, especially since he was carrying a double-barreled shotgun. He came up to Stovepipe and Wilbur, who were standing next to a charred pit in the ground.

"You two again!" Jerrico said. "Stewart, how do you happen to be close by every time hell breaks loose?"

"Just lucky I guess, Sheriff."

"Well, what happened this time?"

Stovepipe nodded toward the crater. "That used to be a fella who had the unfortunate habit of carryin' around dynamite in his pocket."

"Dynamite?"

"Yeah, like this." Stovepipe slid the red paper-wrapped cylinder from his pocket and held it up. Several people were carrying lanterns, and in their light he saw that only about an inch and a half of fuse was left. A couple more seconds and he would have been a hole in the ground himself.

"What the hell! Stop waving that around and do something with it! Get rid of it!"

"I'd be happy to, Sheriff, but I ain't quite sure of the best way to do that."

A heavyset, middle-aged man in a nightshirt stepped forward from the crowd. "I can take it, Sheriff. I sell dynamite in my general store, so I'm used to handling the stuff."

"Thanks, Mr. Bevens," Jerrico said.

Stovepipe put the dynamite in the merchant's outstretched hands, then asked, "Does that look like some you sold recently?"

"A stick of dynamite looks like any other stick of dynamite," Bevens said, "but as a matter of fact, I haven't sold any in several months, so I doubt if it came from my store. Dynamite's not something you leave just sitting around. Most folks don't buy it until they're ready to use it."

That made sense, Stovepipe thought.

As Bevens carried off the explosive, the crowd parted to allow him a wide path.

Jerrico said, "All right. I want to know what happened here and how this fella came to get blown up. First, though"—he turned to the crowd and raised his voice—"everybody clear out! The excitement's over! Go back to bed!"

Many of the bystanders were reluctant to leave, but they slowly did so, some of them muttering as they went. As the crowd cleared out, several figures were left standing there. Helton, the stationmaster, was one of them, along with the night telegraph operator. Keenan Malone was there, too, along with his daughter Rosaleen, who clutched a silk robe around her. Vance Brewster stood beside her.

"Before you go and try to run us off, Sheriff," Malone said, "those are my men you're questionin'. I got a right to be here."

"I'd say so, too," Stovepipe added, "considerin' the trouble was directed at Three Rivers cows."

"Spill it," Jerrico said tautly.

Stovepipe efficiently explained how he and Wilbur had been on guard duty and how he had seen someone light the dynamite and try to throw it into the holding pens. "I figure once the first blast went off, he planned to pull out at least one more stick of dynamite and toss it in there, too. In all the commotion, nobody would've been able to stop him and probably wouldn't have even seen him."

"But you spotted him before he could put his plan into effect."

Stovepipe shrugged. "I've got pretty good eyes. Been told I can see in the dark almost as good as a cat."

"What did you do when you spotted him?"

"I let loose a shot at him. Don't know if I hit him or not, but it made him drop the dynamite, and after that he took off as fast as he could run. I hurried over and put out the fuse. That was the stick I gave to the storekeeper." He flexed his hand, which still stung a little from the burn.

"Good Lord!" Malone boomed. "It could have gone off while you were trying to do that."

"The thought *did* cross my mind," Stovepipe said. "I figured the risk was worth it to keep the pens from bein' blowed up. Not to mention it might've tore up the railroad tracks, too."

Jerrico said, "So how did he wind up being blown to smithereens?"

"I went after him while Stovepipe went after the dynamite," Wilbur looked at his friend and added, "I didn't know what you were doing, you crazy galoot. You might try explaining things now and then."

"Wasn't time for explanations," Stovepipe said. "Anyway, that fella and Wilbur were tradin' shots over by the depot, which I cut through, hopin' I could get the drop on him from the other side."

The telegraph operator said, "I can vouch for that. I saw this scarecrow run through the station lobby just a minute or two before the explosion."

"I might take offense to that scarecrow remark. I ain't quite that skinny." Stovepipe chuckled. "Anyway, I called on the hombre to throw down his gun, and he commenced to shootin' at me instead. He tried to make a run for it, and I aimed to wing him. It, uh, sorta didn't work out that way."

Jerrico snorted. "I reckon not. Is there any of him left?"

Stovepipe grimaced. "A few bits and pieces. Not enough to even come close to sayin' who he was."

"You think he was carrying more dynamite, and that's what you hit?"

"Had to be. Fellas don't just blow up when you shoot 'em, at least none that I've ever seen."

Rosaleen shuddered. "This is terrible."

Her father put his arm around her shoulders and said, "You shouldn't even be here, honey. Go on back to the hotel. Brewster, you go with her."

Looking almost as shaken as Rosaleen did, Vance nodded. "Sure, Mr. Malone." He took Rosaleen's arm and led her away from the station. For once, she didn't argue or put on a display of stubborn pride.

Jerrico asked Stovepipe and Wilbur, "Did either of you happen to get a look at the man's face while you were trying to catch him?"

"The light was too bad," Wilbur said. "He was just a dark shape."

"Same here," Stovepipe said.

Jerrico grunted. "I guess we won't ever know who he was, then, or why he tried to blow up those pens."

"Of course we know," Malone said. "He was one of Mort Cabot's men! Cabot found out his little trick with the railroad didn't work, so he sent that hombre in from the Rafter M to slaughter my cows!"

"What trick with the railroad?"

Malone explained how Cabot had reserved all the rolling stock to prevent the Three Rivers herd from being shipped out. He nodded toward the station-master. "Mr. Helton got the general manager to agree to sendin' more cars here, though."

Helton cleared his throat and said, "Actually, I, uh, I hadn't gotten around to sending that wire to the home office yet, Mr. Malone. The telegram I got from the general manager surprised me as much as it did you."

"What? How in blazes—"

"I don't know and I don't care," Jerrico interrupted. "All I know is that I'm getting damned sick and tired of this feud between you and Cabot, Malone. It's bad enough when your crews take potshots at each other out on the range and steal each other's cattle—"

"By God, you can't accuse me of rustlin'!" Malone said. "I never stole a cow in all my borned days, and neither did any of my men!"

"That's a pretty far-fetched claim to make, considering you don't know everything every one of your riders has ever done. But we'll let it go for now. What I was saying is that the trouble's bad enough out on the range, but when it spills over into town like this— *again!*—I start to lose my patience. I may just establish a deadline at the edge of town. No Three Rivers or Rafter M men allowed in Wagontongue!"

"You can't do that! It ain't legal!"

"Try me and see," Jerrico said. "For now"—he turned, looked at the crater in the ground, and shook his head—"I guess I'll send for the undertaker. He'll sure as hell have his work cut out for him. He may have to just bury a bucket of bloody sand!"

Malone posted extra guards around the holding pens, but Stovepipe and Wilbur weren't among them. "Go on back to the hotel and get some rest," he told them. "I reckon you've done enough for the Three Rivers tonight, and you must be a mite shaken up after nearly gettin' blowed to pieces."

"It ain't my favorite thing I've ever done," Stovepipe said. "I'd just as soon not have to mess with dynamite again any time soon."

As they walked up the street toward the hotel, Wilbur asked, "What do you think, Stovepipe? Was that a Rafter M man who got blasted into a million pieces?"

"Could've been," Stovepipe said. "Might have been somebody else, too. I've got a hunch Mort Cabot ain't the only enemy the Three Rivers has."

"I'm feeling sort of the same way. You think it could have anything to do with that telegram you got?"

Stovepipe tugged at his earlobe. "Don't see how it could have, but right now, we can't rule out anything. We've got some more pokin' around to do."

Wilbur sighed. "That usually works out like poking a bear or a beehive."

"Yeah, but if you do it right, things start to pop."

"Not tonight, I hope. I could use some sleep."

Wilbur got his wish. The rest of the night passed peacefully.

In the morning, Andy Callahan and most of the other members of the Three Rivers crew headed back to the ranch, not too happy because they hadn't gotten a chance to pay a visit to the any of the saloons. Keenan Malone and Rosaleen remained in Wagontongue, as did Stovepipe, Wilbur, Vance, and four other cowboys. They would help the railroad men load the steers when those cattle cars rolled in later in the day.

Workmen had brought in dirt, filled the crater left by the explosion, and smoothed it out, but the memory of what had happened wasn't as easily erased. Men, women, and children gathered around to stare at the place in morbid fascination.

Standing with Stovepipe and Wilbur near the pens, Vance said, "I suppose you can't blame people for being interested. A fella doesn't blow up every day. But I sort of wish they'd go away and stop staring."

"How's Miss Rosaleen doin' this mornin'?" Stovepipe asked.

"She's better. It was a terrible thing for her to see. For anybody to see, I guess. She'll be going back to the ranch this afternoon with her father, once these cows are loaded."

Wilbur said, "Are you gonna ride on the wagon with her again?"

"I suppose I'll have to. I didn't bring a saddle horse with me."

"Tough job, keeping a pretty girl company."

"I'm up to it," Vance said with a smile.

Wilbur looked like he wanted to say something else, but a stern gaze from Stovepipe shut him up.

A short time later, a locomotive's shrill whistle sounded east of town as a train approached.

After the cattle cars rolled in, everybody was too busy to worry about anything else—like getting the steers out of the pens, up the loading chutes, and into the cattle cars. It was bawling, dusty chaos, as well as a lot of hard work. Stovepipe and Wilbur had performed such tasks many times, but Vance only watched. He wanted to help, but his bad arm kept him from getting in the middle of the effort.

After a while, Rosaleen drove up in the wagon and

stopped it where she could sit and watch the cattle being loaded, as well. She beckoned to Vance, who climbed onto the seat beside her.

Wilbur saw that, took off his hat to sleeve sweat from his face, and said to Stovepipe, "Some fellas just have the knack for winding up next to a good-looking gal, don't they?"

Stovepipe grinned. "We ain't ever had to worry about that."

"Speak for yourself! I'd trade places with that youngster . . . even though I guess I'm too old for Rosaleen . . . just like you are."

About to make some rejoinder, Stovepipe looked past the train station and up the street. Half a dozen riders were coming toward the depot. He stiffened and nodded toward them. "Company comin', Wilbur. And that gent in the lead looks like he's mad enough to start chewin' nails. Unless I miss my guess, he's Mort Cabot . . . and he's got some of his gun-wolves with him!"

CHAPTER TWENTY

Cabot appeared to be about the same age as Keenan Malone, a veteran cowman who had been in Montana for a long time. He was stockier, clean-shaven, and had an even redder face than Malone. He wore a brown suit and hat, rather than the range clothes Malone preferred. Cabot might look like he'd be more at home sitting at a desk rather than in a saddle, but his eyes, set deep in pits of gristle and dark and hard as agate, told that he was plenty tough.

Stovepipe did a quick survey of the five men accompanying Cabot. He didn't see Dax Coolidge among them, although several of the men looked vaguely familiar. Likely, he had seen them in the Silver Star on the day of that brawl. They were obvious hardcases, all wearing holstered guns.

Cabot was frowning as he rode up to the train station.

From Stovepipe's vantage point, he could see the owner of the Rafter M rein in, but after that he lost sight of Cabot. "Reckon I'll take a *pasear* into the depot," he said to Wilbur.

"I'll come with you. Those punchers can get along without us for a few minutes."

By the time they reached the lobby, shouting was coming through the open door of Helton's office. A couple Rafter M men stood nearby. The others were over by the door.

"—rightfully belong to me!" Stovepipe heard someone yell inside the office. The voice was considerably deeper than Helton's, so Stovepipe assumed it belonged to Mort Cabot.

"Now, take it easy, Mr. Cabot," Helton said, confirming the guess. "Actually, those aren't the cars you reserved. They're extras that were diverted here from other locations along the line."

"They're the next ones that showed up after I made arrangements with you! I have a right to them, not that damned Malone!"

"But you don't have a herd in town right now, and by the time you do, more cars will be here. You won't be delayed in the slightest." Helton's argument, logical though it was, didn't satisfy Cabot.

Stovepipe hadn't expected it to. As he and Wilbur drifted closer to the open door, Cabot's men moved to block them.

"Get out of here, cowboy," one of them said, scowling. "This is no business of yours." The man's thumbs were hooked in his gunbelt, so his hands were in easy reach of the holstered revolvers on his hips. His stance was casually arrogant, which matched that of his companion.

"Didn't say it is, but this is a free country and a public place, last time I checked," Stovepipe said.

With a sneer on his face, Cabot's man said, "You're one of those Three Rivers riders, aren't you?"

"That's right. Not lookin' for trouble—"

"Then stop trying to eavesdrop on our boss."

Before Stovepipe could deny the accusation—which was, of course, exactly what he and Wilbur were trying to do—Cabot stomped out of the station-master's office.

"If you won't do anything about this, I will, by God!" he flung over his shoulder.

Helton hurried out after him. "Mr. Cabot, please don't do anything rash."

Cabot jerked his head toward the platform. "Come on, boys. We're going out there to those pens and put a stop to this."

The man who had confronted Stovepipe and Wilbur straightened. His hands swung closer to his gun butts. Tight-lipped, he asked, "You gonna try to get in our way, cowboy?"

"Nope." Stovepipe backed off and motioned with his head for Wilbur to come with him.

Cabot stalked past, trailed by all five of his men.

"Blast it, Stovepipe," Wilbur said. "Hell's gonna pop out there."

"Maybe, maybe not. But if it does, we're *behind* those fellas now, where we can get the drop on 'em."

"Oh," Wilbur said, understanding dawning on his freckled face.

"Anyway, I got a hunch certain things have been hangin' fire long enough. Might be *time* for 'em to pop."

They left the station and hurried along the plat-form to the steps at the end. They crossed the tracks between two of the cars and saw Cabot and his men heading along the tracks toward the loading chutes. That took them toward the wagon where Vance and Rosaleen were sitting.

One of the Three Rivers punchers saw the Rafter contingent coming and hustled to tell his boss. Keenan Malone left the chute where he was working and strode toward the wagon. Several of his cowboys followed. With the two forces converging on them, Vance and Rosaleen looked back and forth. Vance seemed a little nervous, but Rosaleen was angry as she glared at Cabot and his men.

Stovepipe and Wilbur continued to drift along behind the group from the Rafter M.

Malone came to a stop at the rear of the wagon, planted his feet solidly, and said in a loud, clear voice that carried over the racket of the cattle, "You ain't welcome here, Cabot. You might as well turn around and go back where you came from."

Cabot waved a hand at the rolling stock lined up along the tracks. "Those are my railroad cars, damn it! You don't have any right to be loading your sorry beef into them."

Malone sneered. "The cars are here, my herd's here. Seems like I got every right to be usin' those cars. If you don't like it, go talk to Helton. He'll tell you about the special deal I got with the railroad."

"Special deal, hell! You're a thief!"

A little muscle jumped in Malone's tightly clenched jaw. "I'd shoot most men for sayin' a thing like that to me, but you ain't worth wastin' a bullet on, Cabot." Malone grinned. "You're just mad 'cause your dirty little trick didn't work."

"I don't know how you did it, but you're crooked. Crooked as a sidewindin' rattlesnake!"

Everybody was tense. Men on both sides had their hands hovering over their guns, ready to hook and draw. It wouldn't take much of a spark to set off an explosion of gunplay to rival the blast that had taken place the night before.

In that breathless atmosphere of impending violence, Stovepipe sidled around until he was close to the wagon. One of Cabot's men stiffened, but Stovepipe held up a hand, palm out, to demonstrate that he wasn't trying to start the ball. In a quiet voice, he said, "I reckon this has gone just about far enough, Vance. You might ought to put a stop to it."

Rosaleen stared at Vance.

"I . . . I can't"—he took a deep breath—"but if they start shooting, Rosaleen will be in danger, too."

"That's what I was thinkin'," Stovepipe said.

She frowned. "What in the world?"

Vance stood up. "Mr. Cabot."

Everyone's eyes jerked toward him. Moving deliberately so no one would think he was trying some sort of trick, Vance climbed down from the wagon and moved toward the back of it where Cabot and Malone had been glaring at each other.

"Who in blazes are you?" Cabot demanded.

"Kid, stay outta this," Malone said. "Look after my daughter—"

"That's what I'm trying to do." Vance faced the owner of the Rafter M. "Mr. Cabot, if you want to blame somebody for this, you should blame me, not Mr. Malone. I'm the one who had those cattle cars brought here."

"You?" Cabot and Malone said at the same time, in astonished unison.

"I don't know you," Cabot said, "but you look like a saddle tramp to me." With a contemptuous look on his face, he ran his gaze over Vance, from the run-down boots to the patched range clothing to the battered old hat.

With a warning edge in his voice, Malone said, "Don't go gettin' too big for your britches, Brewster. I appreciate a man who rides for the brand, but you're stickin' your nose in somethin' that ain't your business."

"Actually, it is," Vance said, a little pale but calm. "Or rather, it will be someday . . . when I own the Three Rivers."

"By the Lord Harry, you've gone too far!" Malone said. "You think because you're sweet on my daughter—"

"That's not it at all," Vance interrupted him. "This has nothing to do with Rosaleen. The reason I say I'll own the Three Rivers someday is because my father is Alfred Armbrister."

Malone's eyes widened. He pulled back like he'd just been punched in the face.

Rosaleen spoke first in response to Vance's statement, exclaiming, "Armbrister! But he's—"

"The fella who owns the Three Rivers," her father said, finding his voice again. "Or most of it, anyway."

Vance nodded. "Eighty percent, I believe. He has a couple partners who own ten percent each, just like in the steel mill he owns in Pittsburgh."

"So your name ain't Brewster."

"No, it's Armbrister. Vance Armbrister."

From the wagon seat, Rosaleen said, "So that means you're a liar."

Vance turned toward her and lifted a hand. "No, wait, I wasn't really trying to deceive anyone—"

"Why should we believe you, when you've been lying to us ever since you rode in?" She leaned forward on the seat, her face set in taut, angry lines. "Or are you still lying? Are you actually the saddle tramp you seemed to be, trying to fool everybody into thinking you amount to something?"

When Vance seemed unable to answer, Stovepipe said, "He's tellin' the truth, miss. He's really Vance Armbrister."

Vance looked puzzled about how Stovepipe knew that, but he said, "It's true. My father has a lot of business holdings, not just the steel mill and the Three Rivers. I've been going around and working in all of them under false names. He wants me to learn all I can about each of them, from the ground up, so I can do a better job of running them when I take over. I wasn't sure about the idea at first, but it's been a wonderful experience. And this . . . my time on the Three Rivers   has been the best so far, Rosaleen, because of—"

She didn't let him finish. She grabbed the reins, slapped them against the backs of the team, and cried out to the horses. The startled animals surged forward, causing the men on both sides of the confrontation to leap out of the way and scatter. Rosaleen whipped the team with the reins and had them galloping along the railroad tracks, away from the loading pens.

"Blast it!" Malone yelled. "The girl's gone loco!"

"No, she's just angry with me," Vance said, "and I don't suppose I blame her. I *did* lie to her. I lied to all of you, although it wasn't my intention to cause any trouble." He took a deep breath and turned back toward Cabot. "So you see, Mr. Cabot, this is my doing, so if you want to be upset with someone, it should be me."

"I still don't believe it," Cabot snapped. "How could you—"

"I sent a telegram to my father yesterday, and he contacted the general manager of the railroad. You think a man who runs a business so dependent on steel wouldn't be happy to do a favor for the man who owns the biggest steel mill in Pittsburgh?"

Cabot's ruddy face was still set in a furious scowl, but he didn't look like he disbelieved Vance's claim anymore.

"I don't care who you are. This still isn't right," Cabot said.

"Everything is perfectly legal. If you and your men try to interfere with the loading of these cows, I'll appeal to the sheriff for help."

"You'd threaten me with *the law*?" Cabot's voice was full of contempt and loathing.

"If I have to."

"Yeah, you're an Eastern businessman, all right. A yellow little weasel who hides behind the law!"

Vance stiffened. His hands clenched into fists, but he controlled the obvious impulse to take a swing at the older man. "You can think whatever you want, Mr. Cabot. But you can't stop this herd from being shipped out today."

"Go to hell!" Cabot turned to his men. "Come on. Let's go up to the Silver Star. I could use a drink to get the foul taste out of my mouth."

The bunch from the Rafter M walked off, casting hostile glances behind them. Malone and the small Three Rivers crew returned the hostility in spades until Cabot and his men crossed the tracks and went out of sight on the other side of the cattle cars.

Malone turned to Vance. "I'm like Rosaleen. I don't cotton to bein' lied to."

"I didn't mean to cause a problem, Mr. Malone. I just wanted to learn how the ranch was run."

"Your pa could've told me you were comin'. You'd have been welcome—"

"That's just the problem. You would have welcomed me, all right. You'd have looked out for me and made sure I never even got my hands dirty, let alone did any actual work."

"You wouldn't have been out tradin' shots with rustlers, that's for damned sure!"

Vance nodded. "Exactly. Now I know firsthand some of the problems and challenges facing you. That's the only way to find out how things really are in a business." He paused. "And one thing I've learned is that a ranch isn't just a business. A lot of the men seem to regard it as a home, and the rest of the crew is their family."

Malone nodded grudgingly. "Fellas get to feelin' that way when they've rode for the same spread a good long time."

"I never would have known that if I hadn't come out here and ridden and worked beside all of you."

"All right, all right." Malone waved a callused hand. "I reckon I see your point. Good luck gettin' Rosaleen to understand that easy, though. Once she gets a burr under her saddle, it's mighty hard to get her to calm down again."

Vance sighed and nodded. "I'll have to try . . . but it might be wise to wait and let her cool off a little bit first."

"I can't argue with you there. Now, we got to get back to loadin' those cows. They ain't gonna climb in those cars by their own selves." Malone started to turn away, then paused and looked back at Vance. "I'm obliged to you for your help, Mr. Armbrister. If you hadn't stepped in, I reckon this rollin' stock wouldn't be here."

"Please, keep calling me Vance. As far as I'm concerned, Mr. Armbrister is my father, and I'd like to keep it that way for a while. I was glad to pitch in and do whatever I could. I have a stake in the Three Rivers' success, too."

"A considerable one, I'd say." Malone gave him a curt nod and went back to the loading chutes.

Stovepipe and Wilbur started to follow him, but Vance put out his good arm to stop them. "Hold on there a minute, you two. I have a question for you, Stovepipe."

"I reckon I've got a pretty good idea what it is," the lanky cowboy said.

"How in blazes did you know who I really am?"

CHAPTER TWENTY-ONE

Stovepipe and Wilbur looked at each other, then at Vance. A long moment ticked by.

Seeing that the young man was determined to get an answer, Stovepipe said quietly, "Well, to tell you the truth, Wilbur and me ain't exactly who we been pretendin' to be, either."

"Who are you? Lawmen?"

"Of a sort. We work for an outfit called the Cattlemen's Protective Association. They send us in whenever and wherever there's bad trouble goin' on involving spreads that belong to the Association. Happens the Three Rivers is a member in good standing." Stovepipe shrugged. "For that matter, so's the Rafter M, but it wasn't Malone nor Cabot who asked the CPA for help. Those old pelicans ain't the sort to do that. They'd rather stomp their own snakes, even if it means a likelihood o' gettin' bit."

"Then who *did* hire you?"

"Your pa. He could tell from the reports Malone sent back to him that bad things were goin' on, and he asked the Association to send somebody to have a look into it."

"Then he didn't send you here to watch over me?" Vance sounded upset if that were the case.

Wilbur said, "Nope. We'd never even heard of you when we rode into Wagontongue and got riding jobs at the Three Rivers." He chuckled. "Once you showed up, though, it didn't take Stovepipe long to catch on that you weren't who you were pretending to be."

"You done a good job of actin' like a cowboy most of the time," Stovepipe said, "but there were little things that made it seem like you were more of a greenhorn than somebody who'd been ridin' the chuck line for years. Your accent was off a mite, too. I've knowed fellas who came from back east, and you reminded me of them now and then."

"But you didn't know I was Alfred Armbrister's son."

Stovepipe shook his head. "Not at first. Didn't know Armbrister even had a son. But when you slipped up and promised Miss Rosaleen you'd do somethin' about the railroad and then went right off to send a telegram, I knew you had to be connected to somebody mighty important, somebody who'd have a lot of influence with the line. I knew Alfred Armbrister owned a steel mill and had his fingers in plenty of other pies, too, so I sent him a wire myself and asked him flat-out if you were related to him."

"Blast it," Vance said. "I fooled everybody else—"

"Don't feel bad," Wilbur said. "Nobody can fool Stovepipe for very long. He can see through a phony story and figure out what's really going on faster than anybody I've ever run into. Reckon that's why we're in the line of work we're in."

"What do you even call the job you do?"

Stovepipe said, "I reckon you can call us range detectives. We started out as genuine cowboys but kept gettin' mixed up in one conundrum after another, so we finally decided to make a career out of it."

"Conundrums with gunplay," Wilbur added. "They seem to follow us around like clockwork."

"Anyway," Stovepipe went on, "your pa wired us back and admitted you were out here pretendin' to be a cowboy. He, uh, asked us to look after you while we were goin' about our other chore."

Vance frowned and shook his head. "I don't need anybody looking after me," he declared. "I've handled myself all right so far, haven't I?"

"Mostly," Wilbur said. "You've got to admit, though, it was a good thing Stovepipe was keeping an eye on you when you had that run-in with Coolidge."

Vance looked a little embarrassed as he nodded. "That's true. I didn't mean to sound ungrateful, Stovepipe—"

"Aw, shoot. Don't think nothin' of it. You want to handle things on your own, and nobody can blame you for feelin' that way."

"So what are you going to do from here on out? Continue investigating Cabot?"

"Maybe. But he ain't the only one who might be behind all the trouble the Three Rivers has been havin'."

Vance looked interested. "What do you mean by that? Who else could be trying to destroy the ranch?"

"I don't rightly know."

"But Stovepipe never rules out anything until he's sure," Wilbur said.

"Mr. Malone doesn't know who you really are?"

Stovepipe shook his head. "Nope. We'd be obliged if you'd keep it that way, too."

"Don't worry. I won't give you away . . . if you let me help you any way I can."

"Right now I reckon you'd be better off tryin' to get back in Miss Rosaleen's good graces. That's liable to be a full-time job by itself."

"But if you need me, you'll call on me?"

Stovepipe nodded solemnly. "You can count on it."

Before any of them could say anything else, Keenan Malone bellowed from the loading chutes, "Stewart! Coleman! You gonna stand there jawin' all day or are you gonna earn your keep?"

"We're comin', boss," Stovepipe said. He pulled his gloves from the place behind his belt where he had tucked them and added, "Come on, Wilbur. Let's go punch some cows."

Mort Cabot and his men galloped out of Wagontongue a short time later. Through the wall slats of one of the cattle cars, Stovepipe saw them go. He didn't figure that was the last he would see of Cabot and the Rafter M gunnies, though.

The rest of the cattle were loaded without incident. The train pulled out in late afternoon, steam whistle blaring, heading east with its four-legged cargo. The cowboys who had worked all day were ready to go back to the hotel, clean up a little, and then blow off some steam of their own.

Vance had been at the loading pens ever since Rosaleen had stormed off. With the job done, he said to Stovepipe and Wilbur, "I suppose I'll spend the evening with you fellows."

"The crew, you mean?" Stovepipe asked with a skeptical frown. "I don't know about that. It don't matter none to Wilbur and me, of course. " He lowered his voice to a conspiratorial tone. "We've got a few secrets of our own, after all, but the rest of the boys might not like it that you ain't what you made yourself out to be."

"How can they be angry with me? Haven't I pitched right in and worked just as hard as anybody?"

Wilbur said, "You sure have, but now that they know, they won't be able to forget that you're rich. To them, you're just *playing* cowboy. You can stop any time you want and go back to a comfortable existence back east. For them, this is their life. They have to keep working hard for forty-a-month-and-found if they want to eat and have a roof over their heads."

Vance thought about that and nodded slowly. "I understand, but I can't really do anything about it. I didn't ask for my life, any more than they did for theirs. It's just the way things worked out."

"You're right," Stovepipe said. "I'm just tellin' you, don't be surprised if they don't see it the same way."

As they all walked back toward the hotel from the depot, Vance could tell Stovepipe and Wilbur were right. The other men talked tiredly but happily among themselves, making a point to exclude Vance from the conversation.

As Vance fell behind the rest of the group, Stovepipe lingered and said quietly, "Don't think they're mad at you. They ain't. They know you've done a lot to help the boss and Miss Rosaleen, and they're obliged to you for it, but to them you're a different breed o' animal now. They don't know how to act around you. So they just shut you out."

"I sort of wish things would go back to the way they were before."

"That's the trouble with life," Stovepipe said. "Things change, and there ain't no puttin' 'em back the way they were. But sometimes that's a blessin', too, and it takes a while to figure out which is which."

Vance could have forced himself in among the crew and they would have had no choice but to accept him, but he didn't want that and figured he might as well move to the Wagontongue Inn for the night. Although the better of the settlement's two hotels, it hardly compared to the hostelries where he had stayed in New York, Boston, Philadelphia, and San Francisco. It was where Malone and Rosaleen had rooms.

"What can we do for you, Mr. Armbrister?" the clerk asked when Vance came up to the desk. The man's use of his real name and the deference he showed made it clear he was aware of Vance's true identity. Evidently, the news had spread all over town already.

"I'd like a room for the night and a hot bath." Vance looked down at his dust-covered garb. "And since I don't have any other clothes with me, could I get these laundered?"

"Absolutely. I'll have a tub brought up to your room and filled with hot water. It shouldn't take too long. We keep some heating all the time for just such a purpose. One of the boys who brings the water can take your clothes over to the laundry and wait for them, so you'll have them back as soon as possible."

"Thanks," Vance said. "About the bill—"

"No need to worry about that now, Mr. Armbrister. We can settle up when you're ready to leave."

Vance nodded distractedly. It was the sort of treatment you got when you were rich. Anybody else would have had to pay in advance.

"Room seven," the clerk said as he handed Vance a key. "Right at the top of the stairs. The boys with the tub will be up there in just a few minutes."

"Thanks," Vance said again. He went up to the room . . . wishing he was at the other hotel, getting ready to head for the Silver Star with the rest of the crew.

The service was as good as the clerk promised. Two boys in their middle teens carried a metal tub up to the room, then lugged buckets of hot water up the stairs to fill it. Vance shed his dirty clothes and sank into the water, which had little wisps of steam curling from its surface. He was careful to keep his bandaged arm from getting wet as he sat with his back to the door.

The boys left with his clothes. Vance sat there soaking with his eyes closed, letting the heat work its way through him. It was the first hot bath he'd had in a couple weeks, and it felt good.

He would have been content to let his mind drift aimlessly, but that was impossible. Too much had happened. His masquerade had been shattered and everything had changed in a matter of moments. From now on, he would never be able to pretend to be a cowboy.

He was going to miss it, he realized. He had worked in his father's steel mill, feeling the heat of the giant forges, sweating and toiling alongside other men. The challenge of it had touched something inside him, something that made him realize he enjoyed the hard work and even the danger. It had certainly been much better than his stints in various offices connected with other enterprises owned by his father.

But the Three Rivers had been different, even better than the mill. Riding out on that range, Vance had felt like he was coming home for the first time in his life. The vast sweep of the mountains and the plains and the sky had touched something inside him he had never known was missing. All the years he had spent among the mansions and tall buildings of the cities had fallen away from him, as if that life had been the masquerade and this the reality.

Simply put, he was cut out to be a cowboy. He was convinced of it.

And of course, Rosaleen made him feel more than ever that the Three Rivers was where he was supposed to be.

She was furious with him, considered him to be nothing more than a no-good liar. Maybe when she calmed down some, he could talk to her, make her see he hadn't lied to hurt her. Hell, it hadn't really been a lie, he thought. Those days he had spent on the Three Rivers, he actually *was* Vance Brewster, grub line rider, or at least he had felt that way. If she would just give him a chance to make her see that . . .

With his mind full of Rosaleen and his feelings for her, he was barely aware of the door opening behind him. He heard a step, figured vaguely it was the boy returning with his clothes, and then realized it couldn't be. Even in his reverie, he knew not enough time had passed for that to be the case.

He started to sit up straighter, and just as he did, a rope dropped past his face, looped around his neck, and jerked tight, cutting off his air.

CHAPTER TWENTY-TWO

Caught by surprise, all Vance could do was react instinctively. His fingers clawed at the rope, but he couldn't get them underneath it to relieve the terrible pressure on his throat. His pulse hammered like a steam engine inside his skull. Water splashed out of the tub as he struggled.

He knew he was going to pass out any moment, and that would be the end of everything. The man holding the rope would finish the job of choking him to death.

With the urgency of that knowledge coursing through him, he summoned all the strength he could get into his legs and pushed down against the bottom of the tub. That brought him up and back in a powerful surge against his attacker. The man couldn't maintain his balance on the wet floor. His feet slipped out from under him and he went over backwards with Vance on top of him.

The tub overturned, flooding the room with water. The would-be killer's grip on the rope slackened just slightly, but it was enough for Vance to get the fingers of his left hand underneath it and pull it away from his neck.

He brought his right elbow back and sank it in the man's belly as hard as he could. Breath gusted from the man's lungs. His grasp weakened a little more. Vance grabbed the rope with both hands and shoved it up and over his head. He twisted away, rolling over on the wet floor.

The man lunged at him and swung a gun he held by the barrel. Vance jerked aside to keep the gun butt from smashing his skull.

Lack of air had caused a red, hazy curtain to drop over his eyes, and he still couldn't see very clearly even though he was gulping down breaths as fast as he could. He struck out almost blindly, his fist thudding against something. The attacker grunted. Vance swung again and landed another blow.

Someone shouted nearby. The would-be killer cursed and scrambled to his feet, leaving the rope tangled on the floor. Vance made a grab for his legs in an effort to tackle him, but he missed. The man darted through the door into the hotel's second-floor corridor.

Vance had managed to push himself to his hands and knees when the clerk from downstairs rushed in, looking shocked and frightened.

He saw Vance on the floor and exclaimed, "Good Lord! Mr. Armbrister, are you all right?"

"Yeah, I . . . I think so," Vance said, his voice raspy from the rope's pressure on his throat.

"I saw water dripping down through the ceiling and knew something was wrong," the man said as he took hold of Vance's arm to help him up.

"Yeah, I'm sorry . . . for the mess." Vance was still a

little breathless, but his pulse was starting to slow down and his vision was clearing.

"What happened? I saw a man run out of here—"

"Where did he go?"

"What? Oh, you mean . . . He went down the rear stairs. I shouted for him to stop, but he never slowed down."

"He tried to kill me." Vance pointed to the rope laying on the floor. "Snuck in while I was in the tub and tried to strangle me with that."

"That's terrible!"

"Yeah, I thought so, too. Did you get a good look at him? Did you recognize him?"

The clerk shook his head. "I'm afraid not. He had his back to me. I never saw his face. He was just a man in jeans and a vest and a brown hat. I think his hair was dark, but I'm not even sure about that. It all happened so fast."

"That's all right." Vance was becoming uncomfortably aware that he was dripping wet and naked. He picked up one of the big white towels the boys had left and wrapped it around his waist, knotting it in place. It seemed pretty obvious he wasn't going to finish his nice peaceful bath.

"I'll send for the sheriff."

Vance shook his head. "No need. The man's gone. We don't have any idea who he was or where to look for him. He might've left some wet footprints on the stairs, but that won't tell us anything. That rope won't, either."

"No, you could find a dozen more just like it on the saddles of horses tied down in the street. There are probably hundreds of lariats like that around here."

Vance suddenly wished Stovepipe and Wilbur were

there. The range detectives might notice some clues he hadn't. But he didn't know where they were. Probably the other hotel or the Silver Star. He could tell them later about the attempt on his life, but by then the trail would be cold.

He looked around the room. "I'll help clean up this mess . . ."

The clerk shook his head. "Absolutely not. This is a terrible thing, and on behalf of the hotel, I can only offer you my profoundest apologies, Mr. Armbrister. You're sure you don't want to report the incident to the sheriff?"

"I'm sure," Vance said. What was that expression Stovepipe had used? *Stomping his own snakes*, that was it. As Vance rubbed his sore throat, he thought for once he was going to stomp his own snakes, and that would start with figuring out who had tried to kill him.

The hotel clerk insisted Vance move to another room so the one he had been in could be cleaned up. That seemed like the simplest solution, so Vance agreed. The clerk also provided a clean shirt and pair of pants from his own clothes so Vance would have something to wear until his clothes got back from the laundry. The borrowed garments were a little too small but better than nothing.

Vance had just gotten his own clothes back and pulled them on when Stovepipe knocked on his door.

The lanky cowboy said, "Thought you might like to know that Miss Rosaleen and her pa are fixin' to sit down to supper in the dining room downstairs. I don't reckon they'd make a scene if you wanted to join them."

"I don't know," Vance said with a faint smile. "Rosaleen was pretty mad."

"Yeah, but she's had time to think about it. She'll have figured out by now that you didn't really mean any harm by pretendin' to be somebody else. If you ask her to forgive you, she might. You never know."

"I suppose that's true." Vance paused. "There's something you don't know about, Stovepipe."

"Reckon there's a whole heap o' things in this world I don't know about. Which one in particular are you talkin' about?"

"The fact that someone tried to kill me a while ago."

Stovepipe stiffened and drew in a deep breath. "What in tarnation? Tried to kill you, you say?"

Vance explained the incident with the would-be strangler. "I didn't get a good look at his face," he concluded, "and neither did the clerk, so I don't have any idea who it could have been . . . but it seems like there's a good chance the man was working for Mort Cabot."

Stovepipe rubbed his chin. "That's a mighty serious accusation. Cabot's rough as a cob and used to gettin' his own way, but I ain't sure he'd try to have a fella murdered in a bathtub."

"Who else would want me dead? I ruined his plan with the railroad cars, after all. And now that he knows who I really am, he might think having me killed would damage the Three Rivers."

"Maybe," Stovepipe said, but he didn't sound convinced. "Sure wish I'd been close by when it happened. Then maybe we'd have some answers . . .

assumin' that fella didn't have a stick of dynamite in his pocket, too."

Stovepipe wanted to check the rear stairs the would-be killer had used when he fled. Any footprints the man had left were gone. Stovepipe and Vance went down the stairs and opened the rear door at the bottom. It led out into an alley. Enough people used it as a shortcut that the dirt was covered with an indistinguishable welter of tracks.

"Fella could've gone anywhere from here," Stovepipe said.

"I guess I should've sent for you right away," Vance said. "You might have been able to locate some clues. I guess I didn't think of it because I was so shaken up from almost dying."

"That'll do it, all right. Well, there's one good thing to consider."

"What's that?"

"If whoever it was wants you dead bad enough, chances are he'll try again." Stovepipe nodded solemnly. "More than likely you'll have another crack at him."

A short time later, Vance entered the hotel dining room, which was small but nicely furnished. The tables had white linen cloths on them, and the room was lit by brass chandeliers.

He spotted Rosaleen and her father at one of the tables right away. They saw him as well. Malone frowned while Rosaleen looked away and wouldn't meet Vance's eyes.

He took a deep breath, gathered his courage, and strode toward them anyway. "Good evening."

They had cups of coffee in front of them but no

food, which meant either their meals hadn't arrived yet or they had finished and the plates had been taken away.

He hoped it was the former. "May I join you?"

"You're the boss," Malone said. "Reckon we can't stop you."

Vance rested his hands on the back of the empty chair in front of him. "I'm not the boss. You don't work for me, Mr. Malone. Not by any stretch of the imagination. My father has always said you have his complete confidence and complete discretion in running the ranch. There's only one boss on the Three Rivers, sir, and that's you."

"Well . . . nice o' you to say so, anyway. Don't reckon I'd ever feel right about givin' orders to the owner's son, though."

"And that's exactly why I didn't tell you the truth about who I am. I wish there had been some other way of handling it, but I wanted an honest, unbiased look at how the Three Rivers is run."

Malone looked at him intently for a moment then said, "Why don't you sit down and tell me what you found out?"

That brought Rosaleen's head around again. "Dad! How can you invite this . . . this liar to join us?"

"Liar's kind of a strong word to use for what he done, Rosie. You got to admit, if we'd knowed who he really is, we wouldn't have treated him the same. He got to learn a lot more about how things actually are on the ranch. I reckon it was more like . . . playactin' than lyin'."

That was a stronger defense than Vance had expected from the cattleman. "Thank you, Mr. Malone. I assure you both I meant no harm."

"And I guess you *did* help some," Rosaleen said grudgingly.

"If he hadn't helped with those railroad cars, that herd wouldn't have been shipped out today, that's for dang sure," her father said.

Rosaleen sighed and nodded. "All right. Sit down, Vance. That *is* your real first name?"

"It absolutely is." He pulled back the chair. "Vance Everett Armbrister."

"Kind of a mouthful," Malone said. "I'm just gonna keep callin' you Vance, like you said to."

"I appreciate it. I'd like it if you'd let me continue working with the crew, too."

Malone looked doubtful. "I dunno about that. Andy told me you had the makin's of a good hand, but now that they all know who you are . . ."

"I can think of one way to win them over. I need to keep going out there on the range and getting as sweaty and dirty and tired as they are. Then they'll see there's really not any difference in us."

"The rich are always different," Rosaleen said.

"They have more money, that's all. They're still as human as anyone else."

She looked dubious but didn't say anything.

A waitress brought Vance a cup of coffee and took his order.

The Malones hadn't eaten yet, so Vance's food arrived only a short time after theirs did. Rosaleen remained quiet for the most part during the meal, but her father and Vance talked at length about the ranch and its operation.

"There are some things we could do to make the spread even better, if your pa don't mind spendin' the money," Malone said.

"I'd love to hear about them. Tell me about it, and I'll write to him and explain the situation. When I see him again, I'll make sure he understands."

By the time the meal was finished and they were lingering over second cups of coffee, Vance could tell that Malone wasn't angry with him anymore. His sincerity had won over the old cattleman . . . but Malone's daughter was a different story. Rosaleen's attitude was still cool. However, she wasn't as angry as she had been earlier in the day, he sensed.

Eventually Malone yawned. "It's been a mighty long day. Reckon I'll turn in. It's been good talkin' to you, son. I've got a hunch you and me can work together."

"I can't tell you how glad I am to hear that, Mr. Malone. That's all I want."

Malone got to his feet. "You comin' on up, Rosaleen?"

"In a minute. I want to talk to Mr. Armbrister, too."

"Vance," he said.

She inclined her head but didn't agree to call him by his first name.

Malone seemed a little reluctant to leave the two of them alone, but they were in the middle of the hotel dining room, after all. That couldn't be *too* improper. "Good night, then," he said gruffly.

When Malone was gone, Vance looked at Rosaleen and said, "You wanted to talk to me?"

"What I really want to do is haul off and punch you."

He couldn't help but laugh a little. "And here I was hoping you would forgive me."

"I didn't say I wouldn't forgive you. I just said I'd like to punch you. That's the way I react when people lie to me."

"You're not ready to accept your father's theory that I was just playacting?"

She gave him a narrow-eyed gaze. "You may have charmed my father, Vance, but as far as I'm concerned, the jury's still out. I'd like to trust you, but how can I ever do that?"

He held up his hands. "I assure you, you know the truth about me now. I'm not hiding anything else."

That wasn't strictly true, he thought. He hadn't said anything to them about the attempt on his life, nor did they know Stovepipe and Wilbur were really range detectives working for his father. But he wasn't actually *lying* about those things, just not telling Rosaleen what she didn't need to know yet.

She was silent for a long moment, then finally said, "I'm inclined to give you a chance. But I'm warning you, Vance Armbrister. You'd better play straight with me from here on out, or I won't just punch you. I'm liable to come after you with a gun."

He couldn't stop himself from smiling as he said, "You've got yourself a deal."

CHAPTER TWENTY-THREE

The next day, everyone returned to the Three Rivers. Vance again rode on the wagon with Rosaleen. They had talked animatedly almost the entire way on the journey into Wagontongue, but she was much quieter on the return trip. Not unfriendly or unpleasant, by any means, but just . . . keeping her distance emotionally.

He could deal with that, for now. He hoped it wasn't going to be a permanent condition.

Anxious to make sure there hadn't been any trouble on the Three Rivers while they were gone, Malone told Stovepipe and Wilbur to come with him, and they weren't able to decline the order without revealing who they really were. The three of them had ridden off ahead. The rest of the hands loafed along with the wagon, matching the vehicle's more deliberate pace.

As they drove up to the ranch house, Rosaleen commented, "Of course you'll have to move into the house now. You can't stay in the bunkhouse anymore."

"Why not?" Vance asked in surprise. "I told your father I want to continue working as one of the hands."

"*I* certainly don't care where you stay, but I don't think the rest of the crew is going to accept you anymore. The first thing the men who were still in town yesterday will do is tell all the others about your real identity."

"I could ask them not to—" Vance stopped. He knew how futile such a request would be, not to mention unfair. He couldn't ask the men to keep his secret from the rest of the crew. That just wouldn't be right. "I still don't think it should matter."

"Spoken like a man who's always had money. Being rich *doesn't* matter to you. You've never known anything else."

"My father came up the hard way. He built that steel mill with a lot of hard work, and with his fists, too, sometimes."

"Yes, but *he* did that, not you. Isn't that right?"

"Well . . . yes," Vance admitted. "But I worked in the mill and the men never knew any different."

Rosaleen brought the wagon to a stop in front of the house and nodded. "That's my point. Maybe Dad was right. Maybe *playacting is* the right word to describe what you do. It certainly isn't genuine."

"Maybe we should leave it up to the men."

"All right," she said with a shrug. "But don't be surprised when things don't turn out like you want them to."

He climbed down quickly from the wagon and was pleased she allowed him to help her to the ground. By that time, the old wrangler arrived to take charge of the team and vehicle. Rosaleen went in the house while Vance walked toward the bunkhouse, where the other cowboys were dismounting.

"Hold up a minute, boss," one of them said. "Where do you think you're goin'?"

"Inside, of course," Vance replied.

"Oh, sure. To get your gear so you can move it into the house, I reckon."

Vance shook his head. "No, I'm going to be staying out here with you fellows, just like I have all along."

A couple men scuffed boot toes in the dirt. All of them looked uncomfortable. The one who had spoken up said, "We sort of didn't figure you'd do that. Don't you reckon you'd be more comfortable in the house?"

"I don't see why. I've been doing just fine out here."

Another man said, "Yeah, but that was before we knew you were the boss."

Vance told himself to stay calm and reasonable. "I had a talk with Mr. Malone about that. I'm not the boss here on the Three Rivers. He is, just like he always has been, and when he's not around to give the orders, Andy Callahan is in charge. Nothing has changed."

"Hard to figure that when all you'd have to do to get us all fired is send a wire to your pa."

"I'd never do that," Vance said. "I wouldn't have any reason to. Even if I had a problem with any of you, I wouldn't go crying to my father. I'd handle it myself."

"That's easy to say, but we know how you rich fellas are. You're used to always gettin' your own way, no matter who you have to run over."

"That's just not true!"

The man who'd been speaking clenched his fists. "Are you callin' me a liar?"

"No more than you're calling me one when I say I want things to go on like they were."

The cowboy shook his head. "You can forget that. You ain't welcome in the bunkhouse anymore."

Mutters of agreement came from several of the other men.

"Andy Callahan has a bunk in there," Vance said, "and he gives orders. Why don't you have a problem with him?"

"Andy's one of us. Always has been."

"When you stay out on the range, Mr. Malone throws his bedroll down with everybody else, doesn't he?"

"Sure."

"And he really is the boss on this ranch, a lot more than I am."

"It's different, that's all."

Vance made a disgusted noise and shook his head. "It's not fair, that's what it is. All I'm asking is that you accept me for who I am, not who my father is or how much money I might have. And it's actually not all that much, you know. Most of it is in a trust—"

He saw the sneers that appeared on several faces and knew he had pushed too far. The man who seemed to be the ringleader of the opposition turned toward the bunkhouse and said, "Come on, boys. We'll pile the gent's gear outside the door so he won't have to breathe the same air as us to get it."

"Wait just a damned minute!" Vance moved quickly after them and grabbed the man's shoulder. "What's your name?"

Instantly, he realized he'd made another mistake.

He should have known the names of all these men, as long as he had been on the Three Rivers. And actually, he did know some of them. But he was upset at the moment and having trouble putting names with faces . . .

The man jerked his shoulder away from Vance's hand and wheeled around. His face darkened with anger. "Hear that? The fancy pants claims he's one of us, but he don't even know my name!"

Vance looked down at his faded and patched denims. "I don't see how you can call these pants fancy—"

"It's Steve," the cowboy said. "Steve Elder. Reckon you can remember that?"

"Steve. Of course. I knew that, I just—"

"You just have trouble tellin' all of us lowly critters apart, right?"

"That's not it at all."

Steve spat, the moisture landing in the dirt an inch away from one of Vance's boots, and he started to turn away again.

Once more Vance reached out to grasp his arm. "Wait—"

Steve whirled, moving fast and bringing his right fist up to smash into Vance's jaw. The powerful blow rocked Vance back several steps and made his head spin crazily.

"You loco fool!" one of the other men said to Steve. "You're gonna get yourself fired!"

"I don't care," Steve raged as he started to come after Vance. Two of the cowboys grabbed his arms to hold him back.

Vance had caught his balance. He raised his right hand and rubbed his jaw where Steve had punched him. The blow hadn't done any real damage, although the jaw likely would be bruised. "It's all right. Let go of him."

"You don't want us to do that, boss," said one of the men holding Steve. "He's a mite out of his head right now."

"No, he's just mad at me," Vance said. "I'll bet all of you are, at least a little. So maybe we should settle this. Maybe I should knock some sense into his head and convince all of you that I'm not the boss of anything."

"You heard him," Steve said. "Let go o' me, blast it! He's just beggin' for it!"

Vance nodded to the men holding him. They looked at each other, one shrugged, and they both released Steve's arms and stepped back.

Roughly the same size, he and Steve were within an inch or so in height. Steve was a little shorter, brawnier, and probably outweighed Vance. As Vance moved, he thought he probably was a bit quicker on his feet. So they were very evenly matched.

Steve charged, yelling as he swung a roundhouse punch at Vance's head. Vance darted to the side to avoid the attack. As the looping punch missed, Vance hooked a hard right into Steve's midsection, and the cowboy jackknifed, bending over so Vance was able to slam a blow down on the back of his neck.

Vance figured Steve would go down and that would end the fight. Steve caught himself, though, with a hand on the ground, and whirled faster than Vance expected. He tackled Vance around the thighs and sent him crashing to the ground.

The other cowboys shouted encouragement to Steve. He was one of them, and although they had all started to accept Vance before the revelation of his true identity came out, he was an outsider again.

Drawn by the commotion, Keenan Malone emerged from the house, followed by Stovepipe and Wilbur. They had been in Malone's office, talking about the attempt on Vance's life in Wagontongue, and the young man from back east was in danger again.

Stovepipe lifted a hand to stop Malone from shouting an order. "That kettle was bound to boil over sometime, boss. Might as well get it outta the way sooner rather than later."

"Blast it. That's Steve Elder he's fightin' with," Malone said. "He's a bare-knuckles brawler from 'way back."

"Vance might have a trick or two up his sleeve. You can't never tell."

Malone waited and watched, but he had a worried expression on his rugged face.

Once Vance was down, Steve tried to scramble on top of him and pin him to the ground, but Vance was able to reach up, grab the front of Steve's shirt, and heave him to the side. As Steve rolled one way, Vance rolled the other to put some distance between them. Both of them made it back to their feet at the same time.

Vance's injured left arm throbbed, but the muscles worked all right as he lifted it and held out his fist in a defensive boxing stance. His right was cocked back and ready. Steve charged again, still in a wild frenzy rather than using any sort of strategy, and Vance was able to block the punch he threw.

With that opening, Vance stepped in and hammered two jabs with his right into Steve's face. One of them split Steve's lip, the other made his left eye swell.

Steve whipped another punch at Vance's head, but the Easterner ducked under it and lifted an uppercut that rocked the cowboy's head back. So far, Vance had used his left arm strictly for defense and went on the offense with his right. As long as he could keep that up, he hoped the wound wouldn't open up again.

He peppered more punches to Steve's head and chest and forced the cowboy to backpedal. Steve caught himself and lunged forward again, ducking instead of trying to absorb whatever punishment Vance could deal out to him. He spread his arms wide and trapped Vance in a bear hug, catching his arms against his sides.

Vance's feet left the ground as his opponent swung him around. The pressure on his injured arm made pain shoot through him. His lips drew back from his teeth in a grimace, and he struck back the only way he could. Lowering his head, he rammed it into the middle of Steve's face.

Hot blood spurted over Vance's forehead as Steve's nose flattened with a crunch of cartilage. Steve howled in pain and let go of him. The cowboy reeled back a step. Setting himself, Vance drove one more powerful blow against Steve's jaw. Steve's feet left the ground as he flew backwards to land in a senseless heap.

Vance stood there, his left arm hanging uselessly at his side, his chest heaving. Sweat covered his face, but he was still on his feet . . . and Steve was on the ground, not moving.

"Holy cow!" said one of the men. "We all forgot the kid's got a bad arm—and he whipped Steve anyway!"

Another man said, "Maybe we were wrong about you, Mr. Armbrister."

"Vance." He was trying not to pant. "Just call me . . . Vance . . . like always."

"I reckon we can do that."

Despite the pain in his arm, Vance started to grin.

That expression disappeared as the front door of the ranch house banged open and Rosaleen exclaimed, "You lunatic! What do you think you're doing?"

CHAPTER TWENTY-FOUR

Rosaleen rushed past her father, as well as Stovepipe and Wilbur, and hurried down the steps from the porch.

Vance came to meet her, holding out his right hand. "Rosaleen—"

"Is your arm bleeding again?"

He forced the arm to work and lifted it. There didn't appear to be any blood on his shirtsleeve. "I don't think so—"

"No thanks to you and your brawling. What were you thinking?"

Vance turned to look at the members of the crew. A couple were hauling the still mostly senseless Steve Elder to his feet. The others just stood there looking uneasy.

"I was thinking there were things the men and I needed to get straight," Vance said. "You told me they might have a problem with me going back to the bunkhouse, and you were right. But we were working it out in the most direct way possible. I figured I would *earn* my right to live and work among them."

"By fighting the biggest and meanest of them?"

One of the men said, "Uh, no offense, Miss Rosaleen, but Steve ain't really what you'd call mean. He's just a mite hotheaded sometimes."

Another man added, "And the way Vance whipped him, even fightin' one-handed, did sort of make us feel more inclined to accept him as one of the bunch."

Keenan Malone came up behind his daughter and said, "A man who's willin' to face up to a challenge is always welcome among fightin' men. And that's what we've got here on the Three Rivers . . . a fightin' crew that still has the bark on!"

Several of the cowboys grinned in agreement.

"Still, you could have been hurt," Rosaleen argued to Vance. "If you keep injuring that arm, it may never heal right and you could wind up losing the use of it! You don't want that."

"No, I sure don't. I'd like to keep working here on the Three Rivers for the time being, and I can't do that one-handed." He gave her a sheepish grin. "I reckon I'd better stop getting in fights for a while."

"Oh"—she blew her breath out and shook her head in exasperation—"maybe you *are* a cowboy. You're as muleheaded as any of that bunch, that's for sure!"

Malone said, "If you want to talk stubborn, honey, I reckon there ain't many in these parts who can hold a candle to you."

She glared at him for a second, then told Vance, "If that arm needs more medical attention, let Aunt Sinead know. I'm sure she'll be glad to take care of you."

"I'll do that," Vance told Rosaleen's back as she swung around and started toward the house.

When he looked at the ranch hands again, he saw

that Steve was standing up under his own power, although the burly cowboy still looked a little groggy. Steve gave a little shake of his head that made droplets of blood fly from his battered nose. He looked up, saw Vance, and came toward him, moving a little shakily.

Vance didn't think Steve was attacking him again, and that proved to be right.

When Steve came close enough to hold out his hand, he said, "Put 'er there, Vance." His voice was thick and the words were slurred from the punishment his face had taken. "I'd be honored to shake the hand of a man who whupped me like that. And I'm sorry I jumped you. I plumb forgot about that bum wing o' yours."

"That's all right, Steve," Vance said as he gripped the other man's hand. "It was a good fight." He paused. "Are you still going to toss my gear out of the bunkhouse?"

"Hell, no! Anybody who can punch like you is more 'n welcome in this crew, no matter who he is or how much dinero he has." Steve looked around at the others. "Ain't that right, boys?"

The emphatic agreement from the men put a grin on Vance's face again. He was confident that with them on his side, he could win over the rest of the crew, too.

As for Rosaleen . . . well, that was only a matter of time.

When Andy Callahan and the rest of the crew came in from the range late that afternoon, they had plenty of stories waiting for them—the confrontation with Cabot and his men over the railroad cars in Wagontongue; the revelation that grub line rider Vance Brewster was actually wealthy Easterner and someday heir to the Three Rivers ranch Vance Armbrister; and the brutal battle between Vance and Steve Elder in which Vance had won his place in the bunkhouse.

When everything settled down, the upshot was that things really hadn't changed all that much. There was still bad blood between the Three Rivers and the Rafter M, and Vance, no matter what his last name was, remained one of them, riding for the brand . . . at least for the time being.

During the next week, things stayed peaceful. No rustlers raided the spread, no one took any potshots at the hands as they rode the range, and Vance's injured arm healed enough he was able to go back to carrying out his share of the work every day. When the men saw that he was willing and able to stay in the saddle for long, hot, dusty hours every day, they gradually forgot where he came from.

And just like Vance hoped, Rosaleen didn't seem to be dwelling on his deception. She might not have forgotten about it, but at least she wasn't furious at him anymore.

Because of that, he expected her to have a smile on her face when he spotted her riding out on the range one day and waved at her. He was on top of a hill, on his way back from checking a stretch of one of the creeks where cows had a habit of getting bogged down in the mud, and she was riding through the valley below. With a smile, he spurred down to meet her.

As soon as he came close enough to make out the expression on her face, he realized something was wrong. She kept looking back over her shoulder as if worried someone might be following her.

Ordinarily, Vance would have had a pleasant greeting for her. When he saw she was upset, he asked as soon as he rode up to her, "What's the matter?"

She looked a little relieved to see him but still worried. "Someone was on my trail. I think it was Dax Coolidge."

Vance stiffened in the saddle. "Coolidge left these parts more than a week ago."

"He *said* he was leaving. We don't have any real reason to think he actually did." She was right about that.

Vance had been hoping Coolidge was really gone, but it was entirely possible he wasn't. "Where did you see him? Where were you headed?"

"I was riding out to Eagle Flats. I haven't been there for a while, and I thought I might catch sight of one of the eagles."

Vance nodded. He knew the area, which was about two miles east of where they currently were, although he had been over there only once. He had heard the men talking about it and knew the place got its name from the birds that sometimes soared majestically over it.

"I came through Aspen Gap," Rosaleen went on. "That was where I looked back and saw a rider through the trees. I didn't get *that* good a look at him, but good enough I'm convinced it was Coolidge. I didn't know what to do except keep going. I couldn't turn back because he was between me and the ranch head-quarters."

"You did the right thing," Vance told her. "There was a good chance you'd run into at least one of the hands if you kept moving, and so you have."

"Just one of you, though." Rosaleen looked around with the worried expression still on her face. "I don't suppose any of the other men are close by?"

"Not that I know of," Vance said, trying not to feel irritated by the fact she obviously thought he couldn't protect her. Logically, he couldn't blame her for that attitude. He *was* only one man, and certainly not a gunfighter.

Dax Coolidge, on the other hand, was a hardened killer. In a battle of Colts, Vance would stand very little chance against Coolidge.

"Keep going to Eagle Flats. Ride hard, and when you get there, you can cut south and circle around to headquarters without going back through the gap."

Rosaleen stared at Vance. "What about you?"

"If Coolidge really is following you, he'll be coming along this valley pretty soon, and he'll have to get past me to go after you."

Rosaleen's face paled as she shook her head. "Vance, no . . ."

He smiled as he said, "Don't worry, I'm not going to have a showdown with him or anything like that. I'm pretty good with a rifle"—he patted the stock of the Winchester sticking up from its saddle sheath—"so I thought I'd fort up in those trees over there and wait for Coolidge. If he shows, I'll take a few warning shots at him so he'll know to turn back."

"What if he doesn't turn back?"

Vance shrugged. "I'll have good cover and plenty of ammunition. I might not be able to take him in a fast-draw contest, but I'm willing to take my chances in a fight like that."

"What if *I'm* not willing?"

He really wanted to ask her what she meant by that. He would have loved to hear her explanation. But they had already wasted too much time talking.

He took his hat off and waved her on. "Ride for Eagle Flats."

She looked like she wanted to argue but leaned forward in the saddle and heeled her pony into a run. Vance swatted at the pony's rump with his hat, just to speed it on its way.

As Rosaleen galloped on down the valley, he headed for the clump of trees he had mentioned. He looked back in the direction Rosaleen had come from, searching for any sign of whoever had been following her. Vance's gut told him she was right about the man being Dax Coolidge, but he would have to see that for himself to be sure.

He continued watching after he'd dismounted, pulled the Winchester from its sheath, and taken cover behind the trees, but he didn't see anyone. Rosaleen was out of sight, and the valley appeared to be deserted except for the cows grazing in the distance.

Worry gnawed at Vance's nerves. Rosaleen was a level-headed young woman. She wasn't the sort to imagine things . . . but maybe she had been mistaken about somebody being on her trail. With all the trouble in recent weeks, she could be forgiven for letting her imagination run away with itself.

She wouldn't be happy, though, if anybody told her that. She would insist she had really seen what she thought she saw.

Problem was, if somebody really had been following her, they should have showed up already.

CHAPTER TWENTY-FIVE

Rosaleen didn't know who she was more afraid for, herself or Vance. If she was right . . . if that really had been Dax Coolidge trailing her and Vance tried to stop him . . . the likelihood of such a confrontation ending well for Vance was very small. He had put up a brave front, but they both knew he was no match for the ruthless gunfighter.

She wanted him to be capable of anything. Even though she wouldn't have admitted it to him, over the past week she had found her affection for hjm growing. She realized she hadn't been fair to him about the way he had concealed his true identity . . . but she wasn't going to admit *that* to him, either, not just yet. She had seen enough to know that he was a kind, intelligent, courageous man. The sort of man she might someday—

She put that thought out of her head as she reached Eagle Flats and paused to look back. She didn't spot any riders back up the valley.

Facing forward again, she looked out over the flats. They stretched for two miles in front of her, ending at another range of low hills. They continued north and south as far as she could see. It was a good place to spot eagles as they flew from one bunch of hills to the other. The sky was open and empty. Rosaleen enjoyed sketching the majestic birds, although she had never told anyone about her artistic efforts or showed them to anybody.

The flats were covered with sage, gray and dry since the time was several months past blooming. She remembered being there when the purple blossoms stretched beautifully as far as the eye could see.

She looked back again and then started across the flats. In those distant hills was a trail that looped around toward the ranch headquarters, but to reach it she had to cross the open ground where any pursuer would spot her instantly. Her best bet, she thought, was to get to the other side of the flats as quickly as she could.

Because she kept looking behind her as she rode, she wasn't watching very carefully in front of her. After glancing over her shoulder for what seemed like the hundredth time, she faced ahead again and gasped in surprise at the sight of a man sitting calmly on his horse about fifty yards in front of her.

Rosaleen hauled back on the reins and brought her pony to an abrupt halt. She could see the man well enough to recognize the arrogant grin and the jaunty way he wore his hat cocked on his head.

Somehow, Dax Coolidge had gotten ahead of her.

He had skirted the valley and ridden past her while she was talking to Vance. She was certain of it. That was the only explanation that made sense.

At least he stayed where he was and didn't ride toward her.

That didn't stop her heart from slugging painfully in her chest. She glanced at the butt of the carbine sticking up from its sheath. Could she pull the rifle out and fire before Coolidge reached her if he decided to attack? He was out of handgun range, so he would have to come closer if he wanted to shoot her.

He didn't make any hostile moves. He took what appeared to be a cigar from his vest pocket, snapped a match to life with his thumbnail, and lit the cheroot. Rosaleen saw the cloud of smoke that wreathed his head as he exhaled.

"Howdy, Miss Malone," he called. "Beautiful day, isn't it?"

She didn't answer the question. She was in no mood for small talk. "I thought you left this part of the country."

"Well, I thought about it. I really did. But then I decided I just couldn't. Too much unfinished business, if you know what I mean."

"I'm sure I don't. Any business you might have is no concern of mine."

"Well, see, you'd be wrong about that," Coolidge said as he gestured with the cigar. "We have a lot in common. You're interested in what happens to the Three Rivers, and so am I."

"You're still working for Mort Cabot! I knew it. That was just an act in town, when you said you were leaving."

"Was it?" The mocking smile was still on his face. "Could be I decided I was on the wrong side all along. Cabot didn't back me up the way a man ought to when you put your life on the line for him. Made me think maybe I ought to be working for the Three Rivers instead."

"We don't hire gunslingers," she said, her voice cold.

"You ought to reconsider. My price is reasonable. I'll work for just regular cowhand's wages . . . plus one little bonus."

"What sort of bonus?"

As soon as she said it, Rosaleen knew she shouldn't have asked the question.

Coolidge's grin became a leer as he said, "You, Miss Malone. I get forty a month and found . . . and you."

"Go to hell!" she cried. "That will never happen. If you were the last fighting man on earth, we'd never turn to scum like you!"

He puffed on the cheroot for a second, then asked, "Is that your final word on the subject?"

"It certainly is!"

"Well, that's too bad." Coolidge put the cigar between his lips again and drew hard on it, making the coal on the end glow so brightly Rosaleen could see it even over the distance separating them. He took the cheroot from his mouth and tossed it on the ground about ten feet in front of him.

Flames shot up with a *whoosh!*

Terror struck through Rosaleen. Like most Westerners, she was more afraid of fire than almost anything else. Prairie fires could wipe out hundreds of thousands of acres, and an uncontrolled blaze in town could burn an entire settlement to the ground in less than an hour.

Even worse, the way the flames were racing along the ground in both directions told her Coolidge had spread something to fuel them, probably black powder or coal oil. With the dry sage catching fire instantly, there would be a wall of flames between them within moments.

Rosaleen whirled her horse. She had to get out of there. The wind was blowing across the flats toward her, but she thought she could stay in front of the blaze.

She heard a couple sharp cracks over the crackling flames. Her pony leaped and then staggered. Instinct made her kick her feet free from the stirrups and she flew from the saddle as the horse collapsed underneath her.

She slammed into the ground, stunning her and knocking the air from her lungs. Rolling over and gasping, she tried to gather her wits. When she lifted her head, she found herself looking back through the leaping flames. Heat blurred the air, but she could make out Dax Coolidge still sitting on his horse, holding a rifle. She knew he had shot her pony out from under her.

Coolidge slid his rifle back in its scabbard and then lifted a hand to his hat brim to sketch a lazy salute to her. With the flames between them, he looked like a devil from hell, she thought.

And hell was closing in on her, consuming the sage in its crackling fury as it rolled across the flats.

The sight of the advancing flames filled Rosaleen with terror that forced her muscles to work. She surged to her feet and looked down at her horse for a second. The pony was dead, beyond anything else Coolidge could do to it. Grief stabbed into her at the loss of her friend, but she had more pressing problems.

She turned and ran.

From the corner of her eye she saw the flames spreading out and curving around to her right. She jerked her head to the left and saw the same thing happening there. Coolidge had laid a trap for her. She had ridden right into it, and it was closing around her with jaws of flame.

Something was bothering him. Vance frowned, stood up straighter, and sniffed the air. He smelled smoke. He hurried out of the trees, knowing he was exposing himself to gunshots if anyone lurking around wanted to harm him, but an urgent need to know where the smoke was coming from gripped him.

As he peered to the east, his fears were realized. Huge billows of grayish-white smoke rose in that direction, drifting toward him on a steady breeze. The clouds of smoke extended for a good distance north and south, curving around to make a cup shape. Anything caught inside that cup would have a hard time getting out.

Vance's heart began to hammer in his chest. As best he could tell, the smoke was coming from Eagle Flats.

Exactly where Rosaleen had gone . . . because he had *told* her to flee there.

Smoke wafted over Rosaleen and clogged the air around her. She coughed and blinked stinging eyes. The fire was still a good distance behind her. She might be able to outrun the flames, but she couldn't outrun the smoke. As she coughed harder and harder, her pace slowed. She pulled her bandana over her nose

and forced herself to run faster again. If she passed
out and fell, the blaze would overtake her in moments
and she would be lost.

She stumbled and barely caught herself before she
dropped to her knees. She looked back to see how
close the fire was. The nearness of it made her leap
ahead. She didn't see Coolidge. He had ridden off,
she thought, abandoning her to an awful death. All
because she had refused his ridiculous offer to go to
work for her father, if she would just give herself to him!

That had been a lie, she thought. Even if she had
agreed, Coolidge would have betrayed them. She was
sure of it. He was probably still working for Cabot.
The whole thing was a trick.

Even with the bandanna over her face, coughs
wracked her with every step. She couldn't see,
couldn't breathe. The world was gray around her,
closing in, nothing left, nothing but smoke.

Rosaleen realized suddenly that she was on the
ground. She had fallen without even being aware of
it. The only thing working slightly in her favor was the
smoke wasn't quite as thick down low. She was able to
breathe a little easier, and that helped clear her head
for a moment.

She wished she had taken the time to soak the
bandanna in water from her canteen before she ran
from where her pony had fallen, but fear of the fire
had been so great she hadn't thought of it. Like it
was, the bandanna probably didn't help much, but it
was better than nothing.

The heat from the blaze washed over her. Stagger-
ing to her feet, she lurched forward again, weaving
back and forth as she tried to run.

It was no use. The smoke was too bad. She slipped to her knees again, then pitched forward. The roar of the flames filled her ears. She seemed to hear something else, some sort of pounding, but the sudden hope she felt evaporated when she realized it was the wild, frenzied beating of her heart. Most of her strength had deserted her, leaving her coughs feeble.

She didn't want to burn to death. Better to die from the smoke before the fire reached her. She took a deep breath, drawing death into her body, and then knew no more.

CHAPTER TWENTY-SIX

Vance rode harder than he ever had in his life. The horse he was mounted on was a big, sturdy one, built for hard work and stamina but not for speed. He wished he had one of the lighter, more nimble-footed cow ponies under him as he raced toward Eagle Flats.

Something seemed unnatural about that fire, he thought as he leaned forward in the saddle. Just a short time earlier, the sky had been clear, no smoke in sight anywhere. The blaze wouldn't have spread out that much, that fast, under normal conditions.

Someone must have set it, and they had to have done something to make it spread like that, too.

Coolidge.

Starting a fire seemed like the sort of reckless, vicious thing he would do.

Vance wondered if Rosaleen had had time to get past the fire's point of origin before it broke out. That seemed unlikely. Probably, she was between him and the flames, trying to get away from them.

He thundered onto Eagle Flats and scanned the ground in front of him, looking for any sign of her.

Smoke blew in his face and stung his eyes, making it hard to see. "Rosaleen!" he shouted at the top of his lungs. "Rosaleen!"

To his right and left, several hundred yards away, flames leaped along the ground with breathtaking speed. The fire was on three sides of him, and the only way out was back the way he had come.

The smoke was getting thicker with each passing second. He pulled his bandanna up over his nose as impenetrable clouds of the choking stuff rolled across the flats.

Through a gap between the clouds, Vance suddenly caught sight of something dark against the sage. He rode in what he hoped was the right direction and then had to haul back hard on the reins to keep the horse from trampling the senseless form lying on the ground.

He dropped from the saddle and cried again, "Rosaleen!" Kneeling beside her, he gripped her shoulders and rolled her onto her back. Her face was pale and still. For a horrible moment, he thought she was already dead. Then she coughed as her body rebelled against the smoke, and he knew she was alive. He pulled her up into his arms.

The swift rataplan of hoofbeats made him look around. Frightened for Rosaleen, he had dropped the reins when he flung himself from the saddle, and his horse was fleeing instinctively from the advancing flames.

"No!" Vance shouted. "Come back here!"

The terrified horse ignored him, of course, and kept going.

Vance fought down the panic welling up inside him. He got one arm around Rosaleen's shoulders, the other under her knees, and scooped her up against him. He lurched to his feet. She was a slender girl, but even so, the weight was considerable as he broke into a run after the horse. Their only hope of salvation was for him to carry her out of the danger zone.

He cradled her against his chest as he stumbled away from the fire. Her head hung loosely, drawing her throat taut, and he could see the pulse beating under her smooth skin. As long as he could see that tiny, vital movement, he figured he could keep his legs moving.

The smoke curling around them stung his nose, made his eyes water, and caused fits of coughing. The air was so hot it seemed to sear his lungs with every deep, ragged breath he drew in. Soon, he didn't have any conscious thought in his brain. He was just a mechanism, arms clamped tight around Rosaleen, legs moving one in front of the other, over and over, as he fled from the roaring conflagration behind them.

In such bad shape, he didn't realize he had lost his footing until it was almost too late. At the last second he twisted so he wouldn't land on Rosaleen. They crashed to the ground with her lying on top of him. He'd cushioned her fall but wasn't sure it mattered. He didn't think he could get back up again.

Her face was only inches from his. He was surprised to see her eyelids flutter, and then they stayed open so he could look into those green eyes that looked like a deep, bottomless lake.

"Vance . . ." she whispered.

"I'm here. I've got you, Rosaleen." He managed to get the words out without coughing, but then another fit of it struck him.

She started to cough, too, as she pushed herself up

a little and looked around them. "We're not . . . getting out of here . . . alive . . . are we?"

"It doesn't . . . look like it. I'm sorry."

"You shouldn't have . . . tried to save me."

"I had to."

She coughed hard again for a moment, then said, "It was Coolidge. I saw him . . . talked to him. He did this."

"He'll pay. Somehow . . . sooner or later . . . he'll pay."

She dropped her head against his shoulder. Even with the smoke all around them, he smelled the clean fragrance of her hair. His arms tightened around her, and she gripped him as well. They were going to die, but they would leave this world together . . .

Vance felt the ground tremble underneath him and watched gigantic figures loom up out of the smoke. They weren't the monsters they seemed at first glance, but turned into men on horseback who quickly dismounted. Strong arms went around Rosaleen and lifted her away from him.

"Wilbur!" Stovepipe Stewart shouted over the roar of the fire. "Give Vance a hand!"

"Save her!" Vance called as the lanky cowboy swung around toward his horse with Rosaleen in his arms.

Stovepipe lifted her onto the horse's back just ahead of the saddle, then climbed on behind her and looped an arm tightly around her waist to hang on to her.

At the same time, Wilbur clasped Vance's uplifted hand and pulled him upright. The stocky redhead was quite strong. Shaky but filled with newfound hope, Vance climbed onto Wilbur's roan and Wilbur swung up behind him.

They pounded after Stovepipe's paint.

The flames had come very close, but the two swift horses soon left them behind. The smoke was still thick around them, but after a couple blinding, choking minutes, they burst out abruptly into clear air. Vance drew in a deep breath and had never experienced anything more intoxicating in his life.

Another coughing spell hit him, and he knew it would take a while for his lungs and throat to get back to normal.

They all kept moving until they were well clear of the smoke. Only then did Stovepipe slow and turn his mount so he could look back toward the fire. Wilbur did likewise.

"That was a mighty near thing," Stovepipe said. "The two o' you were pert near roasted."

"What happened?" Wilbur asked.

"Coo—Coolidge," Rosaleen said around a cough.

"You sure about that?" Stovepipe said.

"I talked to him. There's no doubt."

Stovepipe's craggy face was grim as he said, "I had a hunch he didn't pull up stakes like he said he was gonna. Probably been hangin' around for the past week just waitin' for another chance to get up to some mischief."

"Starting a blaze like that is more than just mischief," Wilbur said.

"He wanted to . . . kill me," Rosaleen said. "He offered to switch sides . . . and work for the Three Rivers . . . but I had to . . . give myself to him . . . if he did."

"The bastard!" Vance couldn't contain his anger.

"I turned him down . . . Didn't believe him anyway."

"Yeah, chances are it was a trick," Stovepipe agreed.

"I think he's still . . . working for Cabot."

Stovepipe didn't say anything in response to that. He pointed at the blaze. "That fire's gonna keep on spreadin', as strong as it's burnin'. We'd better get back and let Mr. Malone and the rest of the crew know. Ain't likely it'd make it all the way to headquarters, but you never know. Anyway, we need to stop it before it burns up too much of the range and kills some cattle."

They rode as hard as they could with the horses carrying double but didn't have to go all the way back to headquarters. After a couple miles they ran into a large group of cowboys led by Keenan Malone. They had spotted the smoke and come to fight the fire. Every man had a shovel.

"Good Lord!" Malone said as he reined in and saw his daughter and Vance riding with Stovepipe and Wilbur. "Rosaleen, are you all right?"

"Thanks to these three I am." She wasn't coughing as badly. "Vance saved me from the fire, and then Stovepipe and Wilbur saved both of us."

"What the hell started it?"

"Not what," Stovepipe said, grim again. "Who. Dax Coolidge."

"Damn it! I knew that devil was still around! Mort Cabot's gonna answer for this! It's war now!"

Andy Callahan said, "We'd better get up there and start diggin' some firebreaks, boss, and worry about the war later."

"Yeah, you're right. Stewart, Coleman, take those two back to the ranch. The rest o' you boys, come on!"

They thundered off toward the fire. Stovepipe, Wilbur, and their two passengers headed toward the ranch house. Their pace wasn't breakneck any longer, but they didn't dawdle since the fire wasn't a great distance behind them.

As they rode, Rosaleen said, "Stovepipe, you and

Wilbur showed up at just the right time again. How is it you have such a knack for doing that?"

"Just lucky, I reckon," Stovepipe said.

"And the fact trouble seems to attract us like a lodestone," Wilbur added.

"Well, I'm glad it does," Vance said. "We'd be in bad shape if it didn't."

He was confident Stovepipe and Wilbur hadn't been far off when the trouble started, even though he hadn't seen them. His father was paying them to keep an eye on his son, and they were sure earning their wages. Vance wasn't going to say anything about that to Rosaleen. It was up to the two range detectives when they would reveal who they really were.

Of course, Vance had a hunch Stovepipe and Wilbur would turn up whenever trouble broke out anyway.

As Rosaleen had said, they had a knack for it.

CHAPTER TWENTY-SEVEN

Knowing Malone and the other men had ridden off in a hurry to check out the giant cloud of smoke, Aunt Sinead was waiting anxiously for news. She was on the porch when Stovepipe and Wilbur rode up with the two young people. She could hear them coughing quite a bit.

"Land's sake!" she said, hurrying down the steps. "What in the world happened?"

"These two got caught in a range fire over on Eagle Flats," Stovepipe said as the older woman lifted her hands to help Rosaleen down from the horse. "As it was, they swallowed a heap o' smoke."

"I can tell," Aunt Sinead said as Rosaleen and Vance coughed again. "I'll brew up some hot tea with honey. That will help, but I'm afraid it will take a while for the damage to heal."

"I know, Aunt Sinead," Rosaleen said. "Thank you."

Vance slid down from Wilbur's roan and put a hand on Rosaleen's arm to steady her as another fit of coughing nearly overcame her.

Aunt Sinead took her other arm and said, "Come on, dear. Let's get both of you in the house."

As they went inside, Stovepipe and Wilbur remained mounted.

Stovepipe thumbed his hat back and grinned. "That was a mighty near thing. Lucky that boy's got hisself a couple o' guardian angels."

Wilbur grunted. "You and me are about as far from angels as you can get, Stovepipe. I'd say we were all lucky. What are we gonna do now?"

"I reckon we can ride back out to the flats and see if Mr. Malone and the rest o' the fellas need any help fightin' that fire."

"Yeah, I was afraid you'd say that. We breathed some smoke, too, you know. I could do with a cup of that tea Aunt Sinead was talking about."

"Later," Stovepipe said as he lifted his reins. "Come on."

As they rode toward Eagle Flats, the smoke rising in that direction diminished. By the time they reached the flats, only a few tendrils curled up here and there from the charred expanse. Malone and the Three Rivers hands stood around, grimy with soot and obviously weary as they leaned on the shovels they had used to beat out the flames and dig firebreaks.

Malone looked up at the newcomers. "Did you get those two young'uns back to the house all right?"

"Yeah, and I expect they'll be fine," Stovepipe said. "Aunt Sinead took charge of 'em. She'll fix 'em right up if anybody can." He looked around. "Appears you got the fire out."

"Yeah, but it wasn't easy, spread over as big an area as it was. We had to hustle to get ahead of it and contain it. Cabot's got a hell of a lot to answer for."

Again, Stovepipe made no response to someone blaming Mort Cabot for what had happened.

"I was thinkin' Wilbur and me might have a look and see if we can track Coolidge. He must've been holed up somewhere for the past week. If we can find his hidin' place it could come in handy."

"He's probably been holed up in the Rafter M bunkhouse, if you ask me," Malone said. "But yeah, see if you can pick up his trail if you want. It can't hurt anything."

Stovepipe nodded. He and Wilbur guided their horses around the huge burned area. With plenty of hot embers out there, crossing it would likely hurt their horses' hooves.

As they rode, Wilbur said, "I've noticed every time somebody says anything about Cabot and Rafter M being behind some new trouble, you don't have much to say, Stovepipe. Why is that?"

"It's hard to put anything past you, ain't it, Wilbur?" Stovepipe said with a chuckle.

"That doesn't answer my question."

Stovepipe looked thoughtful. "I ain't convinced Mort Cabot's as bad as Malone makes him out to be. Maybe they ain't always been friends, but it's hard for two fellas to wind up as mortal enemies unless there's some big blowup to cause it. Things like that just don't happen gradual-like."

"There's bad blood between those two old codgers, though. No doubt about that."

Stovepipe pursed his lips and nodded. "Like you say, no doubt. But is it because somebody else has been pushin' 'em into that bad blood?"

"Who'd do a thing like that, and why?"

"Findin' out is part of the reason we're here. And of course, there's always the chance I'm wrong."

"Sure there is." Wilbur sounded pretty skeptical about that idea.

It took the better part of an hour to make it around to the spot where the fire had started. Spotting the curvature of the burned area, Stovepipe held up a hand to stop Wilbur before they reached the place, then both men dismounted and went forward on foot.

Stovepipe scanned the ground thoroughly until he found what he was looking for. He pointed and said, "Those hoofprints are pretty fresh, and you can tell from lookin' at 'em the fella was facin' where Miss Rosaleen woulda been."

"So it had to be Coolidge. That sort of backs up her story, doesn't it?"

"I didn't have any real doubt about it to start with, but yeah, she would've been close enough to tell who he was, for sure." Stovepipe hunkered on his heels to study the hoofprints more closely then he grunted and pointed again. "Couple empty rifle shells lyin' over yonder. Miss Rosaleen said Coolidge shot her pony out from under her."

"Yeah. The skunk. That's even more proof she was telling the truth."

Stovepipe straightened. "Let's see if we can back-track the varmint."

Coolidge's trail led east, toward the hills that lay beyond Eagle Flats.

As the two range detectives entered that rougher terrain, Wilbur said, "The Rafter M is southeast of here, right?"

"Yep. Handy enough Coolidge could've slipped on

and off the ranch without bein' seen to get his orders from Cabot . . . if Cabot is the one givin' 'em."

Tracking the gunfighter was more difficult up in the hills, but Stovepipe's keen eyes were able to pick up enough sign to keep them on the trail for a couple miles. They reached a steep-walled canyon with a rock floor.

"The tracks lead in there," Stovepipe said as he reined in and nodded toward the canyon mouth.

"Aren't we gonna follow them?" Wilbur asked.

Stovepipe shook his head. "We might be ridin' right into an ambush if we did. My hunch is that Coolidge's hideout is somewhere up that canyon. He'll have picked a spot where he can see anybody who's comin' and throw down on 'em."

The lanky cowboy gazed up at the higher ground on both sides of the canyon. "What we need to do is get up there and work our way around, maybe find some trail where we can come in above wherever Coolidge is holed up. It's too late in the day to do that now, though."

"What if he takes off?"

"He ain't gonna do that," Stovepipe said. "He ain't through raisin' hell around here. Things ain't blowed up all the way yet between the Three Rivers and the Rafter M."

"And you think that's what he's after?"

"I'd bet a hat on it."

They turned and rode back toward the Three Rivers headquarters, planning to continue their search for Dax Coolidge the next day. It was dusk by the time they trotted their horses up to the barn and swung down from their saddles.

Old Asa, the wrangler, came out to take their horses.

The ancient, one-eyed cowboy nodded toward the house and said, "The boss wants to see you two as soon as you get back."

"Figured as much," Stovepipe said. "Thanks, Asa."

"Any luck findin' the stinkin' polecat who tried to hurt Miss Rosaleen?"

"We didn't catch up with him, but we've got a pretty good idea where to look for him."

Asa spat. "If you want to take me along, I reckon I could sit a saddle again, at least for a while. It'd be worth it for a chance to peel that son of a bitch's hide."

"I'll remember that," Stovepipe said, although he had no intention of taking the ancient wrangler along on any hunt for Dax Coolidge.

They went to the ranch house and knocked on the front door.

Aunt Sinead opened it a moment later and said, "I thought it might be you boys. Keenan's in his office, waiting for you."

"Where are Miss Rosaleen and Vance?"

"They're in there with him." The older woman lowered her voice. "There's been a lot of shouting. Keenan's not one to keep his voice down when his dander is up."

Stovepipe laughed softly. The old cattleman wasn't subtle, that was for sure. Men of his breed spoke plainly, said what they meant and meant what they said, often at great volume.

The cowboys went along the hall to the office, where Stovepipe knocked again.

From the other side of the door, Malone bellowed, "Who is it?"

"Stewart and Coleman, boss," Stovepipe said.

"Get in here!"

The tension in the room was obvious. Rosaleen sat in a big leather chair, while Malone and Vance were both on their feet. Vance stood near the chair where Rosaleen sat, while Malone paced back and forth agitatedly.

He swung around to face the newcomers and scowled. "Took you long enough. Did you find Coolidge?"

"Not yet, but we've got a pretty good idea where he's been hidin' out," Stovepipe said.

"He's at the Rafter M, right?"

Stovepipe shook his head. "I don't reckon he is. I think he's got a camp up in those hills on the other side of Eagle Flats. That's about the end of Three Rivers range, ain't it?"

"Yeah, but it ain't far from Rafter M range, either." Malone made a curt slashing gesture. "It don't matter. Coolidge ain't our real problem. Mort Cabot is . . . and I got just the solution for him."

"What's that?" Stovepipe asked, but he had a hunch he already knew the answer . . . and didn't think he was going to like it.

"We're ridin' over there tonight, and I'm gonna blow a hole in Cabot and any of his men who get in my way. Then I'm gonna burn the place to the ground. He wants to fight with fire, damn it, so I'm gonna give him fire right back!"

CHAPTER TWENTY-EIGHT

Stovepipe exchanged a glance with Wilbur, then said, "Hold on, boss. You ain't got no proof Cabot had anything to do with Coolidge startin' that fire. You go over there and fill him full o' lead, Sheriff Jerrico's liable to arrest you for murder. You don't want Miss Rosaleen havin' to attend a necktie party where you're the guest of honor."

"That's what I've been trying to tell him, Mr. Stewart." Rosaleen's voice was still hoarse from all the smoke she had breathed. "I thought Vance might talk him out of this foolishness, but I was mistaken about that."

"Darn right you were." Vance was hoarse, too. "Coolidge came mighty close to killing both of us, and if Cabot was responsible, he deserves whatever happens to him."

Malone gave an emphatic nod. "Those are fightin' words, son . . . and I like 'em."

"Most important word there is *if*," Stovepipe said. "*If* Cabot's to blame. You don't know that he is. Could be Coolidge was actin' on his own. You all know how touchy the varmint is. He's pretty close to bein' plumb loco."

Malone glared coldly at him. "I don't take kindly to the hands who ride for me puttin' up arguments and contradictin' what I say. Especially ones who ain't been on the Three Rivers for more 'n a month. You better keep that in mind, Stewart."

Stovepipe looked at Vance. He was the only one who knew who the two range detectives really were. If he wanted to reveal that fact, Stovepipe and Wilbur couldn't stop him.

However, Vance didn't say anything. He just stood there looking as angry and determined as Malone.

"Sorry, boss," Stovepipe said. "Didn't mean to argue with you. It's just that Wilbur and me like ridin' for the Three Rivers, and we don't want nothin' to jeopardize that. I ain't sayin' Cabot's innocent. I just figured it'd be a good idea to have some proof before we headed off to war."

"What sort of proof?" Malone asked with a frown.

"Since Wilbur and me have a pretty good idea what area Coolidge has been hidin' out in, why don't you let us scout around some more, locate the place, and then keep an eye on it? If Coolidge actually is workin' for the Rafter M, he'll have to ride down there sooner or later. If he does, we'll have proof Cabot's behind what happened today. You could go to the sheriff with that."

"You mean sic the law on him?" Malone glowered. "I don't cotton to that. Goes against the grain not to handle trouble on my own."

Rosaleen said, "That's what the law is for, Dad. Things aren't like they were when you and Mr. Cabot and all the other pioneers started your ranches here years ago."

"Maybe they ain't the same in some ways, but some things never change," Malone insisted.

Rosaleen turned to look at Vance. "Please. You understand what I'm saying, surely."

"Why? Because I'm from back east and have never really had to fight for anything I wanted? That may be true, but I come from fighting stock, Rosaleen. My father battled for his fortune. Maybe it's time I started fighting some real battles of my own."

"By getting yourself killed?"

Malone said, "What in blazes has happened here? I've always been the one who's had to stop you from flyin' off the handle, gal, not the other way around."

"Maybe coming so close to dying today made me realize how precious—and how fragile—life really is."

"Maybe so, but what good is life if you have to back down from challenges in order to live it?"

Not knowing how much longer they might go on wrangling, Stovepipe interrupted. "Give Wilbur and me one more day, boss. If we don't find Coolidge and prove one way or the other whether he's still workin' for Cabot, you can raise hell and shove a chunk under the corner all you want to."

Malone snorted. "Mighty generous of you to give me permission to do that, Stewart, when last time I checked you worked for me and not the other way around!" His angry expression eased slightly, though, as he shrugged and went on. "But I suppose another day wouldn't hurt nothin'. Shoot, by waitin' to strike back, it might even throw Cabot off his guard a little. What do you say, Vance?"

Clearly, Vance was furious over what had happened.

He didn't want to calm down and wait. He wrestled with his emotions and finally, reason won out and he agreed. "One more day. But if you don't show any results, Stovepipe . . . well, I don't know what's going to happen. It won't be peaceful, I can promise you that."

Stovepipe had won. "Deal."

Fortified by a hearty breakfast and several cups of strong black coffee, the two detectives rode out before sunup the next morning. Wilbur had a bundle of Aunt Sinead's biscuits and some bacon in his saddlebags so they wouldn't go hungry at lunchtime.

"You reckon Malone will keep his word and not attack the Rafter M?" Wilbur asked as they rode east away from the ranch headquarters.

"He ain't a man to go back on his word without a mighty good reason," Stovepipe replied. "Before yesterday, I might've said Vance would keep him reined in, but ol' Vance was as walleyed as a spooked horse himself. He was every bit as ready to go to war as the old man was."

"Well, sure. He's in love with the girl, and Coolidge nearly killed her, not to mention how close Vance came to dying himself. It was a near thing, Stovepipe. The range could've run red with blood last night."

"We've headed it off for the time bein'. Now we've got to deliver, though. If we don't find that gun-wolf's hideout, things could still go to hell."

They angled north through the hills before they ever reached Eagle Flats, then cut east so as to cross the open ground several miles away from the scene of the fire that had almost taken the lives of Vance and

Rosaleen. Stovepipe's sense of direction was unerring. He led Wilbur into the rugged landscape and they began working their way south toward the narrow canyon where Coolidge's trail had taken them.

Any time there was a chance for them to move to higher ground, they did so, climbing gradually until they were well above the area where they had been the day before. As they rode onto a broad bench, Stovepipe wasn't surprised to see a chasm cutting across the ground in front of them. He pointed it out to Wilbur and said, "Unless I miss my guess, that's the other end of the canyon we found yesterday. Let's get closer on foot and see if we can tell anything."

They dismounted, pulled their Winchesters from the sheaths, and let the reins dangle. The paint and the roan were well-trained and wouldn't wander. With the caution they had developed over years of work that often required stealth, Stovepipe and Wilbur catfooted toward the canyon.

Before they reached the brink, they dropped to hands and knees and covered the last few yards. Stovepipe took off his hat, set it aside, and risked a look. He could see about a hundred yards back up the canyon.

There was no sign of Dax Coolidge or anybody else.

Stovepipe turned to look at Wilbur and shook his head. He frowned and then sniffed the air. Pointing behind him, he indicated they should back off from the edge.

When they had pulled back, Stovepipe whispered, "I didn't see nobody, but I think I caught a whiff of wood smoke. Don't see no smoke comin' up, so Coolidge is probably keepin' his fire pretty small, but he can't get rid of the smell completely."

"I thought I smelled it, too," Wilbur agreed, also in a whisper. "What do we do now?"

"Let's head back the other direction. Stay as quiet as you can."

They crawled along the top of the canyon, picking up the rifles and setting them down carefully so the metal didn't clink against any rocks. After a few minutes, Stovepipe could tell the smell of wood smoke was getting stronger and figured Coolidge had fed a few twigs into his fire, maybe to boil a pot of coffee.

Motioning for Wilbur to stop, Stovepipe dropped all the way to his belly and eased forward to look over the brink again. On the other side of the canyon, the rock wall bulged out enough for the overhang to form a cavelike area underneath it. A few curls of smoke drifted from under the rock. he heard a horse stamping and blowing. The animal sounded restless and impatient, probably with good reason. Likely, there wasn't any graze up in that gloomy enclosure.

Stovepipe slid back to join Wilbur and whispered, "He's there, all right, or at least somebody is." Quickly, he explained what he'd seen.

"Now what?"

"Now you're gonna stay here and keep an eye on the place while I go back the other way and find a spot where I can climb down."

"You're going after Coolidge on his own ground?" Wilbur didn't think that was a very good idea. "Why don't we just call on him to surrender? With us up here, he can't get away. If he tries, we'll drill him."

Stovepipe shook his head. "I want to take the varmint alive. That's the only way he can answer questions. If we holler down at him, he'll just fort up in there and we won't have any way of gettin' him out."

"We could bounce some slugs in there and make him think twice about being stubborn."

"And one of those ricochets might blow a hole clean through him, too." Stovepipe shook his head. "Nope, I don't want to risk it. You give me time to get in position and then chunk a rock down in the canyon to get his attention. He'll come out to make sure nobody's tryin' to sneak up on him, and when he does, I'll jump him and hogtie him."

"He'll put up a fight, you know."

"Why, sure he will. But I'll take my chances."

"And what if he kills you?"

"Then it'll be up to you, Wilbur. You can capture him or you can blow his lights out, whichever one seems like the thing to do at the time."

"Would it do any good to tell you to be careful?"

Stovepipe shook his head. "Not a whole heck of a lot."

CHAPTER TWENTY-NINE

Leaving Wilbur above Dax Coolidge's camp, Stovepipe went back the other way, still being careful not to make any more noise than necessary. He didn't want Coolidge to know anybody was around until he was ready to make his move.

When he had put enough distance between himself and the camp, he stood up and loped the rest of the way. The canyon had enough bends in it that he was out of sight of Coolidge's hideout. When he reached the end of the chasm, where the two sides pinched together, Stovepipe knelt and looked for a way to climb down. The rock wall had enough cracks, fissures, and knobs to provide handholds and footholds. He wasn't very fond of climbing, but it had to be done. Not able to take it with him, he set the rifle aside.

He searched for a good foothold. Spotting one, he rolled to his belly, slid his legs over the edge, and wedged the toe of his right boot into a crack. He grabbed hold of a tree root and reached down with his left foot to find another. His heart pounded in his chest as he slowly lowered himself. The canyon was a good forty feet deep, and its floor was stone. If he lost his grip and fell, the landing would bust him all to pieces, if not kill him outright.

"Just make sure you don't fall, old son," he told himself under his breath to counter that grim thought.

The descent was a slow, nerve-racking business.

Finally, Stovepipe dropped the last few inches and heaved a sigh of relief when his boots were firmly on solid ground again. He stood there for a moment, breathing hard as his racing pulse slowed. When his nerves had settled down, he drew his Colt and started along the canyon toward Coolidge's camp.

He had told Wilbur to watch for his signal before tossing a rock into the canyon. Knowing his friend and partner was as reliable as the sun coming up in the east every morning, it was unlikely he would get impatient.

Stovepipe reached a bend about fifty yards from the cavelike area under the overhang. He took his hat off and edged an eye around so he could take a look. A tiny fire flickered in the back of the shadowy area under the bulge of rock.

Stovepipe caught a glimpse of Wilbur's hat on the opposite wall. He reached around the bend and waved his own hat. A second later, Wilbur's hat waved in a return signal to let him know the redhead had seen him.

A few seconds went by, then a fist-sized rock arched out over the canyon and dropped down to strike the other wall, bounce off, and land on the canyon floor with a clatter.

For a moment nothing happened. Then Dax Coolidge appeared, slipping out from under the overhang in a gliding crouch. Gun in hand, he turned toward the spot where the rock had fallen. He wasn't wearing his hat, so Stovepipe got a good look at his face and recognized the hired gun beyond any doubt.

As Coolidge stalked toward the area where he had heard the racket, Stovepipe eased around the bend. Moving as quietly as an Apache, he began closing the distance between himself and the gunman.

Coolidge crouched, twisting from side to side as he searched for whatever he had heard. About twenty yards from his camp, he decided the noise hadn't amounted to anything, probably just a rock that had fallen. He straightened from his crouch.

Stovepipe had almost reached the overhang. He would have liked to be closer, since he was armed only with the Colt. All Coolidge had was a revolver, too, so they were on even terms.

And with the element of surprise, Stovepipe had the advantage.

He waited until Coolidge slid his gun into leather then leveled his own Colt and called out, "Hold it right there, Coolidge! Don't make a move!"

Most men would have followed orders when somebody had the drop on them, but Dax Coolidge wasn't most men. He twisted toward the range detective and his hand moved to his gun in a blur of speed.

Stovepipe had no choice but to press the trigger of his Colt. The gun roared and bucked in his hand, but Coolidge's swift pivot had thrown off his aim. Blood flew as Stovepipe's bullet nicked Coolidge's left arm. The revolver in the man's right fist still roared and spat flame.

Stovepipe fired again as the slug whined past his ear. He wanted to wound Coolidge, not kill him. A dead man couldn't answer any questions. He aimed low and fired. The bullet kicked up rock splinters inches from Coolidge's foot as he moved.

Coolidge fired again. Mixed with the boom of his revolver as it bounced off the canyon walls was the sharp crack of Wilbur's rifle. The stocky redhead had joined the fight.

The canyon's close confines made a horrible racket of the echoes. The deafening reports were disorienting, pounding like fists against Stovepipe's ears. Even worse, Coolidge was like a blasted phantom as he weaved back and forth. His reputation as a gunwolf was well-deserved. He was as dangerous as any man Stovepipe had ever faced.

Stovepipe whirled and darted under the overhang, figuring he might find some cover in the cavelike area. He wanted to prevent Coolidge from retreating in there, too. As long as Coolidge was out in the open in the canyon, Wilbur would bring him down eventually.

As Stovepipe jumped into the shadows under the bulging rock, a huge shape loomed up out of the gloom. Spooked by the gun-thunder, Coolidge's horse had bolted. Stovepipe barely had time to get out of the way as the animal charged out. As it was, the horse's shoulder clipped him with enough force to knock him off his feet.

Stovepipe's wrist slammed against a rock when he landed. The Colt slipped out of suddenly nerveless fingers and slid away. He grimaced in a mixture of pain and exasperation. His plan had been a good one, he knew, and should have worked, but it seemed like everything that could possibly go wrong was trying its damnedest to do so.

More shots crashed out from Wilbur's rifle. Knowing

his friend was giving him covering fire, Stovepipe came up on hands and knees and scrambled after his gun.

Before he could reach it, something crashed into his back. He landed hard on his face, the impact stunning him for a second, but instinct made his elbow drive back against the man who had tackled him. He wasn't sure why Coolidge wanted to fight hand to hand instead of just shooting him, but Stovepipe was grateful he didn't have a slug in him. He twisted and threw Coolidge to the side. As the gunman toppled, he grabbed Stovepipe's shirt collar and hauled the range detective with him.

Up on the canyon rim, Wilbur couldn't risk any more shots. Coolidge and Stovepipe were close together as they wrestled on the rocky ground.

Stovepipe caught a glimpse of a bloodstain on Coolidge's right sleeve, matching the one on the gunman's left arm. Wilbur must have winged Coolidge, Stovepipe thought, and forced him to drop his revolver. That explained why Coolidge had tackled him rather than ventilating him. Staying close to Stovepipe was the only way Coolidge could keep Wilbur from drilling him.

It was a desperate battle, there on the floor of the canyon.

Coolidge snarled in fury as he got a hand on Stovepipe's face and tried to hook fingers in his eyes and gouge them out. Stovepipe hammered a punch into Coolidge's throat, making the gunman gag and pull back. He clamped fingers around Coolidge's wrist and jerked the clawlike fingers away from his eyes. Coolidge went for Stovepipe's throat with his other hand. Stovepipe slammed another punch into Coolidge's face before the man's choking grip could lock in place.

Stovepipe heaved and bucked, and they rolled again. Coolidge snatched up a rock big enough to crush a skull and swung it at Stovepipe's head. He jerked his head aside just in time for the rock to smash into the ground beside his ear. Coolidge brought it back to try again, but before the blow could fall, Stovepipe drove his knee into Coolidge's belly. Coolidge gasped and turned pale.

Stovepipe laced his hands together and brought them up in a clubbing blow under Coolidge's chin. The punch jerked Coolidge's head far back and sent him sprawling on the ground. Not giving him any chance to recover, Stovepipe went after him and buried a fist in the midsection . . . where he had just hit him with his knee. Coolidge's struggles were growing weaker.

The realization he was about to lose the fight caused Coolidge to summon up all his remaining strength. He grabbed the front of Stovepipe's shirt and slung him to the side. Stovepipe landed on his shoulder and rolled. He came up and saw Coolidge about to stomp him in the face. He got his hands raised and caught the gunman's boot, stopping it when the heel was only a couple inches away. Stovepipe heaved and Coolidge went over backwards again.

The will to fight was running out of him like water.

Stovepipe landed on top of him, straddling him with a knee on each side, and smashed a left and a right into the man's face. Coolidge's eyes rolled up in their sockets and he went limp.

Stovepipe stayed where he was for a moment, his chest heaving as he tried to catch his breath. His cheeks stung where Coolidge's clawing fingernails had left scratches. Battling the gunfighter had been a little like fighting a wildcat, Stovepipe thought. It had taken every bit of his own strength and determination to come out on top.

Sure Coolidge was out cold, Stovepipe pushed himself to his feet and looked around for the gun he had dropped earlier. Spotting it, he scooped it from the ground.

"Stovepipe!" Wilbur called from the rim. "Are you all right?"

"Yeah. A mite battered and bruised, but nothin' that won't heal. Get the horses and bring 'em back around to the mouth of this canyon. I'll tie up Coolidge, get him in his saddle, and meet you there."

"What are we gonna do with him? Take him to Wagontongue and turn him over to the sheriff?"

"Not just yet," Stovepipe said. "We're headed for the Three Rivers, and Mr. Coolidge here is gonna answer a few questions first."

CHAPTER THIRTY

Using a piece of rope from Coolidge's own lariat, Stovepipe bound the gunman's hands behind his back, then retrieved the runaway horse about a hundred yards down the canyon. He got the saddle cinched into place and lifted Coolidge onto the animal's back. That was quite a chore, but luckily Stovepipe's lanky frame was deceptively strong.

With another piece of rope, he tied the man's feet together under the horse's belly. Coolidge was starting to groan and mutter as he regained consciousness, but he couldn't go anywhere.

Stovepipe picked up his hat, batted it against his thigh to get the dust off, and punched its crown back into shape. He had just settled it on his head when Coolidge started bitterly cursing him.

"You're just wastin' your time and breath, mister," Stovepipe said. "I've done heard all them words before, and they don't bother me none . . . but since there's nothin' else you can do, you go right ahead and cuss if it makes you feel better."

"You're a dead man," Coolidge said as his lips twisted

into a snarl. "I promise you that, Stewart. I'm gonna watch you die, slow and hard, and I'm going to enjoy every second of it."

Stovepipe ignored the threat, took hold of the reins, and led the horse with its captive rider toward the mouth of the canyon. By the time they got there, Wilbur was waiting for them, sitting on the roan and holding the reins of Stovepipe's paint.

As Coolidge paused for breath, Wilbur grinned. "I could hear this fella ranting all the way out here. I don't think he's too happy with you, Stovepipe."

"No, I reckon not."

"You want me to gag him? We're liable to get a mite tired of listening to his filth before we get back to the Three Rivers."

Coolidge said, "You can't take me there. Old man Malone's crazy! He'll shoot me on sight."

"I don't reckon he will," Stovepipe said. "He's as eager to find out who you're workin' for as we are."

"Hell, is that all you want to know? I'll tell you. I take orders from Mort Cabot."

Stovepipe swung up into his saddle and squinted at the gunman. "You're mighty quick to confess."

Coolidge made a disgusted sound. "You think Cabot would cover for me if it was the other way around? You know good and well he wouldn't. I haven't killed anybody in these parts. I'll take my chances with the law. Just don't turn me over to that madman Malone."

Wilbur said, "You tried to kill Rosaleen Malone yesterday when you started that fire."

"So I started a fire," Coolidge said with a sneer. "You can't prove that was attempted murder."

"What about shootin' her horse?" Stovepipe asked.

Coolidge shrugged. "So I'll do a couple years in the pen. That's still better than dying."

"You'll repeat all this to Sheriff Jerrico if we take you to Wagontongue?"

"Sure, why not? Like I said, taking my chances with the law is better than the alternative."

"I'll think on it," Stovepipe said. He took hold of Coolidge's reins and led the gunman's mount as the three of them started out of the hills toward Eagle Flats.

Now that Coolidge believed he had struck a deal, he stopped the torrent of profanity. The silence, broken only by the thudding of the horses' hooves, was a welcome relief.

For his part, no matter what Coolidge thought, Stovepipe didn't intend to deliver the man to Sheriff Jerrico in Wagontongue. Not just yet, anyway. He was still bound for the headquarters of the Three Rivers ranch.

They reached the flats and started out onto the sage-covered plain. Up ahead, the burned area was visible as a dark smudge. It had cooled enough that they didn't have to go around it.

A couple hundred yards onto the flats, the whip crack of a rifle shot sounded somewhere behind them. At the same instant, Stovepipe heard the ugly sound of a bullet hitting flesh and jerked his head toward Coolidge.

The gunman had stiffened in the saddle and arched his back. His eyes were wide with pain and shock, and when he opened his mouth to say something, the only thing that came out was blood welling over his lips. He slumped forward and then toppled out of the saddle. With his legs tied under the horse's belly, all he could do was slide to one side.

Stovepipe caught a glimpse of the back of Coolidge's shirt and knew from the bloodstain blooming on it like a crimson flower that the gunfighter was done for. The bullet had gone straight to Coolidge's heart.

Another bullet whipped through the sage and kicked up dirt only a few feet away.

Stovepipe dropped the reins of Coolidge's horse and shouted to Wilbur, "Ride!"

He leaned forward in the saddle as he jabbed his boot heels into the paint's flanks. There was no point in waiting around for the rifleman back in the hills to kill him and Wilbur, too.

It wasn't the first time they'd had to make a run for their lives. They juked the horses back and forth, angling from side to side in an effort to make themselves more difficult targets. Stovepipe felt the wind-rip of another slug as it whipped past his ear. Another came close enough that it sounded like the hum of a giant hornet.

They spread out. More than fifty yards separated them. Stovepipe glanced at his friend. Bent in the saddle, the redhead seemed to be unhurt. He rode his galloping horse like he and the mount were one creature instead of two.

Suddenly, Stovepipe's hat flew in the air and something smashed against the side of his head with stunning force. He grabbed the saddlehorn and managed not to fall off, but it took a supreme effort not to pass out. He felt a warm flood down the side of his face and knew he was bleeding badly.

His strength deserted him just as rapidly as his

blood. The reins slipped out of his hand. Instead of dodging back and forth, the paint ran straight ahead. Stovepipe leaned forward until he was lying on the horse's neck and grasped the paint's mane with both hands to keep from toppling out of the saddle. He couldn't see anything. A red curtain had dropped in front of his eyes, and it was being swallowed on both sides by encroaching blackness.

When those two waves of oblivion met in the middle, Stovepipe was gone.

As Wilbur jerked his head back and forth, he tried to watch everything around him. He had to keep an eye on the ground in front of him for any holes or other irregularities that might trip up his horse. Running at top speed, a fall could be fatal for both of them.

He checked on his friend to make sure he was still all right just as Stovepipe's hat sailed into the air and blood flew from his head. "Stovepipe!" Fear exploded through Wilbur as he immediately veered toward his friend.

Stovepipe slumped far forward in the saddle. The bright red splash of blood on his face stood out plainly even at a distance. A bullet zinged past Wilbur so close he felt its heat against his cheek. The bushwhacker was one hell of a shot.

Wilbur had seen the same thing Stovepipe had. He knew the first shot had killed Dax Coolidge. What he didn't know was if the killer had been trying to silence Coolidge and he and Stovepipe were just bonus targets, or if the man had set out to kill all three of them. He was sure as blazes making a good try at the latter.

None of that mattered at the moment.

Wilbur angled farther toward Stovepipe, trying to intercept the paint with the lunging strides of the roan.

He knew the paint was faster, though. They had argued about that in the past and even had a few races. Although Wilbur would always defend his roan, he knew Stovepipe's mount possessed more speed.

Wilbur was able to close up the gap enough to see how Stovepipe lay stretched out on the horse's neck with one side of his face covered in blood. The son of a bitch had drilled him through the head. The realization chilled and sickened Wilbur.

They reached the burned area. Clouds of dust, gray from the ashes mixed with it, rose from the horses' hooves. Wilbur figured that would spoil the rifleman's aim, but a second later his hat leaped from his head as a bullet bored through the crown. That slug had practically parted his hair.

There was nothing he could do for Stovepipe, but he couldn't bring himself to abandon his friend. As the paint veered away and began to slow, Wilbur rode harder and tried to catch up.

A bullet slammed into his left hip like a giant fist. The impact twisted him halfway around, but he didn't fall out of the saddle. His whole left leg was numb, which threw him off balance. As he struggled to stay mounted, the roan began to slow. Another bullet plucked at the side of Wilbur's shirt.

He had no choice but to keep going. If he stayed where he was, the rifleman was going to blow him out of the saddle. He heeled the roan into a gallop again and hung on for dear life as choking clouds of ashes and dust rose around them.

"Stovepipe," Wilbur whispered in anguish at leaving his friend behind even though the lanky cowboy was already dead.

A couple more slugs whined past Wilbur's head then he didn't hear any more. He figured he was finally out of range. The bushwhacker must have been using a Sharps for the shots to carry that far, he thought.

He didn't stop until he reached the far side of Eagle Flats. Feeling had returned to his left leg and it throbbed in agony with each beat of his heart. As he reined in, Wilbur reached down, expecting to find his pant leg soaked with blood, but instead it was dry. He moved his hand up to his hip and searched for the wound. He didn't find that, either.

What he found was a rip in the thick leather of his gunbelt. To his amazement, Wilbur realized he hadn't been wounded after all. The heavy slug had struck him a glancing blow that failed to penetrate the gunbelt. Even so, it had been enough to almost cripple him.

Despair welled up inside him. He turned his horse and looked back out across the flats, searching for Stovepipe and the paint.

They were gone. The paint had continued running and was out of sight. Wilbur had no way of knowing where they had gone. If he rode back out there to search, he would be putting himself right back in the sights of that bushwhacker.

With the bitter taste of ashes and defeat on his tongue, Wilbur turned the roan toward the Three Rivers headquarters.

Chapter Thirty-one

When Stovepipe came to, he didn't know where he was or what had happened to him. All he knew was that some blacksmith from hell seemed to be hammering out a horseshoe, and the anvil was the inside of his skull.

Something brushed against the side of his face and tickled. He moved his head to get away from whatever it was, and that imp of a blacksmith started whaling away harder with his hammer. Stovepipe groaned.

A moment later, something wet nudged insistently against his cheek. Despite the pain, he turned his head again, but whatever was bumping against him kept doing it.

Finally, the knowledge that he wasn't dead soaked into his brain. He forced his eyes open and found himself looking up into the eyes of his paint.

The horse snuffled its lips against his cheek again and bumped its snout against him.

The paint was trying to wake him up, Stovepipe realized. How in blazes wasn't he dead? That blasted bushwhacker had shot him in the head. Thinking about the bushwhacker jogged the rest of the memories back into place for Stovepipe. He remembered starting across Eagle Flats with Wilbur. Dax Coolidge had been their prisoner . . . until he had been shot in the back and killed. Stovepipe and Wilbur had tried to get away, but Stovepipe had been hit . . .

"Wilbur," Stovepipe muttered. He wanted to know if his friend was still alive. The only way to find out was to get up and start moving around again, even if it hurt like hell.

With the paint still hovering over him, Stovepipe reached up and got hold of the horse's headstall. The paint tried to pull away, but Stovepipe hung on tight and let the horse lift him. He got his feet underneath him, pushed up, and stood next to the paint. The smell of blood coming from Stovepipe seemed to make the horse more nervous than usual.

Stovepipe hung on for a few moments while his head settled down and the world stopped spinning crazily. As he got his wits back about him, he reached up to find out just how badly he was hurt and winced. In the hair just above his right ear, his fingertips explored a sticky gash on the side of his head. Just touching it made the mad throbbing inside his skull worse, but he realized the bullet had just grazed him. The heavy-caliber bullet had packed so much punch it had felt like his head was smashed to pieces.

He had bled like a stuck pig, too, he thought as he touched the drying blood all over the side of his face. Head wounds always bled a lot, even the nonfatal ones, and this one had been particularly gory. He figured he looked a pretty grisly sight but didn't think he was going to die from it, so he wasn't going to worry about the injury. He had more important things on his mind, like trying to find Wilbur.

Still leaning on the paint for support, Stovepipe looked around. He was still out on Eagle Flats but couldn't see the burned area, which meant the paint had traveled for quite a distance before its senseless rider had finally fallen off . . . into a dried sage plant. That was what had been tickling his face when he woke up.

His searching gaze went from horizon to horizon without seeing any sign of Wilbur. Stovepipe's heart sank. His friend might well be dead, cut down by the same drygulcher who had wounded him.

The pain in his head had subsided slightly, and he forced his thoughts into more productive channels. Studying the hills on both sides of the flats gave him a rough idea of where he was—a couple miles north of the area Coolidge had burned. If he was going to start looking for Wilbur, he needed to head south.

Climbing into the saddle seemed like a formidable task, but Stovepipe knew he had no choice. "Steady there, old hoss," he told the paint. "I know you're a mite spooked on account of I probably smell like a slaughterhouse, but this ain't the time to cut any capers."

He got a foot in the stirrup, held on tight to the horn, and swung up into the saddle. The paint moved around a little, which caused Stovepipe's head to spin again, but it settled down after a moment. He took up the reins and said, "All right. Let's go."

Every time a hoof hit the ground, a fresh jolt of pain went through his skull. He ignored them as best he could and kept moving. As he rode south, the hills began to look more familiar, and he knew his guess about the location was correct. After a while, the large burned area came into sight.

Off to the east, he spotted a horse grazing. As he rode closer, he recognized Coolidge's mount, but he didn't see the gunfighter. He left the horse and headed toward the hills.

He found Coolidge's body before he reached them. The piece of rope holding him on the horse had given out. Broken pieces of it were still attached to each ankle. Coolidge had been busted up quite a bit by being dragged, but he hadn't bled all that much. The only really bloody place on his clothes was on the back of his shirt where he'd been shot. Stovepipe figured that the gunman was already dead while he was bouncing along tied to the horse, his heart stilled by the high-caliber round that had cored through it.

Coolidge wouldn't be answering any questions, but that didn't mean Stovepipe was at the end of the trail. Somebody had lurked in those hills and taken advantage of the opportunity to ambush them. The fact that Coolidge had been shot first told Stovepipe it hadn't been a rescue attempt. Above all else, the rifleman had wanted to make sure that Coolidge died.

To Stovepipe, that smacked of an effort to be certain Coolidge wouldn't talk. The gunfighter's allies, whoever they were, hadn't been exactly loyal to him.

Having seen no sign of Wilbur, Stovepipe was starting to hope the redhead had gotten away. He knew that under normal circumstances, Wilbur would never desert him, no matter what. But . . . if Wilbur had seen him shot in the head, had seen all that blood covering his face, and been convinced he was dead, it was possible he might have lit a shuck.

In that situation, he just might have headed back to the Three Rivers to fetch help.

Since he couldn't be sure of that, Stovepipe wasn't going to wait around for anybody to show up. He squinted at the hills to the east.

That blasted bushwhacker had been up there somewhere, lurking around until he could carry out his deadly errand. He was bound to have left a trail when he rode off, satisfied that at least Coolidge was dead, anyway.

Stovepipe intended to find that trail.

Wilbur thought he might run into some of the Three Rivers punchers before he got all the way back to headquarters, but as luck would have it, he didn't. It was the middle of the afternoon when he rode in. Most of the crew was out on the range somewhere else.

Rosaleen and Aunt Sinead were home, as was Asa. The two women and the old wrangler stepped out of the house and barn, respectively, to see who was riding in. Rosaleen realized something was wrong as soon as she saw Wilbur, hatless and riding stiffly because of the pain in his left hip and leg.

"Wilbur!" she exclaimed as she rushed down the steps. "Where's Stovepipe?"

"Dead," Wilbur said in a voice strained with painful emotion. "He was bushwhacked and shot in the head."

Rosaleen stopped short, gasped, and brought a hand to her mouth in horror. "Dead?" she repeated in a half-whisper, clearly unable or at least unwilling to accept it.

"I reckon so."

Asa had reached the side of Wilbur's roan. He reached up and said, "Let me give you a hand there, son."

With the wrangler's help, Wilbur climbed down from the saddle.

Rosaleen couldn't help but see how awkwardly he was moving. "You've been hurt, too."

"It's nothing," Wilbur said in a gruff voice. He touched his gunbelt where the thick leather was torn. "A slug glanced off my hip and banged it up a mite. I'll be all right. All the crew out working?"

"That's right. Dad and Vance are with them." Rosaleen paused. "Did you find Coolidge?"

"We found him, all right."

"And . . . and he's the one who killed Stovepipe?"

Wilbur shook his head. "No, that was somebody else, some bushwhacker we never even caught a glimpse of. He killed Coolidge first, then shot Stovepipe. Nearly ventilated me." He took a deep breath. "I need to round up the other fellas. We can go back over there, maybe pick up the varmint's trail. Somebody . . . somebody will need to bring in Stovepipe . . . and Coolidge, too, I suppose. I'll just get a fresh horse—"

"You won't do any such thing," Rosaleen broke in. "You can barely stay on your feet, Wilbur."

"Rosaleen is right, Mr. Coleman." Aunt Sinead had come down from the porch to join them. "You need to come inside. I'll give you some coffee with a nice jolt of Irish whiskey in it, and I should probably take a look at that injury, too, just to make sure you're not hurt worse than you think you are."

"Blast it," he said, "I need to fetch the hands—"

"I'll do that," Rosaleen said. "Asa, saddle a horse for me while I go get my riding gear on."

The old wrangler looked and sounded hesitant as he said, "I dunno, Miss Rosaleen—"

"Dad's not here and neither is Andy Callahan . . . or Vance, for that matter. That means *I'm* in charge."

"Do what she says, Asa," Aunt Sinead said. "She's just going out on Three Rivers range to look for her father and the other men. That shouldn't be dangerous."

"I dunno," Asa said again. "Bushwhackers runnin' around and folks gettin' shot . . . seems like all hell's bustin' loose, ladies, if you'll pardon my French."

"It's busting loose, all right," Wilbur said. "And after what happened to Stovepipe, I intend to see that it blows sky high."

CHAPTER THIRTY-TWO

A short time later, Rosaleen was on her way, riding hard toward the south where most of the crew was working. Vance and her father were there, and she wanted to see both of them very much. She was upset at the news Wilbur had brought, and it would help to see the two men she cared the most about in the world.

She hadn't really thought about it, but even though she had known Vance for only a couple weeks, he had risen to that level in her estimation. Sure, she'd been angry with him for lying about who he really was, but she had known from the first she would forgive him for that . . . as soon as enough time had passed. Evidently, she had reached that point, because she really wanted him to put his arms around her and tell her everything was going to be all right.

It seemed impossible to believe Stovepipe Stewart was gone. Rosaleen hadn't known him all that much longer than she'd known Vance, but even so, she had grown quite fond of him. Already, he had become like an uncle to her. Despite his easy drawl and low-key manner, he had such a commanding presence that any time he was around he made everyone feel like things were under control.

Rosaleen wasn't sure she would ever feel that way again.

She came in sight of several men on horseback and recognized them as Three Rivers punchers. As she rode up to them, they touched the brims of their hats and nodded to her.

She didn't have time for pleasantries. "Where are my father and Mr. Armbrister?"

"Last time we saw 'em, they were over yonder about half a mile," one of the cowboys said as he pointed to the west. "Is somethin' wrong, Miss Rosaleen?"

She didn't answer, galloping off in the direction the man had indicated. A few minutes later she found Vance and her father riding together, hazing a small bunch of cattle along one of the streams.

"Rosaleen, honey, what's wrong?" Malone greeted her as she galloped up to them.

"Mr. Stewart's been killed," she said bluntly.

"Stovepipe!" Vance exclaimed. "No!"

Rosaleen nodded. "Mr. Coleman brought the bad news back to the house. They found Dax Coolidge over in the hills east of Eagle Flats and captured him, then someone ambushed them and killed Coolidge and Stovepipe. Wilbur barely got away."

Malone couldn't stop the curses that erupted from his mouth. Vance was silent, but he got a grim and determined look on his face.

When Malone paused, Vance said, "Does Wilbur know who ambushed them?"

Rosaleen shook her head. "They never got a look at him. He shot Coolidge first, so Wilbur thinks the man's real goal was to shut him up. They were bringing Coolidge back here to question him about who he's been working for."

"We all know the answer to that!" Malone said. "Rafter M! Cabot's behind this, sure as hell! He probably had a man watchin' Coolidge with orders to shut him up if he got caught."

Vance nodded. "That makes sense." He sighed. "Stovepipe . . . I can't believe he's dead. He just seemed . . . I don't know . . . indestructible, like he'd just go on forever."

"We can't let Cabot and his bunch get away with this," Malone said. "So far, everything they've done has been bad enough, but now they've killed one of us. We can't let that stand."

"No, we can't," Vance agreed. He looked up at the sky. "It'll be dark before we can round up all the men and get back to the ranch. But that's all right. Cabot probably won't expect us to do anything once night has fallen."

"Are you sayin' what I think you're sayin', son?"

"I'm saying every man needs to strap on a gun and fill his pockets with ammunition. The Three Rivers crew is riding tonight . . . and we're going to rain down hell on Rafter M!"

Stovepipe had a pretty good idea where he, Wilbur, and Coolidge had been when the ambush took place. Judging from that, he estimated the bushwhacker's line of fire. His eyes followed that mental line and saw that it ran almost across the top of a knoll covered with boulders, brush, and trees. He nodded. That was close enough to be within the margin of error, and the knoll was certainly a good place for the hidden rifleman to have lurked while he drew a bead on Coolidge's back.

Stovepipe headed for that brushy height. The terrain forced him to weave back and forth some, but it didn't take him long to reach the knoll. He dismounted and went up the slope on foot, leading the paint.

His head still hurt, but having a puzzle to solve always distracted him from whatever physical woes he might be suffering. This case was no different. He ignored the pain and concentrated on searching for the trail he hoped to find.

At the top of the knoll, he hunkered on his heels and studied the ground. It was too rocky to take many prints, but as he looked around, he spotted something gleaming in the late afternoon sunlight and reached under a bush to pull out a long brass cartridge case.

It was from a .50 caliber round, all right. Considering the distance and the accuracy the bushwhacker had displayed, Stovepipe had had a hunch the man was using a Sharps buffalo gun. This confirmed it. There was a good reason for calling a rifle like that a Big Fifty.

Stovepipe didn't find any other shells. He figured the ambusher had picked up the rest of them but missed this one because it had rolled under the bush. A few more minutes of searching turned up the butt of a quirly, which meant nothing—most men rolled their own instead of smoking store-boughts—but it was another indication that someone had waited there for a while.

Standing up, Stovepipe turned and looked out across Eagle Flats. The marksman had had a perfect field of fire from up there. Killing Coolidge with one round had been good shooting. Coming so close to ventilating the two range detectives while they were on the move was even better. But Stovepipe had survived, and since he hadn't seen any sign of Wilbur, he hoped his partner had, too.

Stovepipe led the paint down the far side of the hill. He found hoofprints under a tree at the bottom of the slope where the bushwhacker had left his horse. Stovepipe grunted as he looked at the prints. He recognized them, which came as no real surprise.

He had seen these same hoofprints before, more than once.

Stovepipe roamed around until he found tracks leading away from the spot then mounted up and followed the trail deeper into the hills. The bushwhacker had headed northeast.

That wasn't the way to Rafter M headquarters, Stovepipe mused. That didn't surprise him, either, since he had never been convinced Mort Cabot was behind all the trouble. Blaming Cabot for everything was just too damned convenient, in Stovepipe's opinion.

The sun continued to sink toward the mountains in the west. Stovepipe felt frustration growing inside him. He didn't know how long he lain unconscious in the sage, but it seemed likely the bushwhacker had a good-sized lead on him. He probably wouldn't be able to catch up before nightfall, and in the rugged terrain he couldn't hope to track his quarry in the dark.

While it was still daylight, he would close the gap as much as he could. He had forgotten all about the ache in his head as he focused his attention on following the sign the bushwhacker had left behind. The man hadn't been very careful about covering his trail. More than likely, he had figured he was safe from any pursuit.

That sort of overconfidence could prove fatal.

Stovepipe still hadn't caught up when the shadows of dusk settled down over the landscape. He followed the trail as long as he could but finally had to rein in and heave an exasperated sigh. He would have to wait until morning to resume his task. Wandering all over those hills in the dark wouldn't accomplish anything.

He leaned forward, patted the paint on the shoulder, and said quietly, "Looks like you'll get to rest up for a spell, old hoss."

Suddenly, he lifted his head sharply and sniffed the air. It carried a faint tang of smoke. He might not be able to *see* well enough to trail anymore, but he could still follow his nose.

Somebody had built a campfire up above him. There was no guarantee it was the man who had shot him and killed Dax Coolidge . . . but who else would be roaming around those hills tonight?

"Sorry, son," he told the horse. "Looks like we ain't stoppin' just yet, after all."

He rode forward slowly, trying not to make too much noise. Sound carried at night, and Stovepipe didn't want whoever had made that camp to know anyone was around until he was sure who it was.

The smell of smoke grew stronger. Stovepipe tracked it just as he had the smoke from Coolidge's campfire earlier that day. When he thought he was close enough, he tied the paint's reins to a sapling and went ahead on foot. Too close and the quarry's horse might scent the paint and raise a ruckus, warning the man someone else was around.

When Stovepipe was close enough to hear the faint crackling of flames from the campfire, he dropped to hands and knees and crawled forward until he could peer through a small gap in some brush. He saw the glow of the fire, which had been built in front of a huge outcropping of rock.

A horse was picketed over to one side. The animal had been unsaddled, and lying next to the saddle on the ground was a scabbard containing a Sharps buffalo gun. As far as Stovepipe was concerned, that was proof positive he had found the bushwhacker.

As he watched, a man walked over to the fire and hunkered down beside it to put a coffeepot at the edge of the flames. The man's hat was pushed back on curly dark hair. The reddish light from the fire revealed an angular, lantern-jawed face. Stovepipe had seen the man first in the Silver Star saloon and on a few occasions since then, in Wagontongue. He didn't know the man's name, but he knew who he was.

The bushwhacker was one of Sheriff Charlie Jerrico's deputies. He was so confident no one would find him up here, he hadn't even removed his badge.

Before Stovepipe could do anything else, the thud of hoofbeats drifted to him through the night air. The deputy heard it, too, and moved his hand to rest on the butt of the revolver at his hip.

Someone was coming.

CHAPTER THIRTY-THREE

Vance hadn't calmed down any by the time they got back to the ranch house. He still couldn't believe Stovepipe was dead. In a short period of time, the two range detectives had become his best friends. They had saved his life several times, and saved the life of the woman he loved as well.

And now Stovepipe was gone. Someone had to pay for that. Since Mort Cabot was the most likely person to be responsible for the ambush, that put him squarely in Vance's sights.

At least, it would before the night was over, Vance vowed as he rode in at the head of the group of cowboys, along with Keenan Malone.

Wilbur limped onto the front porch as the men rode up.

Vance dismounted and hurried to the stocky redhead's side. He gripped Wilbur's shoulder and said, "Is it true?"

"Yeah, I'm afraid so," Wilbur said, nodding. "Shot in the head and bleeding like that, I don't see how he could have survived."

Vance frowned. "But you didn't actually see his dead body? Didn't check to see if he was breathing or his heart was beating?"

"Damn it! Don't you think I've been kicking myself ever since I got back for not doing exactly that? That bushwhacker had a bead on me, though. He'd already come within a fraction of an inch of shooting me out of the saddle a couple times. And by the time I finally got out of range, Stovepipe's horse had run off and I didn't know where they'd gone."

"I'm sorry, Wilbur," Vance said. "I know I sounded like I was blaming you, and I didn't mean to."

"It's all right." Wilbur sighed. "I'm blaming myself, and I reckon I always will be from now on." He squared his shoulders as Malone joined them on the porch. "What are you going to do?"

"We're ridin' on the Rafter M. I figure we'll go fast, hit 'em hard, take over the place, and then put a gun to Mort Cabot's head and make him confess to all the evildoin' he's responsible for."

"And then?"

"I reckon a rope and a tree limb will do just fine for the son of a bitch."

Vance said, "Hold on. I agree we're going to ride over to the Rafter M and put a stop to this trouble once and for all, but I don't know about lynching Cabot." He shook his head. "I admit, when I first heard Stovepipe was dead, I would have gone along with that and never complained. I've had time to think about it a little, though. I'm still not sure we shouldn't turn Cabot over to the law once he confesses."

"And if he don't confess?" Malone asked with a challenging jut of his jaw.

"If it comes down to a fight . . . don't hold back," Vance said. "Whatever happens, I'm taking the responsibility for it."

"The hell you are! You may own the place someday, but I'm still the manager of this spread." Malone turned to look at Andy Callahan, who still sat his horse in front of the porch. "Andy, tell the boys to grab their guns and throw their saddles on fresh horses. Time's a-wastin'!"

Callahan nodded curtly. "You got it, boss." He turned his horse and rode toward the bunkhouse, where the other cowboys were waiting.

"I'm coming with you," Wilbur declared.

Rosaleen asked, "What did Aunt Sinead say about your injury?"

"I've got a good-sized bruise on my hip already," Wilbur replied with a shrug. "It's sore, and the leg's stiff. But there's no reason I can't sit a saddle, and my gun hand's not hurt a bit. I owe it to Stovepipe."

"Then I'm coming, too," Rosaleen said.

"The hell you are!" her father said.

"You're not coming, Rosaleen, and that's final," Vance added.

"He saved my life. He saved Vance's life more than once. And I'm a good shot with my carbine." She glared at Vance. "And who are you to make decisions for me, Vance Armbrister?"

"I'm the man who loves you, that's who," he answered without hesitation.

"You listen to the boy," Malone said. "He's right."

Rosaleen looked back and forth between them and said, "So you're ganging up on me."

"Looking out for your safety, that's all," Vance said. "We don't have time for this argument, Rosaleen."

"The boy's right. We got to get ready to ride."

She let out a clearly frustrated sigh. "All right. I don't want to waste a lot of everybody's time. Just put an end to this—"

"We intend to," Malone said.

"And stay safe."

"I don't reckon we can promise that," Vance said.

Rosaleen turned to Wilbur. "Look out for these two, will you? They're stubborn as mules."

"I would, but right now I'm feeling pretty mule-headed myself," Wilbur said. "I've got a score to settle . . . for Stovepipe."

Stovepipe didn't move and barely breathed as the rider came up to the deputy's camp. The newcomer was mounted on a big chestnut. The deputy seemed to relax at the sight of it. Whoever the rider was, the deputy recognized him and had expected to see him.

As the newcomer reined in and swung down from his saddle, the deputy stood up and said, "Howdy, Garrity."

"MacDonald." The man's voice was cool and businesslike. He wore a buckskin shirt and a brown hat and had a close-cropped, reddish-brown beard. "I saw your signal fire earlier. You got a message for me from the boss?"

"You bet I do. He was here a little while ago and had plenty to say."

Hidden in the brush, Stovepipe frowned. He was

close to finding the mastermind behind all the trouble. Even though he had a pretty good idea who that was, proof would be nice.

"You want some coffee first?" MacDonald went on.

For a second Garrity looked like he was going to refuse, but then he shrugged and said, "Why not?"

"Let me get another cup."

While MacDonald was digging in his saddlebags for a tin cup, Garrity squatted beside the fire and warmed his hands. It wasn't a particularly cold night, but at that elevation the air had a nip to it once the sun went down, no matter what time of year it was.

The pause gave Stovepipe time to think. Something about the name *Garrity* was familiar to him. He rifled through all the information he had stored in his brain and after a moment came up with a first name to go with the last one: *Cort.*

Months back, in a U.S. marshal's office over in the Dakotas where he and Wilbur had been working on a different case, Stovepipe had seen a wanted poster with Cort Garrity's name on it, as well as a description that matched the man hunkered by the fire. Garrity was an outlaw and killer, wanted in numerous states and territories for murder, rustling, train robbery, and assorted other crimes. He had been reported to be the leader of a gang of desperadoes who were almost as bad as he was.

In other words, just the sort of men who'd be good at stirring up trouble between a couple ranchers and playing the two cattle barons against each other.

MacDonald came back to the fire with two cups. Using a piece of leather to protect his hand as he picked up the coffeepot, he filled both cups with the strong black brew.

Garrity took one of them, sipped, and made a face. "It ain't exactly good, but I suppose I've had worse."

"That's what I told the last whore I was with." MacDonald threw back his head and laughed more than the jest deserved.

Stovepipe's jaw clenched. Mere hours earlier, he had been wounded—had come within a whisker of dying, in fact—Dax Coolidge had been killed, and for all Stovepipe knew, Wilbur had been slain, too, although he hoped with all his heart that wasn't the case. All at the hands of McDonald—the man sitting there drinking coffee and making jokes about whores.

Stovepipe had never considered blowing a hole in a man without giving him a fair shake, but if he was ever going to, that might have been the time.

He shoved that thought out of his head and re turned his attention to what MacDonald and Garrity were saying.

"What is it the boss wants us to do next?" Garrity asked. "Steal some cattle from the Rafter M? It's been a while since we hit Cabot." The outlaw chuckled. "Wouldn't want the old bastard to feel neglected."

"Naw. Things are comin' to a head, Garrity. I killed Coolidge this afternoon."

Garrity's bushy red eyebrows rose in surprise. "Coolidge?" he repeated. "Why in the hell did you kill Coolidge? He's working for the same fella we are, or at least he was."

MacDonald took a sip of his coffee, then said, "I don't know what you were complainin' about. This tastes just fine to me."

Garrity waved a hand. "Forget about the damn coffee and answer my question."

"I killed Coolidge because he'd outlived his usefulness and the boss didn't trust him not to talk," MacDonald answered. His jovial voice had turned cold and hard. "Besides, he'd been captured by a couple Three Rivers men. Stewart and Coleman." The deputy frowned. "I don't trust those two. There's somethin' off about 'em"—he shrugged—"but I don't suppose I have to worry about them anymore. Not about Stewart, anyway. I killed him, too."

"Well, hell, it sounds like you've been on a butcherin' spree. What about Coleman?"

"I let him go."

A wave of relief went through Stovepipe. But it wasn't *exactly* true, he thought. MacDonald had been trying to kill Wilbur, too. In the conversation he'd had with his boss, he must have made it sound like he'd let Wilbur go on purpose to excuse his failure to kill both range detectives.

Stovepipe was so glad to hear Wilbur was still alive he had to force himself to concentrate in order to hear what MacDonald said next.

"With Stewart dead, all hell's likely to break loose now. When they hear about it, Malone and the Armbrister kid will fly off the handle and head for the Rafter M with the whole crew."

"What's that have to do with me and my boys?" Garrity wanted to know.

"The boss wants you to go back to the hideout, get everybody together, and ride for the Rafter M. If you can head off the bunch from the Three Rivers, take care of them and then go on to the Rafter M and do the same there. If Malone and his men get there first, they can shoot it out with Cabot's crew, and then you can swoop in and wipe out whoever's left."

"Then this is the big cleanup," Garrity said.

"Damn right. The boss figures we might as well go ahead and turn this to our advantage. One way or another, he wants every man from the Three Rivers and the Rafter M dead by morning."

CHAPTER THIRTY-FOUR

A chill went through Stovepipe at the deputy's words. Once again he thought about how he had never shot anyone from ambush . . . but if there was ever a time to do so, it was now. Chances were, he could draw his gun and kill both MacDonald and Garrity before they had a chance to fight back. Both men were cold-blooded murderers and deserved to die. With both of them dead, their boss's orders to wipe out everyone from the Three Rivers and the Rafter M would never be delivered.

Those were good reasons, good enough to make Stovepipe reach down to his hip and close his hand around the well-worn walnut grips of his Colt.

Then more hoofbeats sounded close by in the night.

MacDonald dropped his coffee cup and came quickly to his feet like a snake uncoiling. His hand flashed to his gun.

Garrity stayed where he was and said sharply, "Take it easy. Those are just a couple of my men."

"What are they doin' here?" the deputy wanted to

know. "You usually come alone when I've got a message for you."

"No rule says I have to," Garrity snapped. "I wasn't expecting to see a signal from you tonight. Didn't know what was going on. For all I knew, things had gone to hell and we all needed to hightail it out of these parts." He shrugged. "So I brought a couple men with me, just in case."

The riders reined to a halt at the edge of the circle of light cast by the fire

One of them asked, "Everything all right here, Cort?"

"Yeah." Garrity straightened and tossed what was left of his coffee into the fire, where it sizzled among the flames. "The boss has run out of patience. We're moving in and taking over both ranches."

"Damn well about time," the second outlaw said. "I never liked the whole idea of proddin' them into wiping out each other. Too many things might go wrong with that plan. It never pays to be too fancy."

"Hey, it's come mighty close to workin'," MacDonald said in protest. "We're just seizin' the opportunity to speed things up a little."

Garrity grunted. "Whatever you say." He headed for his horse. "Come on, boys. There's plenty of work to do before morning."

Hidden in the brush, Stovepipe took his hand off his gun. The arrival of the other two outlaws had changed things. Even with surprise on his side, four against one made for steep odds. Too steep. He could kill some of them, but they would get lead in him, too.

And if he died there, the attack on the Rafter M would go on as planned. He had to survive in order to get back to the Three Rivers, let Wilbur and the others know he was still alive, and stop them from riding into the trap.

He stayed where he was as Cort Garrity mounted up and rode off with his two men.

Once they were gone, MacDonald picked up the cup he had dropped, shook out the dregs from it, and refilled it. He looked very satisfied with himself as he sat there sipping the coffee. After a few minutes, he said out loud, "Reckon I can head back to town now. This was a pretty good day's work, if I do say so myself. Won't be long now until I've got more money than I've ever seen at one time before. I can afford to get myself a really *good* whore for a change!"

Stovepipe could still hear the hoofbeats of the outlaws' horses fading into the distance. If he made a move against MacDonald and gunplay erupted, Garrity and the others would come rushing back to see what was going on. Stovepipe knew he had to wait, although the delay gnawed at him.

By the time MacDonald finished the coffee, Stovepipe couldn't hear Garrity and the others anymore. They probably weren't completely out of earshot yet, but they would be before too much longer. He bided his time while MacDonald stowed away the cups and prepared for the return trip to Wagontongue.

Stovepipe waited until MacDonald had his hands full lifting the saddle onto the chestnut's back before he stepped out of the brush, lined his Colt on the crooked deputy, and said, "Hold it right there, mister. Try anything funny and I'll blow your spine in two."

The unmistakable menace in Stovepipe's voice froze MacDonald right where he was. Without looking around, he said, "Who the hell—"

"A ghost, I reckon you could say."

"Stewart?" MacDonald turned his head enough to see over his shoulder. "But you're dead!"

"Not hardly," Stovepipe said. "Go ahead and put that saddle on your horse, but keep both hands on it."

MacDonald did as Stovepipe ordered.

"Now, use your left hand and reach over to take your gun out of its holster. Make sure it's nice and easylike, or I'll pull the trigger."

The deputy lowered his left arm and moved his hand toward his gun the way Stovepipe had told him. Then he paused. "I can't reach it like this. Can't I take my right hand off the saddle so I can turn a little more? I'll keep my arm up."

"Careful," Stovepipe warned.

MacDonald raised his right arm and twisted his body as he reached for the gun again with his left hand.

Suddenly he whirled around and whipped his right arm toward Stovepipe. Seeing something flicker redly in the firelight, Stovepipe jerked to the side and pulled the trigger. The Colt blasted as the knife MacDonald had thrown flew past his right ear, missing by only a couple inches. The small blade had been hidden up his sleeve.

The bullet flew over MacDonald's head as he had already ducked. He threw himself forward in a diving tackle aimed at Stovepipe's legs and rammed into the range detective's knees. Stovepipe went over backwards to crash into the brush.

For the second time that day, Stovepipe found himself in a desperate hand-to-hand battle. MacDonald scrambled up and grabbed the wrist of Stovepipe's gun hand. He shoved the Colt to the side while aiming a punch at Stovepipe's face. Stovepipe turned his head to avoid the blow and threw a left that caught MacDonald on the jaw and knocked him to the side. MacDonald didn't loosen his grip on Stovepipe's wrist, though.

The two men thrashed in the brush as they struggled for the upper hand. Losing so much blood earlier in the day had left Stovepipe weaker than usual, and he was still a little loopy from the head injury. MacDonald had a lot of strength packed into his wiry frame. All things being equal, the two men would have been evenly matched.

As it was, Stovepipe was at a disadvantage, and the crooked deputy fought to seize that opportunity. MacDonald had to know his freedom and probably his very life were at stake.

A wicked hook slammed into Stovepipe's midsection. He gasped for breath but got his left hand locked around MacDonald's throat. When he rolled over, MacDonald went with him and wound up on the bottom. Aware he might be running out of time, Stovepipe bore down, trying to choke the deputy into unconsciousness.

It was possible Garrity and the other outlaws had heard that shot and were on their way back to the camp. Stovepipe needed to end the fight as quickly as he could.

MacDonald's knee rose and dug into Stovepipe's stomach. The brutal blow made Stovepipe's grip slip just enough for MacDonald to tear free. He risked letting go of Stovepipe's gun hand and rocketed a hard right to his jaw. The slugging punch knocked Stovepipe off him.

As Stovepipe fell to the side, MacDonald jerked his leg up and snapped it out in a kick. His boot heel caught Stovepipe on the right wrist, making the gun fly out of his hand. MacDonald swarmed after him, kicking and punching.

Stovepipe's injury had dulled his reactions, leaving him unable to block all the blows. A couple smashed into his head. Coupled with the damage the bullet graze had already done, that was too much. Stovepipe's head spun crazily and his strength deserted him. MacDonald hit him again, and Stovepipe slumped back in a limp heap.

He didn't pass out entirely. He was aware of what was going on. As MacDonald took hold of his ankles and dragged him closer to the fire, something jabbed painfully into Stovepipe's hip and brought him out of his stupor.

The crooked deputy picked up the gun Stovepipe had dropped and stuck it behind his belt. With that done, he turned toward Stovepipe and laughed. "You're mighty stubborn, Stewart. By all rights, you ought to be dead. What happened? That bullet just graze your skull?"

Stovepipe summoned enough strength to push himself up on an elbow. He shook his head groggily and said, "Yeah. You came close, mister, but no see-gar."

"I could say the same about you. Maybe you tracked me up here, but it ain't gonna do you any good. Everybody already thinks you're dead, and pretty soon that's what you're gonna be."

"Reckon you'll find a ravine to dump my carcass in, so Jerrico won't ever know I got away the first time after all." Stovepipe had two reasons for saying that. He was trying to slide his other hand under his hip without MacDonald noticing, so he needed to stall and distract the deputy. And if he could surprise

MacDonald into confirming his theory, so much the better.

MacDonald frowned. "So you know about the sheriff bein' the boss. Reckon that's no real surprise, me bein' his deputy and all."

"Is everybody who wears a badge in Wagontongue really an outlaw?"

That brought a laugh from MacDonald. "Naw. Just me and Cousin Charlie."

"You and Jerrico are cousins?" Stovepipe knew MacDonald was a garrulous sort and counted on that.

"Sure. Garrity's kin, too, although more of the shirt-tail sort. I ain't sure how he's related, exactly. We all rode together when we were kids, before Charlie decided to pin on a badge and ride the law-and-order trail."

"So Jerrico really was an honest lawman?"

"For a while," MacDonald answered with a shrug. "But a fella can't escape his breedin' forever. Garrity and his bunch drifted over here when things got too hot for 'em in the Dakotas. He sized things up and saw there were two big spreads hereabouts just ripe for lootin'. He thought Cousin Charlie and me would throw in with him, but Charlie said he'd only do it if he was the boss of the operation and we did things his way. Said he'd built up some trust among the folks around here and didn't want to ruin it in case things went bad. So that's what we did. Nobody ever figured a couple star packers were tied up with all the rustlin' and trouble-makin'."

"I did," Stovepipe said. "I've known it for quite a while now."

"The hell you say! Ain't no way you could've."

"Sure there is. The shoe on your horse's left hind

hoof has got a peculiar nick on it. I spotted it on some of the tracks you left behind when you and Garrity's bunch tried to rustle those cattle from the Three Rivers a week or so ago. You were one of the varmints who got away. When I saw the same hoofprint later on in the corral behind the sheriff's office in Wagontongue, I knew there had to be a connection. Then Jerrico found an excuse to turn Coolidge loose. I reckon it happened the way he said it did, but if it hadn't, he would've found some other way. I've been suspectin' Jerrico was the ringleader for a while now, and thanks to you, I know for sure."

MacDonald scowled and reached for the gun he had shoved behind his belt. "That knowledge ain't gonna do you a damn bit of good, Stewart, because I'm fixin' to blow a hole through you with your own six-shooter!"

He jerked the gun out and swung the barrel toward Stovepipe.

CHAPTER THIRTY-FIVE

Even as flame spouted from the gun muzzle, Stovepipe was on the move. He wasn't quite as weak and addled as he'd been making out while he talked to MacDonald. He had been in pretty bad shape when the outlaw deputy dragged him, but as soon as he realized what was poking his hip, he had kept the conversation going as he tried to get his hand on the knife without MacDonald noticing.

Stovepipe wasn't as good with a knife as he was with a gun, but he was better than most men. As he rolled swiftly to the side and the shot MacDonald fired kicked up dirt and stone mere inches from him, his arm flashed up and back and then forward. The knife spun through the air in a perfect throw that ended with MacDonald's own blade buried in his throat.

MacDonald pulled the trigger again as he staggered back a step, but his gun hand had already sagged and the slug went into the ground between him and Stovepipe. With his left hand, he pawed at the knife's handle, got hold of it, and pulled it free.

That was a mistake. Blood fountained from the

wound, spraying out several feet in front of him. The odds were he wouldn't have survived anyway, but that action cinched it. MacDonald made a gagging, choking noise as dark crimson continued to well from his throat. He dropped the gun and it thudded to the ground.

His knees buckled, and he pitched forward onto his face. A pool of blood began to form under his head as it continued to leak from his body.

Stovepipe pushed himself to his feet and stood there without moving for a few moments until his legs steadied underneath him. A lot of blood had been spilled—his own, Dax Coolidge's, and now MacDonald's. Somehow Stovepipe was still alive, and the other two weren't. He felt pretty good about that.

He didn't have time to congratulate himself on surviving. Cort Garrity was on his way to ambush the Three Rivers crew as they rode toward the Rafter M. If that didn't prove possible, Garrity would wait until the cowboys from the two ranches had shot it out and then kill anyone who lived through the battle.

Stovepipe knew he was the only one who could head off that massacre.

He left MacDonald's body where it had fallen and picked up his gun. He pouched the iron and then returned to the spot where he had left the paint.

"More work for both of us, old hoss," he told the animal as he settled into the saddle. "Reckon we'll get to rest for a spell one of these days. Right now, though, we got to light a shuck. We'll get back to Eagle Flats and head south. Maybe if we move fast enough we can run across Vance and Malone and the other fellas before they get to the Rafter M."

As he rode away from the camp, however, he was

well aware that he was in a race . . . and he was probably starting out behind. Somewhere in the night, Garrity and the other outlaws who worked for Sheriff Charlie Jerrico had already set out on their deadly errand.

Vance, Wilbur, and Keenan Malone rode at the front of the cowboys from the Three Rivers as they headed for the Rafter M. Rosaleen, Aunt Sinead, and Asa had been left behind, but everybody else was going off to war.

Vance worried a little about leaving the ranch practically defenseless, but Malone had assured him that wasn't actually the case.

"Rosaleen's a fine shot, and so's Asa. And Sinead . . . well, I never saw a woman who could handle a double-barreled shotgun like she can. If there's trouble, they can fort up in the bunkhouse. It's sturdy and has just the one door and only a few windows. They'll hold out. But I don't think it'll come to that. Cabot won't be expectin' us."

Vance wasn't sure about that, either. Cabot had to know that one of his men had killed Stovepipe. He would be figuring the Three Rivers would try to avenge their fallen comrade. The code of honor rough frontiersmen followed demanded such a response.

That thought made something tickle at the back of Vance's mind as he rode through the night with nearly two dozen heavily armed fighting men at his back. Something wasn't right . . .

He was riding in the middle, with Malone to his right and Wilbur to his left. Wilbur was a veteran range detective. He had to have encountered all sorts of plots and schemes over the years he and Stovepipe had worked together. Stovepipe might have been the brains of the duo, but that didn't mean Wilbur wasn't experienced and canny.

"Wilbur," Vance said, "I've been thinking. It seems like some of the things that have happened have been mighty convenient."

"You mean like somebody's maneuvered Malone and Cabot into fighting with each other?" the redhead asked.

"That's exactly what I mean!"

"Stovepipe did some pondering along the same lines," Wilbur said. "He didn't have any real proof yet, or at least none he was ready to share with me, but I got the feeling he was leaning in that direction. And you know how Stovepipe's hunches always turned out to be right!"

"If that's true, riding in on the Rafter M with all guns blazing might not be the best idea—"

"What are you two jabberin' about?" Malone broke in.

Earlier, Vance had been just as hot-tempered as the old cattleman, but he'd had a chance to cool off a little and do some thinking. He wasn't sure they were on the right path. "Mr. Malone, attacking Cabot and his men might not be the wisest idea. We could have been tricked—"

"Tricked! Is Stovepipe dead or ain't he?"

"He's dead," Wilbur said grimly, "and I'm gonna settle the score for him. But it could be we're playing right into somebody else's hands, Mr. Malone."

"Who the hell else is there to blame except Cabot?"

"I don't know," Wilbur admitted, "but what if somebody's been playing the two of you against each other?"

"Pshaw! Nobody's that tricky. It'd take a plumb sidewinder to come up with an idea like that."

That simple, straightforward attitude was one good reason such a scheme might work, Vance thought. Men like Malone and Cabot were used to being honest and blunt, even in their hostility toward each other. They couldn't conceive of just how warped some intellects could be. Vance had seen it, though, in big business dealings back east, where no one's word could be trusted about anything.

He might be able to explain that to Malone, given enough time, but at the moment, the most important thing was to throw the brakes on the assault on the Rafter M. They needed to talk things over, investigate further—

Gunfire ripped through the night.

Muzzle flames bloomed in the darkness on both sides of the broad, shallow cut they were riding along. Bullets whined through the air and thudded into flesh and bone. Men grunted and cursed. Horses screamed.

They had ridden into an ambush. That played into the discussion Vance and Wilbur and Malone had been having, but there was no time to think about that with the air filled with lead.

"Head for those trees!" Wilbur yelled as his horse leaped forward. The clump of trees was up ahead on their left, about fifty yards away.

Fifty yards was a long way to go with bullets whining around your head. Vance leaned forward in the saddle and urged his horse into a gallop. Malone thundered along beside him, and behind them came the rest of the crew . . . except for the handful who had already toppled from their saddles, mortally wounded.

Malone suddenly grunted and swayed. Vance reached over to grab his arm and steady him. "Mr. Malone!" he called over the gun-thunder and the hammering hoof-beats. "Are you hit?"

"Keep goin', boy!" Malone said. "Don't worry about me!"

Vance wasn't about to do that. He tightened his grip on Malone's arm and kept riding.

Wilbur had pulled ahead slightly. The redhead had his revolver out and fired back at the gunmen hidden on the ridges of the cut, twisting back and forth in his saddle as he triggered the weapon. It probably wouldn't do any good, but the wild shots might make one or two of the bushwhackers duck for cover and slow down the assault.

Some of the Three Rivers punchers managed to put up a fight, too, as they raced for cover. Wilbur reached the trees and darted among them, followed closely by Vance and Malone. Vance had to let go of Malone's arm to rein his horse to a stop, and as he did the old cattleman toppled from his mount.

Vance was kneeling beside him an instant later, lifting him and asking, "How bad is it, Mr. Malone?"

"Don't know," Malone replied in a strained voice. "I'm hit in the body, but I ain't dead so it didn't get my heart, and I can still breathe so it ain't my lungs. Prop me up against a tree, son, and put a gun in my hand. I'll fight to the end."

Vance didn't doubt that for a second. He got hold of Malone under the arms and positioned him against a tree as the rancher had asked. Even in the thick shadows under the trees, Vance could see the dark stain on Malone's shirt and knew he was bleeding heavily. Such a wound might well be fatal.

But the way things were going, it was entirely possible none of them would live through that night, so with grim resolve Vance pulled Malone's Colt from its holster and pressed the gun into the old man's hand.

"We rode into a trap . . . didn't we?" Malone said. "Looks like you were . . . right after all, Vance. Sorry I was . . . too stubborn to listen to you."

"Don't worry about that. I was just as furious with Cabot as you were, just as ready to attack the Rafter M. And that was just what somebody wanted us to do."

"Too late now . . . all we can do is . . . make 'em pay in blood . . . for their damn trickery . . ."

Malone's head slumped forward and the hand holding the gun fell into his lap. For a terrible moment Vance thought he was dead, but when he pressed a hand against Malone's chest he felt the old heart still beating steadily. The cattleman had just passed out.

Vance stood up and drew his own revolver. Bullets whipped through the branches and thudded into the tree trunks around him. The other survivors from the crew had reached the shelter, such as it was, and were firing back at the ridges on both sides of them.

Vance darted from one tree to another until he found Wilbur crouched behind one of the trunks, cranking off rounds from a Winchester. "Looks like Stovepipe was right," he called to the redhead.

"He usually is," Wilbur said. "I mean, was." His voice caught a little. "Doesn't do us any good now. We're outnumbered and outgunned. These trees will protect us for a while, but if those bushwhackers have enough ammunition, they'll shoot this grove to pieces, sooner or later."

"Do you think it's Cabot and the men from the Rafter M or somebody else?"

Wilbur took another shot, lowered the rifle, and started thumbing fresh rounds from his pocket into the loading gate. "I don't know what to think anymore. All I know is there's a bunch of varmints out there who want us dead—and I'm going to do my damnedest to disappoint them!"

Stovepipe heard the gunfire quite a while before he spotted muzzle flashes in the distance. That gave him something to steer by as he tried to find Wilbur, Vance, and the men from the Three Rivers.

There was no doubt in Stovepipe's mind that his friend and the others were right in the middle of that battle royal he was hearing.

From the sound of it, several dozen guns were in action. That was encouraging, in a way. It meant the Three Rivers crew was putting up a fight against Garrity's outlaw band and hadn't been wiped out in the first volley. Wilbur would battle until his last breath, and from what Stovepipe had seen of them, so would Keenan Malone and the rest of the Three Rivers punchers. Stovepipe was confident Vance wouldn't back down, either.

He just hoped he could get there in time to lend them a hand. He kept the tired paint moving at as fast a clip as he dared.

CHAPTER THIRTY-SIX

Rosaleen's nerves were stretched taut. The men she loved—her father, Vance, and yes, Wilbur, Andy Callahan, and the rest of the Three Rivers crew—were out there somewhere in the night, headed toward a showdown. Would they live through it and come back to the ranch? She could only pray that would be the case.

In the meantime, there was no guarantee she and her aunt and the old wrangler weren't in danger, too. She sensed there might be some deep currents under the surface of this affair. Someone else might have been able to sort them out, but she couldn't. All she could do was wait and be watchful.

For that reason, she was on the front porch of the ranch house with the carbine in her hands when she heard hoofbeats approaching in the darkness. All the lamps were out in the house behind her. Aunt Sinead was sitting in a rocking chair beside an open window with a Greener in her lap, and Asa was in the bunkhouse with a Winchester. If any enemies rode up, they would be caught in a crossfire.

Rosaleen stiffened at the sound of the horse coming closer. Her hands tightened on the carbine. She listened intently and could tell it was only one rider. Her keen eyes probed the shadows and spotted him as he neared the ranch house.

She lifted the carbine to her shoulder, drew a bead, and called out in a clear, strong voice, "Hold it right there, mister! Don't come any closer."

The rider reined in. "Miss Rosaleen? Is that you?"

Relief washed through Rosaleen as she recognized the voice. It belonged to Sheriff Charlie Jerrico from Wagontongue.

Lowering the carbine, Rosaleen breathed easier "It's all right, Sheriff. You can come ahead. I didn't know who you were, and things are pretty tense tonight."

She heard Jerrico chuckle. "I can imagine." He rode up to the front porch and reined to a halt again. Solemn now, he said, "I heard what happened to Stewart. Where is everybody, Miss Malone?" The lawman's voice hardened. "They haven't ridden over to the Rafter M to raise hell, I hope."

"You know my father, Sheriff. Somebody hits him, he's going to hit back."

"Take the law in his own hands, you mean." Jerrico shook his head. "I was hoping I could get out here in time to talk some sense into his head. The days of open warfare between ranches are over. We have law and order in these parts now."

"I wish that was true. I'm not sure my father will ever feel that way, though. He believes a man has to fight his own battles and not rely on someone else to do it for him."

"How long ago did he and the rest of the crew leave?"

"More than an hour ago."

"Then it's too late to stop things now. They've got too big a lead on me. It's not likely they'd listen to me, anyway."

"No, it's not," Rosaleen agreed.

Jerrico took off his hat and ran a hand over his close-cropped dark hair. He sighed as he put the hat back on. "Why don't you come back to Wagontongue with me, Miss Malone?" he suggested. "I'd feel better if I knew you were safe tonight."

"There's no need for that," Rosaleen said. "I'm perfectly safe right here, Sheriff. The Three Rivers is my home."

"I know that, but what if things go bad for your father and the rest of his bunch? Some of the men from the Rafter M might ride over here looking to finish the job."

"You really think they'd attack the ranch and hurt me?"

"I don't know what to think anymore, miss. The way things are blowing up tonight, I'd say almost anything could happen."

Maybe he was right, Rosaleen thought. If the raid on the Rafter M backfired, she might be in danger. But she wasn't going to abandon Aunt Sinead and Asa. And if they all went into town with the sheriff, that really would leave the ranch undefended . . .

That thought made up her mind. She shook her head. "I'm sorry, Sheriff. I appreciate you looking out for my safety, but I can't leave."

"Blast it, Miss Malone." Jerrico swung down from

the saddle and stepped up onto the porch. "I just want to make sure nothing happens to you—"

"I can protect myself." She patted the carbine's smooth stock.

"Who else is here? You're not alone, are you?"

"My aunt is in the house, and our wrangler is over in the bunkhouse."

"They can all come into town with us. You'll all be safe."

"And if we did that, Mort Cabot could come in here and burn everything to the ground." Rosaleen shook her head. "I can't allow that to happen."

"Why don't you ask the other two? Find out what they want to do."

"They're going to agree with me. I'm sure of that."

Aunt Sinead had been listening through the open window. She appeared in the doorway with the shotgun tucked under her arm. "That's right, Sheriff. We're not leaving the Three Rivers."

Jerrico began, "Ma'am, I'm just trying to talk sense here—"

"Wait a minute, Sheriff." Something had occurred to Rosaleen that made her back stiffen again. "You said you heard about what happened to Mr. Stewart. *How* did you hear?"

"It's my job to keep up with everything that goes on in the county," Jerrico answered gruffly. "Some range rider drifted into town and was talking about it in one of the saloons. Word got back to me pretty quickly. I keep my ear to the ground, you know."

"It doesn't matter where you keep your ear, Sheriff. You couldn't have known about Stovepipe being killed. Wilbur brought the bad news straight back here. The only ones who knew about it were here on the

Three Rivers, and they all went with my father and Vance to the Rafter M."

"No offense, miss, but you've got to be mixed up on that. Maybe Coleman ran into somebody on the way here and said something to them about it—"

"Wilbur would have mentioned that," Rosaleen said.

Aunt Sinead said, "Dear, what are you talking about? I'm confused."

"You're not the only one, ma'am." Jerrico reached for Rosaleen's arm. "Now come on. We'll sort all this out back in Wagontongue—"

"No." She took a swift step backward and raised the carbine. "I'm not going to Wagontongue or anywhere else with you. I've finally figured it out. The only way you could know what happened to Stovepipe is if you talked to the man who ambushed him . . . or if you killed him yourself!"

"Rosaleen!" Aunt Sinead said. "You can't think—"

Even in the dim light, Rosaleen had seen the way Jerrico's muscles grew taut at the accusation.

A cold edge came into his voice as he said, "That's just loco, Miss Malone. I told you what happened. I'm sorry if you don't want to believe me. But either way, it's still too dangerous for you to stay out here tonight. You're coming to town with me."

"No, I'm not," Rosaleen said. "Get on your horse and get out of here, Sheriff. I'm giving you just enough benefit of the doubt that I don't shoot you down right here and now."

"Threatening the law isn't a very smart thing to do, little lady."

"Is that what I'm doing? Threatening the law? Or are you really something else, *Sheriff*?"

The cold contempt she packed into the last word made Jerrico glare at her. He started to turn away toward the edge of the porch . . . only to whirl back, taking her by surprise as he grabbed the barrel of her carbine, shoved it to the side, and then wrenched it out of her hands before she could pull the trigger.

"Oh!" Aunt Sinead said. She might not understand what was going on, but Jerrico's sudden violence spurred her into action. She lifted the scattergun.

Jerrico swung the carbine by the barrel. The stock slammed into the older woman's head. Aunt Sinead dropped the shotgun and fell to the porch, knocked senseless by the vicious blow.

"No!" Rosaleen cried. She threw herself at Jerrico, grabbed the carbine, and tried to wrestle it away from him.

Asa charged out of the bunkhouse carrying his rifle. He was confused, but he knew he was going to protect the boss's daughter if he could. "Get away from him, Miss Rosaleen!" the wrangler yelled. "I can't get a shot—"

Jerrico stopped trying to keep Rosaleen from taking the carbine away from him. He let go of the weapon and threw a punch. His right fist crashed into Rosaleen's left cheek and knocked her back. She hit the wall behind her as the carbine fell to the porch between them. Stunned, she lost her balance and fell.

She saw Jerrico whirl around as Asa's rifle cracked. The bullet smacked into the wall. Jerrico palmed out his revolver and fired twice from the hip. Asa cried out as the bullets ripped through him. The impact twisted him around. He dropped the Winchester and collapsed with his face in the dirt of the ranch yard.

Rosaleen regained her wits enough to make a

lunge for the carbine. Jerrico's foot came down on it before she could grasp it. With a shove, he sent it sliding away. It fell off the end of the porch.

"You're too damn smart for your own good, Miss Malone," he said as he bent over to grab her arm with his free hand. Cruelly, he jerked her to her feet. She swayed and would have fallen again if not for his painful grip on her arm.

With his other hand, he jabbed the muzzle of his Colt under her chin and tilted her head back. "You're my hole card," he told her. "No matter how things play out the rest of the night, I've got the upper hand as long as I have you. That's why you're coming back to Wagontongue with me." He laughed. "I reckon I was telling the truth in a way. All I want to do is keep you safe—because that's the easiest way for me to stay alive!"

Her eyes flicked one way, saw Aunt Sinead's motionless form on the porch, looked the other at the crumpled heap that was Asa, the old wrangler. Fury filled her and she started to struggle despite the gun threatening her.

Jerrico cursed. "I don't have time for this." He pulled the gun back and chopped viciously with it, slamming the barrel against her head. A fiery explosion went off behind Rosaleen's eyes, and then blackness closed in around her.

CHAPTER THIRTY-SEVEN

Echoes of the booming shots rolled like thunder across the plains. At the edge of the Three Rivers range, about halfway between the headquarters of the adjoining ranches, Stovepipe reined in as he came to the eastern end of a long, shallow gap between two ridges. The scene of the ambush was far enough away from the Rafter M that Cabot and his men wouldn't hear the shooting. If everything went according to Jerrico's plan, Garrity's gang would wipe out the men from the Three Rivers and then descend on the Rafter M to take Cabot by surprise and continue the slaughter.

Then, when the killing was finished, the outlaws could get to work on stripping the range of cattle, looting both ranches until nothing was left. Once they disposed of the resulting massive herd, they would have enough money to slip over the border into Canada or go anywhere else they liked.

Muzzle flashes came from the heights on both sides as the outlaws poured lead into a small clump of trees.

Obviously, the men who had survived the initial ambush had taken cover in that growth.

In the light from the moon and stars, Stovepipe spotted several dark, unmoving shapes lying in the gap. Dead men and dead horses, he thought grimly. There was no way he could tell if Wilbur was among the slain.

The muzzle flashes from the ridges told him there were at least two dozen killers up there. Even taking them by surprise, Stovepipe couldn't hope to deal with all of them before he was gunned down. He might be able to call on the paint for the last of its strength and make a dash for the trees, so he could join the men there, but one more gun wouldn't help them.

Although the idea of leaving his friends to carry on the fight stuck in Stovepipe's craw, he knew it was the only chance for any of them to survive. He needed more men if he was going to turn the tables on the outlaws, and there was only one place he could get them.

He turned the paint toward the Rafter M.

By having the men call out to each other during lulls in the firing, Wilbur had been able to do a head count of the defenders. Ten men were in the trees, not counting Keenan Malone, who had passed out from being wounded. A few of them had been winged, but not seriously.

Andy Callahan was not among the defenders. The segundo hadn't made out of the ambush. He had to be one of the men lying out there in the gap, dead or badly wounded.

"Looks like you're in charge, Vance," Wilbur told the young man.

"I don't think that's a good idea," Vance replied. "You've got a lot more experience at this sort of thing than I do, Wilbur. If you have any ideas, I'm perfectly willing to go along with them."

"That's just the problem," Wilbur said. "We're pinned down here, and there's not a damned thing we can do other than what we're already doing. In the long run, that's not going to do us any good. They'll pick us off one by one."

"They haven't so far. We need to hang on and keep fighting. Maybe something will happen."

Wilbur laughed. "See, I told you, you need to be in charge. You're a lot more optimistic than I am." He lifted the Winchester to his shoulder again and squeezed off another shot as he aimed at a muzzle flash on the northern ridge. "What we need is a miracle, and I reckon they're gonna be in short supply tonight!"

During the time Stovepipe had been in those parts, he had never paid a visit to the Rafter M, but he knew where the ranch headquarters was. He had studied maps of the area before he and Wilbur had set out on their assignment. He always liked to have at least an idea of the lay of the land before he wound up hip deep in a case.

Knowing where the Rafter M was and finding it in the dark were two different stories, though. Stovepipe had to rely on instinct as much as knowledge as he rode through the night.

After a while he spotted the glow of lamplight in

the distance. He patted the paint on the neck and said, "Not much longer now, old hoss."

Even in the darkness, Stovepipe could tell the headquarters of the Rafter M bore a distinct resemblance to that of the Three Rivers. The main house was built of logs rather than whitewashed planks, but the bunkhouse, the barns, the corrals, the smokehouse, and all the other outbuildings were arranged in a similar layout.

Several dogs set up a barking fit as he rode in. Knowing that commotion would attract the attention of the spread's residents, he brought the paint to a halt and sat in plain sight, unmoving so Cabot and his crew would see he wasn't a threat.

Men clad in long underwear and carrying guns emerged from the bunkhouse. The front door of the main house opened and Mort Cabot stepped out, wearing a long nightshirt and carrying a rifle.

He called, "Who in blazes is out there?"

"Hold your fire, Mr. Cabot. My name's Stewart. I ride for—"

"I know who you ride for! You're one of those Three Rivers bastards, and you're not welcome here! Talk quick or we'll blow you out of the saddle!"

"There's a gap about five miles west of here, between a couple long ridges—"

"Tomahawk Gap," Cabot broke in. "I know it. What about it?"

"Most of the Three Rivers crew is trapped there in some trees. They were ambushed by a bunch of outlaws and are tryin' to hold them off."

Cabot snorted. "Why should I care about that?"

"Because when those desperadoes finish wipin' out

Malone's bunch, they'll be on their way here to raid your ranch and kill you and all your crew."

Cabot was silent for a couple seconds, then he burst out in a laugh. "Haw! What a load of horse crap! The only varmints in these parts who want to kill me are Keenan Malone and his no-good polecat crew!"

"You're wrong," Stovepipe said, remaining calm despite Cabot's stubborn attitude. "The leader of the gang that ambushed the Three Rivers is a fella named Cort Garrity. You might have heard of him."

Cabot came closer. In the light that came through the open door behind the rancher, Stovepipe could see the frown creasing Cabot's forehead.

"I've heard of Garrity. Didn't know he was in this part of the country."

"You weren't supposed to know. Nobody knew except a couple of Garrity's relations who threw in with him on a scheme to set you and Malone against each other and wind up lootin' both ranches."

"Who in blazes are you talkin' about?"

"Sheriff Jerrico and one of his deputies, an hombre named MacDonald," Stovepipe said.

Silence hung over the ranch yard. After a moment, some of the cowboys who rode for Cabot started to mutter to each other.

Cabot found his voice. "That's the craziest story I've ever heard! Jerrico and MacDonald are lawmen."

"Pinnin' on a badge don't mean a man can't break the law, as well as upholdin' it. Everything I've just told you is true, Mr. Cabot. You've got my word on that."

"And just why the hell should I take the word of a shiftless grub line rider like you, Stewart?"

Stovepipe took a deep breath. "Because my pard Wilbur and I actually work for the Cattlemen's Protective Association. We're range detectives, not just cowboys."

"You have any proof of that?"

Stovepipe was glad Cabot hadn't dismissed the possibility out of hand. "The boss of the Montana branch over in Billings is a man named Riley Wheelock. You're probably acquainted with him, seein' as you're a member in good standin' of the CPA."

"Yeah, I know him, but I reckon a lot of people do."

Stovepipe took a deep breath, not liking the card he was about to play but knowing it was the only one left in his hand. "Not everybody knows about his son Danny, though. Just his close friends, and some of the fellas who work for him, like me and Wilbur."

Cabot had taken a sharp breath at the mention of Danny Wheelock's name. "That . . . unfortunate young man . . . is in an institution. Riley and his poor wife knew they couldn't care for him properly. I don't like to hear a friend's bad luck bandied about."

"And I didn't like bringin' it up, but I needed to convince you I'm tellin' the truth, Mr. Cabot. There's a lot more goin' on around here than you know about. You and Malone are the victims of a plot. I can tell you all about it, but I'd rather do that once you've gathered up your crew and we've headed out to Tomahawk Gap to turn that trap around on Garrity and his gang."

"You want us to risk our lives rescuing that son of a bitch Malone?"

"I reckon he'd do it for you if the situation was the

other way around and he was convinced it was the right thing to do."

Cabot stared up at Stovepipe as several seconds ticked by slowly. Then he turned toward the bunkhouse and shouted at his men, "Get dressed and get ready to ride! We're heading for Tomahawk Gap!" He looked at Stovepipe again and added, "You'd better be telling the truth, Stewart. If this is a trick I'm gonna take great pleasure in skinning you alive!"

CHAPTER THIRTY-EIGHT

Rosaleen groaned as consciousness seeped back into her brain. Her head pounded painfully. She didn't know where she was, but she was lying on something scratchy and uncomfortable.

When she forced her eyes open, the first thing she saw was a door made of iron bars. She was in a jail cell, a fact she confirmed by pushing herself up on an elbow and looking around. The scratchy surface underneath her was a cheap wool blanket spread on a thin bunk bolted to the stone wall.

Iron bars formed the walls of the cell as well as the door. An empty cell was beside hers, and across an aisle were two more. A heavy wooden door with a small, barred window in it separated the cell block from the rest of the building. She knew she was in the jail in Wagontongue, even though she had never set foot in there.

As Rosaleen sat up, that door swung open and Sheriff Charlie Jerrico sauntered through. He grinned at her through the bars and said, "I thought I heard a little noise back here. You're awake, eh?"

Rosaleen stood up. The pain in her head made the world swim dizzily for a moment, but anger kept her on her feet. She grasped the bars and glared at Jerrico. "You're a disgrace to that badge you're wearing."

The crooked lawman's grin disappeared. "No, what's a disgrace is how a man can risk his life over and over to keep folks safe, then have them begrudge him the sort of wages they'd pay a swamper to sweep out a saloon. I stayed on the right side of the law for ten years, and what did it get me? Not a damned thing!"

"What about your self-respect?"

A bitter laugh came from Jerrico. "Yeah, that and a nickel'll buy a man a beer. I probably would have gone along like I was doing anyway, if some distant kin of mine hadn't showed up with an idea for making all of us rich."

Rosaleen forced her brain to work. "By setting the Three Rivers and the Rafter M against each other? Is that the idea you mean?"

"Like I told you, miss, you're too damn smart for your own good. But that doesn't matter anymore. By morning, the crews from both ranches will be dead, and I'll be well on my way to being a rich man. In a week or so, I'll slip away, meet up with my cousins, and claim my share of the loot. Then Wagontongue will never set eyes on me again."

"You're forgetting one thing. I'll tell everyone what you really are."

He smiled again, sadly this time, and shook his head. "I don't reckon you'll have a chance to do that. It's a pity, too. You're a mighty pretty girl." Jerrico shrugged. "But there are a lot of mighty pretty girls in this world, and most of them will be happy to enjoy the company of a man with plenty of money."

She had known right away that he planned to kill her, but hearing him put it plainly made a chill go through her. She backed away from the bars and said, "If you come near me, I'll start screaming. Someone will hear me and come to see what's wrong. They'll want to know why you've got me locked up, and I'll tell them everything."

"The town's asleep. Nobody's going to hear you. Anyway, I'm not going to hurt you . . . yet. I need to keep you alive, just in case everything doesn't work out quite like I've planned. I told you, you're my hole card." Jerrico's eyes were cold as ice as he added, "But once I've gotten word everything's taken care of, I won't need you anymore. It'll be easy enough to wrap you up, put you in the back of a wagon, and take you somewhere you'll never be found."

He was talking about disposing of her body, Rosaleen realized. She was sick with fear, but she wasn't going to let him see that. She lifted her chin defiantly and said, "Somebody's going to stop you. You can't get away with something so awful."

"People get away with doing awful things all the time. You think there's some rule saying only people who stay on the straight and narrow ever get rewarded?" Jerrico laughed. "You're young and ignorant, girl. Too bad you won't have a chance to learn more. I would've enjoyed teaching you." He started to turn away.

Desperately, Rosaleen said, "You've forgotten about Aunt Sinead and Asa. They know what you did."

He looked back over his shoulder at her. "Neither of them will talk . . . ever again."

As the horrible implication of his statement soaked in on her, Rosaleen backed up until her knees hit the bunk. She sat down, put her face in her hands, and began to sob. She barely noticed when Jerrico went out and slammed the cell block door closed behind him.

Stovepipe asked Cabot if he could switch his saddle to a fresh horse, and the ranch owner agreed.

"I'm obliged to you," Stovepipe said. "This ol' paint o' mine has had a long, hard day."

"You look like you have, too," Cabot said. "Is that dried blood all over your face?"

"Yeah. Got a bullet graze on my head. Good thing my skull's hard as a rock."

"So you get shot in the head and just keep going?"

"Hell of a thing, ain't it?" Stovepipe said with a grin.

By the time he had his saddle on a fresh mount, the Rafter M crew was ready to ride. Cabot had gone back into the house and returned fully dressed and carrying his rifle.

One of his men—Stovepipe figured it was the foreman—said, "There's no need for you to come along, boss. We'll see if there's any truth to what this hombre told you."

"The hell there's no need!" Cabot said. "If Stewart's right, those buzzards have been plotting against me, too. I'll be in on the finish. I never ducked a fight, and I'll be damned if I'll start now!"

Stovepipe said, "That sounds just like somethin' Keenan Malone would say."

"Don't compare— Ah, the hell with it! Let's go."

Counting Stovepipe, nineteen men swung up into

their saddles and galloped away from the Rafter M. Based on Stovepipe's earlier estimate, the outlaws would outnumber them, but not by much. If they could take Garrity's gang by surprise, the battle would be close enough to call it even.

Since Cabot and his men knew that range so well, they were able to travel at a faster pace than Stovepipe had while he was looking for the ranch headquarters. He hoped they would get back to Tomahawk Gap before the outlaws wiped out the men who had taken cover in the trees.

He could only pray that Wilbur was among the defenders, and not one of the men who had been cut down in the opening volley of the ambush.

From time to time, Cabot called a halt to listen, and when they finally heard the sound of gunfire in the distance, the cattleman said to Stovepipe, "Well, you were telling the truth about some sort of fight going on, anyway. Still don't know for sure who's mixed up in it, though."

"You'll see I'm right when we get there," Stovepipe told him. "Right now, I'm just mighty glad to hear those guns goin' off. That means the fight ain't over yet."

"Let's don't waste any more time." Cabot sent his horse lunging ahead through the darkness.

Stovepipe knew it wasn't very likely the outlaws would hear the hoofbeats of the approaching riders over all the gun-thunder, but it was possible, so they needed to be careful. When he figured they were within half a mile of the gap, he told Cabot, "We'd better go the rest of the way on foot."

"You're right." Cabot signaled for a halt.

The Rafter M cowboys dismounted and shucked their rifles from saddle boots.

Cabot said to Stovepipe, "They're on the ridges on both sides of the gap?"

"They were when I headed for your spread," the range detective replied.

"We'll split up, then. Richards, you take eight of the boys and sneak up on the ridge to the north. The rest of us will take the south side."

The Rafter M foreman said, "I don't much cotton to skulkin' around like an Injun, boss."

"Neither do I, but we've got to take those owlhoots by surprise if we're gonna have a chance to beat them."

From the sound of that, Cabot had accepted his story, Stovepipe thought. That was good. They didn't need any hesitation. Such a delay at the wrong moment could prove fatal to their plans.

"Wait until you hear my signal to throw down on them," Cabot continued. "I'll fire three shots as fast as I can. You move in then."

"Do we give 'em a chance to surrender?"

Cabot sighed. "I suppose you'd better . . . but not much of one."

Richards picked the men to go with him.

Stovepipe said to Cabot, "I reckon I'll go with you and your bunch."

"Damn right you are. If this is a trick of some sort, you'll be getting a bullet before anybody else, Stewart."

"Reckon I'll take that chance. You'll see I was tellin' the truth."

The men tied their horses to some brush and set off into the night, carrying their rifles as they trotted through the darkness. The two groups angled away from each other when they approached the gap. Stovepipe and Cabot led his men up the ridge on the southern side and catfooted toward the rim overlooking Tomahawk Gap.

Stovepipe put out a hand and touched the cattleman's arm. "Horses up ahead," he whispered.

"I see 'em. Did they leave a man to watch them?"

Stovepipe's keen eyes searched the darkness and spotted a tiny orange glow that flared up and then died down again.

"Yeah, there's a man smokin' a quirly up there. I'll take care of him."

"Better be quiet about it," Cabot said. "If you raise a ruckus, it'll warn the rest of them and we'll lose what little advantage we have."

"I know." Stovepipe handed his rifle to Cabot. It would be close work.

He drew his Colt from its holster as he slipped up behind the outlaw guarding the gang's horses. The man was leaning against the trunk of a small tree as he smoked. Stovepipe moved with all the stealth he was capable of, and when he was close enough, he reversed the gun in his hand, lifted it, and struck swiftly, bringing the butt down on the man's head with a solid thud.

The outlaw's hat might have cushioned the blow a little, but not enough to keep him from being knocked senseless. His knees buckled, dropping him to the ground. Stovepipe leaned over and walloped him again, just for good measure. Then he tied the man's hands behind him with his own belt and stuffed his bandanna in his mouth as a gag.

Returning quickly to Cabot's side, Stovepipe took his rifle back from the rancher and told him, "The way ahead is clear now, as far as I can see."

"How far is it to where those owlhoots are dug in?"

"Maybe fifty yards."

Cabot nodded. "All right. Let's get a little closer, and then I'll give the signal."

"Hold on a second. You believe me now, don't you?"

"Everything you said about what's going on here looks to be true. I'm giving you the benefit of the doubt, Stewart, even though it's hard for me to trust anybody who rides for the Three Rivers. What you said about the CPA and Riley Wheelock carries a lot of weight, though. I don't see how you could have known about his boy unless you're really who you say you are. And I can't bring myself to believe that anybody who works for the CPA is crooked."

"I'm obliged to you for believin' me, then. Before the night is over, I'll show you and Malone the proof that Jerrico's been playin' you for fools."

"If he has, he's going to be damned sorry," Cabot said in a grim, flint-hard voice. "Let's clean up this rat's nest."

With the Rafter M punchers right behind them, Stovepipe and Cabot crept closer to the rim. The shots from up ahead continued as the outlaws poured lead into the grove of trees. The defenders down there didn't know it, but help was at hand, finally.

Cabot paused and looked over at Stovepipe, who nodded in the moonlight. Cabot drew his pistol, pointed it into the air, and fired three shots as fast as he could pull the double-action revolver's trigger. Even with all the other gunfire going on, the signal was unmistakable.

While the echoes of the three shots were still booming, Stovepipe rushed forward with his Winchester and shouted, "Throw down your guns! It's over, Garrity!"

He didn't know if the outlaw leader was on this

ridge or the one on the other side of the gap, but he didn't figure it mattered. None of the desperadoes was likely to surrender, anyway.

Shouts of alarm and curses came from the men kneeling behind rocks along the rim. They whirled around as Stovepipe shouted again, "Elevate! Throw down your guns!"

Orange bursts of muzzle flame split the darkness, and the fight was on.

CHAPTER THIRTY-NINE

Stovepipe snapped his Winchester to his shoulder and opened fire, swinging the barrel from left to right and spraying bullets at the outlaws along the rim. After cranking off five rounds as fast as he could work the rifle's lever, he slowed down and started aiming at the muzzle flashes he saw ahead of him.

Slugs whipped past his ears, close enough he could hear them sizzling through the air. He dropped to one knee and felt another bullet stir the thick, gray-streaked hair on his head. All around him, Cabot and the other Rafter M men were firing, as well. The night was a hellish blend of flame and racket.

As Stovepipe's Winchester ran dry, he dropped the rifle and pulled his Colt. Across the way, orange flashes erupted all over the ridge as Cabot's men on that side of the gap attacked the outlaws over there.

Down in the trees, two of the defenders had been killed and several more were wounded by the almost continual barrage from the ridges. Wilbur figured it was only a matter of time before the bullets flying around found him or Vance . . . or both of them.

The sound of slugs whipping through the branches or smacking into tree trunks was almost constant. After a while the brain grew numb to the never-ending danger. Wilbur forced himself to stay behind cover the best he could. A part of him wanted to charge toward one of the ridges, shouting out his defiance as he emptied his gun at the enemy.

At least that would get the ordeal over with in a hurry.

In the past, whenever things had gotten bad, he'd had Stovepipe to keep him steady and on an even keel. His anger over Stovepipe's death fueled his rage and made him even more irrational.

"I'm going up there," he told Vance as he paused in his firing to reload yet again. His voice was an angry growl.

"What are you talking about?" Vance asked. "At least we've got a chance here, Wilbur. If you step out of these trees, you'll be riddled with lead before you get ten feet."

"I'm not sure I give a damn anymore—" He stopped short as the gunfire from the ridges took on a new tone.

There was a lot more of it, for one thing, almost as if the number of bushwhackers had suddenly doubled . . . but the bullets weren't zipping through the trees anymore. After living with that sound for what seemed like days, even though actually it had only been about an hour, the sudden lack of those deadly whispers was dramatic.

"What's going on?" Vance said into the relative silence. "They're not shooting at us anymore."

"Sounds like they're not," Wilbur agreed in amazement, "but they're sure as hell shooting at *somebody.*"

Only one explanation made any sense. Another force had arrived out of nowhere and was attacking the bushwhackers. Who those reinforcements were—and the very identity of those who'd ambushed the Three Rivers men—were still mysteries, but as far as Wilbur could see, the men from the Three Rivers had gotten a reprieve somehow.

Stovepipe surged to his feet and darted forward, gun in hand. Two outlaws stood up to his left and blazed away at him. Close enough to pick his targets, he twisted in their direction and hammered a pair of shots at them. One man went over backwards, driven off his feet by the impact of a slug smashing into his chest, while the other doubled over as Stovepipe's second bullet plowed into his gut.

The injury, the weariness from loss of blood, and the long day of rushing around on the range were all forgotten in the heat of battle. Stovepipe swung the Colt toward another outlaw who charged at him. The flames that spouted from both weapons almost touched. Stovepipe felt the hot kiss of the enemy's bullet as it barely scraped the side of his neck.

The outlaw's head jerked back as Stovepipe's bullet caught him between the eyes and bored on through his brain to explode out the back of his skull. Already dead, he stumbled and pitched forward, causing Stovepipe to leap out of his way.

He had three bullets remaining, counting the one he had slipped into the Colt's sixth chamber before the fighting started. Usually, he left that empty so the hammer could rest on it. Three bullets remaining, he thought, before he would have to reload. In the middle of this melee, he might not have a chance to do that.

Suddenly, a man dashed past him. Stovepipe barely caught a glimpse of the fleeing outlaw's face, but he saw enough to recognize the man as Cort Garrity. The gang leader was abandoning his men and trying to get away.

Since it was Garrity who had led Jerrico and Mac-Donald to cross back over to the lawless side of the street, Stovepipe didn't intend to allow the man to escape. He wheeled around and ran after the outlaw.

Cabot hadn't left anyone to guard the outlaws' horses. He'd needed all of his men to battle the ambushers. If Garrity reached the animals, he could vault into a saddle and gallop away before anyone could stop him . . . unless Stovepipe prevented that, since he seemed to be the only one who'd seen Garrity making a break for it.

Stovepipe heard the horses moving around in front of him, no doubt spooked by all the gunfire crashing nearby. He spotted Garrity, who hadn't quite reached the horses, and shouted, "Hold it, mister!"

Garrity spun around. The gun in his hand blared death. Stovepipe weaved to the side as a bullet whined past his head. He thrust out his Colt and triggered twice, aiming just above Garrity's muzzle flash.

Garrity grunted and stumbled back a step. The bullets hadn't knocked all the fight out of him. His gun blasted again. The slug plucked at Stovepipe's sleeve. Stovepipe fired his final shot.

Garrity went up on his toes. His finger closed spasmodically around the trigger, but the gun was pointed at the ground and the shot went harmlessly into the dirt. Garrity tottered forward and gasped. "Who . . . who . . ."

"Stovepipe Stewart," the range detective said.

"MacDonald said . . . you were dead!"

"Not hardly."

Those words were the last thing Cort Garrity heard. He folded up on himself, crumpling to the ground, and his final breath rattled in his throat. Stovepipe heard that and knew the threat from the boss outlaw was over, but that didn't mean he and his allies were out of the woods. Shots still blasted along both ridges, although the fighting seemed to be trailing off. Stovepipe plucked fresh cartridges from the loops on his shell belt and thumbed them into the Colt's cylinder before he turned back toward the rim.

It was time for him to find out if his friend and partner was still alive.

The storm of gunfire continued on both ridges for several minutes and then began to fade away. Scattered shots still boomed here and there, but Wilbur could tell by the sound of them one side or the other had emerged victorious and was engaged in mopping up.

"Pass the word for everybody to be ready," he told

Vance. "We don't know who won up there or which side they're on."

Finally, an odd hushed silence hung over Tomahawk Gap. That silence was broken after a few minutes by the *clip-clop* of hoofbeats approaching the trees.

"Howdy in there!" a man sang out. "Hold your fire! We're friends!"

Wilbur's breath froze in his throat. He felt like he'd just been punched in the gut. His heart began to slug heavily in his chest. Unable to hold back, he burst out of the trees and shouted, "Stovepipe! Stovepipe, over here!"

Half a dozen men on horseback rode quickly toward the trees. The one in the lead, a tall, lanky figure, swung down from his saddle before his mount even stopped moving. He threw his arms around Wilbur and started pounding the stocky redhead on the back.

Wilbur returned the rough greeting. "Damn it, I thought you were dead!"

"Figured you must have thought that," Stovepipe told him. "If I'd seen me floppin' around on that horse o' mine, out cold and covered in blood, I reckon I'd have figured I was dead, too!"

Wilbur took a sudden step back and gripped his friend's arms. "Good Lord, Stovepipe!" he said in a horrified voice. "I deserted you! You were alive and I left you to die!"

"Not a bit of it," Stovepipe insisted. "You didn't have any reason in the world to believe I was alive. Not only that, but you had to get back to the Three Rivers to tell 'em what happened. If you think I'm holdin' any sort of grudge against you, you're just plumb wrong."

"That's because you're the best friend an hombre could ever have."

Stovepipe grinned. "Well, I ain't denyin' that."

Vance stepped up and thrust out his hand. "Stovepipe, I can't tell you how happy I am you're still alive."

"I'm a mite pleased with that turn of events my own self," Stovepipe said as he clasped the young man's hand. "Where's Mr. Malone?"

"Back in the trees," Wilbur said as he nodded in that direction. "He's wounded. We don't know how bad he's hurt, but he's alive. At least he was the last time anybody checked on him."

"We'll get him to the ranch. There's a lot to tell you . . . and the job ain't over yet, neither."

One of the men who had ridden up with Stovepipe nudged his horse forward. "Now that you're finished with this reunion, Stewart, hadn't we better do something about the man behind all this trouble?"

"Cabot!" Vance dropped his hand to the gun he had returned to its holster.

Quickly, Stovepipe lifted a hand. "Take it easy, Vance. You fellas are on the same side now. I was right about somebody else pullin' the strings behind all this trouble. I had a hunch who it might be, but now I'm sure."

"Wait a minute," Vance said. "It was the crew from the Rafter M that rescued us just now?"

"That's right," Cabot said. "It was a bitter pill to swallow, too, throwing in with the Three Rivers, but I see it was the right thing to do."

Stovepipe pointed a thumb at one of the ridges. "Those bushwhackers came from a gang o' rustlers

and outlaws headed up by a fella named Garrity.
They're the ones who've been wideloopin' cows from
both spreads. Garrity wasn't the big boss, though.
That's Charlie Jerrico."

"The sheriff?" Wilbur practically yelped.

"It's a long story," Stovepipe said. "I'll tell you all
about it once we've gathered up the wounded and are
headin' back to the Three Rivers."

CHAPTER FORTY

Now that they didn't have to worry about getting shot because Cabot's men were standing guard over the few outlaws who hadn't been killed in the battle, Stovepipe, Wilbur, and Vance were able to check on Keenan Malone's condition.

Wilbur lit a match and held it up while Stovepipe knelt next to the unconscious cattleman. He pulled Malone's bloodstained shirt aside to reveal the puckered bullet hole in the older man's torso. There was no exit wound on Malone's back.

"Bullet's still in there," Stovepipe said. "No way of knowin' how much damage it's done. I hate to move him because that might make the slug shift around, but there ain't nothin' else we can do. We need to get him back to the Three Rivers and get the doc out from Wagontongue." Stovepipe rested his hand on Malone's chest above the wound. "Heart's beatin' pretty good, and he seems to be breathin' all right. I reckon he's got a chance . . . if we don't kill him gettin' him back there."

Mort Cabot came up behind the three men. "I can

go back to the Rafter M and bring a wagon out here. Might be easier for him to ride in it."

Stovepipe considered the idea and then shook his head. "Obliged to you for the offer, Mr. Cabot, but that'd take too long. We're as close to the Three Rivers headquarters as we are to yours. We'll put him on a horse in front of me, so I can hang on to him and keep him from bouncin' around too much."

"I'll do that, Stovepipe," Vance said. "You're wounded, too, you know, and probably exhausted on top of it."

"I *am* startin' to feel a mite tired. All right, Vance, bring your horse up and get on. Some of the rest of us will lift him in front of you."

That delicate operation was accomplished quickly but carefully, without jolting Malone any more than necessary.

Cabot said to Vance, "I saw that Andy Callahan was killed in the ambush. Sorry. He was a good man . . . for a Three Rivers man. I guess that leaves you in charge, since Malone is laid up."

"I suppose there's no getting around it," Vance said. "So, speaking for the Three Rivers . . . thank you for your help, Mr. Cabot."

"Don't go getting the idea we're all gonna be friends now," Cabot said gruffly. "But I don't suppose it'll hurt to give each other a hand now and then, when it's really necessary. We'll gather up the wounded and the dead and bring them back to your spread, along with those prisoners." He shook his head. "Not sure what we'll do with them, since we can't trust the law in Wagontongue anymore."

"There'll be new law in Wagontongue before mornin'," Stovepipe said as he swung up into the saddle of his borrowed horse. "I reckon you can count on that." He set off along with Wilbur and Vance, leaving the other Three Rivers hands behind to help Cabot and his men.

Wilbur glanced back and said, "You think they can get along and work together after they've been at each other's throats for so long?"

"Cabot knows what's been goin' on," Stovepipe said. "He'll keep both sides in line, I reckon."

"Speaking of what's been going on . . . you said you'd spill the story once we started back," Wilbur reminded him.

"Yeah, I did, didn't I?"

For the next several minutes, Stovepipe explained everything that had happened since Wilbur had ridden away from Eagle Flats. Stovepipe told his companions about backtracking the bushwhacker who had turned out to be the deputy named MacDonald, and everything he had learned from eavesdropping on MacDonald's conversation with Cort Garrity.

"Wait a minute," Wilbur said. "They're all related? Garrity, MacDonald, and Charlie Jerrico?"

"That's right. Jerrico and MacDonald used to ride the owlhoot trail themselves, before they started packin' stars."

Wilbur shrugged. "Some men go back and forth across that line. I never saw how they could, myself."

"Most of 'em go back to their roots, sooner or later. Jerrico and MacDonald surely did. MacDonald confessed the whole thing to me later, when I got the drop on him."

"Where is he now?"

"He figured to turn the tables on me." Stovepipe shook his head. "Turned out to be a bigger job than he could manage."

Wilbur grunted. "Can't say as I'm sorry about that. So who does that leave on the loose? Just the sheriff?"

"As far as I know. We got to rattle our hocks into Wagontongue anyway to fetch the sawbones for Mr. Malone. We'll round up Jerrico while we're at it."

"You really think he'll let himself be rounded up peacefully?"

"Probably not likely," Stovepipe said.

As they approached the Three Rivers headquarters, Vance said, "Rosaleen's going to be upset when she sees her father is hurt. We need to let her know right away that he's still alive."

"She and Aunt Sinead will take good care of him while Wilbur and me are fetchin' the doc," Stovepipe said.

"What about me? I'm coming with you."

"No need for that. You can stay at the ranch in case the ladies need any help."

"You're just trying to protect me," Vance said. "You think you'll have to shoot it out with Jerrico."

"Could happen," Stovepipe said with a shrug. "Somebody's got to keep the Three Rivers runnin' for a while, Vance, and I reckon that job's gonna fall to you. Otherwise your pa's gonna have to find somebody else to take over, and he might not be happy with Wilbur and me if he does."

"You might need help—" Vance began, then stopped abruptly. "What am I saying? You've been two or three steps ahead of everybody all along, Stovepipe. You don't need my help."

"I wouldn't go so far as to say that. Seems I recollect

plenty of times it came in mighty handy havin' you around." Stovepipe's voice hardened. "But this final hand is our game, mine and Wilbur's. We'll play it out."

They came in sight of the ranch buildings a few minutes later. The dogs barked, as usual, but the place was dark, surprising them. No one emerged from the house or the bunkhouse, either.

Stovepipe spotted a couple of dark shapes on the porch. "Hold on," he said as he reined in. "Vance, you stay here with Malone."

"Is something wrong?" Vance asked.

"That's what we're gonna find out."

Stovepipe and Wilbur dismounted and stalked toward the house with drawn guns. The shapes on the porch didn't move, and as the two range detectives came closer, Stovepipe smelled something that made an icy finger drag along his spine.

The scent was like copper, and it set his teeth on edge. He had smelled it before and knew what it was.

Wilbur sniffed the air and said quietly, "Stovepipe, is that . . . ?"

"Yeah. Fresh blood. A lot of it."

They had reached the bottom of the porch steps. The two shapes still hadn't moved. Stovepipe reached in his shirt pocket with his left hand and fished out a lucifer. He snapped the match to life with his thumbnail and held it up so its garish light splashed over the two bodies lying on the porch.

Aunt Sinead and Asa, the old wrangler, were both dead, their throats slit in hideous wounds that had caused blood to pool around them. It looked like Asa had been shot a couple times, too.

"My God," Wilbur whispered. "Who . . . who'd do such a terrible thing?"

"I reckon we both know the answer to that," Stovepipe said. "There's only one hombre who could've done this."

"Jerrico. But why?"

From where he sat on horseback with Malone, Vance called, "Stovepipe, what's wrong? Is that . . . is that someone lying on the porch?"

"It's Aunt Sinead and Asa," Stovepipe replied. "Sorry to tell you this, son, but they're both dead. Murdered."

"Oh, God." Vance's voice was taut with pain and grief. "Is . . . is Rosaleen with them?"

"No sign of her. Stay out here. Wilbur and me will go in and have a look around."

The next few minutes were sheer torture for Vance as he waited for the two range detectives to come back out of the house.

Finally, they emerged and Stovepipe said, "She ain't here."

Vance heaved a sigh of relief. "You looked everywhere?"

"Everywhere in the main house. I reckon we'd better check the bunkhouse and the barns."

That took even longer, but when they were finished, they were confident Rosaleen was no longer at the ranch headquarters.

"Let's get Malone inside," Stovepipe said as he came up to the horse where Vance sat holding the wounded old cattleman. "We'll put him on that big sofa in the front room. It's practically a bed, and it'll be easier than carryin' him upstairs. Easier on him, too."

"We have to find Rosaleen," Vance said as he carefully lowered Malone into the arms of the range detectives.

"I got a pretty good idea where to look," Stovepipe assured him. "Jerrico's got her."

"Why?" Vance asked, repeating the same question Wilbur had voiced earlier.

"To use as a hostage in case things didn't work out the way he wanted them to. I reckon he's waitin' in Wagontongue to get word from MacDonald or Garrity. He don't know yet they're both dead."

"He plans to kill her," Vance said, anguish in his voice.

"Not as long as she's still some use to him. She'll be all right until he finds out what happened."

Grunting a little under Malone's considerable weight, Stovepipe and Wilbur carried him into the house and gently placed him on the sofa. Wilbur lit a lamp, and Stovepipe took a quick look at Malone's wound.

"Don't look like it's been bleedin' again. Still appears he's got a chance if we can get the doc out here to tend to him pretty quicklike." Stovepipe turned to Vance. "You're gonna have to stay here so you can keep an eye on him. Make sure he's as comfortable as you can get him. That's all any of us can do for him."

"Stay here?" Vance repeated. He shook his head. "I can't do that. Jerrico has Rosaleen. I'm going to Wagontongue to kill him."

"You're a brave young fella, Vance, but you're no gunfighter. Jerrico's a hardcase killer. You best leave him to me and Wilbur. He's our meat."

"But Rosaleen—"

"We'll bring her back safe to you. You got my word on that." Stovepipe paused. "Besides, how do you reckon she'd feel about you if she knew you rode off and left her pa here badly wounded with nobody to look after him?"

Vance glared at him for a moment, then said, "Damn it. You're right about that. And I suppose you're right about me not being any match for Jerrico, too. But be careful, Stovepipe. Once he realizes the game is over and he's lost, there's no telling what he might do. He might kill her just for spite."

"I doubt that. He won't hurt her as long as he thinks he can use her to get away with a whole hide." Stovepipe clapped a hand on Vance's shoulder, gave it a reassuring squeeze for a second, then he and Wilbur strode back out to their horses and mounted up.

"You must be done in, Stovepipe," Wilbur said as they rode away from the Three Rivers. "All you've done for more than twelve hours straight is ride and fight."

Stovepipe chuckled. "Naw, you're forgettin' I got to rest for a spell when I passed out from bein' shot in the head." His voice hardened. "I'll be all right as soon as I finish this one last chore."

CHAPTER FORTY-ONE

It was after midnight by the time Stovepipe and Wilbur reached Wagontongue. The buildings were dark, even the Silver Star and the other saloons. Those establishments might stay open all night on Saturday and payday, but not otherwise.

The exception was the sheriff's office and jail, where a light still burned dimly in the front window.

"Jerrico's waitin' up for news from his kin," Stovepipe said quietly to Wilbur when they had dismounted a couple blocks away. "If he was to hear that everything went off as planned, he'd kill the girl and dispose of her body."

"Hard to believe anybody's that cold-blooded, even a crooked lawman," Wilbur said. "But after I saw what he did out there at the Three Rivers . . ."

"He'll get what's comin' to him." Stovepipe drew his gun and checked the loads. "Let's go see what we can find out. We'll stay in the back alley for now."

They approached the jail from behind, gliding through the shadows like ghosts. Stovepipe spotted a faint glow up ahead. After a moment he could tell it came through a barred window. That window must open into one of the cells, he thought, and the light filtered back from the lamp that was burning in Jerrico's office.

Wilbur was too short to peer through the window, but Stovepipe was able to grasp the bars and lift himself high enough. His eyes were adjusted to the dim light, but from this angle there was nothing to be seen. He took a chance and hissed, "Miss Rosaleen!"

A startled gasp came from inside the cell. Stovepipe heard some rustling around, and then suddenly the young woman's face appeared on the other side of the bars.

"Stovepipe!" she whispered urgently. "Is that really you?"

"It sure is," he told her. "Wilbur's with me, too."

"And Vance?"

"No, he had another chore to take care of, but he's all right. The trouble's almost over, Miss Rosaleen."

"Sheriff Jerrico is the one behind all of it. He . . . he's really an outlaw. He's an evil man."

"Yes'm, we know." Stovepipe didn't tell her about the murders of Aunt Sinead and Asa. Time enough for that grief later, after Rosaleen was safe. "We're gonna deal with him right now. You just hold on a few more minutes, and we'll have you outta there."

"I . . . I don't know how to thank you, Stovepipe—"

"Don't worry about that. Just keep your chin up." He let go of the bars and came down off his toes. Turning to Wilbur, he said, "We need to find a crate or somethin' for you to stand on. That way you can guard the gal through this window. If Jerrico tries to come into the cell block after her, you fill him full o' lead."

"I'd be mighty happy to," Wilbur said with grim resolve.

However, before they could find anything for Wilbur to stand on, they heard the swift rataplan of hoofbeats entering the settlement.

"Somebody's in a hurry," Wilbur said. "That's usually not good."

"No, it ain't," Stovepipe agreed. "Come on."

They started to circle the jail, but before they reached the mouth of the dark passage beside the stone building, the hoofbeats came to a stop and Vance Armbrister called, "Jerrico! Come out of there, you murdering skunk!"

"Blast it," Stovepipe muttered. "The boy couldn't do what he was told." He yanked his gun from leather and charged forward.

Shots blasted from inside the jail.

Stovepipe and Wilbur reached the corner in time to see Vance fling himself from the saddle and weave toward the building, returning Jerrico's fire. The youngster didn't lack for courage. He was charging right into a hail of bullets and hammering out return shots of his own.

Then Vance cried out. He fell to a knee and dropped his gun, but he didn't go all the way to the ground.

The door of the sheriff's office swung open. Charlie Jerrico stepped out, a sneer on his face. "You're a fool, kid," he called to Vance. "Riding into town and trying to shoot up the sheriff's office. It's no wonder you got yourself killed. You must have gone loco. That's what people will think, anyway."

Jerrico hadn't noticed the two range detectives.

Wilbur started to lift his gun, but Stovepipe put out a hand to stop him.

Vance looked up at the crooked lawman. Blood dripped down his left sleeve as he said, "You've lost, Jerrico. Everybody knows what you did—Malone, Cabot, Stovepipe and Wilbur, the rest of the crews from the Three Rivers and the Rafter M. It's over. Garrity and MacDonald are dead. The rest of your bunch is either dead or taken prisoner. You're the only one left, you son of a bitch. Where's Rosaleen?"

Clutching the bars of her cell door, she was listening to the confrontation through the window in the cell block door and the open front door. She cried, "Vance! Vance, I'm in here!"

Jerrico's face twisted in a hate-filled snarl as he half-turned toward the door, then tried to snap back around. Vance was already lunging for the gun he had dropped, scooping it up and angling the barrel toward Jerrico as the lawman pulled the trigger. Vance's shot crashed out a hair after Jerrico's.

The slug from the sheriff's gun plowed into the street inches from Vance, but the young man's bullet went home, ripping into Jerrico's torso and slanting up through his heart. Jerrico took a stumbling step forward and tried to lift his gun for another shot, but it slipped from his nerveless fingers before he could pull the trigger. He reached the edge of the boardwalk in front of the office and plunged off, falling facedown in the street.

He didn't move again.

Wilbur hurried to Vance's side and helped the young man to his feet. "How bad are you hit?"

Vance's face was pale and drawn from pain, but his

voice was strong as he said, "Not too bad. He just drilled me through the arm. What about him?"

"Dead," Stovepipe reported from where he had just toed Jerrico's body over onto its back. "You were supposed to stay at the Three Rivers and look after Mr. Malone."

"Mort Cabot and his men rode in with those prisoners not long after you left. They locked the outlaws in the smokehouse, and I figured they could look after Mr. Malone. I headed for town as fast as I could."

Stovepipe chuckled and inclined his head toward the open door. "Rosaleen's back in one of the cells. She's fine, but I reckon she'll be even better once she sees you. Keys ought to be hangin' in there somewhere."

Vance holstered his gun and hurried inside. He would need some medical attention, but that could wait until after he and Rosaleen had been reunited.

Stovepipe and Wilbur stood together in the street. "You took a mighty big chance, letting Vance shoot it out with Jerrico after all," Wilbur said. "We could have blasted Jerrico to hell from that alley mouth."

"Yeah, but I changed my mind about the boy. I had a hunch Vance has what it takes. He's gonna need to be pretty tough, since he's gonna be runnin' the Three Rivers from now on."

"You don't think he'll go back east and take over his father's steel mill?"

"What do you think?"

Wilbur laughed. "I've got a hunch of my own that says you're right, Stovepipe."

* * *

Wagontongue's sawbones patched up the bullet hole in Vance's arm, then headed out to the Three Rivers to see what he could do for Keenan Malone. Stovepipe and Wilbur followed, along with Vance and Rosaleen.

It was a long, tense night. The four of them waited on the porch with Mort Cabot while the doctor worked on Malone. The bodies of Aunt Sinead and Asa had been wrapped in blankets and taken inside, and the blood had been cleaned from the planks as best it could be.

Exhaustion claimed Stovepipe as he sat in one of the rocking chairs on the porch. He fell sound asleep and didn't wake up until dawn was creating a reddish-gold spectacle in the eastern sky.

He jerked awake when the front door opened. The doctor stepped out onto the porch as he wiped his hands on a bloody piece of cloth.

Vance, Rosaleen, and Wilbur had been sitting down, too, but they came quickly to their feet.

The doctor gave them a weary smile. "He's going to be all right. I got the bullet out and it doesn't appear to have done any major damage."

"Oh, thank God," Rosaleen said in a hushed voice. Vance put his arm around her shoulders and drew her against him.

"Mr. Malone did lose quite a bit of blood, though, and getting shot is a shock," the gray-haired medico went on. "He'll be laid up for a while, and he'll have to take it easy even longer. It'll be months before he's back out riding the range . . . but I'm confident he will be."

"I'll make sure the spread is in good shape for

him," Vance said. He looked down at Rosaleen. "That's a promise."

"*We'll* make sure," she said.

Vance grinned and nodded. "That's what I meant."

The doctor turned to Stovepipe. "You need to let me clean that wound on your head and see if it needs any stitches, Mr. Stewart. Head injuries are dangerous."

"Shoot, not with a skull like mine. It's mighty thick, and hard as a rock."

Wilbur's snort showed what he thought of that claim.

"All the same, you need some medical attention," the doctor insisted. "Honestly, I don't see how you kept going like you did."

"That's what Stovepipe's like when he's got his jaws locked on a mystery," Wilbur said. "Nothing can get him to turn loose, not even a bullet."

"Is it true that Sheriff Jerrico was behind all the trouble around here in recent months?"

"Yep," Stovepipe said. "You're gonna be needin' a new lawman."

Vance said, "Maybe once you've recuperated a little, you could take the job, Stovepipe. And Wilbur could be your deputy."

"The two of us settle down and pin on law badges?" Stovepipe shook his head. "We're too fiddlefooted to let grass grow under our boots. Anyway, I reckon there's some other bad hombres out there somewhere, gettin' ready to raise all sorts o' hell, and it'll be up to Wilbur and me to stop 'em. Ain't no shortage o' trouble on the frontier."

Wilbur agreed. "And that's just the way we like it."

CUTTHROATS
A SLASH AND PECOS WESTERN

JOHNSTONE. KEEPING THE WEST WILD.
*Not every Western hero wears a white hat or a tin star.
Most of them are just fighting to survive. Some of them
can be liars, cheaters, and thieves. And then there's a
couple of old-time robbers named Slash and Pecos . . .*

Two wanted outlaws. One hell of a story.
After a lifetime of robbing banks and holding up
trains, Jimmy "Slash" Braddock and Melvin "Pecos
Kid" Baker are ready to call it quits—though not
completely by choice. Sold out by their old gang,
Slash and Pecos have to bust out of jail and pull one
last job to finance their early retirement . . .

The target is a rancher's payroll train. Catch is:
the train is carrying a Gatling gun and twenty
deputy US marshals who know Slash and Pecos are
coming. Caught and quickly sentenced to hang,
their old enemy—the wheelchair-bound bucket of
mean, Marshal L. C. Bledsoe—shows up at the last
minute to spare their lives. For a price. He'll let
them live if they hunt down their old gang,
the Snake River Marauders. And kill those
prairie rats—with extreme prejudice . . .

**Look for *Cutthroats*.
Coming in July, wherever books are sold.**

CHAPTER ONE

In the early morning hours, the bounty hunters gathered around the remote mountain cabin, crouched in a shadowy clearing. They were thirteen in number—a dozen-plus wolves on the blood scent.

Ray Laskey walked up to where Jack Penny crouched in the pines roughly fifty yards from the cabin, running an oily rag down the barrel of his Henry repeating rifle.

"All the boys are in position, boss," Laskey said, slicing a hunk of wedding cake tobacco onto his tongue and chewing.

Penny turned to Laskey and winked in acknowledgment with the rheumy blue eye that always seemed to roll to the outside corner of its socket and that always made Laskey feel vaguely uneasy, for some reason. That wandering eye seemed like some separate living thing, rolling and bobbing around in Penny's ugly, bearded head . . . like some ghastly thing that lived inside a log at the bottom of a murky lake and only came out to rend and kill. . . .

Both men crouched lower behind their covering

...ne when the cabin's front door latch clicked. Laskey ...rew a sharp breath as he turned to see the door ...pen. He squeezed his Spencer tightly but then eased his grip when he saw that the person stepping out onto the cabin's small stoop was a woman with long, thick, copper-red hair.

The woman, nicely put together and clad in a man's wool shirt and tight denim trousers, turned toward the split firewood stacked against the cabin's front wall. When she had an armload, she straightened, turned back to the door, and stopped abruptly.

No, Laskey thought. *Don't do that. Keep goin'. Get back inside the cabin, dearie. . . .*

The woman turned ever so slowly to stand staring straight off into the trees, directly toward where Laskey and Penny crouched behind a stout ponderosa.

Laskey's gut tightened.

Had she heard or in some other way sensed the killers crouched in the forest around the cabin? Had she smelled their unwashed bodies made even whiffier from their long, hard ride over the course of the long night lit only by a small and fleeting powder-horn moon?

Penny glanced at Laskey. The bearded bounty hunter smiled darkly, then raised his Henry to his shoulder. He slid the barrel up over a feathery branch and leveled his sights on the woman. He crouched low over the long gun, resting his bearded cheek up snug against the stock.

Slowly, almost soundlessly, he ratcheted back the hammer with his thumb.

Laskey looked at the woman. His heart thudded. She appeared to be staring straight at him. Straight at Penny steadying his sights on her chest.

No, no, no, dearie. You didn't hear nothin'. You didn't smell nothin'. No one's out here. A coyote, maybe. A rabbit, maybe—up and out too early for its own damn good . . .

That's all.

Go on inside, stoke your stove, start cookin' breakfast for them two cutthroats in there. It's them we want. Not you, purty lady.

We got other plans for you . . . dearie. . . .

As though obeying Ray Laskey's silent plea, the woman turned slowly, stepped back toward the door, nudged it open, and stepped inside. She turned to look outside once more, then closed the door and latched it with a soft *click.*

Penny eased his Winchester's hammer down against the firing pin.

Laskey released a breath he hadn't realized he'd been holding.

Penny turned to him, spreading his ragged beard as he grinned. "She almost joined the angels."

"When, uh . . ." Laskey said, pressing the wedding cake up tautly against his gum, "when do you want to . . . ?"

"Start the dance?"

"Yeah, yeah. Start the dance."

"As soon as they show themselves. Best odds, that way. Won't be too long now, most like. We got time."

"What, uh . . . what about the woman?" Laskey said.

"What about her?" Penny asked him.

Laskey shrugged, toed a pinecone. "She's too purty to kill. Outright, I mean . . ."

Laskey grinned, juice from the wedding cake bleeding out from between his thin lips.

Penny scowled down at the shorter man. "We came here to kill, an' that's what we're gonna do, Ray, my boy. She's with them cutthroats, so she dies with them cutthroats. Hell, there's a reward on her head, too. Dead or alive. Same as them."

"Oh, boy," Laskey said. "The woman, too, huh? Seems a shame's all."

Penny placed a big, strong, gloved hand on Laskey's shoulder and squeezed. "The woman, too, Ray. We ain't here for none o' that nonsense you're thinkin' about, you randy scoundrel."

Penny brushed his gloved fist across Laskey's pointed chin.

He winked his weird fish eye again, and it rolled like that living thing in the dark lake, fleeing back to its log after feeding.

CHAPTER TWO

"What you two old cutthroats need is a job," said Jaycee Breckenridge.

James "Slash" Braddock lifted his head from his pillow, frowning at the pretty woman forking bacon around in the cast-iron skillet sputtering atop her coal-black range. "Jay, honey, please don't use such nasty language so early in the morning. Pecos an' me got *sensitive ears*!"

"What'd she say?" asked Melvin Baker, better known for the past thirty years of his outlaw career as the Pecos River Kid.

He lay belly down on the cot on the far side of the small cabin from Slash Braddock. His blue eyes were open, regarding his longtime outlaw partner in shock and disbelief. "I didn't just hear her use the bad word again—did I, Slash?" He closed his hands over his ears. "Oh, please, tell me I didn't!"

"Now, look what you done, Jay! Poor ole Pecos is beside himself over here! He's likely ruined for the whole dang day! I might have to hide his guns from him, so he don't blow his brains out!"

Pecos buried his face in his pillow and pretend bawled.

At the range, one hand on her hip as she continued to flip and shuttle the bacon around in the same pan in which potatoes and onions fried, Jay shook her long, copper-red hair back from her hazel-eyed face and laughed. "Look what time it is, you old mossyhorns!"

She glanced at the windows behind her through which slanted the crisp, high-altitude sunlight of the Juan Valley of southern Colorado Territory. "It's nigh on midmorning and you two are still lounging around like a pair of eastern railroad magnates on New Year's Day!"

"Lounging around—nothin'!" Pecos lifted his head from his pillow and looked over his shoulder at Jay. "I was dead asleep not more'n two minutes ago. You done woke me up with your foul language. You oughta be ashamed of yourself, woman. What would Pistol Pete think of such talk?"

"Ha!" Jay threw her head back, laughing. "Whenever I mentioned the word 'job' to that old rascal—as in he might want to quit ridin' the long coulees and try an honest job for a change—he'd howl like a gut-shot cur an' skin out of here like a preacher caught in a parlor house. He'd run clear across the yard and throw himself in the creek. Didn't matter what time of year it was. Spring, summer, winter, or fall—that's just what he'd do, Pete would."

Jay threw her head back again, laughing.

But then she turned a thoughtful look over her shoulder, gazing out the window toward the lone grave standing on a knoll about sixty yards out from the cabin, in a little pocket of ponderosas and cedars. Jay's shoulders, clad in a plaid work shirt tucked into tight denims, rose and fell slowly, heavily. Her lower lip trembled. She stifled a sob, clamping her hand over her mouth, then wheeled from the range and hurried to the cabin's front door.

"Excuse me, boys!" she said in an emotion-strangled voice as she opened the door and stepped out onto the small front stoop. She slammed the door behind her.

Through the door, Slash heard her sobbing.

He turned to his partner, scowling, and said, "Pecos, what'd you have to go and do that for?"

"Ah, hell!" Sitting up now, clad in his wash-worn longhandles that clung to his big, rawboned frame, Pecos slapped the cot beside him and hung his gray-blond, blue-eyed head like a young man fresh from the woodshed. "I reckon Pete's name just slipped out. I mean, hell, he *was* her man. And, hell, we rode with him for nigh on thirty years before he . . . well, you know . . . before he got himself planted over there in them trees."

Pecos turned a disgruntled look at Slash. He kept his voice down so he wouldn't be heard on the stoop from where Jay's sobs pushed softly through the door. "Come on, pardner, Pete's been dead almost five years now. We should be able to mention his name from time to time."

"Dammit, Pecos." Slash tossed his animal skin covers aside and dropped his bare feet to the timbered floor still owning the chill of the crisp mountain morning. "You an' I both know Pete didn't get himself planted in them trees over there. *I* did!" Slash jabbed his thumb against his chest that bore the hooked knife scar that gave him his nickname. "I'm the one that got him planted. My own damn carelessness did."

"It was a bullet from the gun of one of Luther Bledsoe's deputies that killed Pete, Slash, you stupid devil. Don't you start in with all this old Pete stuff now, too!"

"I didn't," Slash said, rising in disgust and grabbing his brown whipcord trousers off a chair. "You did!"

"Ah, hell!" Pecos twisted around and flopped belly down on his cot, burying his head in his pillow. His big Russian .44, snugged inside its brown, hand-tooled leather holster, hung by its shell belt hooked over elk horns mounted on the wall above his head, within an easy grab if needed. Such a move had been needed more than a few times in his and Slash's long careers as riders of the long coulees, or the owlhoot trail, as some called the life of a professional western outlaw.

Slash quickly stepped into his pants. Then his boots. He left his blue chambray shirt on the chair but he strapped his twin, stag-butted Colt .44s around his waist, which was solid as oak at his ripe age of fifty-seven, which he was not above crowing about to Pecos, who'd grown a little fleshy above the buckle of his own cartridge belt.

Slash rarely walked more than five steps without either the revolver or his Winchester Yellowboy repeater. As he grabbed his hat off the kitchen table his bone-handled bowie knife, also strapped to his shell belt, rode high on his left hip, behind the .44 positioned for the cross-draw on that side. He swept a hand through his dark-brown hair, still thick, he was proud to know, but well streaked with gray—especially up around the temples and in his long sideburns that sandwiched a broad, strong-jawed, brown-eyed face—the face of a handsome albeit middle-aged schoolboy.

One who'd spent the bulk of his life out in the blazing western sun.

That he was no longer a schoolboy, however, made itself obvious once again as it always tended to do upon his first rising. As he tramped across the kitchen, his hips and knees and ankles popped and cracked, stiff from too long in the mattress sack after too many years forking a saddle and sleeping on the hard, cold ground of one remote outlaw camp or another. An old back injury, the result of being thrown from a horse during a run from a catch party nearly twenty years ago, made Slash curse under his breath as he lifted the popping skillet off the range and slid it onto the warming rack, so the vittles wouldn't burn.

He pulled a couple of heavy stone mugs down from a shelf near the range and set them on the table. He dumped two heaping helpings of sugar into one, because he knew Jay liked her mud a little sweet—"Just like her men," she often quipped—then used a deer hide swatch to lift the hot black coffeepot from the range, and filled both mugs to their brims.

"Is Jay gonna be all right?" Pecos asked, his chagrined voice muffled by his pillow.

"Of course, she's gonna be all right," Slash said, heading for the door. "She's Jay, ain't she?"

He fumbled the door open and stepped out, drawing the door closed behind him with a hooked boot. Jay stood ahead and to his right, her back to him, staring out over the porch rail toward the lone grave on the knoll.

The sun glowed in her hair. Birds flitted about the sunlit yard around the cabin ringed with pine forest. Tall stone escarpments flanked the place. The cabin, originally built by a hermetic, now-dead fur trapper, was situated here on this mountain shoulder in such a way that it couldn't be seen from any direction unless you rode right up on it. And the only way you were likely to ride up on it was either by accident or if you'd already known it was here and you were headed for it.

That's what had made the place such a prime hideout over the years. After a bank or train job, the Snake River Marauders, as Slash and Pecos's old gang called themselves, often split up their booty and then separated themselves into small groups of twos, threes, and fours, scattering and holing up till their trail cooled. They'd meet up again later at some far-flung, prearranged place to plan their next job.

Sometimes Slash, Pecos, and Pistol Pete, the old outlaw from the far northern Dakota country, would meet Jay in Mexico, and they'd spend their winnings in Durango, Loreto, or Mazatlán. Sometimes they'd sun themselves on the beaches of the Sea of Cortez, drinking pulque and tequila and feasting on spicy Mexican dishes like *tortas ahogadas* and *chilorio*.

Sometimes they'd hole up here for weeks or months at a time, hunting in the San Juans and the Sawatch to the north, and fishing and swimming in the pure, cold mountain streams. It was the time between jobs spent either here or in Mexico that Slash had always preferred over the jobs themselves, but he could never deny his almost primal attraction to the danger and excitement, as well as the money, that had always lured him back to the outlaw trail.

Now he set the cup of sugary coffee on the rail in front of Jay and kissed her tear-damp cheek. "Cup o' mud for you, darlin'," he said. "Put hair on your chest."

Staring toward the grave atop the knoll, Jay laughed at the old joke she and her old friend Slash had shared all the years they'd known each other—going on fifteen now—and offered her usual retort, "I don't want hair on my chest, Slash. That doesn't sound appealing to me at all!"

Slash gave a wry snort and sipped his coffee. "How you doing?"

"Look at me," she said, still staring toward the grave. "It's been how long, now? Going on five years? And I'm still pining for that man turned to dust under those mounded rocks over there."

"That's all right. He was a good man. He deserves pining for."

"Yes, he does, at that." Jay hardened her voice as well as her jaws as she turned to her old friend. "But it's time for me to move on, dammit, Slash."

"You're right on that score, too, Jay." Again, Slash sipped the rich black coffee.

"I'm still young . . . sort of," she said with proud defiance. "I still have my looks. Or most of them, barring a few crows-feet around my eyes and a little roughness to my skin . . . as well as to my tongue," she added drolly.

Slash looked at her, which was one of his favorite things to do. She was a slight, petite woman but with all the right female curves in all the right female places. She wore each of her forty-plus years beautifully on a face richly tanned by the frontier sun. The lines and furrows had seasoned her, refining her beauty and accentuating her raw, earthy character. Her hazel eyes were alive with a wry, frank humor.

She was the most sensuous and alluring woman Slash had ever laid eyes on, and he'd first laid eyes on her when she was well past thirty.

"Hellkatoot," he said. "You're still a raving beauty, Jay. There's not many women over forty who've kept their looks as well as you have. You'll find a man. You just gotta start lookin' for one, that's all."

Jaycee Breckenridge drew a deep, slow, fateful breath. "I'm not gonna find one out here, am I? The only men who come around here anymore are you and that lummox lounging around inside like Diamond Jim."

Slash smiled.

"And you two don't deserve me," Jay said with another laugh.

"We sure don't!" Slash chuckled and shook his head.

Besides, he knew, they shared too much history. Good history and bad history. He'd once gotten his hopes up about Jay, a long time ago. But then she'd tumbled for the older, wiser "Pistol" Pete Johnson, five years Slash's senior, old enough to have been Jay's father.

She'd preferred the astuteness and assuredness of the older man. She'd been taken by the burly Pete's rough-sweet ways and his bawdy humor. Mere days after she'd met the man at the country saloon she'd been singing in, she never looked back. At least, not as far as Slash knew, and he thought he knew her as well or better than anyone on earth, now that Pete was gone.

"I'm so sorry, Jay," he said, looking off in frustration.

She frowned at him, puzzled. "For Pecos? Don't be silly. He only mentioned his old friend's name."

"No, not for Pecos." Slash turned to her. "For me."

Jay looked at him askance, with sharp admonishment. "Let's not go down that trail again, Slash."

CHAPTER THREE

"Pete's death wasn't your fault," Jay said. "It was the fault of the man—that deputy U.S. marshal riding for Chief Marshal Bledsoe—who shot him from that ridge. Cowardly devil!" she added hatefully, tears glistening in her eyes once more.

Slash shook his head. "I led us into that trap. I knew those mountains we were riding in. I knew 'em like the back of my hand! At least, I thought I did."

"It was a box canyon," Jay said. "The box canyons are filled with lunatics."

"I took a wrong turn. I was hungover from the night before. I shouldn't have been drinking the night before a job, but I did. I took a wrong turn and led Pete an' Pecos an' Arnie and Devlin into that box canyon and couldn't find my way out again before that no-account lawdog that was shadowin' us fired down at us from that ridge.

"To put the cherry on it, that bullet wasn't even meant for Pete. It was meant for me! That marshal wanted to cut the head off the snake, to take me out, the gang's leader, but Pete rode in front of me when we were all looking for another way out of that canyon. He's the one whose ticket got punched when it should've been mine."

Slash gritted his teeth and shook his head as he stared toward the grave, the old sorrow and self-recrimination having returned full-blast. "Dammit!"

"Slash, now—"

"No." Slash shook his head defiantly. "I reckon I should've retired back then, nigh on five years ago. I got careless in my old age. Overly confident. If I'd called it quits, let one of the others take over—one of the younger men that was *qualified* to take over—Pete might still be alive today." He turned to the woman, placed his hands on her arms. "I hope to God you can find it in your heart to forgive me one day, Jay."

She studied Slash thoughtfully. Slowly, a sad smile stretched her lips and she placed a gentle hand on his cheeks, staring deeply into his own sad eyes. "I'll make a deal with you, Slash."

He cleared emotion from his throat. "Anything . . ."

"I'll forgive you if you forgive yourself." Jay's smile grew, and warmth filled her hazel-eyed gaze. "How 'bout that? Oh, and I'll add one more thing. I promise not to break down like a damn weeping fool every time I hear his name. Maybe *sometimes*, but not every time," she added, chuckling. "All right, Slash? Do we have a deal?"

Slash gazed back at her, his heart lightening ever so gradually. He removed her hand from his cheek and kissed it. "All right." He chuckled with genuine relief. "All right. We got ourselves a deal."

Connect with

Visit us online at
KensingtonBooks.com
to read more from your favorite authors, see books
by series, view reading group guides, and more.

Join us on social media

for sneak peeks, chances to win books and prize packs,
and to share your thoughts with other readers.

facebook.com/kensingtonpublishing
twitter.com/kensingtonbooks

Tell us what you think!

To share your thoughts, submit a review,
or sign up for our eNewsletters, please visit:
KensingtonBooks.com/TellUs.